Vol. One

STORY	RODNEY BARNES	EDITOR	GREG TUMBARELLO
ART	JASON SHAWN ALEXANDER	PUBLISHING COORDINATOR	SHANNON BAILEY
COLOR	LUIS NCT	LOGO & PUBLICATION DESIGN	BRENT ASHE
LETTERING	MARSHALL DILLON		

IMAGE COMICS, INC.

Robert Kirkman: Chief Operating Officer | Erik Larsen: Chief Financial Officer | Todd McFarlane: President | Marc Silvestri: Chief Executive Officer | Jim Valentino: Vice President | Eric Stephenson: Publisher / Chief Creative Officer | Jeff Boison: Director of Publishing Planning & Book Trade Sales | Chris Ross: Director of Digital Services | Jeff Stang: Director of Direct Market Sales | Kat Salazar: Director of PR & Marketing | Drew Gill: Cover Editor | Heather Doornink: Production Director Nicole Lapalme: Controller
IMAGECOMICS.COM

KILLADELPHIA, VOL. 1. First printing. July 2020. Published by Image Comics, Inc. Office of publication: 2701 NW Vaughn St., Suite 780, Portland, OR 97210. Copyright © 2020 Rodney Barnes & Jason Shawn Alexander. All rights reserved. Contains material originally published in single magazine form as KILLADELPHIA #1-6. "Killadelphia," its logos, and the likenesses of all characters herein are trademarks of Rodney Barnes & Jason Shawn Alexander, unless otherwise noted. "Image" and the Image Comics logos are registered trademarks of Image Comics, Inc. No part of this publication may be reproduced or transmitted, in any form or by any means (except for short excerpts for journalistic or review purposes), without the express written permission of Rodney Barnes & Jason Shawn Alexander, or Image Comics, Inc. All names, characters, events, and locales in this publication are entirely fictional. Any resemblance to actual persons (living or dead), events, or places, without satirical intent, is coincidental. Printed in the USA. For international rights, contact: foreignlicensing@imagecomics.com. ISBN: 978-1-5343-1569-3.

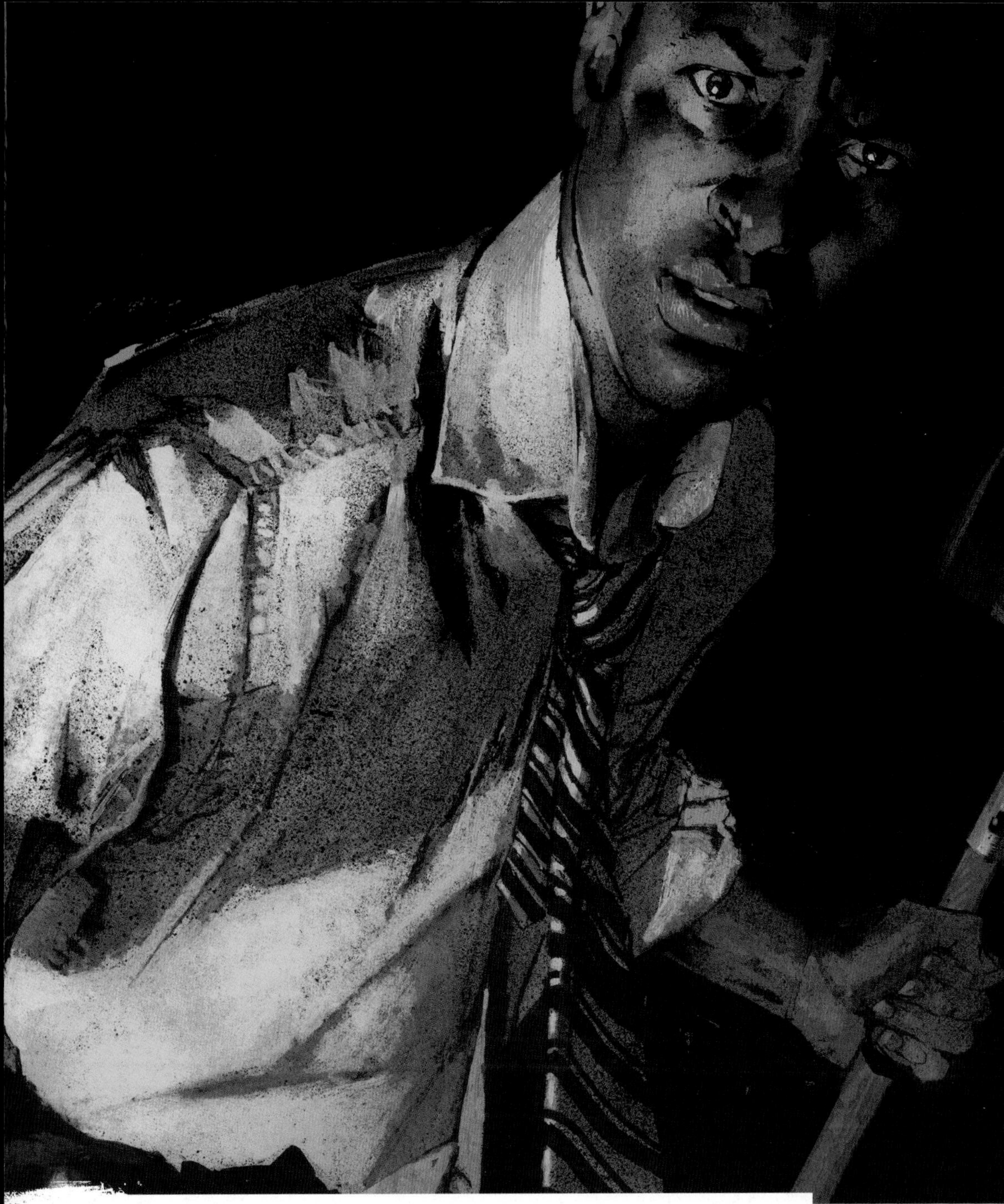

"THE KEY TO SOLVING THIS NIGHTMARE IS IN THERE."

A CALL TO ARMS

Chapter I

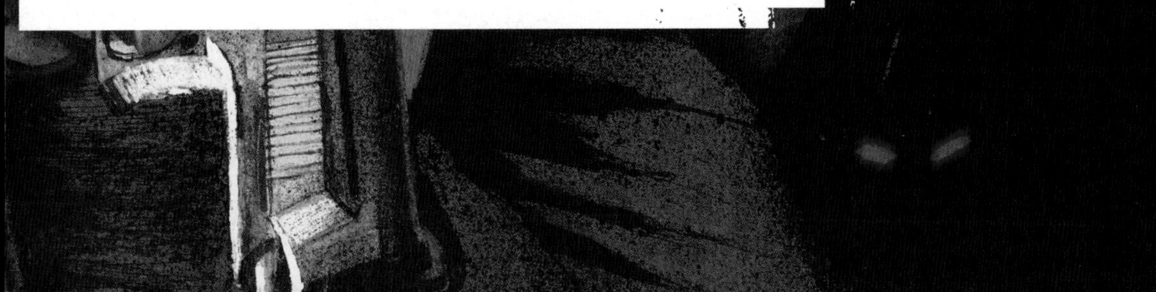

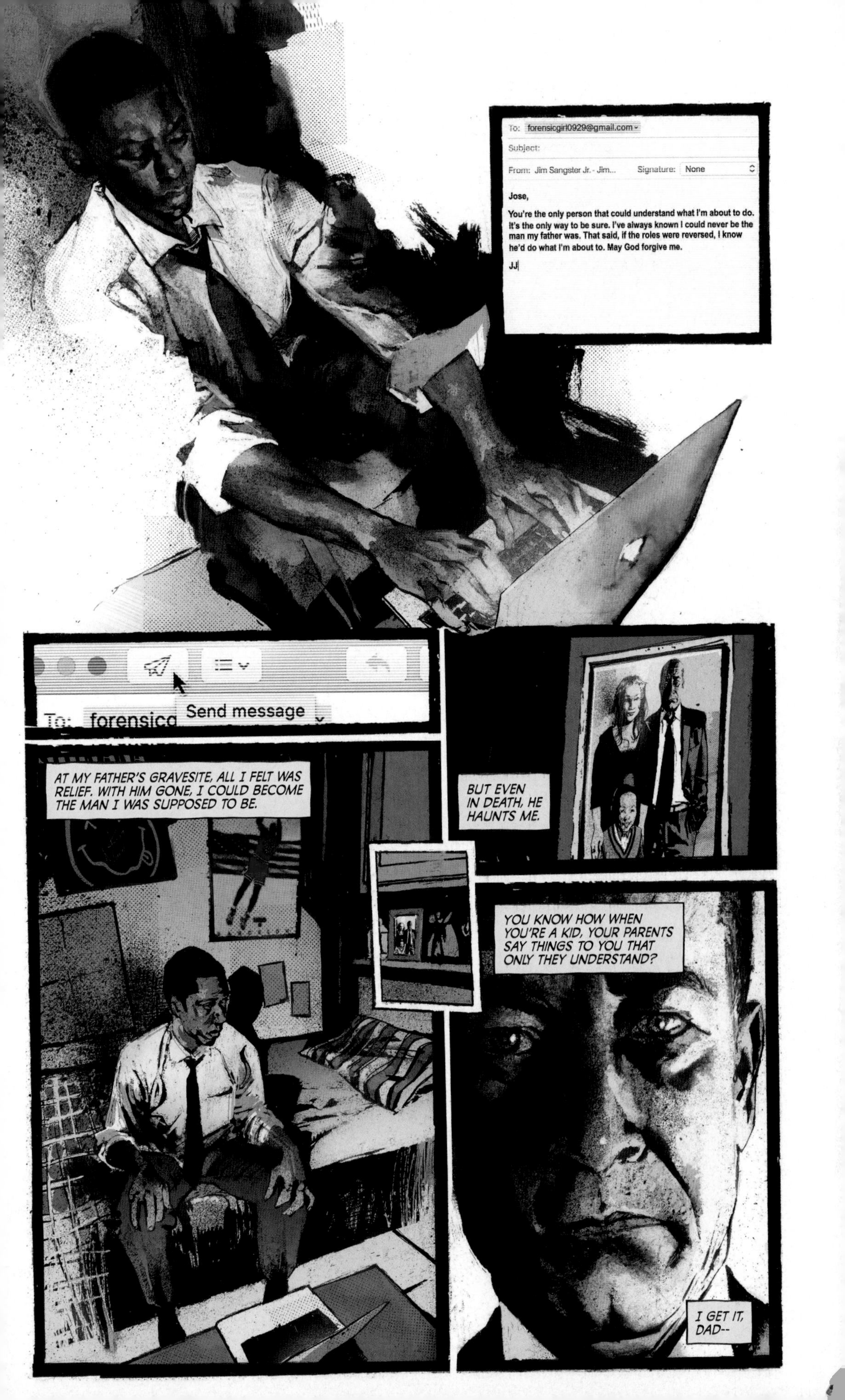

To: forensicgirl0929@gmail.com
Subject:
From: Jim Sangster Jr. - Jim... Signature: None
Jose,
You're the only person that could understand what I'm about to do. It's the only way to be sure. I've always known I could never be the man my father was. That said, if the roles were reversed, I know he'd do what I'm about to. May God forgive me.
JJ
To: forensicg
Send message
AT MY FATHER'S GRAVESITE, ALL I FELT WAS RELIEF. WITH HIM GONE, I COULD BECOME THE MAN I WAS SUPPOSED TO BE.
BUT EVEN IN DEATH, HE HAUNTS ME.
YOU KNOW HOW WHEN YOU'RE A KID, YOUR PARENTS SAY THINGS TO YOU THAT ONLY THEY UNDERSTAND?
I GET IT, DAD--

--IT'S FINALLY COMING INTO FOCUS...
DIDN'T THINK ANYTHING COULD BE WORSE THAN THE NINETIES. CRACK TURNED THIS CITY UPSIDE DOWN.
TEN DAYS EARLIER.
MISSING
THOUGHT I'D SEEN EVERY TYPE OF DEATH IMAGINABLE...
...UNTIL NOW.
WELL PLAYED, MOTHERFUCKER.
TRUST AND BELIEVE I'M GONNA FIND YOU.
AND SOMEHOW, SOME WAY...
...I'M GOING TO KILL YOU.

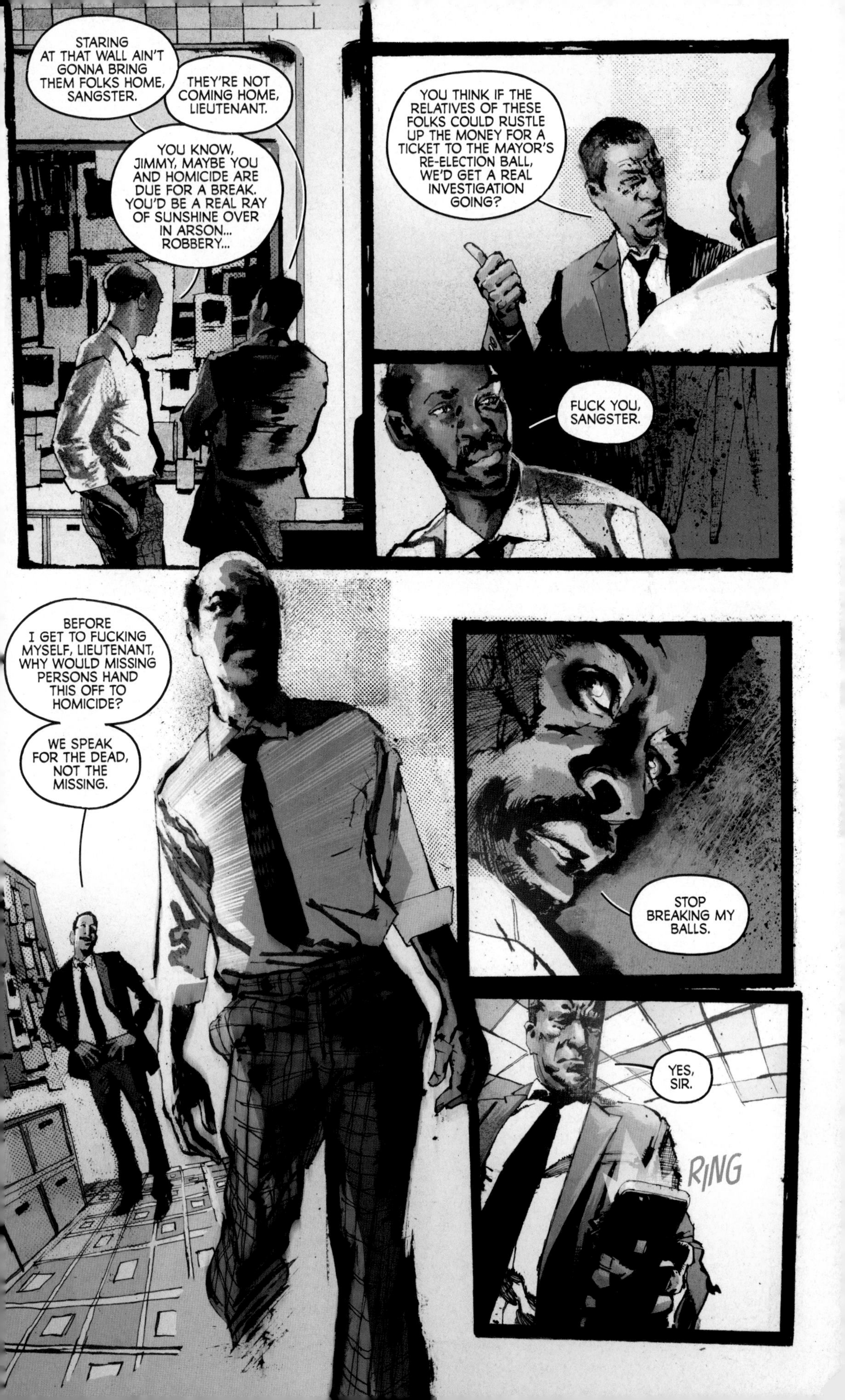
STARING AT THAT WALL AIN'T GONNA BRING THEM FOLKS HOME, SANGSTER.
THEY'RE NOT COMING HOME, LIEUTENANT.
YOU KNOW, JIMMY, MAYBE YOU AND HOMICIDE ARE DUE FOR A BREAK. YOU'D BE A REAL RAY OF SUNSHINE OVER IN ARSON... ROBBERY...
YOU THINK IF THE RELATIVES OF THESE FOLKS COULD RUSTLE UP THE MONEY FOR A TICKET TO THE MAYOR'S RE-ELECTION BALL, WE'D GET A REAL INVESTIGATION GOING?
FUCK YOU, SANGSTER.
BEFORE I GET TO FUCKING MYSELF, LIEUTENANT, WHY WOULD MISSING PERSONS HAND THIS OFF TO HOMICIDE?
WE SPEAK FOR THE DEAD, NOT THE MISSING.
STOP BREAKING MY BALLS.
YES, SIR.
RING

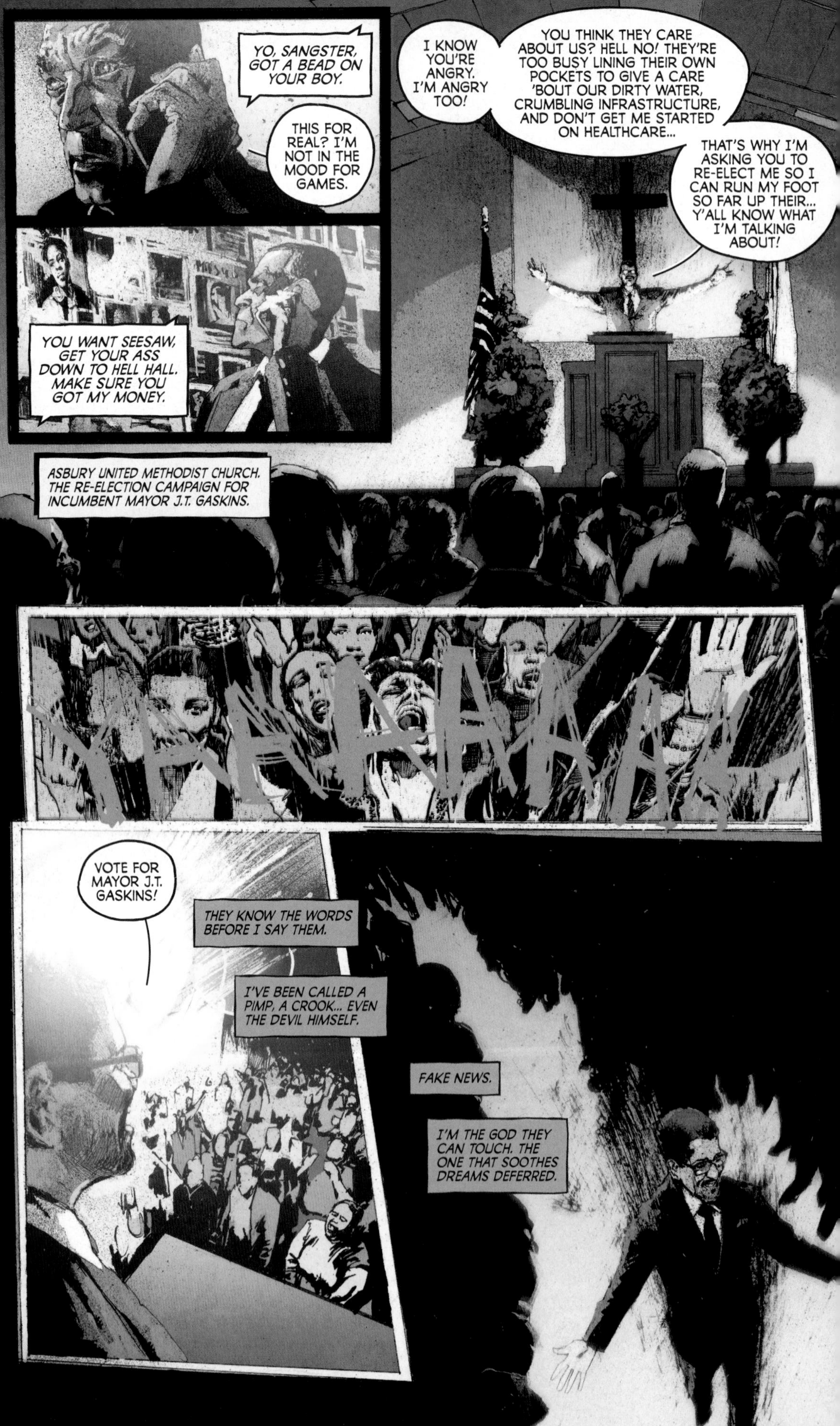
YO, SANGSTER, GOT A BEAD ON YOUR BOY.
THIS FOR REAL? I'M NOT IN THE MOOD FOR GAMES.
YOU WANT SEESAW, GET YOUR ASS DOWN TO HELL HALL. MAKE SURE YOU GOT MY MONEY.
I KNOW YOU'RE ANGRY. I'M ANGRY TOO!
YOU THINK THEY CARE ABOUT US? HELL NO! THEY'RE TOO BUSY LINING THEIR OWN POCKETS TO GIVE A CARE 'BOUT OUR DIRTY WATER, CRUMBLING INFRASTRUCTURE, AND DON'T GET ME STARTED ON HEALTHCARE...
THAT'S WHY I'M ASKING YOU TO RE-ELECT ME SO I CAN RUN MY FOOT SO FAR UP THEIR... Y'ALL KNOW WHAT I'M TALKING ABOUT!
ASBURY UNITED METHODIST CHURCH. THE RE-ELECTION CAMPAIGN FOR INCUMBENT MAYOR J.T. GASKINS.
YAAAAAA!
VOTE FOR MAYOR J.T. GASKINS!
THEY KNOW THE WORDS BEFORE I SAY THEM.
I'VE BEEN CALLED A PIMP, A CROOK... EVEN THE DEVIL HIMSELF.
FAKE NEWS.
I'M THE GOD THEY CAN TOUCH. THE ONE THAT SOOTHES DREAMS DEFERRED.

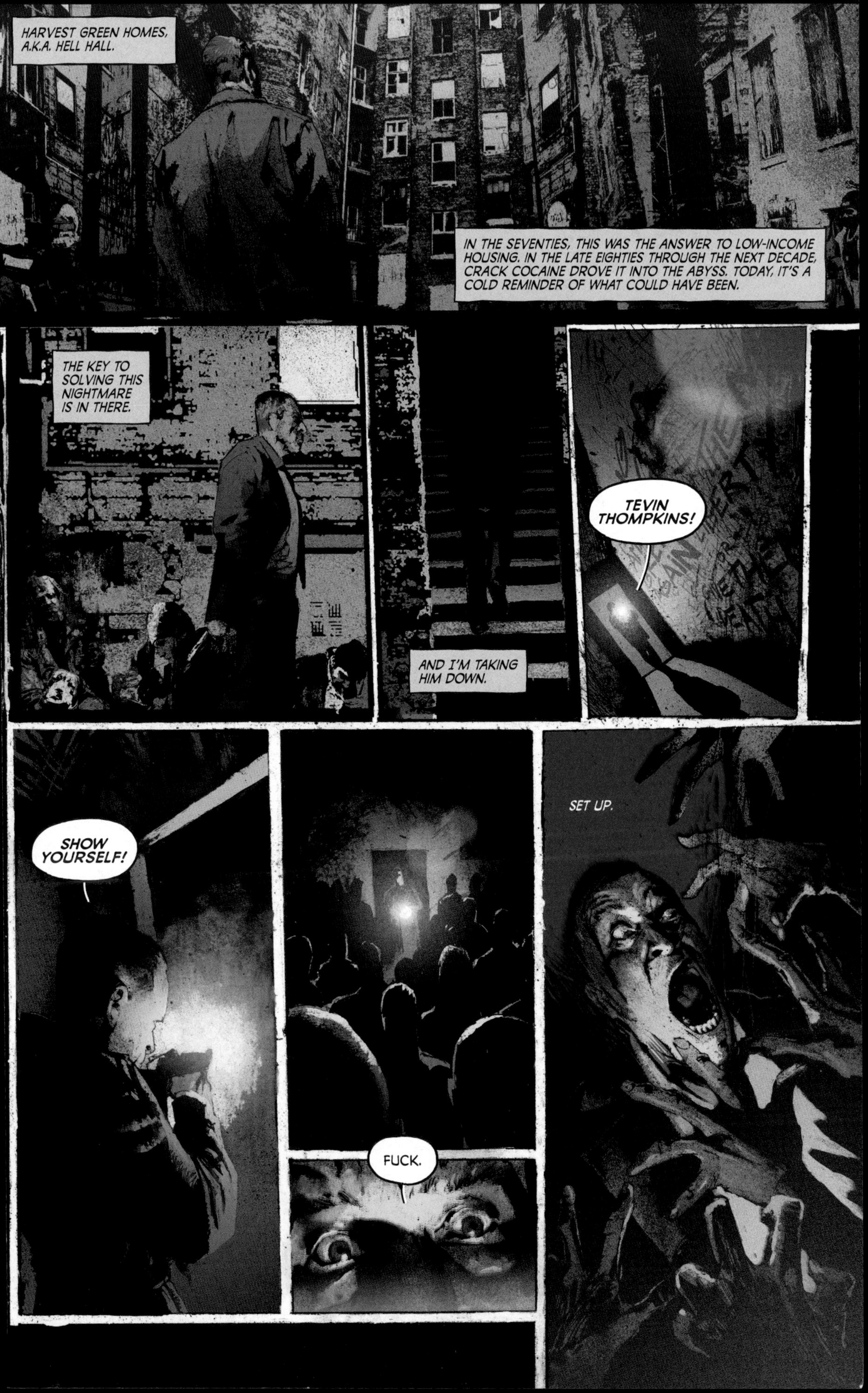
HARVEST GREEN HOMES, A.K.A. HELL HALL.
IN THE SEVENTIES, THIS WAS THE ANSWER TO LOW-INCOME HOUSING. IN THE LATE EIGHTIES THROUGH THE NEXT DECADE, CRACK COCAINE DROVE IT INTO THE ABYSS. TODAY, IT'S A COLD REMINDER OF WHAT COULD HAVE BEEN.
THE KEY TO SOLVING THIS NIGHTMARE IS IN THERE.
AND I'M TAKING HIM DOWN.
TEVIN THOMPKINS!
SHOW YOURSELF!
FUCK.
SET UP.

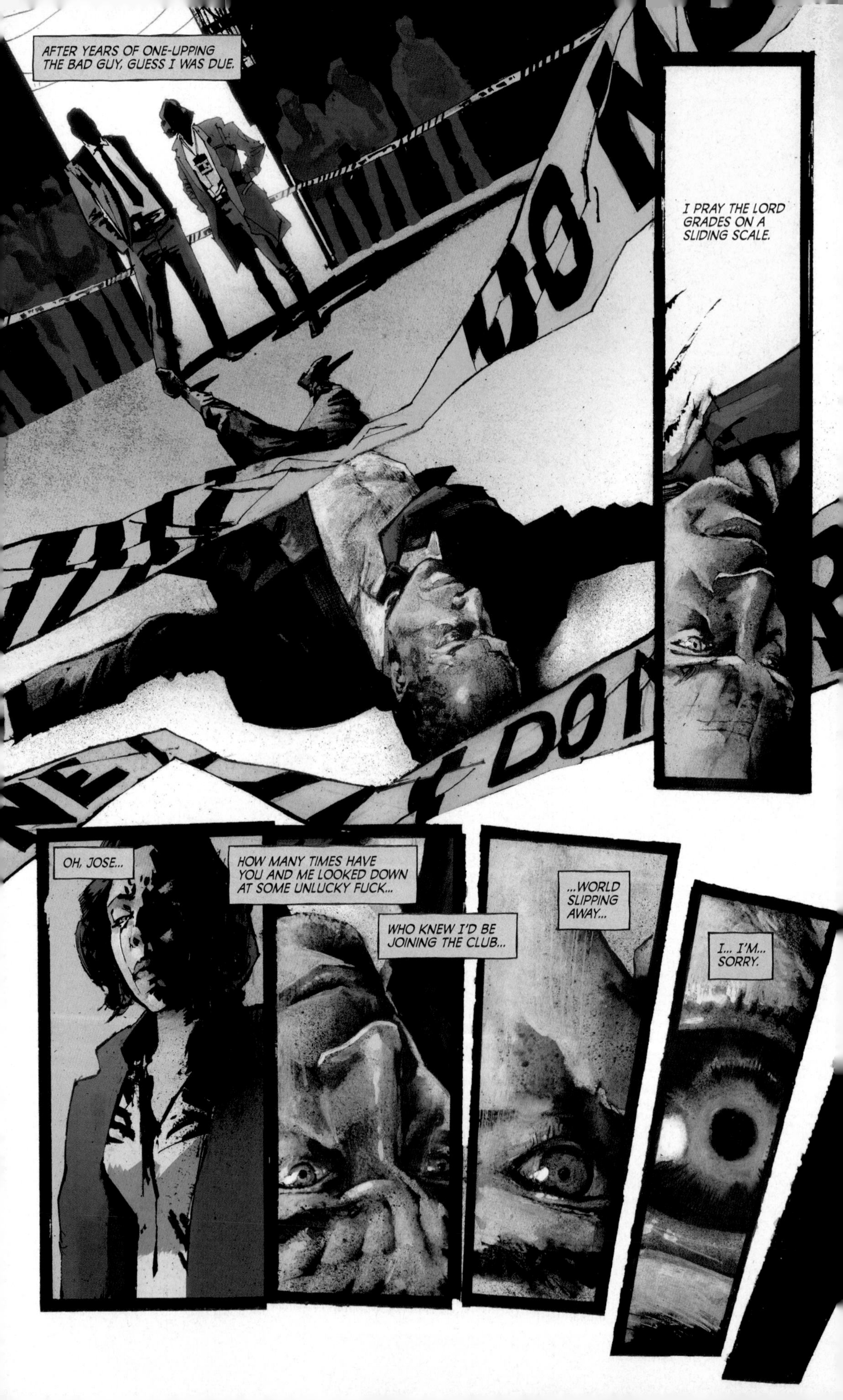
AFTER YEARS OF ONE-UPPING THE BAD GUY, GUESS I WAS DUE.
I PRAY THE LORD GRADES ON A SLIDING SCALE.
OH, JOSE...
HOW MANY TIMES HAVE YOU AND ME LOOKED DOWN AT SOME UNLUCKY FUCK...
WHO KNEW I'D BE JOINING THE CLUB...
...WORLD SLIPPING AWAY...
I... I'M... SORRY.

PUT POP IN THE GROUND AND GET MY ASS BACK TO BALTIMORE.

BACK TO BEING A NO-NAME BEAT COP GOING NOWHERE FAST.

ON THE BRIGHT SIDE, I'LL NEVER SEE PHILADELPHIA AGAIN.

HAPPY TO CLOSE THIS CHAPTER OF MY LIFE.

I HATED MY FATHER.

FOR HIS SAKE, I HOPE HELL AIN'T AS HOT AS THEY SAY.

JAMES SANGSTER SR.

BORN SEPTEMBER 19, 1963
DIED AUGUST 1, 2017

THE TIRED MAN RESTS

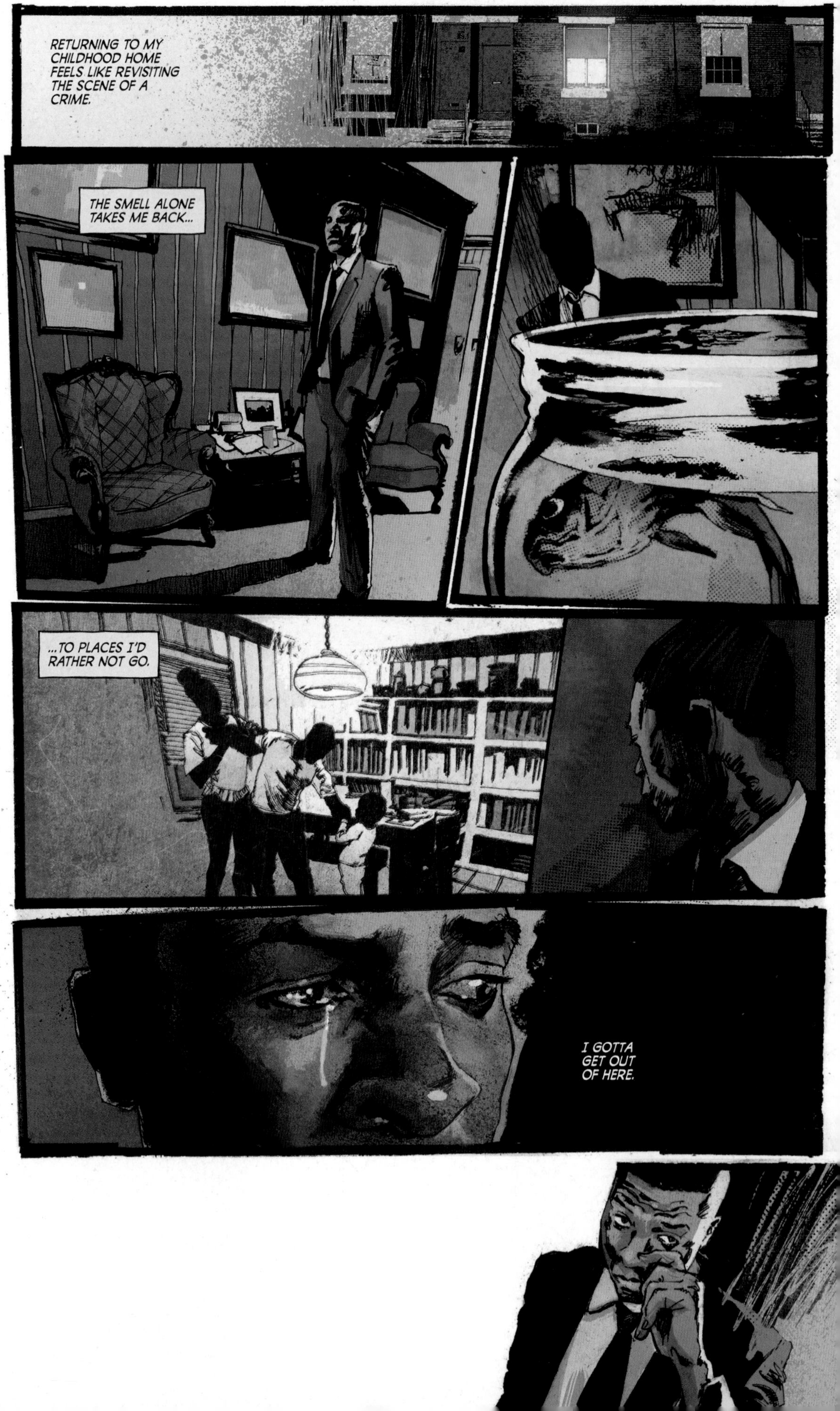
RETURNING TO MY CHILDHOOD HOME FEELS LIKE REVISITING THE SCENE OF A CRIME.
THE SMELL ALONE TAKES ME BACK...
...TO PLACES I'D RATHER NOT GO.
I GOTTA GET OUT OF HERE.

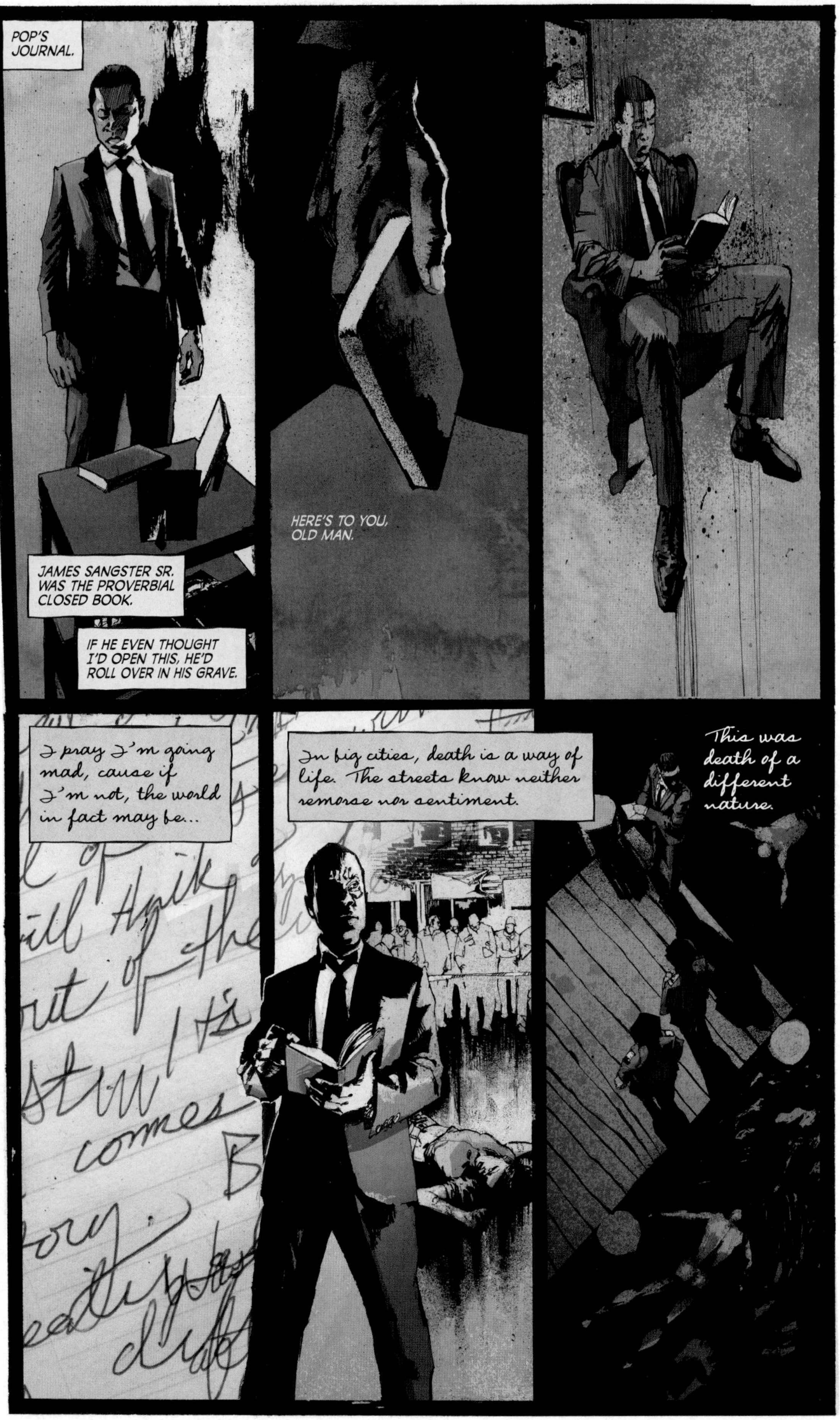
POP'S JOURNAL.
JAMES SANGSTER SR. WAS THE PROVERBIAL CLOSED BOOK.
IF HE EVEN THOUGHT I'D OPEN THIS, HE'D ROLL OVER IN HIS GRAVE.
HERE'S TO YOU, OLD MAN.
I pray I'm going mad, cause if I'm not, the world in fact may be...
In big cities, death is a way of life. The streets know neither remorse nor sentiment.
This was death of a different nature.

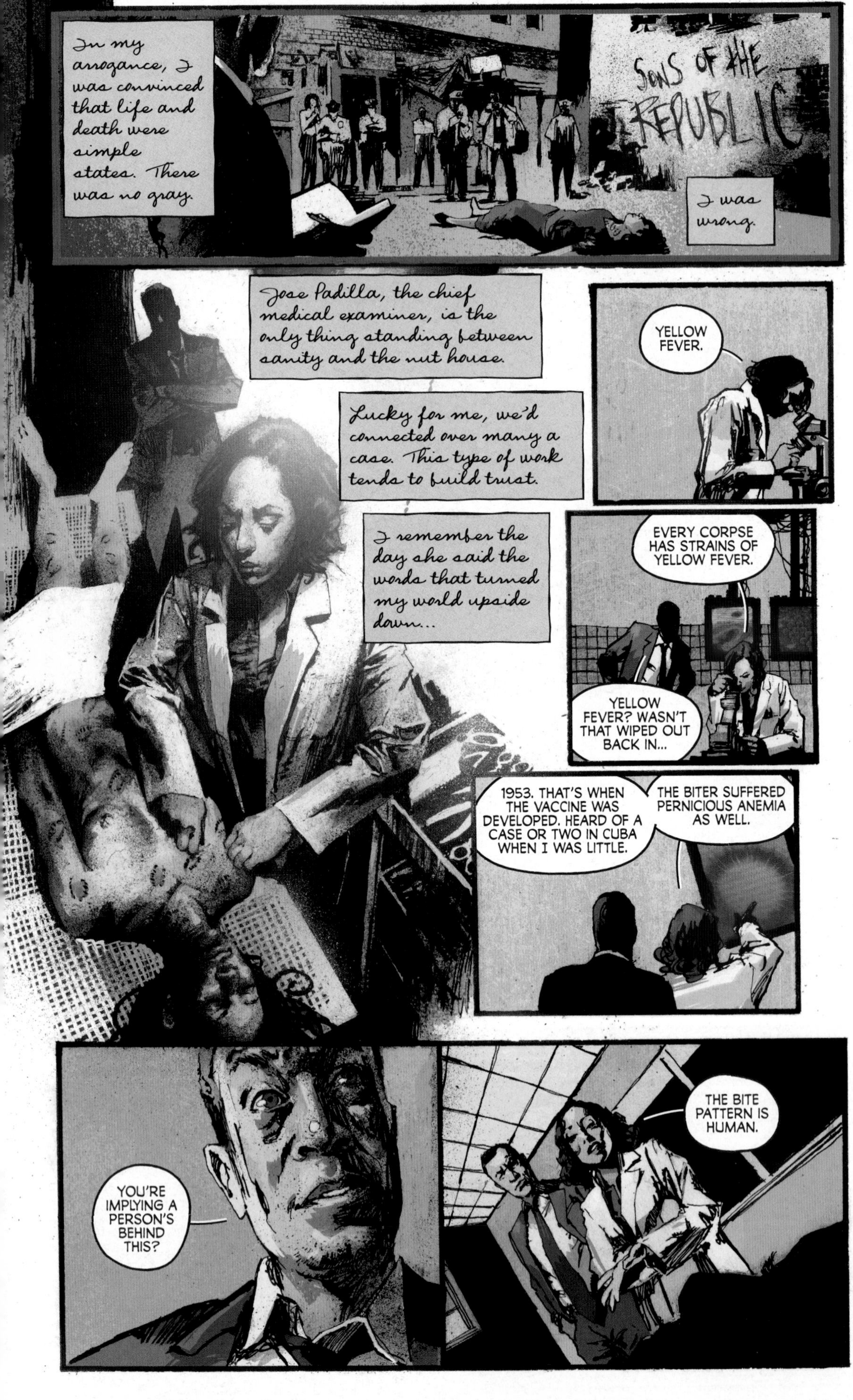

In my arrogance, I was convinced that life and death were simple states. There was no gray.
SONS OF THE REPUBLIC
I was wrong.
Jose Padilla, the chief medical examiner, is the only thing standing between sanity and the nut house.
Lucky for me, we'd connected over many a case. This type of work tends to build trust.
I remember the day she said the words that turned my world upside down...
YELLOW FEVER.
EVERY CORPSE HAS STRAINS OF YELLOW FEVER.
YELLOW FEVER? WASN'T THAT WIPED OUT BACK IN...
1953. THAT'S WHEN THE VACCINE WAS DEVELOPED. HEARD OF A CASE OR TWO IN CUBA WHEN I WAS LITTLE.
THE BITER SUFFERED PERNICIOUS ANEMIA AS WELL.
YOU'RE IMPLYING A PERSON'S BEHIND THIS?
THE BITE PATTERN IS HUMAN.

SO... TO BE CLEAR, SOMEONE'S GOING AROUND BITING PEOPLE?

MULTIPLE PEOPLE ARE BITING MULTIPLE PEOPLE.

YELLOW FEVER ONLY EXISTS IN THE CARIBBEAN AND THIRD WORLD COUNTRIES TODAY. ALTHOUGH PHILADELPHIA AND THE VIRUS HAVE A HISTORY OF SORTS.

1793. FIVE THOUSAND PEOPLE DIED AND SEVENTEEN THOUSAND FLED THE CITY.

IF YOU ASK ME, WHICH YOU WILL, THE PERSON OR PERSONS BEHIND THIS HAVE DEVELOPED A RESISTANCE.

AND WITH THE AMOUNT OF OPEN WOUNDS, THOSE CRIME SCENES SHOULD BE A MESS.

"AT DEATH, THE HEART STOPS. THAT COULD EXPLAIN THE LACK OF SPILLAGE."

"BUT THE BODIES... THEY'RE ON 'E' BY THE TIME I GET 'EM."

"DRAINED SOMEPLACE ELSE AND THE BODY DUMPED?"

"WOULD REQUIRE TIME."

"AND PRECISION."

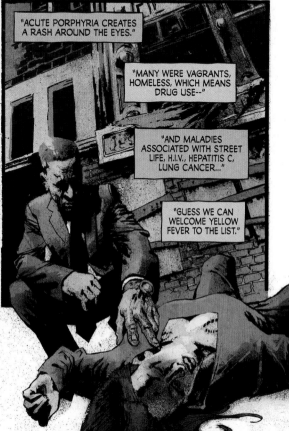

"ACUTE PORPHYRIA CREATES A RASH AROUND THE EYES."

"MANY WERE VAGRANTS, HOMELESS, WHICH MEANS DRUG USE--"

"AND MALADIES ASSOCIATED WITH STREET LIFE, H.I.V., HEPATITIS C, LUNG CANCER..."

"GUESS WE CAN WELCOME YELLOW FEVER TO THE LIST."

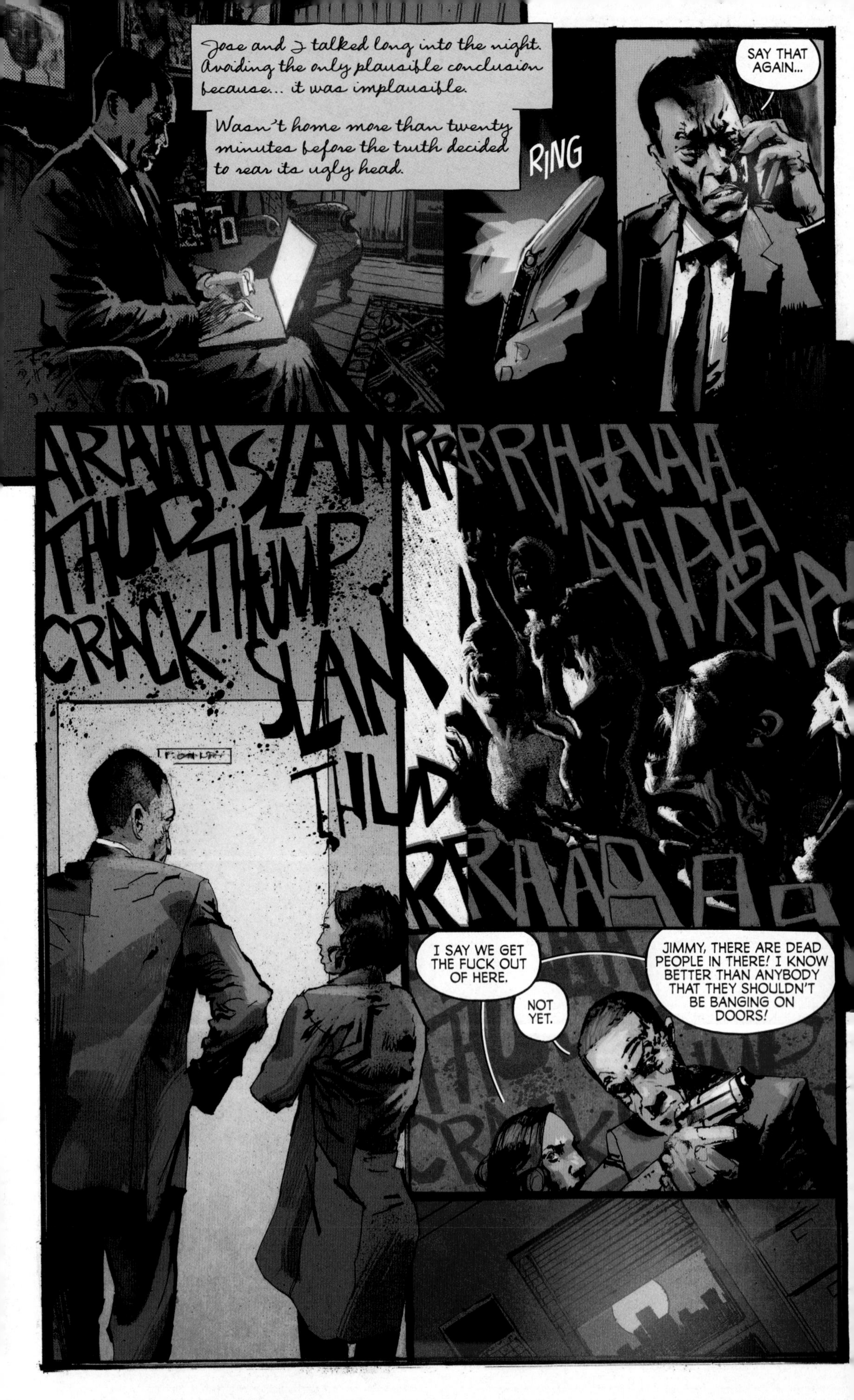
Jose and I talked long into the night. Avoiding the only plausible conclusion because... it was implausible.
Wasn't home more than twenty minutes before the truth decided to rear its ugly head.
RING
SAY THAT AGAIN...
ARRHH SLAM
THUD
THUMP
CRACK
SLAM
THUD
RRRRH RAAA
RRRAAAA
I SAY WE GET THE FUCK OUT OF HERE.
NOT YET.
JIMMY, THERE ARE DEAD PEOPLE IN THERE! I KNOW BETTER THAN ANYBODY THAT THEY SHOULDN'T BE BANGING ON DOORS!

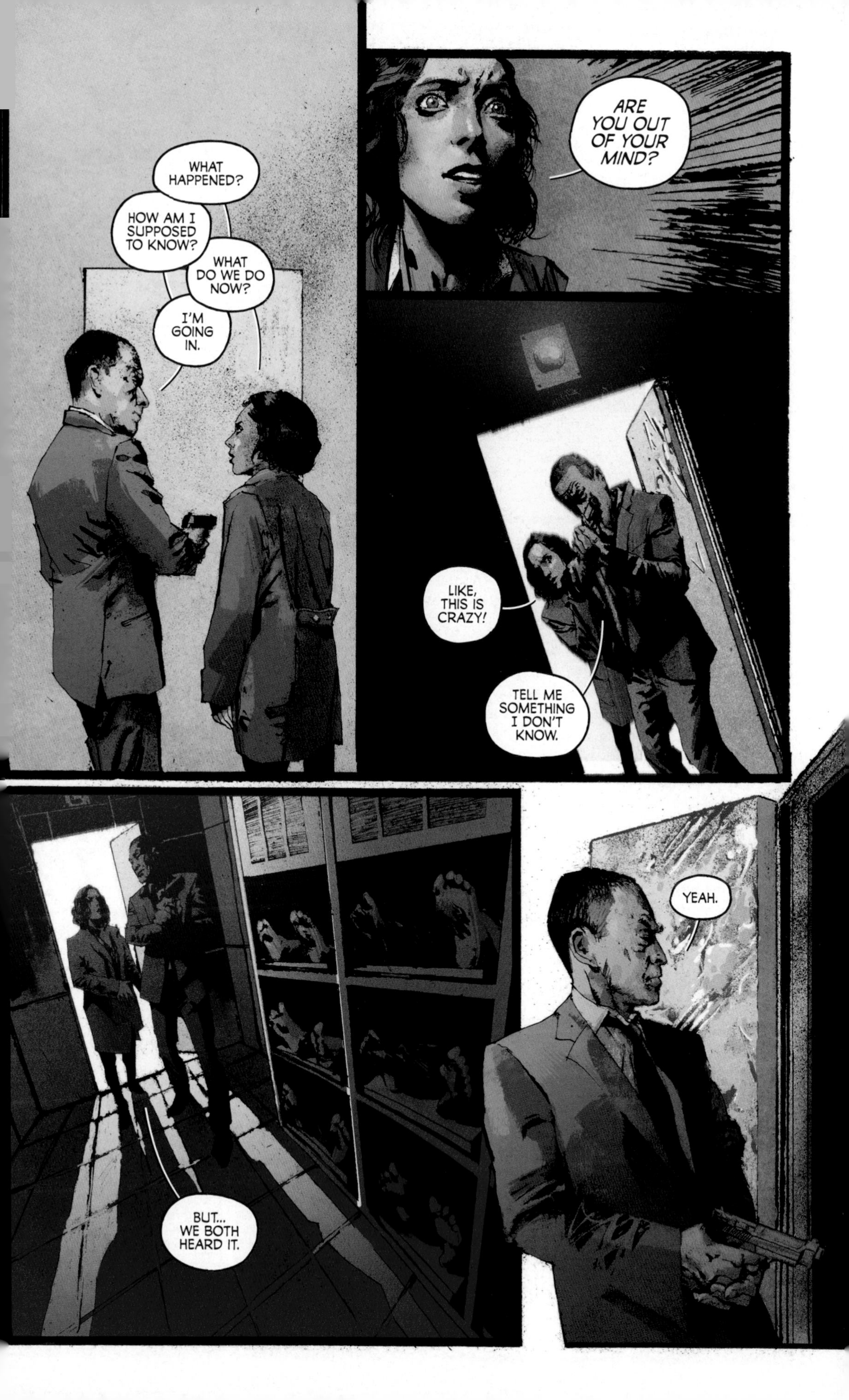
WHAT HAPPENED?
HOW AM I SUPPOSED TO KNOW?
WHAT DO WE DO NOW?
I'M GOING IN.
ARE YOU OUT OF YOUR MIND?
LIKE, THIS IS CRAZY!
TELL ME SOMETHING I DON'T KNOW.
BUT... WE BOTH HEARD IT.
YEAH.

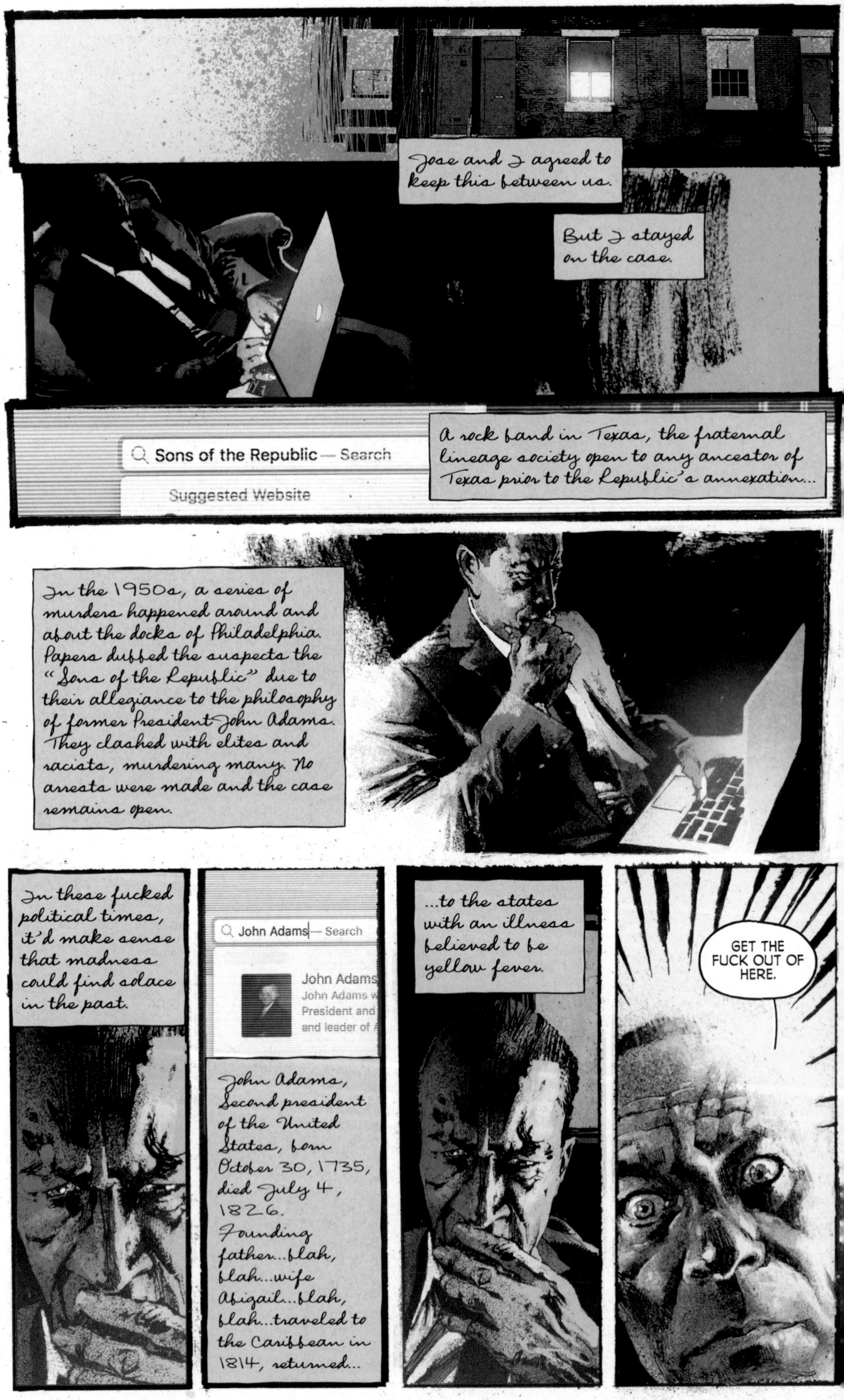
Jose and I agreed to keep this between us.
But I stayed on the case.
Sons of the Republic — Search
Suggested Website
A rock band in Texas, the fraternal lineage society open to any ancestor of Texas prior to the Republic's annexation...
In the 1950s, a series of murders happened around and about the docks of Philadelphia. Papers dubbed the suspects the "Sons of the Republic" due to their allegiance to the philosophy of former President John Adams. They clashed with elites and racists, murdering many. No arrests were made and the case remains open.
In these fucked political times, it'd make sense that madness could find solace in the past.
John Adams — Search
John Adams
John Adams w
President and
and leader of A
John Adams, Second president of the United States, born October 30, 1735, died July 4, 1826. Founding father...blah, blah...wife Abigail...blah, blah...traveled to the Caribbean in 1814, returned...
...to the states with an illness believed to be yellow fever.
GET THE FUCK OUT OF HERE.

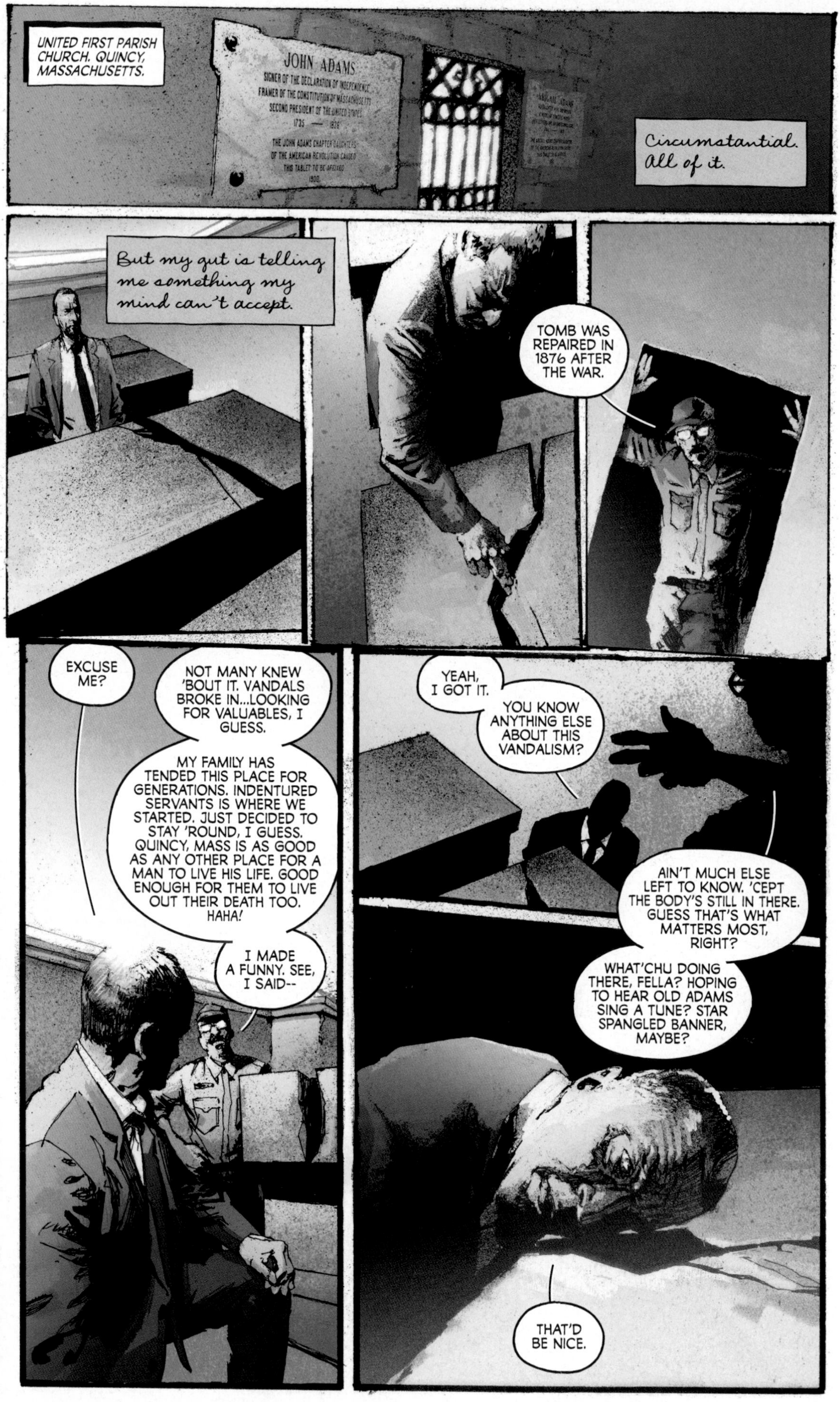
UNITED FIRST PARISH CHURCH. QUINCY, MASSACHUSETTS.
JOHN ADAMS
SIGNER OF THE DECLARATION OF INDEPENDENCE
FRAMER OF THE CONSTITUTION OF MASSACHUSETTS
SECOND PRESIDENT OF THE UNITED STATES
1735 — 1826
THE JOHN ADAMS CHAPTER DAUGHTERS OF THE AMERICAN REVOLUTION CAUSED THIS TABLET TO BE AFFIXED 1900.
Circumstantial. All of it.
But my gut is telling me something my mind can't accept.
TOMB WAS REPAIRED IN 1876 AFTER THE WAR.
EXCUSE ME?
NOT MANY KNEW 'BOUT IT. VANDALS BROKE IN...LOOKING FOR VALUABLES, I GUESS.
MY FAMILY HAS TENDED THIS PLACE FOR GENERATIONS. INDENTURED SERVANTS IS WHERE WE STARTED. JUST DECIDED TO STAY 'ROUND, I GUESS. QUINCY, MASS IS AS GOOD AS ANY OTHER PLACE FOR A MAN TO LIVE HIS LIFE. GOOD ENOUGH FOR THEM TO LIVE OUT THEIR DEATH TOO. HAHA!
I MADE A FUNNY. SEE, I SAID--
YEAH, I GOT IT.
YOU KNOW ANYTHING ELSE ABOUT THIS VANDALISM?
AIN'T MUCH ELSE LEFT TO KNOW. 'CEPT THE BODY'S STILL IN THERE. GUESS THAT'S WHAT MATTERS MOST, RIGHT?
WHAT'CHU DOING THERE, FELLA? HOPING TO HEAR OLD ADAMS SING A TUNE? STAR SPANGLED BANNER, MAYBE?
THAT'D BE NICE.

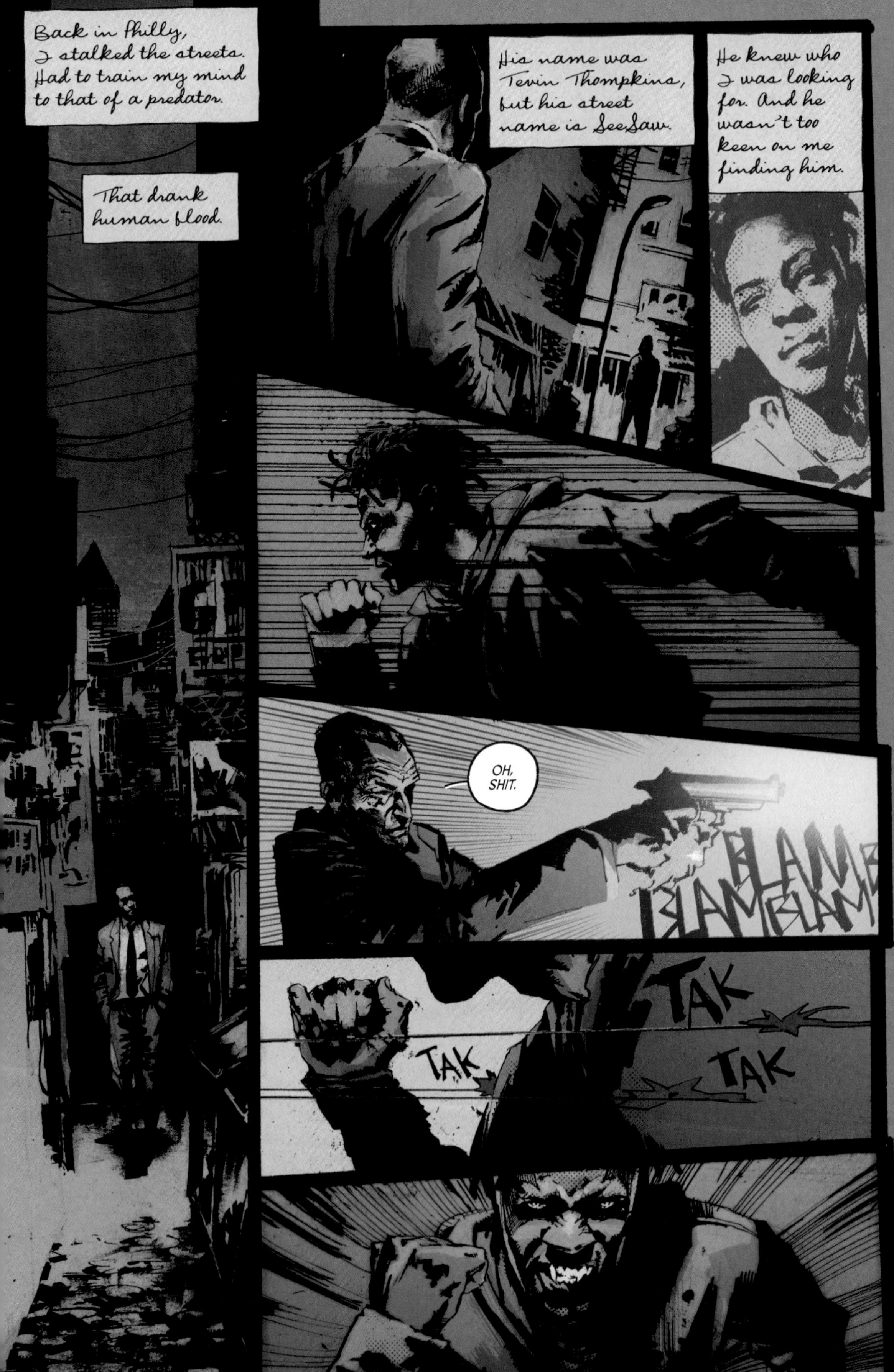
Back in Philly, I stalked the streets. Had to train my mind to that of a predator.
That drank human blood.
His name was Tevin Thompkins, but his street name is SeeSaw.
He knew who I was looking for. And he wasn't too keen on me finding him.
OH, SHIT.
BLAM
BLAM BLAM
TAK
TAK
TAK

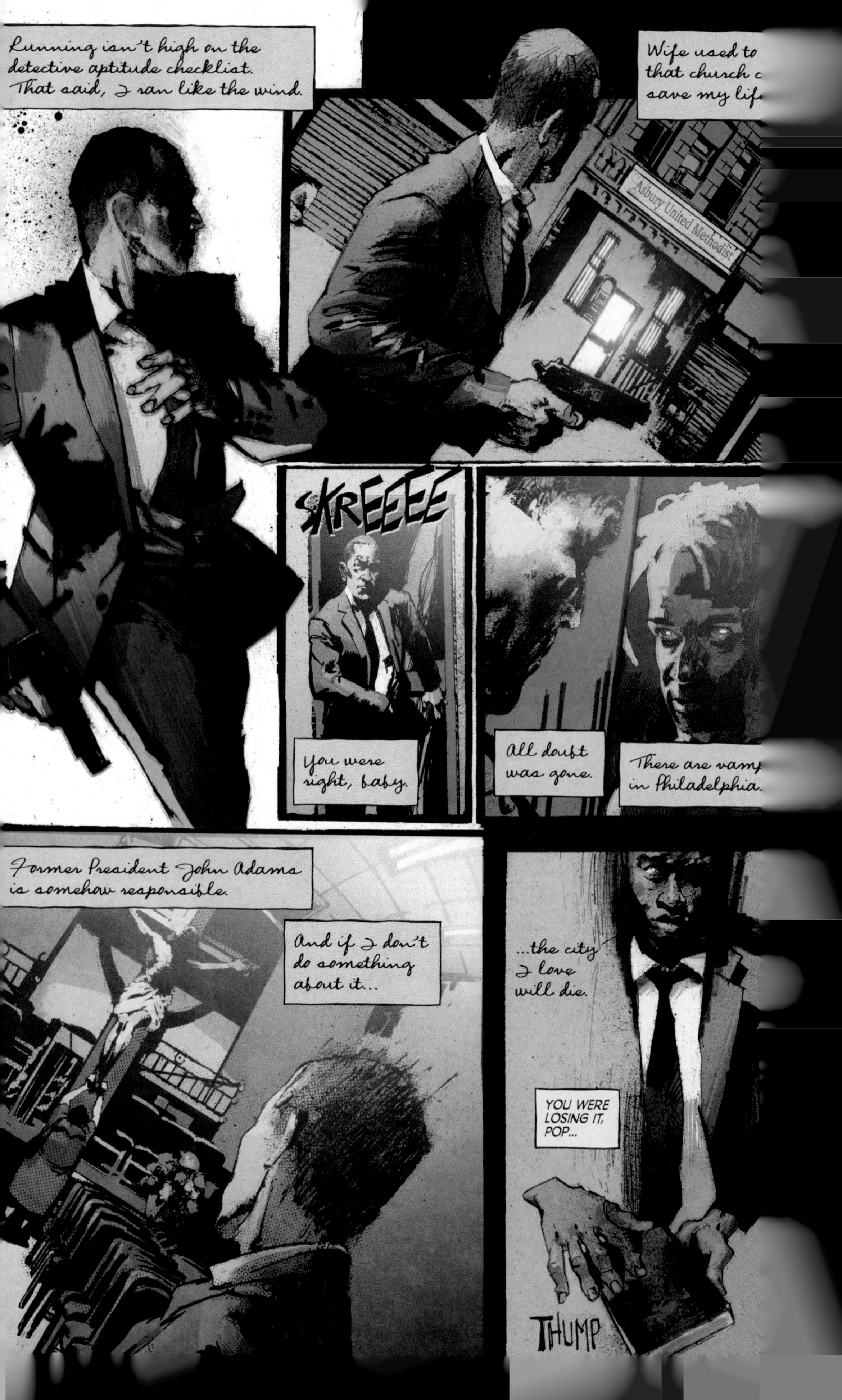
Running isn't high on the detective aptitude checklist. That said, I ran like the wind.
Wife used to
that church
save my lif
Asbury United Methodist
SKREEEE
You were right, baby.
All doubt was gone.
There are vamp
in Philadelphia.
Former President John Adams is somehow responsible.
And if I don't do something about it...
...the city I love will die.
YOU WERE LOSING IT, POP...
THUMP

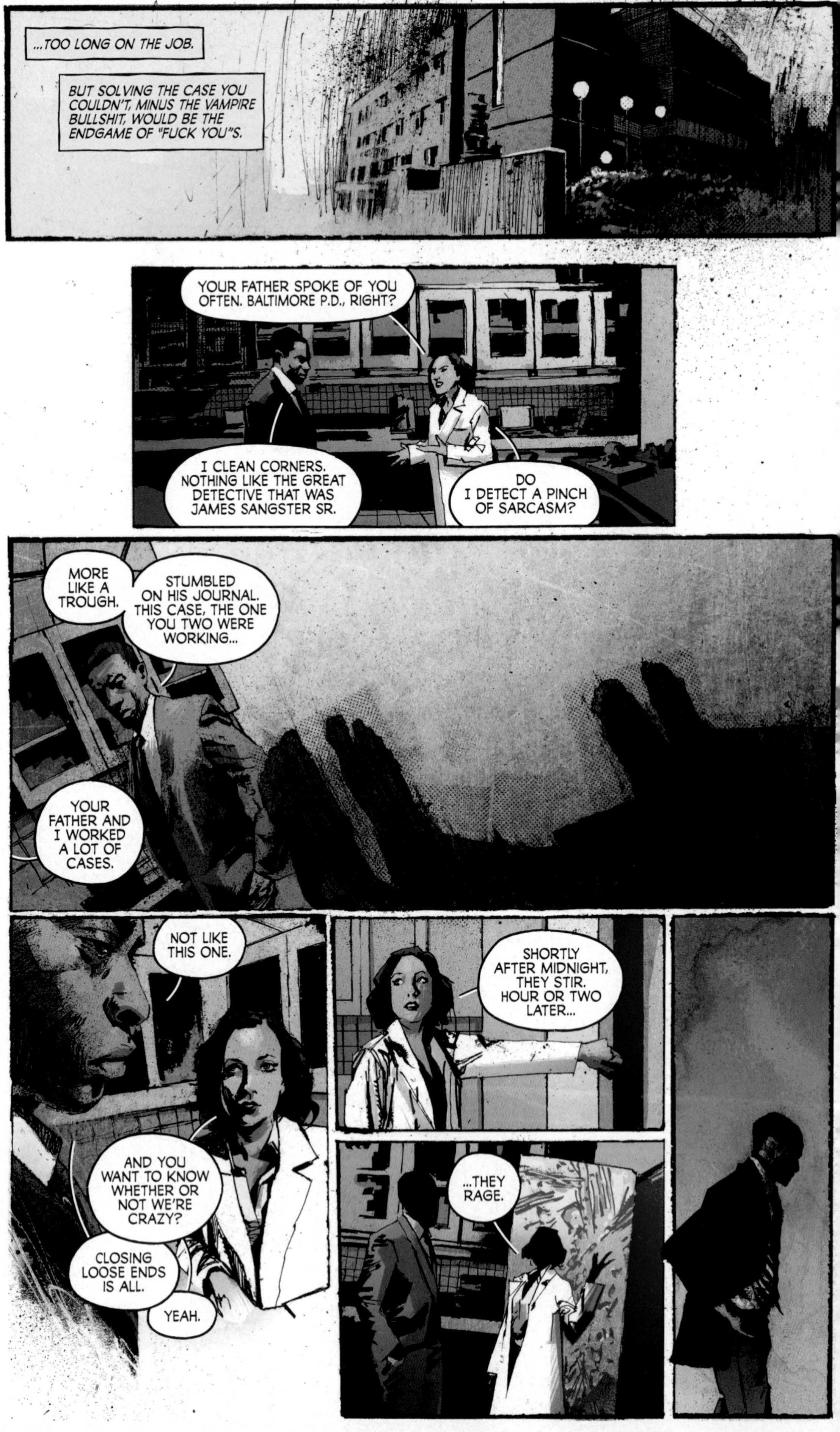

...TOO LONG ON THE JOB.
BUT SOLVING THE CASE YOU COULDN'T, MINUS THE VAMPIRE BULLSHIT, WOULD BE THE ENDGAME OF "FUCK YOU"S.
YOUR FATHER SPOKE OF YOU OFTEN. BALTIMORE P.D., RIGHT?
I CLEAN CORNERS. NOTHING LIKE THE GREAT DETECTIVE THAT WAS JAMES SANGSTER SR.
DO I DETECT A PINCH OF SARCASM?
MORE LIKE A TROUGH.
STUMBLED ON HIS JOURNAL. THIS CASE, THE ONE YOU TWO WERE WORKING...
YOUR FATHER AND I WORKED A LOT OF CASES.
NOT LIKE THIS ONE.
AND YOU WANT TO KNOW WHETHER OR NOT WE'RE CRAZY?
CLOSING LOOSE ENDS IS ALL.
YEAH.
SHORTLY AFTER MIDNIGHT, THEY STIR. HOUR OR TWO LATER...
...THEY RAGE.

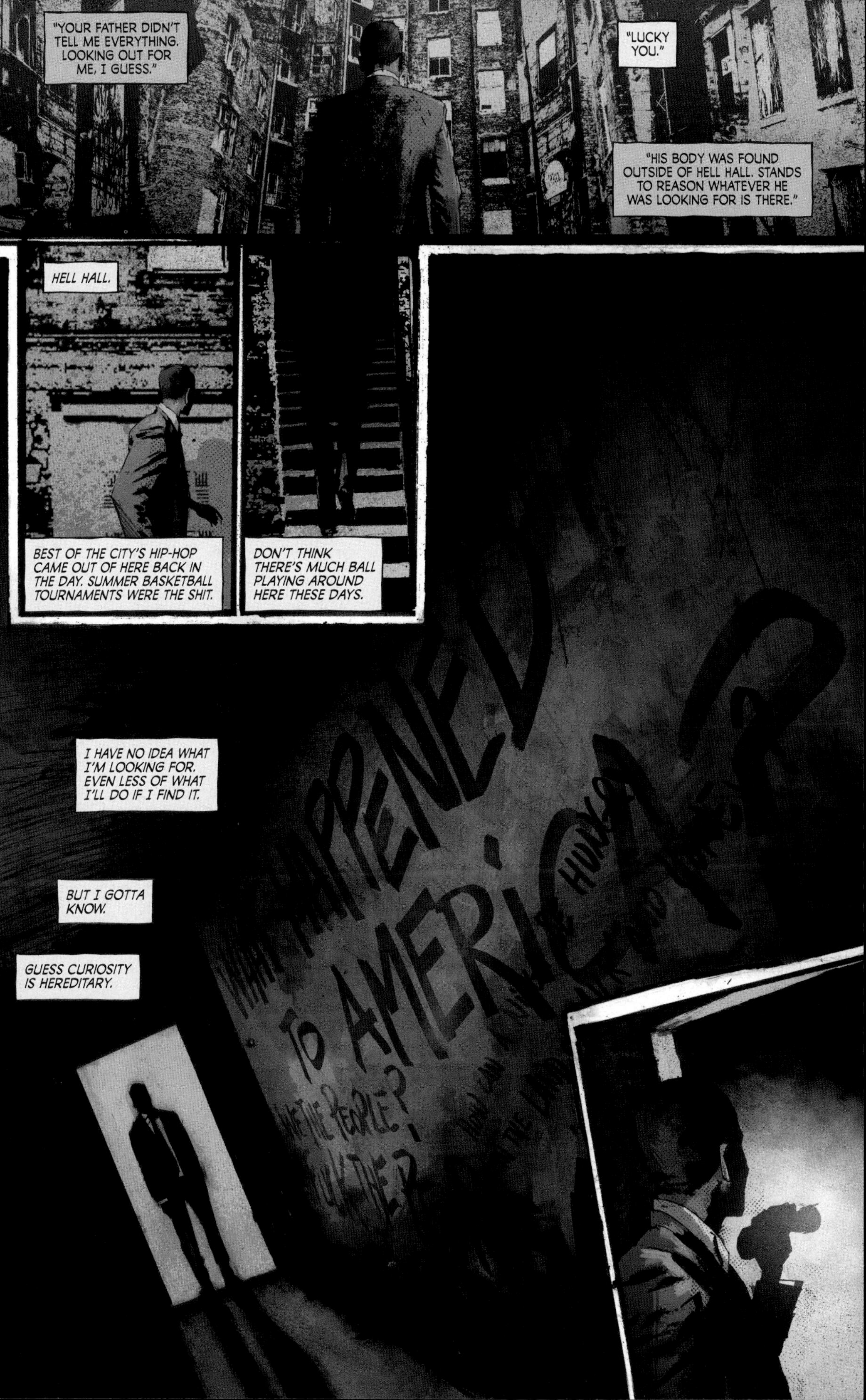

"YOUR FATHER DIDN'T TELL ME EVERYTHING. LOOKING OUT FOR ME, I GUESS."
"LUCKY YOU."
"HIS BODY WAS FOUND OUTSIDE OF HELL HALL. STANDS TO REASON WHATEVER HE WAS LOOKING FOR IS THERE."
HELL HALL.
BEST OF THE CITY'S HIP-HOP CAME OUT OF HERE BACK IN THE DAY. SUMMER BASKETBALL TOURNAMENTS WERE THE SHIT.
DON'T THINK THERE'S MUCH BALL PLAYING AROUND HERE THESE DAYS.
I HAVE NO IDEA WHAT I'M LOOKING FOR. EVEN LESS OF WHAT I'LL DO IF I FIND IT.
BUT I GOTTA KNOW.
GUESS CURIOSITY IS HEREDITARY.

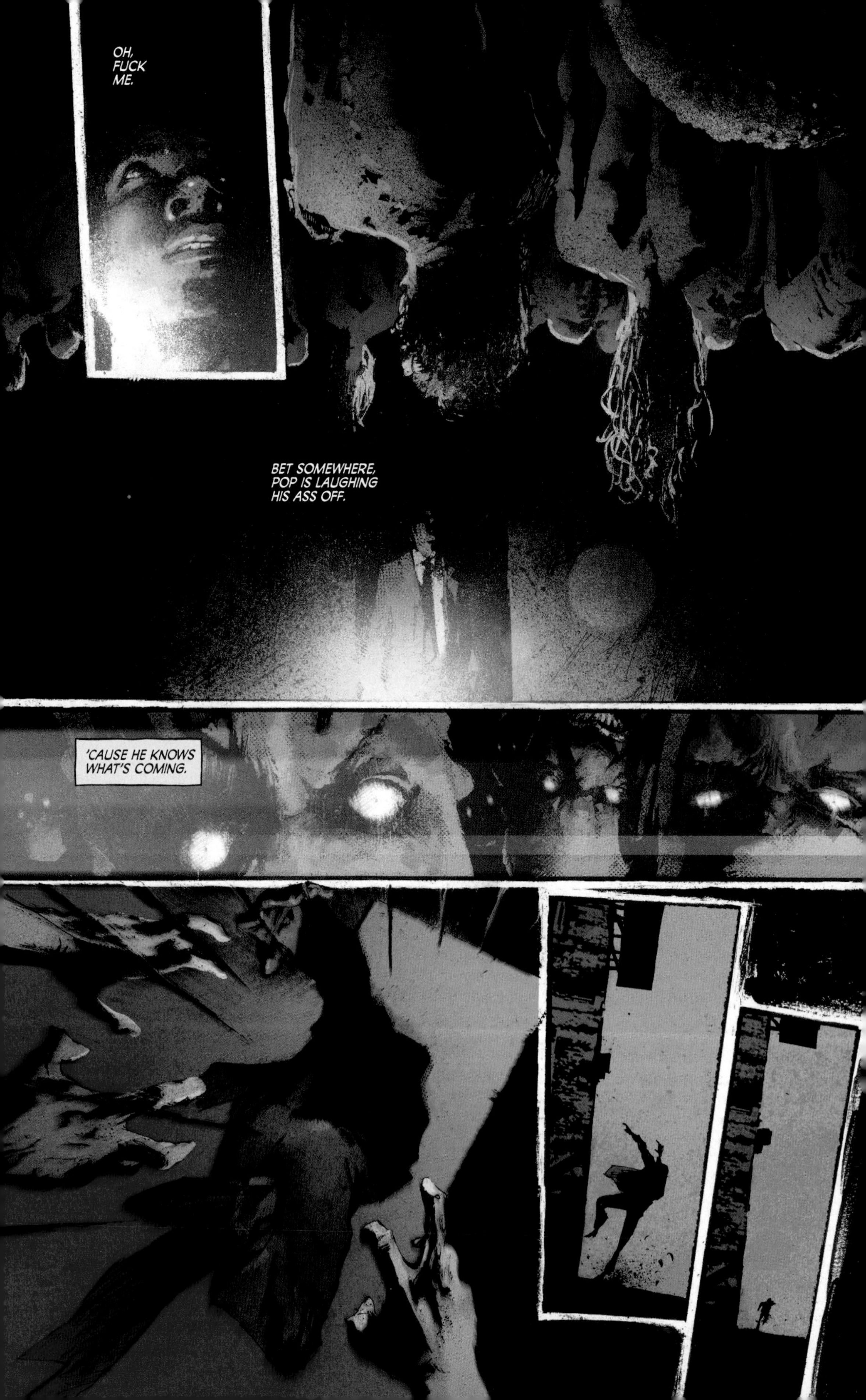
OH, FUCK ME.
BET SOMEWHERE, POP IS LAUGHING HIS ASS OFF.
'CAUSE HE KNOWS WHAT'S COMING.

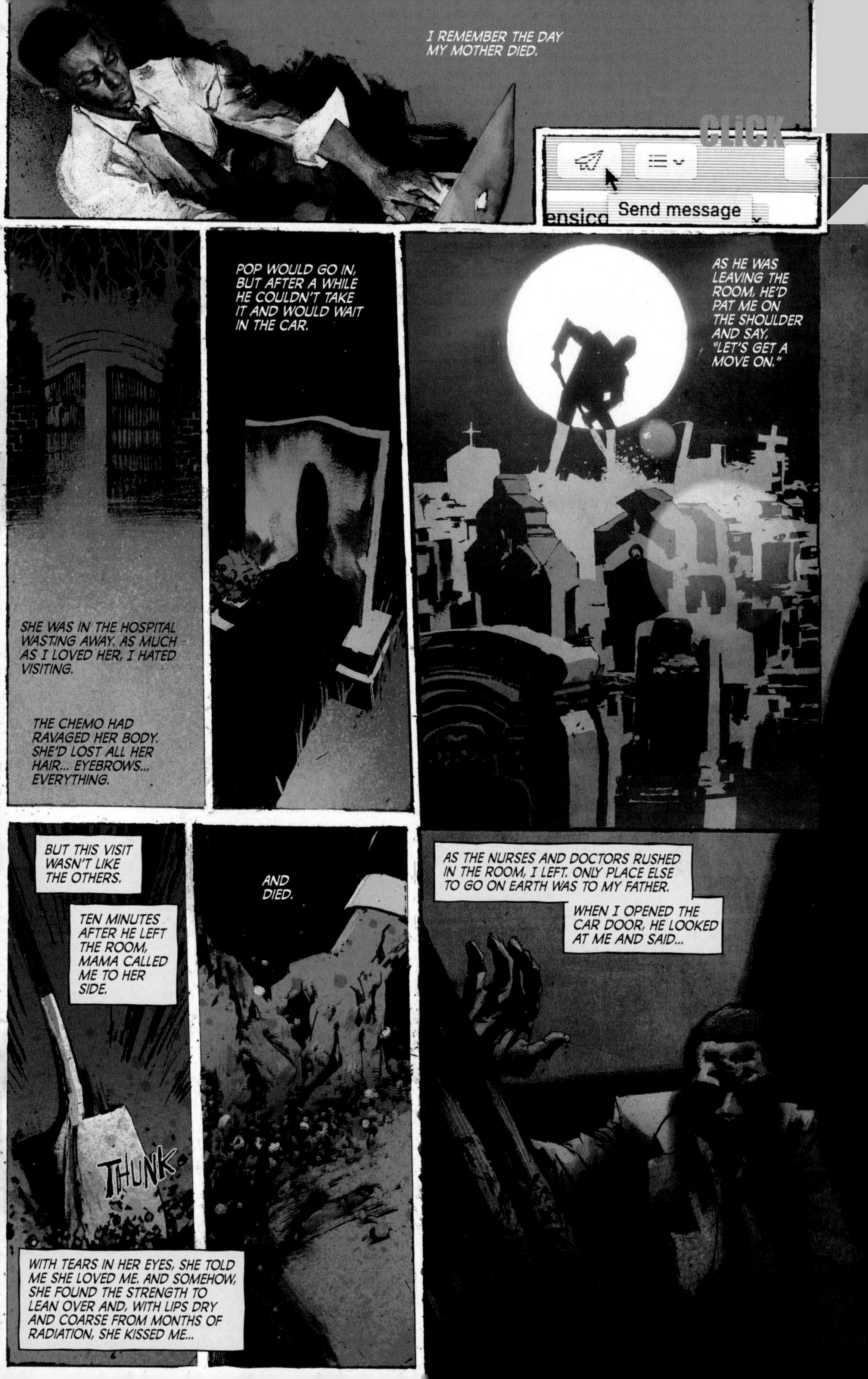
I REMEMBER THE DAY MY MOTHER DIED.
CLICK
Send message
SHE WAS IN THE HOSPITAL WASTING AWAY. AS MUCH AS I LOVED HER, I HATED VISITING.
THE CHEMO HAD RAVAGED HER BODY. SHE'D LOST ALL HER HAIR... EYEBROWS... EVERYTHING.
POP WOULD GO IN, BUT AFTER A WHILE HE COULDN'T TAKE IT AND WOULD WAIT IN THE CAR.
AS HE WAS LEAVING THE ROOM, HE'D PAT ME ON THE SHOULDER AND SAY, "LET'S GET A MOVE ON."
BUT THIS VISIT WASN'T LIKE THE OTHERS.
TEN MINUTES AFTER HE LEFT THE ROOM, MAMA CALLED ME TO HER SIDE.
THUNK
WITH TEARS IN HER EYES, SHE TOLD ME SHE LOVED ME. AND SOMEHOW, SHE FOUND THE STRENGTH TO LEAN OVER AND, WITH LIPS DRY AND COARSE FROM MONTHS OF RADIATION, SHE KISSED ME...
AND DIED.
AS THE NURSES AND DOCTORS RUSHED IN THE ROOM, I LEFT. ONLY PLACE ELSE TO GO ON EARTH WAS TO MY FATHER.
WHEN I OPENED THE CAR DOOR, HE LOOKED AT ME AND SAID...

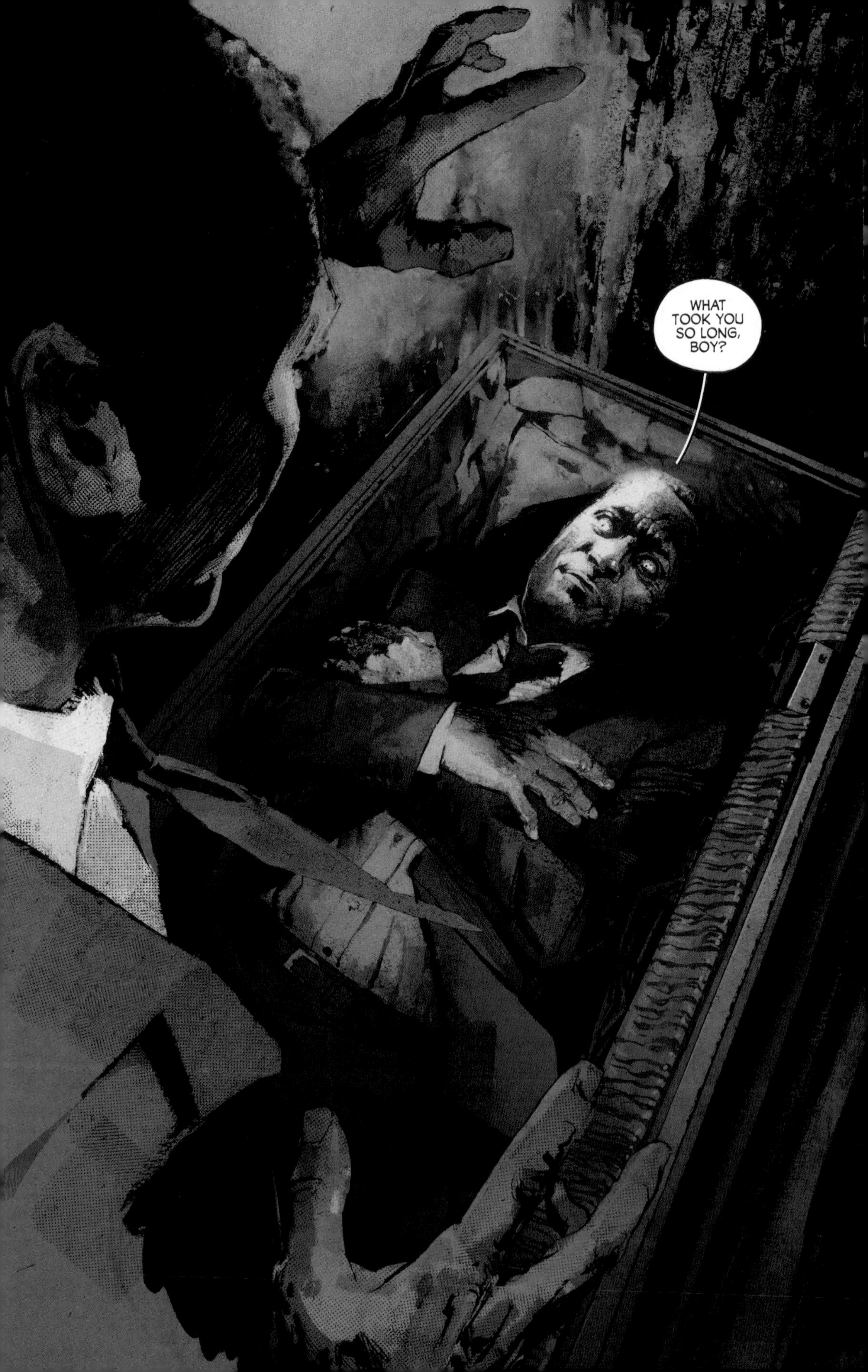
WHAT TOOK YOU SO LONG, BOY?

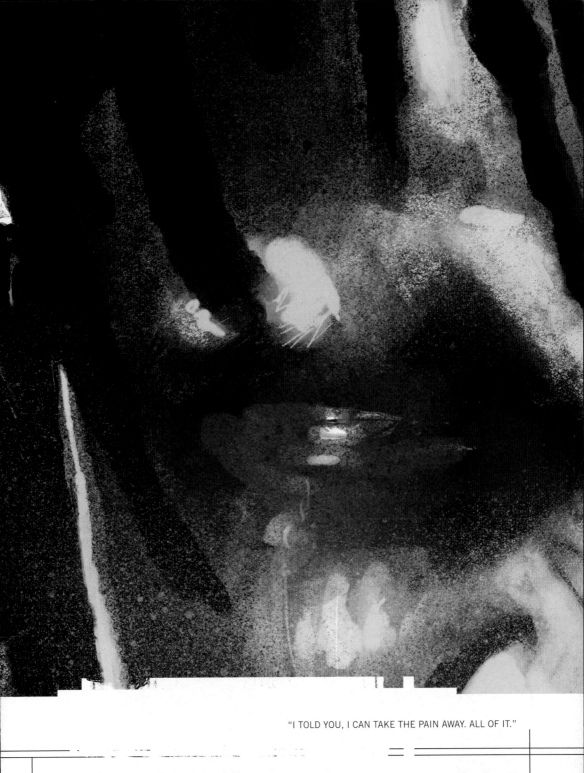

"I TOLD YOU, I CAN TAKE THE PAIN AWAY. ALL OF IT."

DEATH, MY SWEET SAVIOR

Chapter II

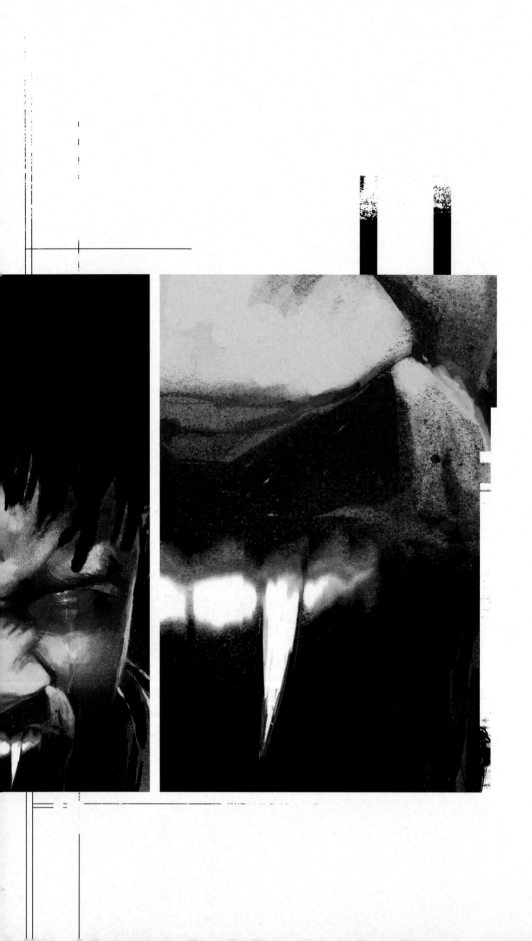

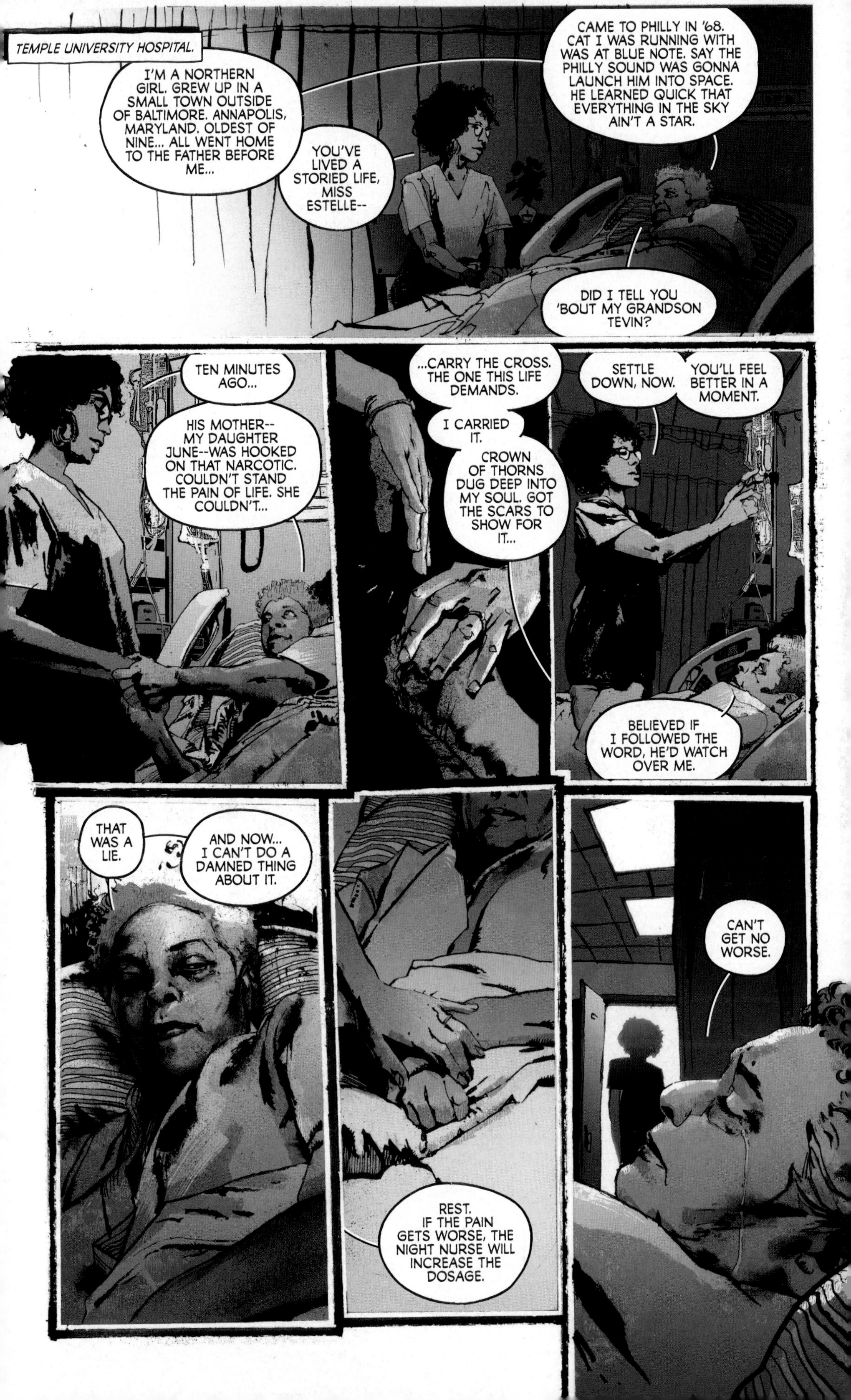
TEMPLE UNIVERSITY HOSPITAL.
I'M A NORTHERN GIRL. GREW UP IN A SMALL TOWN OUTSIDE OF BALTIMORE. ANNAPOLIS, MARYLAND. OLDEST OF NINE... ALL WENT HOME TO THE FATHER BEFORE ME...
YOU'VE LIVED A STORIED LIFE, MISS ESTELLE--
CAME TO PHILLY IN '68. CAT I WAS RUNNING WITH WAS AT BLUE NOTE. SAY THE PHILLY SOUND WAS GONNA LAUNCH HIM INTO SPACE. HE LEARNED QUICK THAT EVERYTHING IN THE SKY AIN'T A STAR.
DID I TELL YOU 'BOUT MY GRANDSON TEVIN?
TEN MINUTES AGO...
HIS MOTHER--MY DAUGHTER JUNE--WAS HOOKED ON THAT NARCOTIC. COULDN'T STAND THE PAIN OF LIFE. SHE COULDN'T...
...CARRY THE CROSS. THE ONE THIS LIFE DEMANDS.
I CARRIED IT.
CROWN OF THORNS DUG DEEP INTO MY SOUL. GOT THE SCARS TO SHOW FOR IT...
SETTLE DOWN, NOW.
YOU'LL FEEL BETTER IN A MOMENT.
BELIEVED IF I FOLLOWED THE WORD, HE'D WATCH OVER ME.
THAT WAS A LIE.
AND NOW... I CAN'T DO A DAMNED THING ABOUT IT.
REST. IF THE PAIN GETS WORSE, THE NIGHT NURSE WILL INCREASE THE DOSAGE.
CAN'T GET NO WORSE.

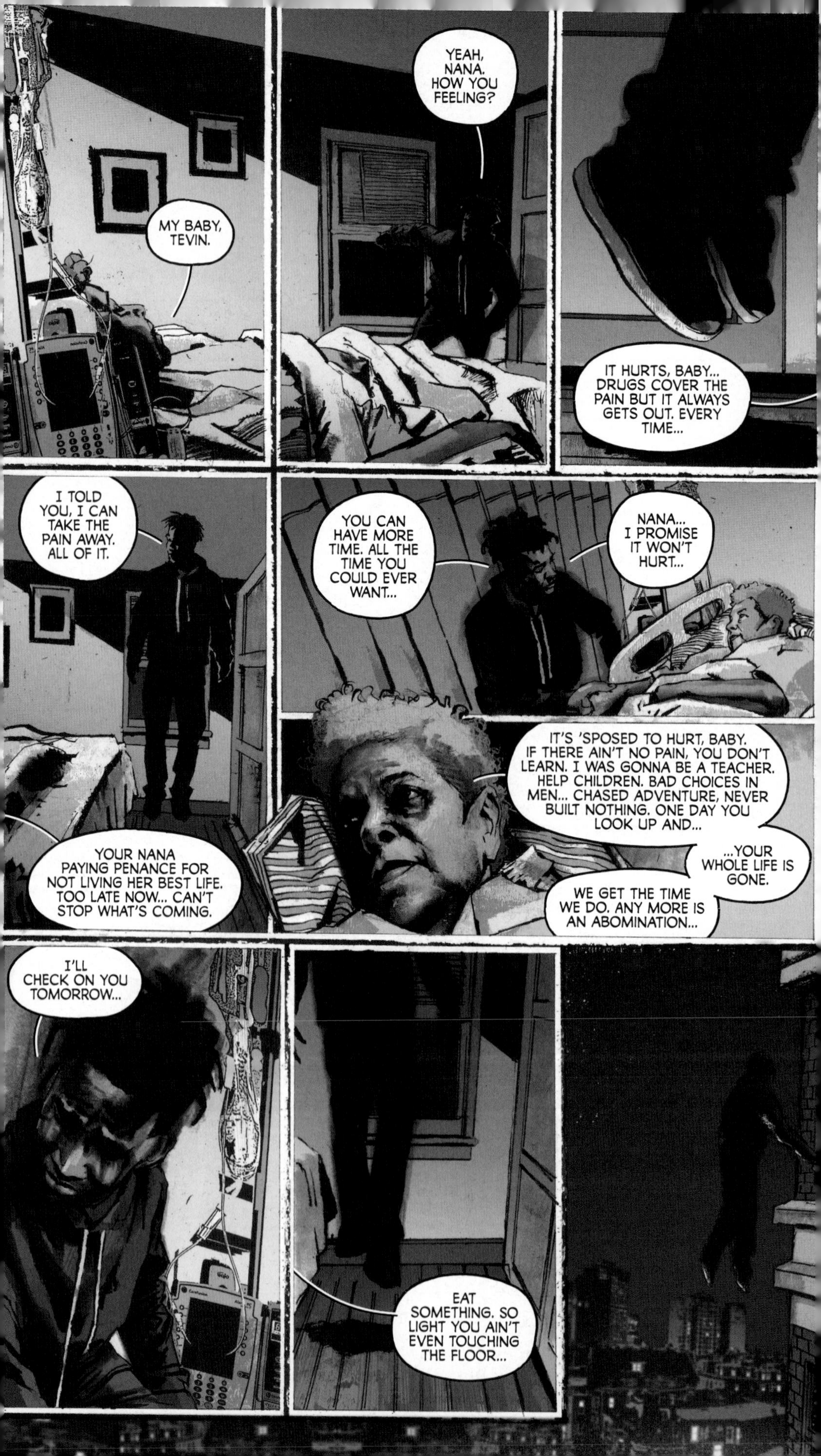
MY BABY, TEVIN.
YEAH, NANA. HOW YOU FEELING?
IT HURTS, BABY... DRUGS COVER THE PAIN BUT IT ALWAYS GETS OUT. EVERY TIME...
I TOLD YOU, I CAN TAKE THE PAIN AWAY. ALL OF IT.
YOUR NANA PAYING PENANCE FOR NOT LIVING HER BEST LIFE. TOO LATE NOW... CAN'T STOP WHAT'S COMING.
YOU CAN HAVE MORE TIME. ALL THE TIME YOU COULD EVER WANT...
NANA... I PROMISE IT WON'T HURT...
IT'S 'SPOSED TO HURT, BABY. IF THERE AIN'T NO PAIN, YOU DON'T LEARN. I WAS GONNA BE A TEACHER. HELP CHILDREN. BAD CHOICES IN MEN... CHASED ADVENTURE, NEVER BUILT NOTHING. ONE DAY YOU LOOK UP AND...
...YOUR WHOLE LIFE IS GONE.
WE GET THE TIME WE DO. ANY MORE IS AN ABOMINATION...
I'LL CHECK ON YOU TOMORROW...
EAT SOMETHING. SO LIGHT YOU AIN'T EVEN TOUCHING THE FLOOR...

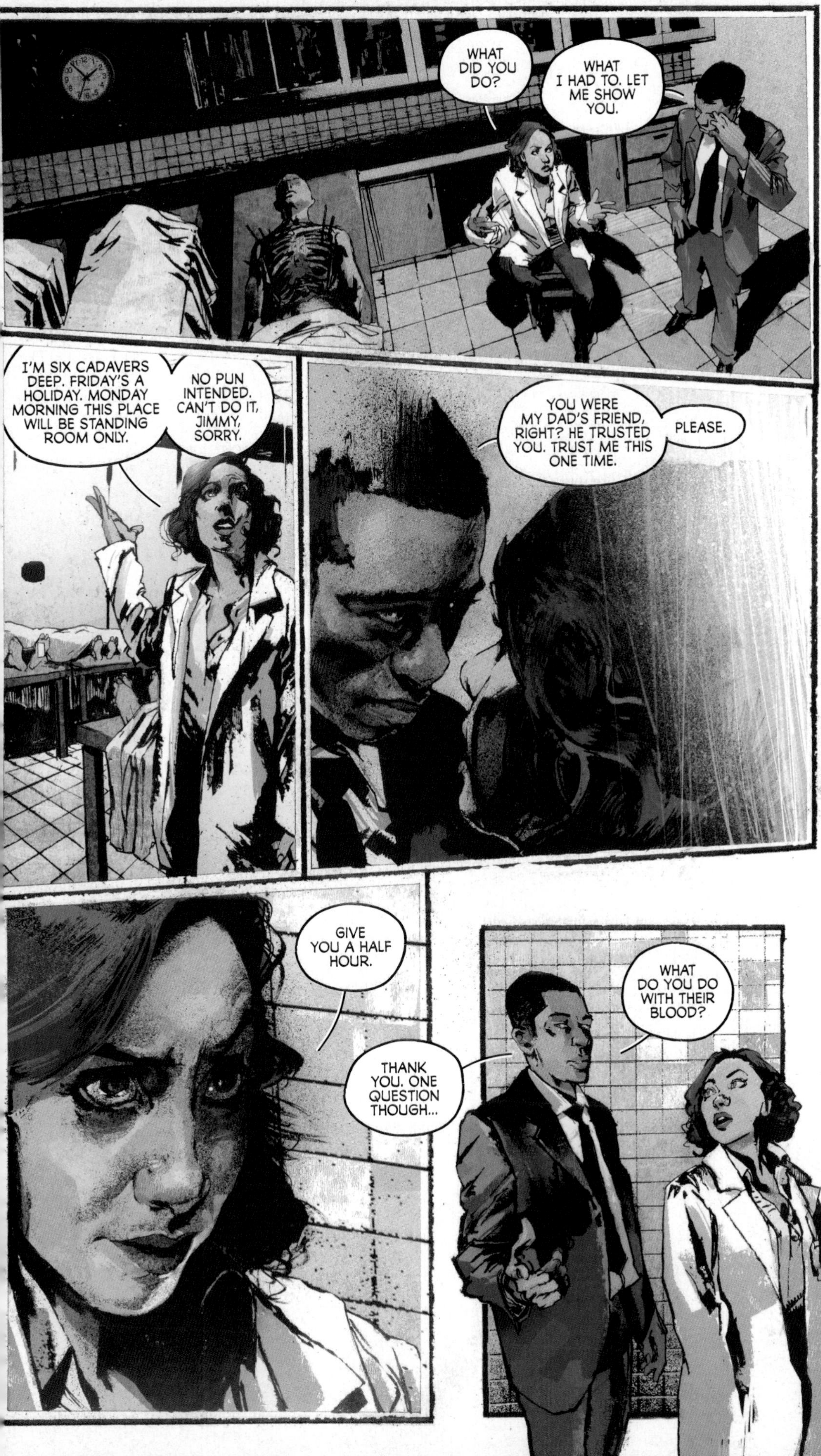

WHAT DID YOU DO?
WHAT I HAD TO. LET ME SHOW YOU.
I'M SIX CADAVERS DEEP. FRIDAY'S A HOLIDAY. MONDAY MORNING THIS PLACE WILL BE STANDING ROOM ONLY.
NO PUN INTENDED. CAN'T DO IT, JIMMY, SORRY.
YOU WERE MY DAD'S FRIEND, RIGHT? HE TRUSTED YOU. TRUST ME THIS ONE TIME.
PLEASE.
GIVE YOU A HALF HOUR.
THANK YOU. ONE QUESTION THOUGH...
WHAT DO YOU DO WITH THEIR BLOOD?

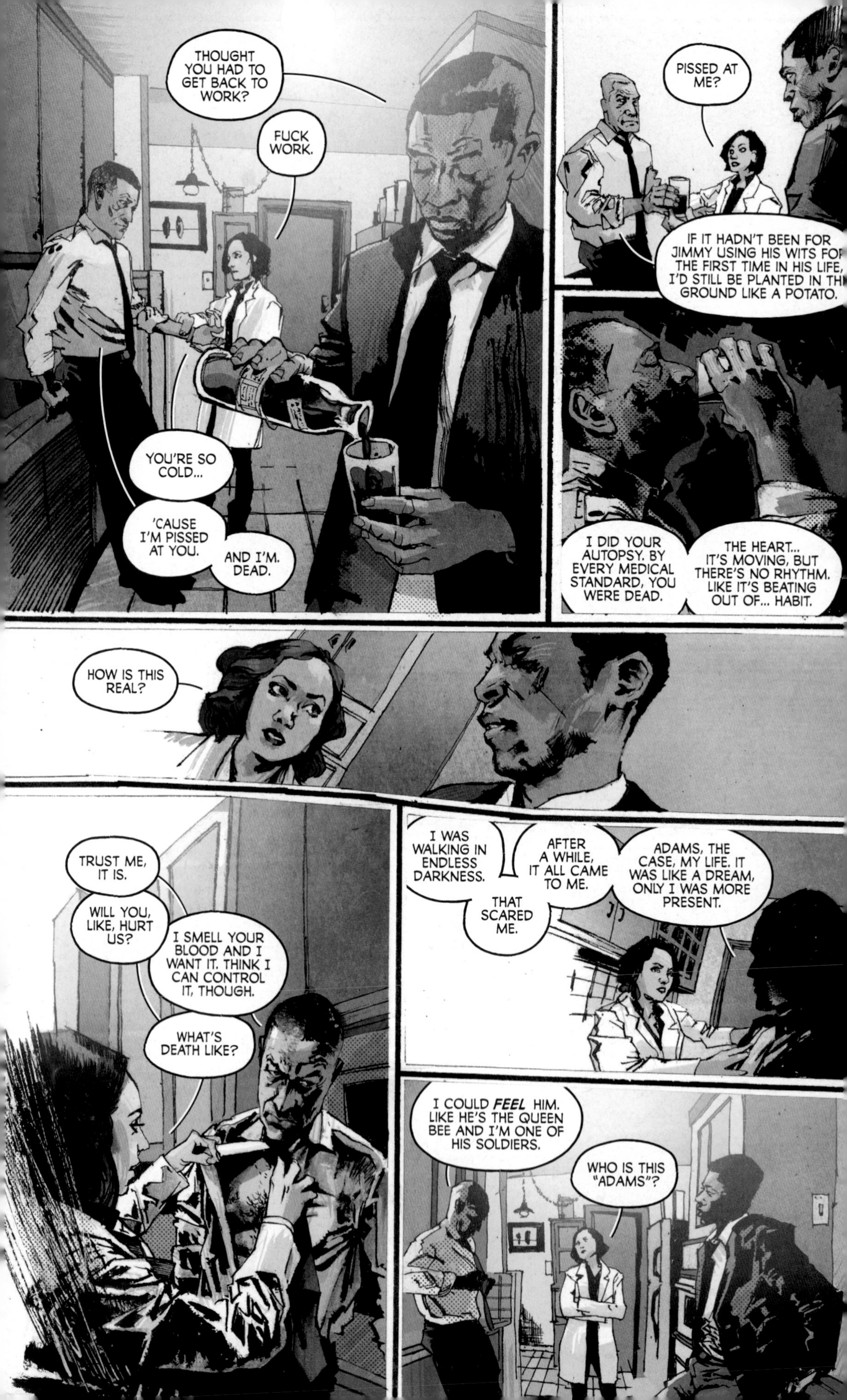
THOUGHT YOU HAD TO GET BACK TO WORK?
FUCK WORK.
YOU'RE SO COLD...
'CAUSE I'M PISSED AT YOU.
AND I'M. DEAD.
PISSED AT ME?
IF IT HADN'T BEEN FOR JIMMY USING HIS WITS FOR THE FIRST TIME IN HIS LIFE, I'D STILL BE PLANTED IN THE GROUND LIKE A POTATO.
I DID YOUR AUTOPSY. BY EVERY MEDICAL STANDARD, YOU WERE DEAD.
THE HEART... IT'S MOVING, BUT THERE'S NO RHYTHM. LIKE IT'S BEATING OUT OF... HABIT.
HOW IS THIS REAL?
TRUST ME, IT IS.
WILL YOU, LIKE, HURT US?
I SMELL YOUR BLOOD AND I WANT IT. THINK I CAN CONTROL IT, THOUGH.
WHAT'S DEATH LIKE?
I WAS WALKING IN ENDLESS DARKNESS.
THAT SCARED ME.
AFTER A WHILE, IT ALL CAME TO ME.
ADAMS, THE CASE, MY LIFE. IT WAS LIKE A DREAM, ONLY I WAS MORE PRESENT.
I COULD *FEEL* HIM. LIKE HE'S THE QUEEN BEE AND I'M ONE OF HIS SOLDIERS.
WHO IS THIS "ADAMS"?

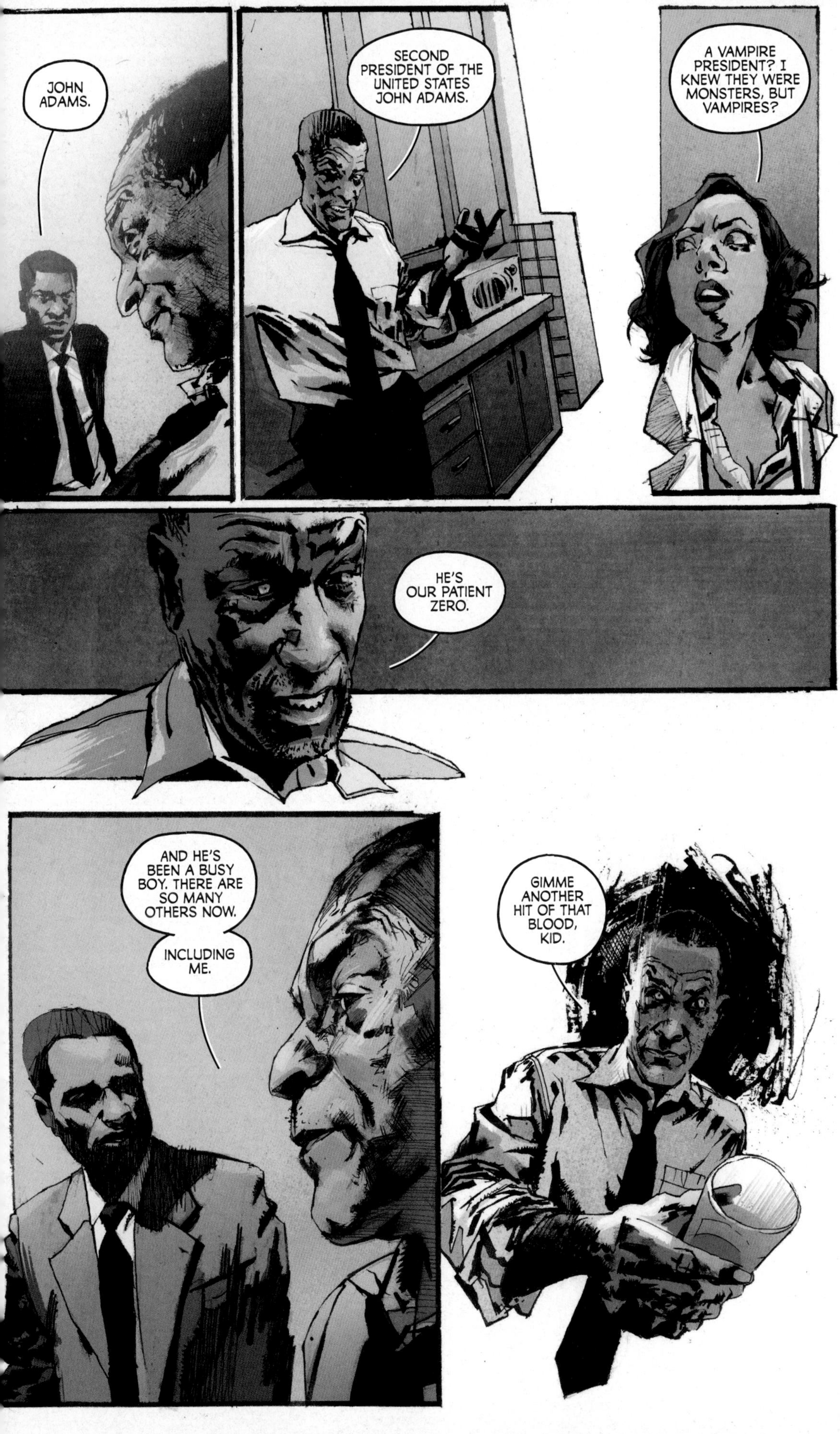

JOHN ADAMS.
SECOND PRESIDENT OF THE UNITED STATES JOHN ADAMS.
A VAMPIRE PRESIDENT? I KNEW THEY WERE MONSTERS, BUT VAMPIRES?
HE'S OUR PATIENT ZERO.
AND HE'S BEEN A BUSY BOY. THERE ARE SO MANY OTHERS NOW.
INCLUDING ME.
GIMME ANOTHER HIT OF THAT BLOOD, KID.

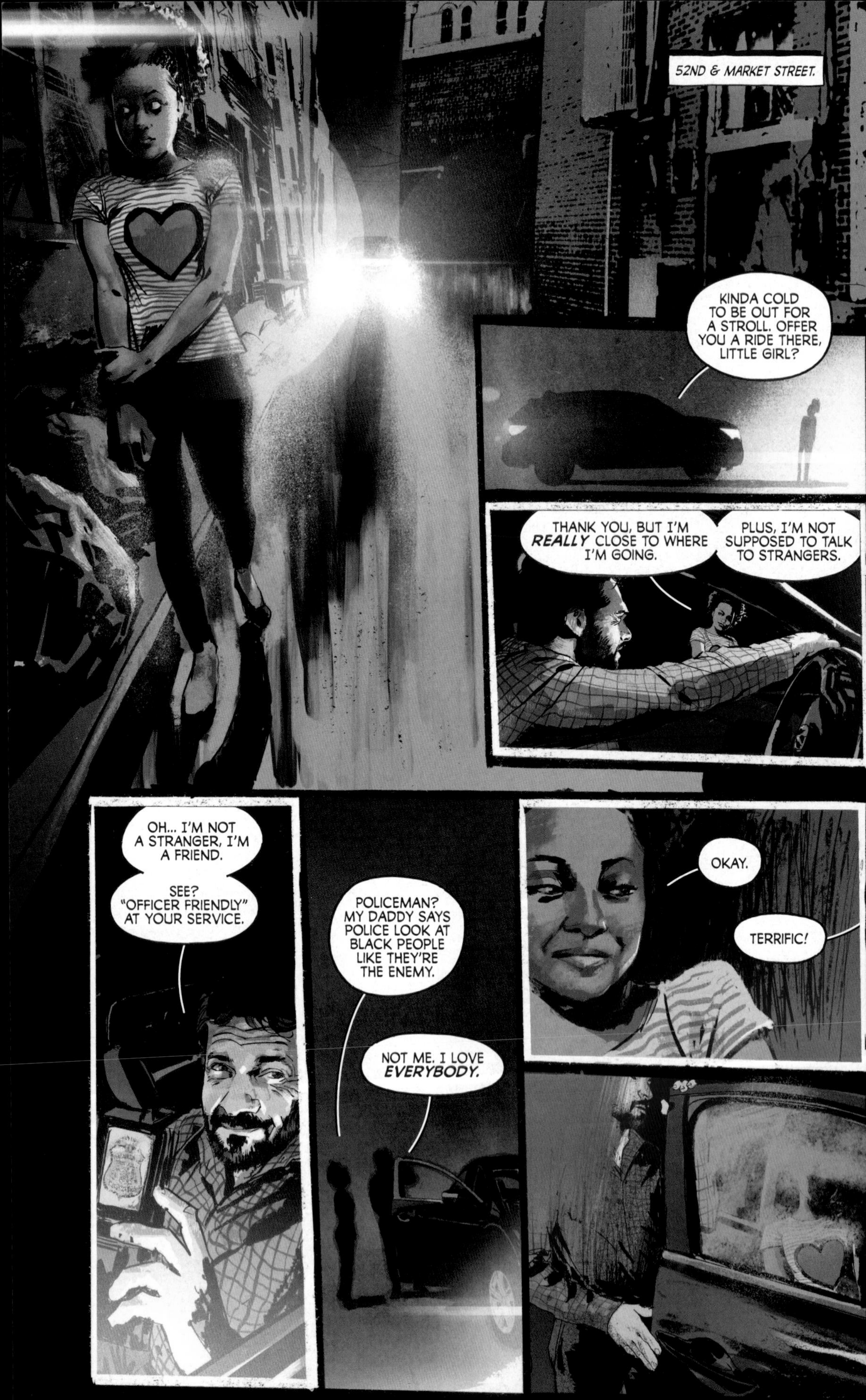
52ND & MARKET STREET.
KINDA COLD TO BE OUT FOR A STROLL. OFFER YOU A RIDE THERE, LITTLE GIRL?
THANK YOU, BUT I'M *REALLY* CLOSE TO WHERE I'M GOING.
PLUS, I'M NOT SUPPOSED TO TALK TO STRANGERS.
OH... I'M NOT A STRANGER, I'M A FRIEND.
SEE? "OFFICER FRIENDLY" AT YOUR SERVICE.
POLICEMAN? MY DADDY SAYS POLICE LOOK AT BLACK PEOPLE LIKE THEY'RE THE ENEMY.
NOT ME. I LOVE *EVERYBODY.*
OKAY.
TERRIFIC!

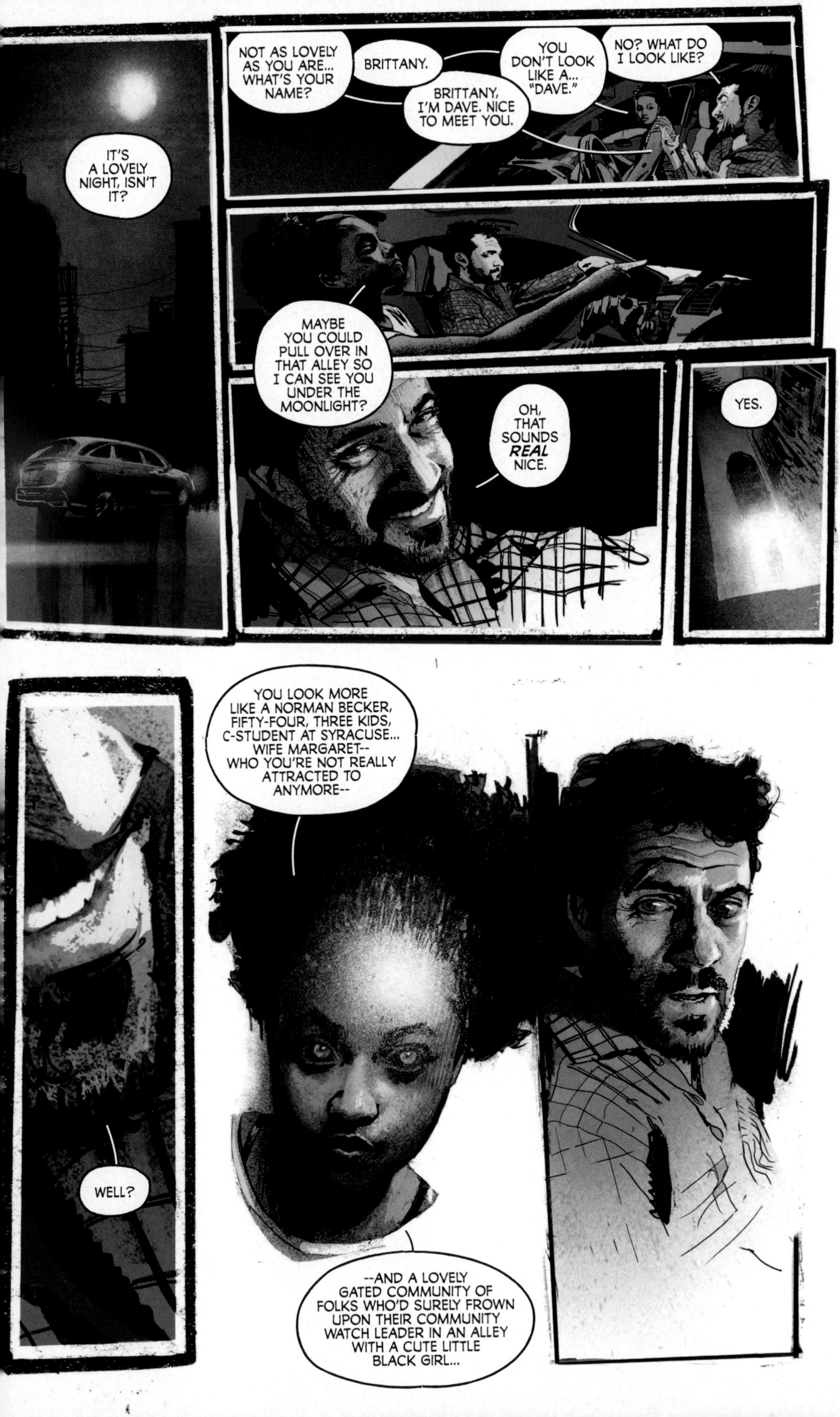
IT'S A LOVELY NIGHT, ISN'T IT?
NOT AS LOVELY AS YOU ARE... WHAT'S YOUR NAME?
BRITTANY.
BRITTANY, I'M DAVE. NICE TO MEET YOU.
YOU DON'T LOOK LIKE A... "DAVE."
NO? WHAT DO I LOOK LIKE?
MAYBE YOU COULD PULL OVER IN THAT ALLEY SO I CAN SEE YOU UNDER THE MOONLIGHT?
OH, THAT SOUNDS *REAL* NICE.
YES.
WELL?
YOU LOOK MORE LIKE A NORMAN BECKER, FIFTY-FOUR, THREE KIDS, C-STUDENT AT SYRACUSE... WIFE MARGARET-- WHO YOU'RE NOT REALLY ATTRACTED TO ANYMORE--
--AND A LOVELY GATED COMMUNITY OF FOLKS WHO'D SURELY FROWN UPON THEIR COMMUNITY WATCH LEADER IN AN ALLEY WITH A CUTE LITTLE BLACK GIRL...

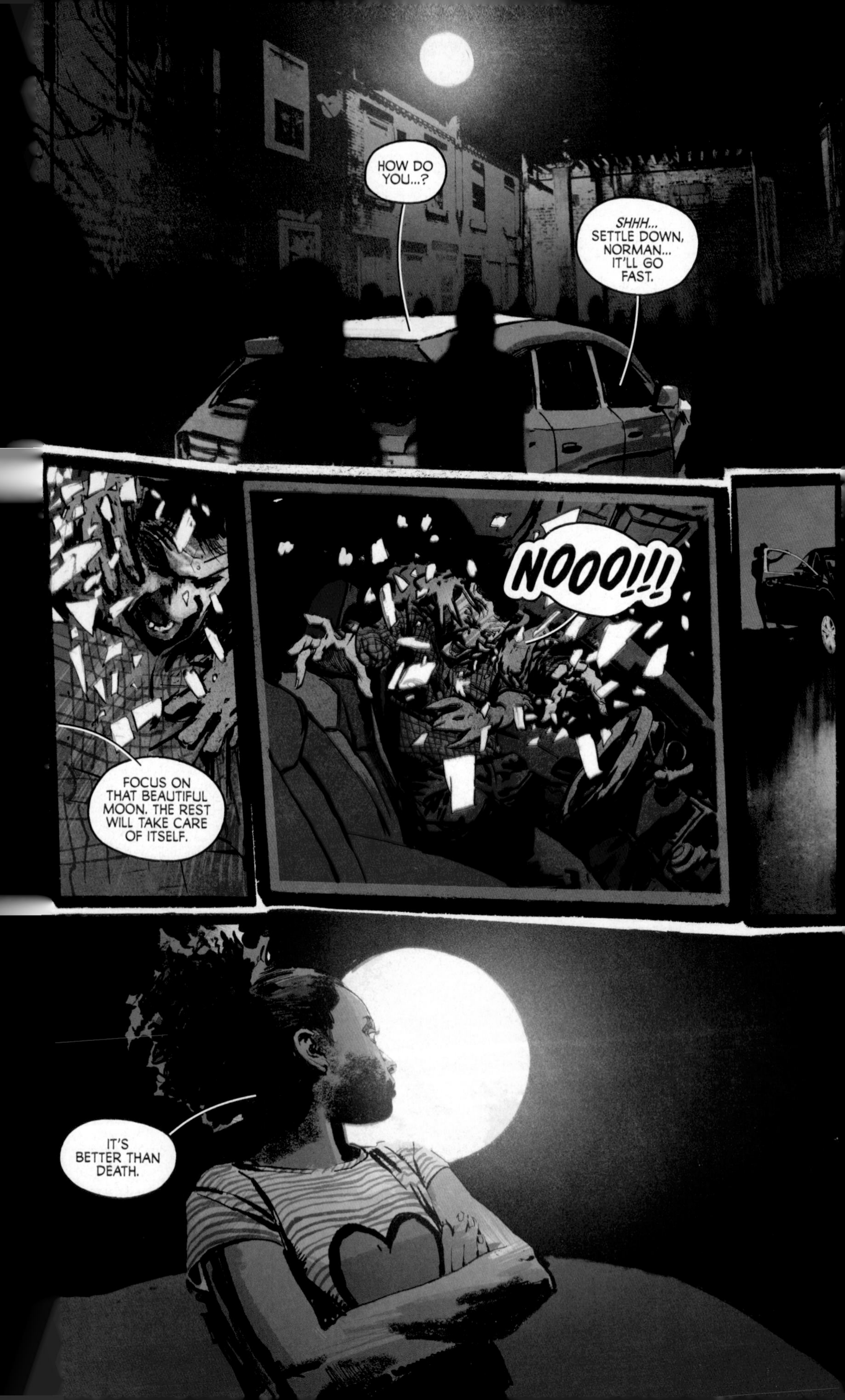
HOW DO YOU...?
SHHH... SETTLE DOWN, NORMAN... IT'LL GO FAST.
FOCUS ON THAT BEAUTIFUL MOON. THE REST WILL TAKE CARE OF ITSELF.
NOOO!!!
IT'S BETTER THAN DEATH.

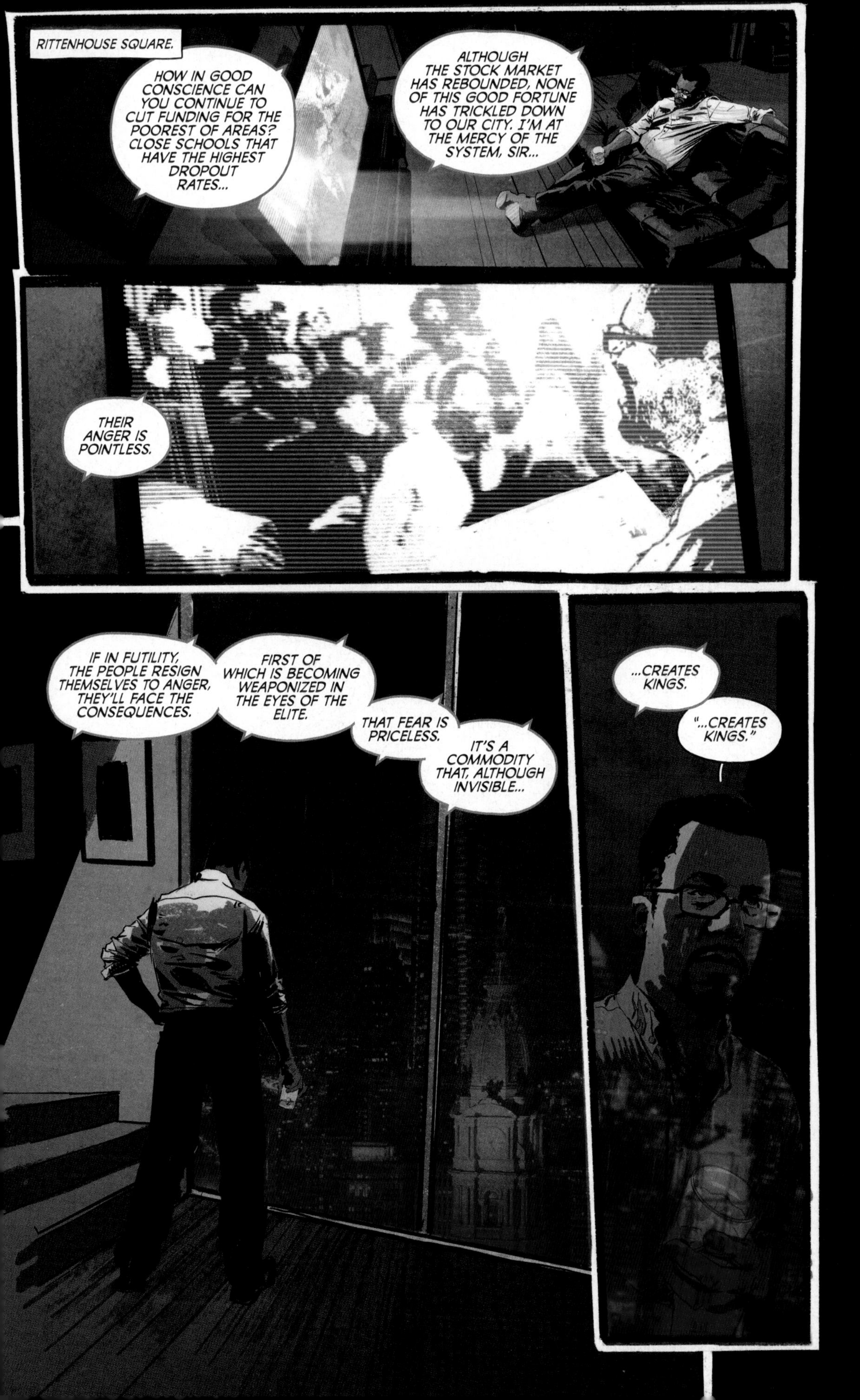
RITTENHOUSE SQUARE.
HOW IN GOOD CONSCIENCE CAN YOU CONTINUE TO CUT FUNDING FOR THE POOREST OF AREAS? CLOSE SCHOOLS THAT HAVE THE HIGHEST DROPOUT RATES...
ALTHOUGH THE STOCK MARKET HAS REBOUNDED, NONE OF THIS GOOD FORTUNE HAS TRICKLED DOWN TO OUR CITY. I'M AT THE MERCY OF THE SYSTEM, SIR...
THEIR ANGER IS POINTLESS.
IF IN FUTILITY, THE PEOPLE RESIGN THEMSELVES TO ANGER, THEY'LL FACE THE CONSEQUENCES.
FIRST OF WHICH IS BECOMING WEAPONIZED IN THE EYES OF THE ELITE.
THAT FEAR IS PRICELESS.
IT'S A COMMODITY THAT, ALTHOUGH INVISIBLE...
...CREATES KINGS.
"...CREATES KINGS."

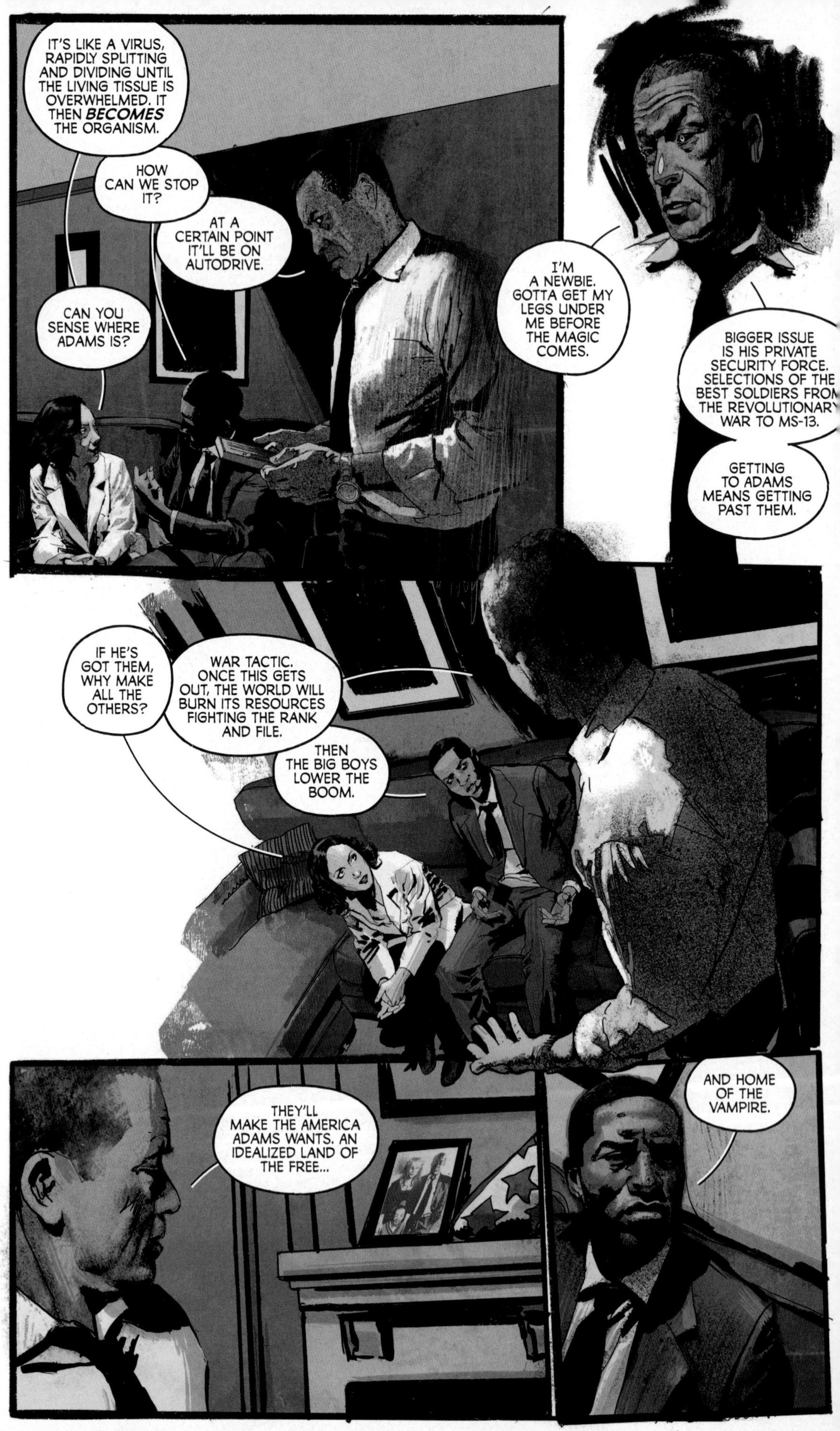
IT'S LIKE A VIRUS, RAPIDLY SPLITTING AND DIVIDING UNTIL THE LIVING TISSUE IS OVERWHELMED. IT THEN *BECOMES* THE ORGANISM.
HOW CAN WE STOP IT?
AT A CERTAIN POINT IT'LL BE ON AUTODRIVE.
CAN YOU SENSE WHERE ADAMS IS?
I'M A NEWBIE. GOTTA GET MY LEGS UNDER ME BEFORE THE MAGIC COMES.
BIGGER ISSUE IS HIS PRIVATE SECURITY FORCE. SELECTIONS OF THE BEST SOLDIERS FROM THE REVOLUTIONARY WAR TO MS-13.
GETTING TO ADAMS MEANS GETTING PAST THEM.
IF HE'S GOT THEM, WHY MAKE ALL THE OTHERS?
WAR TACTIC. ONCE THIS GETS OUT, THE WORLD WILL BURN ITS RESOURCES FIGHTING THE RANK AND FILE.
THEN THE BIG BOYS LOWER THE BOOM.
THEY'LL MAKE THE AMERICA ADAMS WANTS. AN IDEALIZED LAND OF THE FREE...
AND HOME OF THE VAMPIRE.

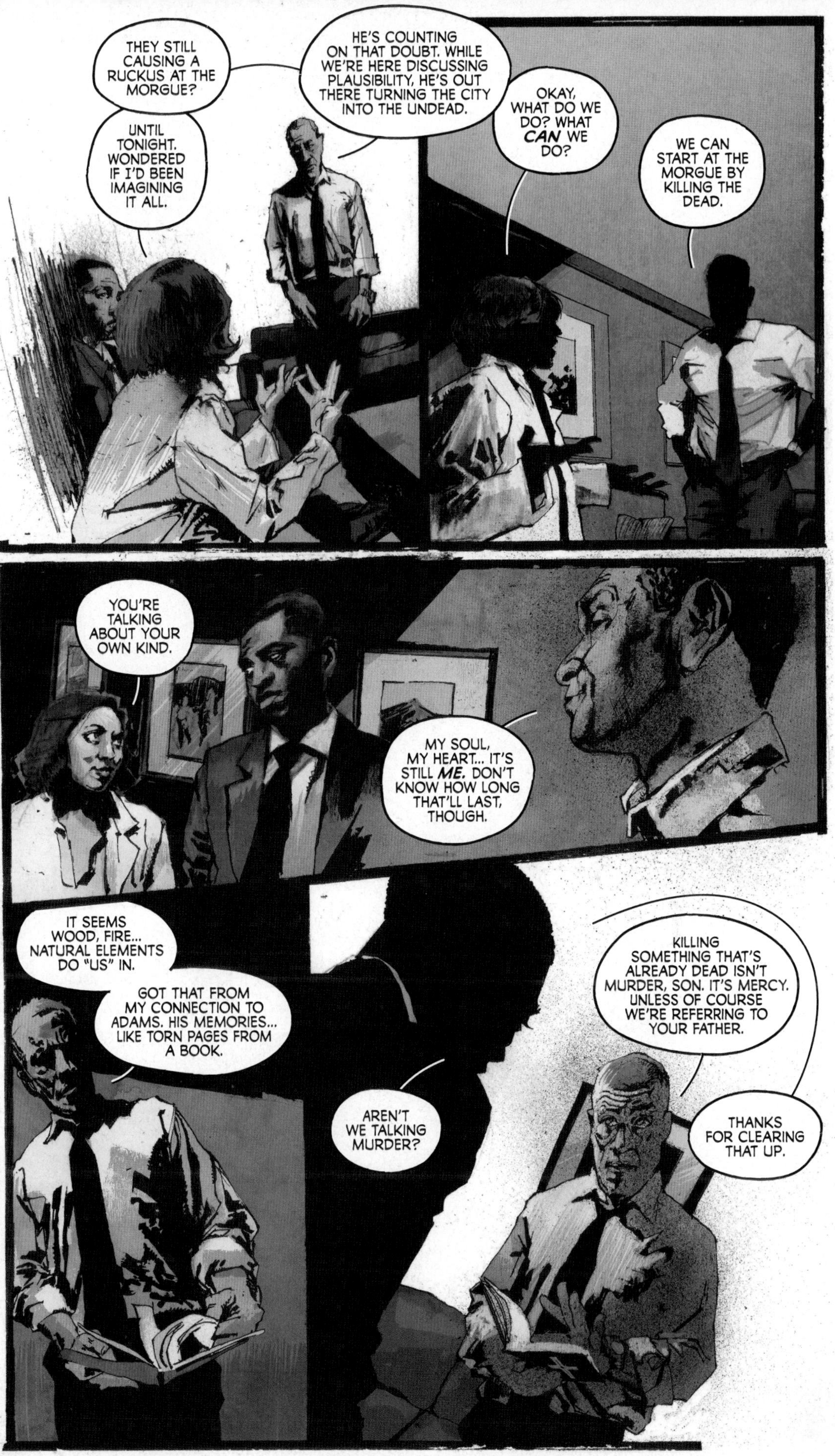
THEY STILL CAUSING A RUCKUS AT THE MORGUE?
UNTIL TONIGHT. WONDERED IF I'D BEEN IMAGINING IT ALL.
HE'S COUNTING ON THAT DOUBT. WHILE WE'RE HERE DISCUSSING PLAUSIBILITY, HE'S OUT THERE TURNING THE CITY INTO THE UNDEAD.
OKAY, WHAT DO WE DO? WHAT *CAN* WE DO?
WE CAN START AT THE MORGUE BY KILLING THE DEAD.
YOU'RE TALKING ABOUT YOUR OWN KIND.
MY SOUL, MY HEART... IT'S STILL *ME.* DON'T KNOW HOW LONG THAT'LL LAST, THOUGH.
IT SEEMS WOOD, FIRE... NATURAL ELEMENTS DO "US" IN.
GOT THAT FROM MY CONNECTION TO ADAMS. HIS MEMORIES... LIKE TORN PAGES FROM A BOOK.
AREN'T WE TALKING MURDER?
KILLING SOMETHING THAT'S ALREADY DEAD ISN'T MURDER, SON. IT'S MERCY. UNLESS OF COURSE WE'RE REFERRING TO YOUR FATHER.
THANKS FOR CLEARING THAT UP.

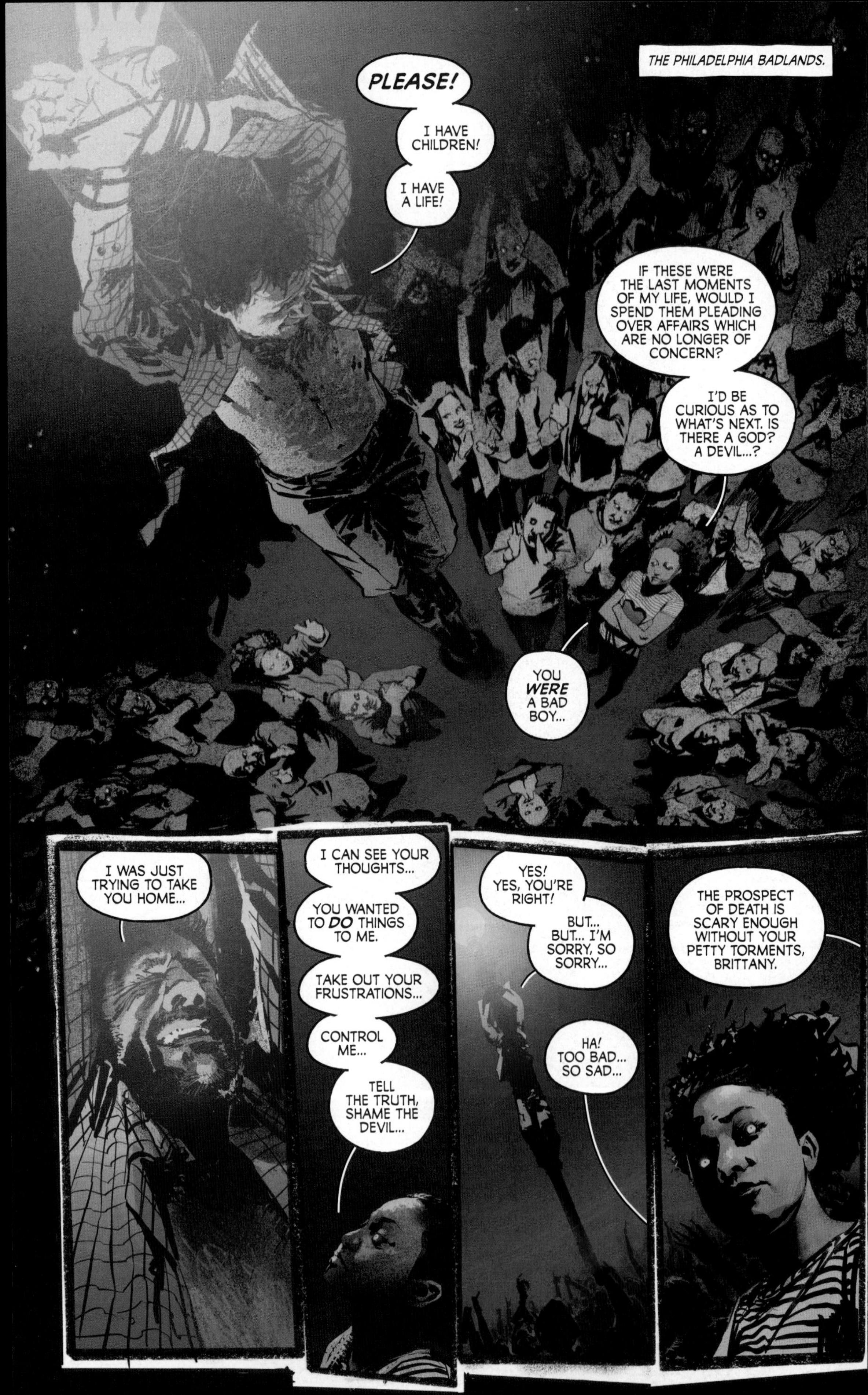
THE PHILADELPHIA BADLANDS.
PLEASE!
I HAVE CHILDREN!
I HAVE A LIFE!
IF THESE WERE THE LAST MOMENTS OF MY LIFE, WOULD I SPEND THEM PLEADING OVER AFFAIRS WHICH ARE NO LONGER OF CONCERN?
I'D BE CURIOUS AS TO WHAT'S NEXT. IS THERE A GOD? A DEVIL...?
YOU *WERE* A BAD BOY...
I WAS JUST TRYING TO TAKE YOU HOME...
I CAN SEE YOUR THOUGHTS...
YOU WANTED TO *DO* THINGS TO ME.
TAKE OUT YOUR FRUSTRATIONS...
CONTROL ME...
TELL THE TRUTH, SHAME THE DEVIL...
YES! YES, YOU'RE RIGHT!
BUT... BUT... I'M SORRY, SO SORRY...
HA! TOO BAD... SO SAD...
THE PROSPECT OF DEATH IS SCARY ENOUGH WITHOUT YOUR PETTY TORMENTS, BRITTANY.

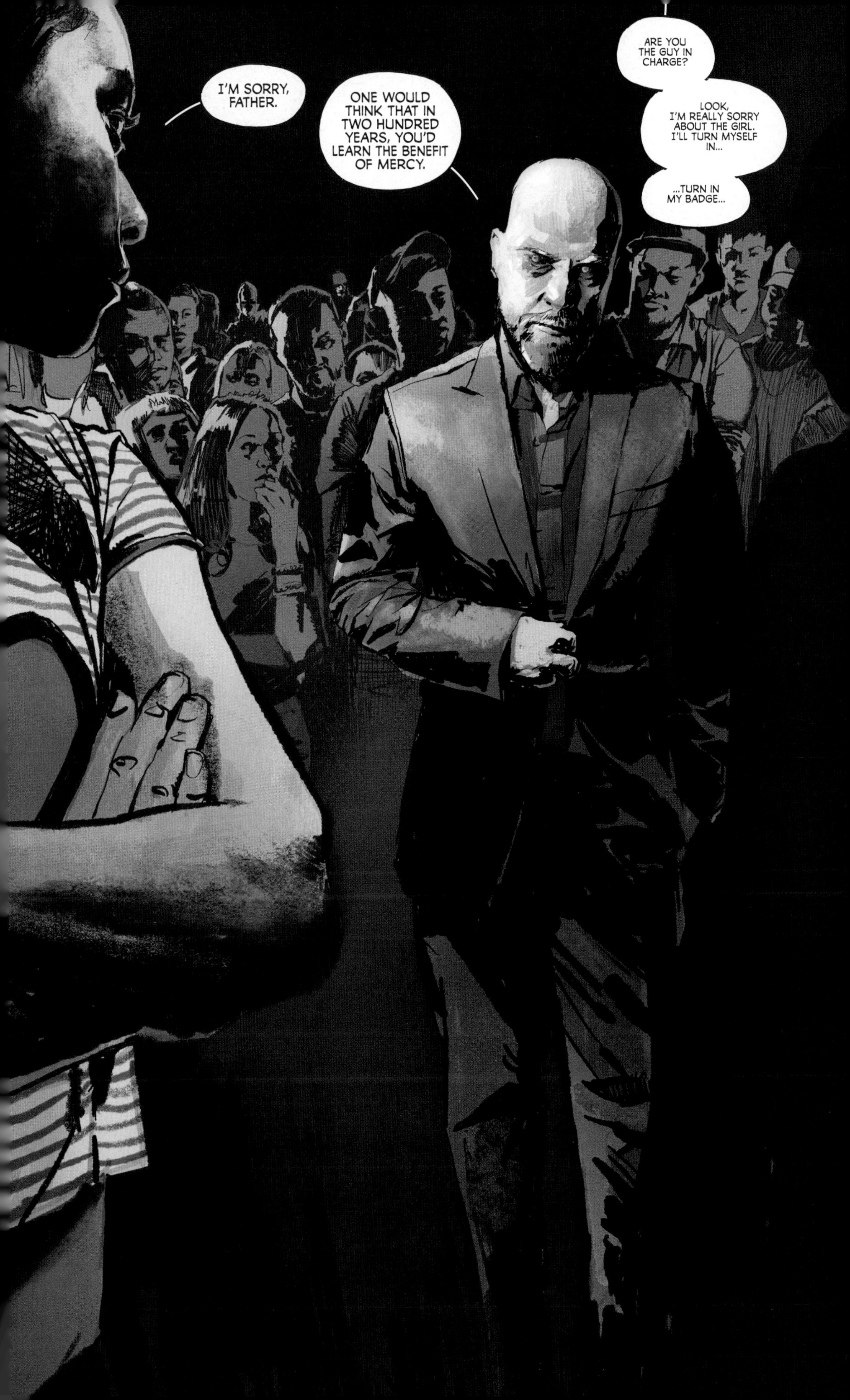
ARE YOU THE GUY IN CHARGE?
I'M SORRY, FATHER.
ONE WOULD THINK THAT IN TWO HUNDRED YEARS, YOU'D LEARN THE BENEFIT OF MERCY.
LOOK, I'M REALLY SORRY ABOUT THE GIRL. I'LL TURN MYSELF IN...
...TURN IN MY BADGE...

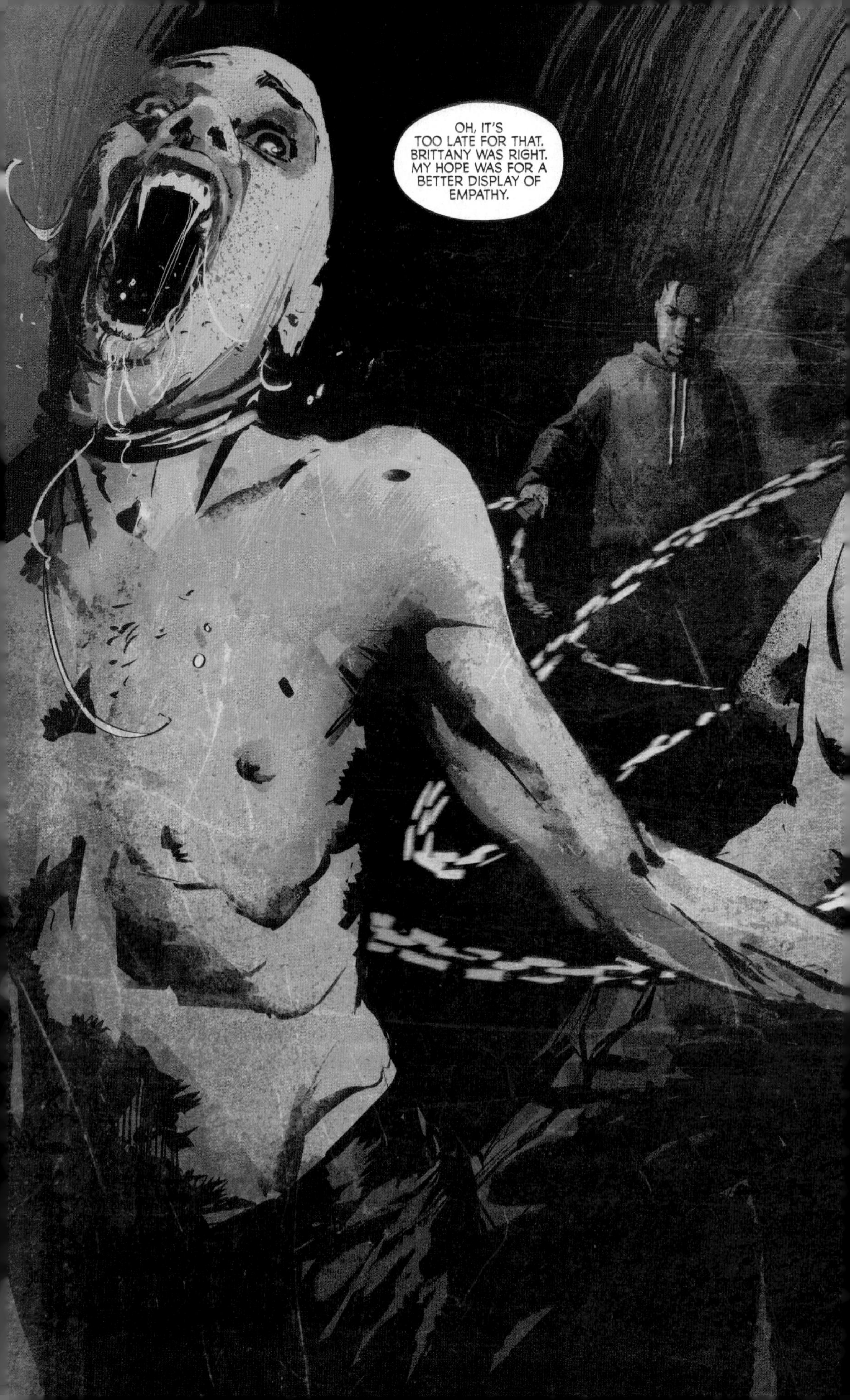
OH, IT'S TOO LATE FOR THAT. BRITTANY WAS RIGHT. MY HOPE WAS FOR A BETTER DISPLAY OF EMPATHY.

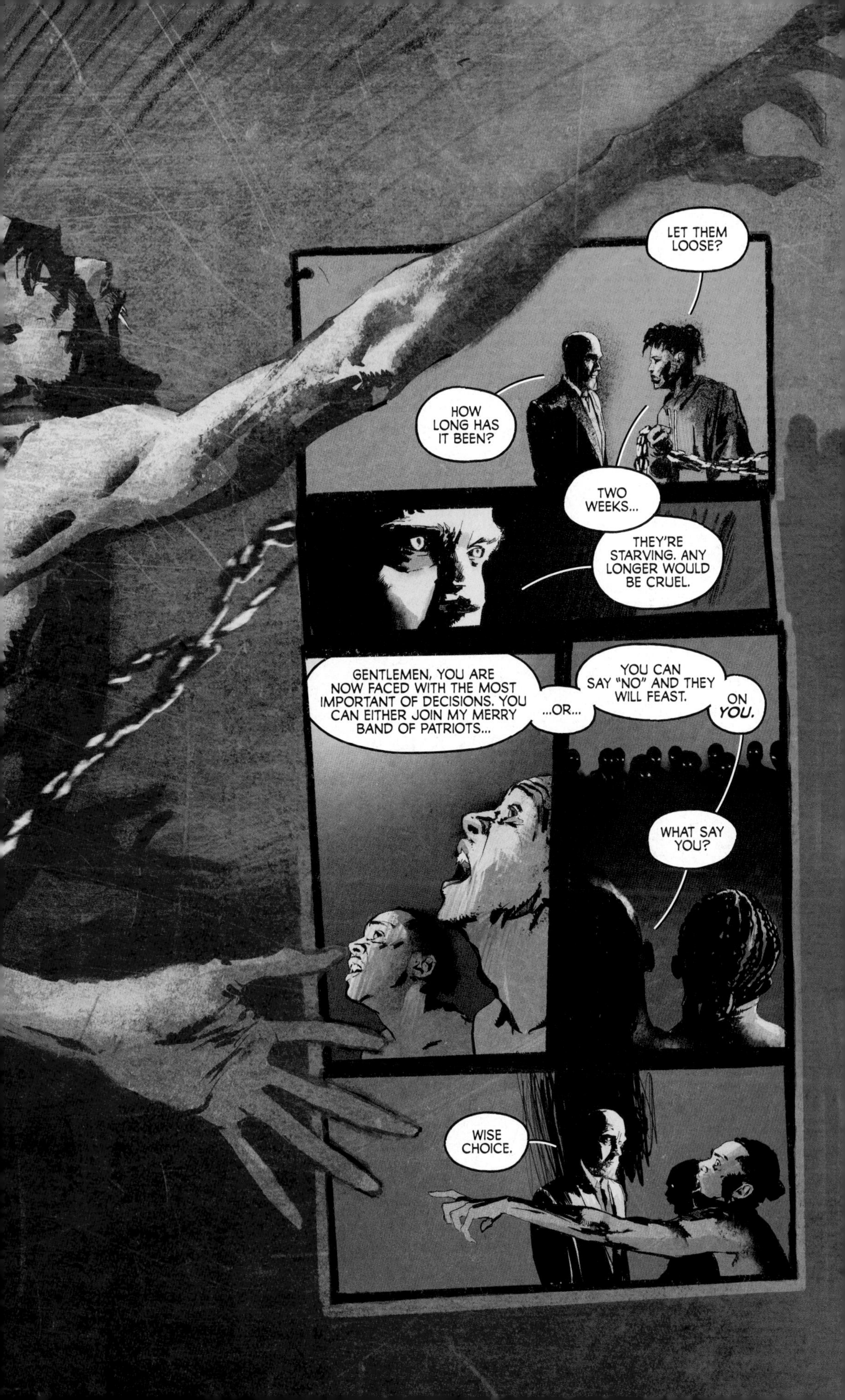

LET THEM LOOSE?
HOW LONG HAS IT BEEN?
TWO WEEKS...
THEY'RE STARVING. ANY LONGER WOULD BE CRUEL.
GENTLEMEN, YOU ARE NOW FACED WITH THE MOST IMPORTANT OF DECISIONS. YOU CAN EITHER JOIN MY MERRY BAND OF PATRIOTS...
...OR...
YOU CAN SAY "NO" AND THEY WILL FEAST.
ON *YOU.*
WHAT SAY YOU?
WISE CHOICE.

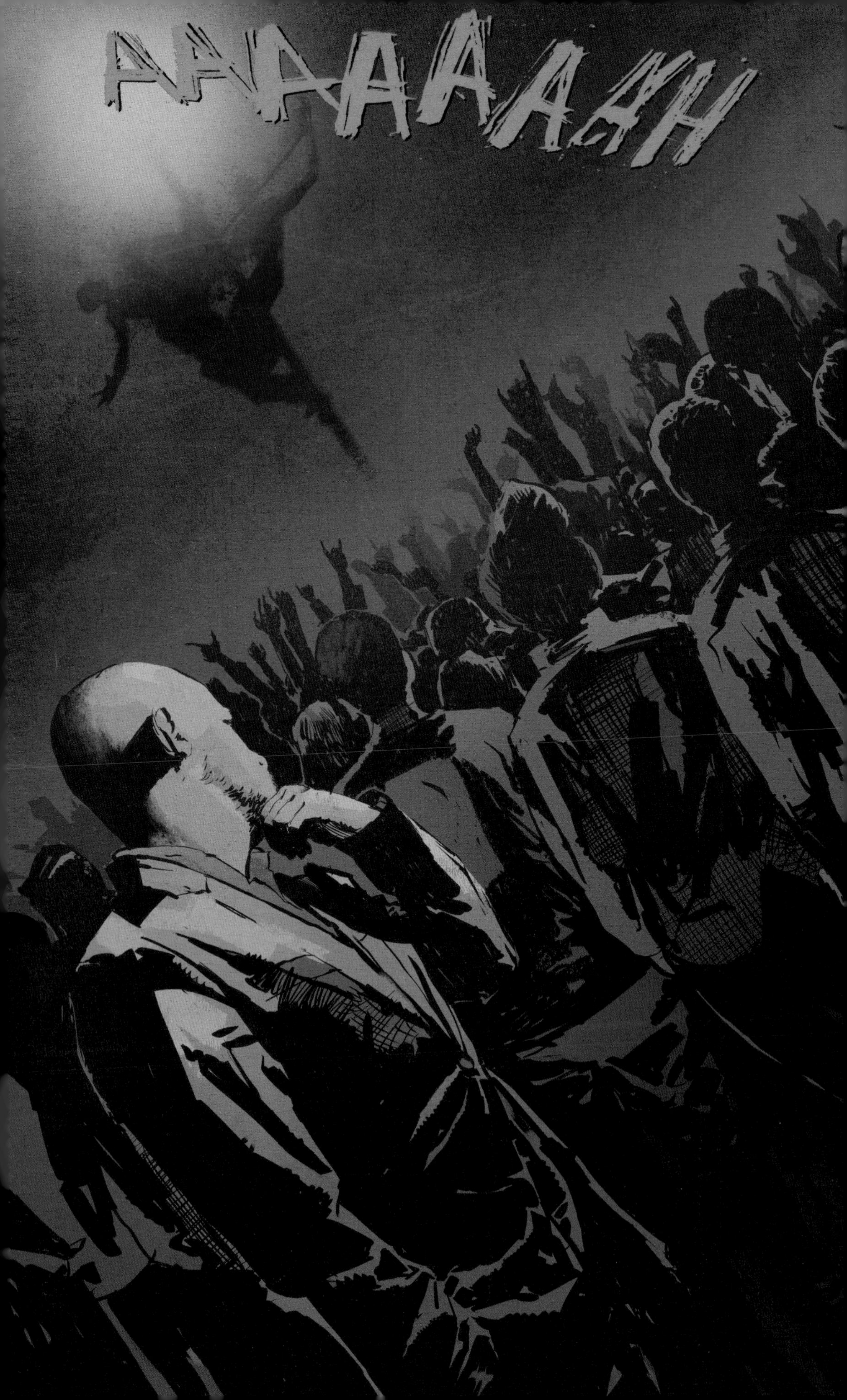
AAAAAAAH

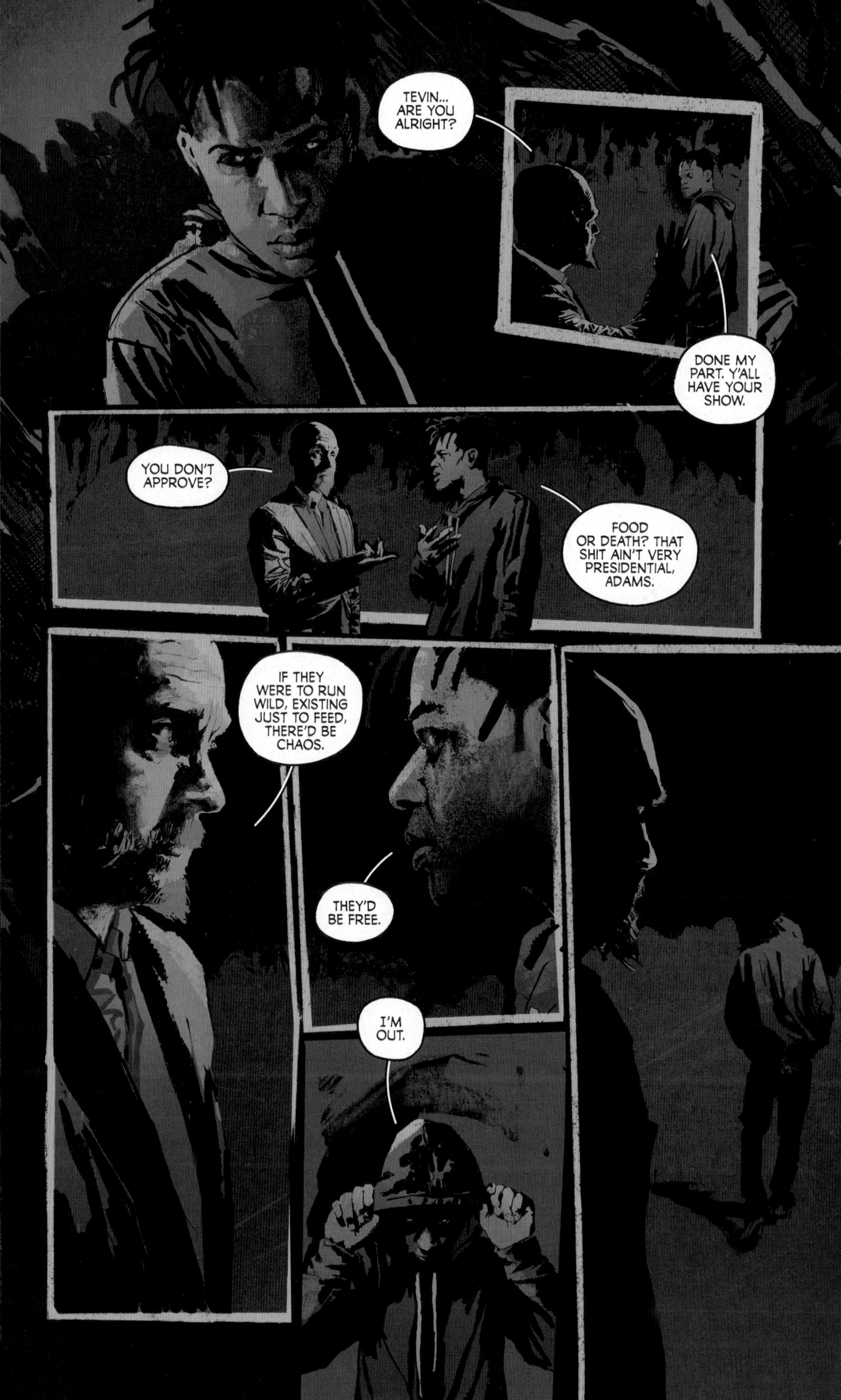
TEVIN... ARE YOU ALRIGHT?
DONE MY PART. Y'ALL HAVE YOUR SHOW.
YOU DON'T APPROVE?
FOOD OR DEATH? THAT SHIT AIN'T VERY PRESIDENTIAL, ADAMS.
IF THEY WERE TO RUN WILD, EXISTING JUST TO FEED, THERE'D BE CHAOS.
THEY'D BE FREE.
I'M OUT.

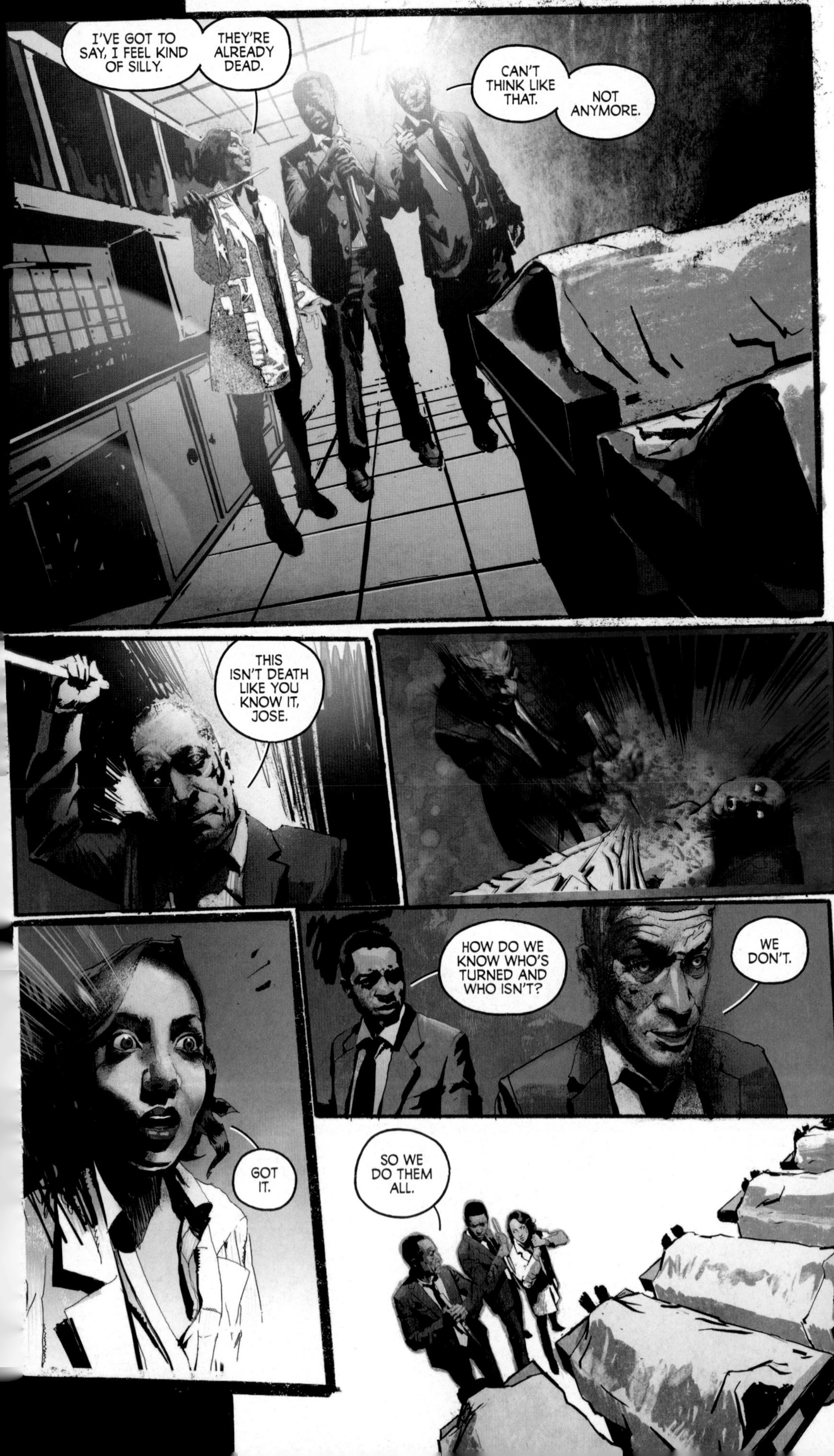
I'VE GOT TO SAY, I FEEL KIND OF SILLY.
THEY'RE ALREADY DEAD.
CAN'T THINK LIKE THAT.
NOT ANYMORE.
THIS ISN'T DEATH LIKE YOU KNOW IT, JOSE.
GOT IT.
HOW DO WE KNOW WHO'S TURNED AND WHO ISN'T?
WE DON'T.
SO WE DO THEM ALL.

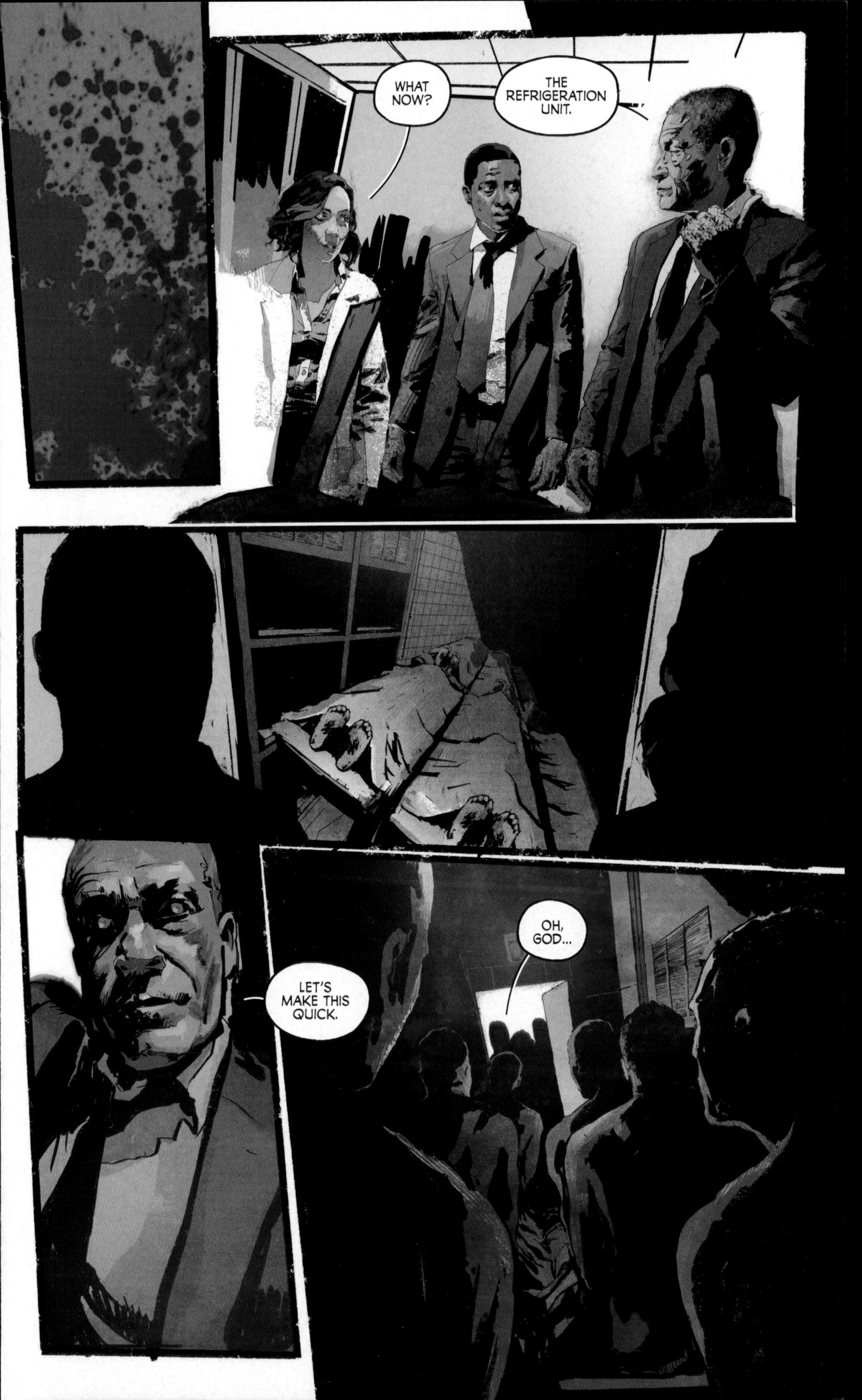
WHAT NOW?
THE REFRIGERATION UNIT.
LET'S MAKE THIS QUICK.
OH, GOD...

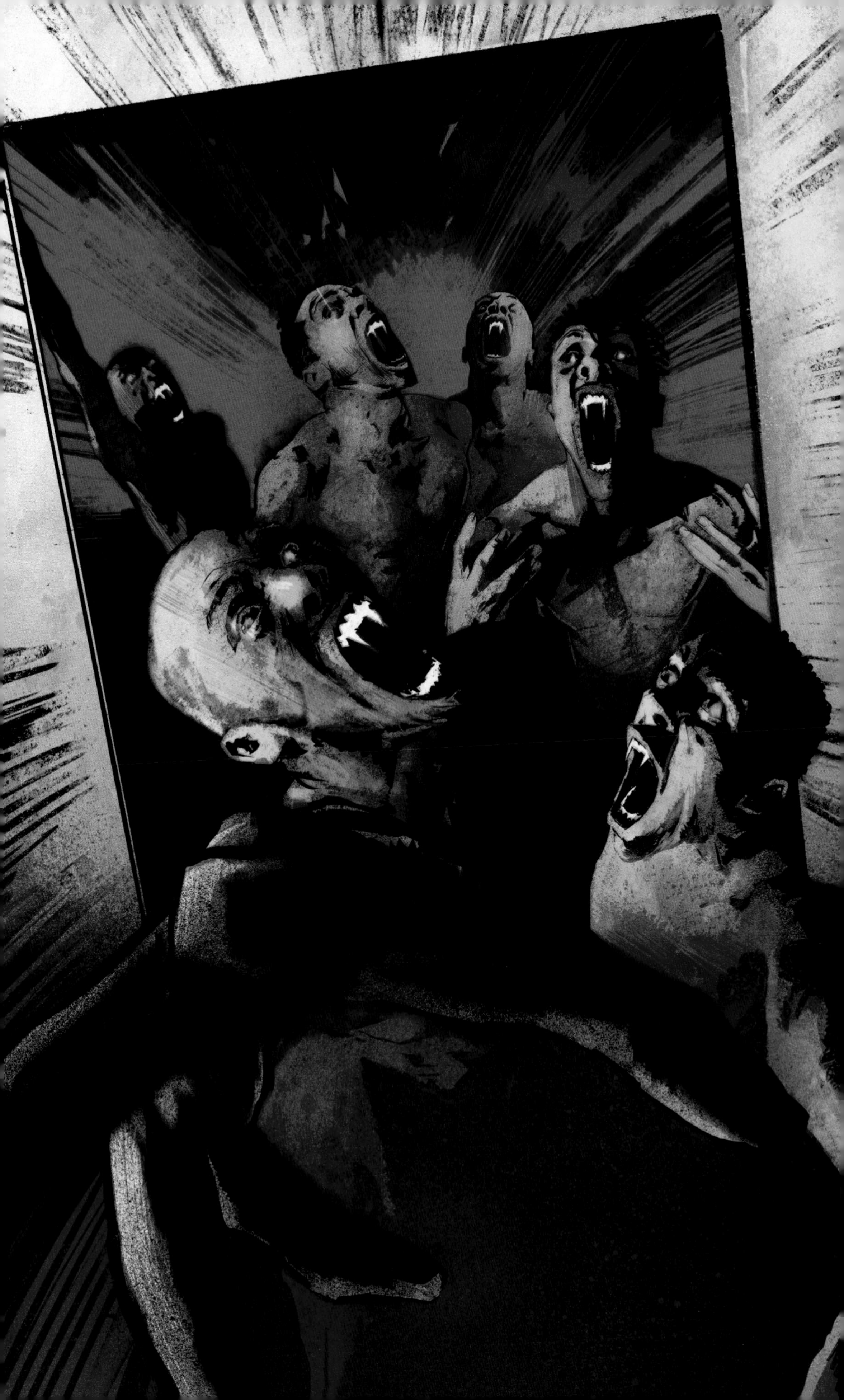

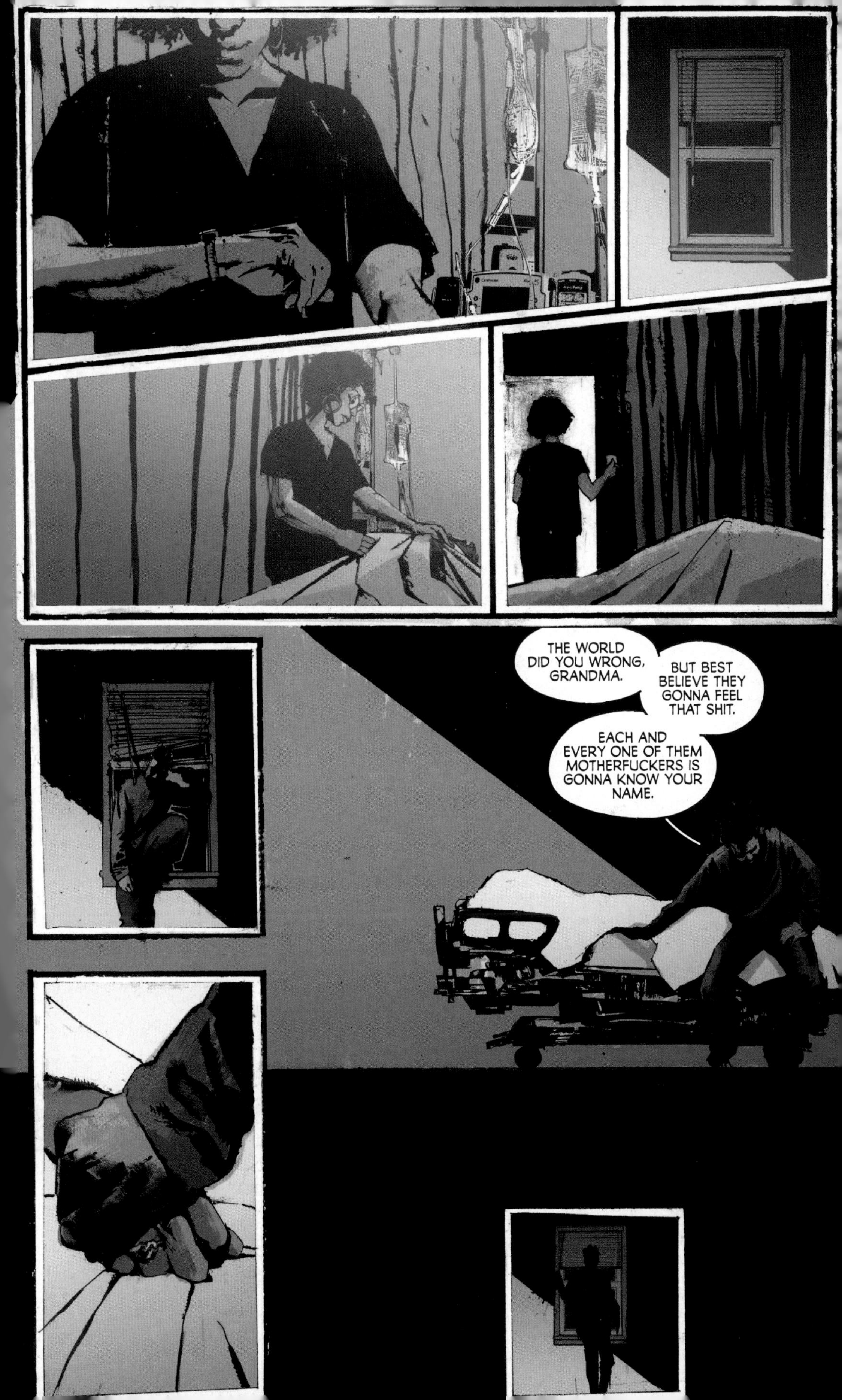
THE WORLD DID YOU WRONG, GRANDMA.
BUT BEST BELIEVE THEY GONNA FEEL THAT SHIT.
EACH AND EVERY ONE OF THEM MOTHERFUCKERS IS GONNA KNOW YOUR NAME.

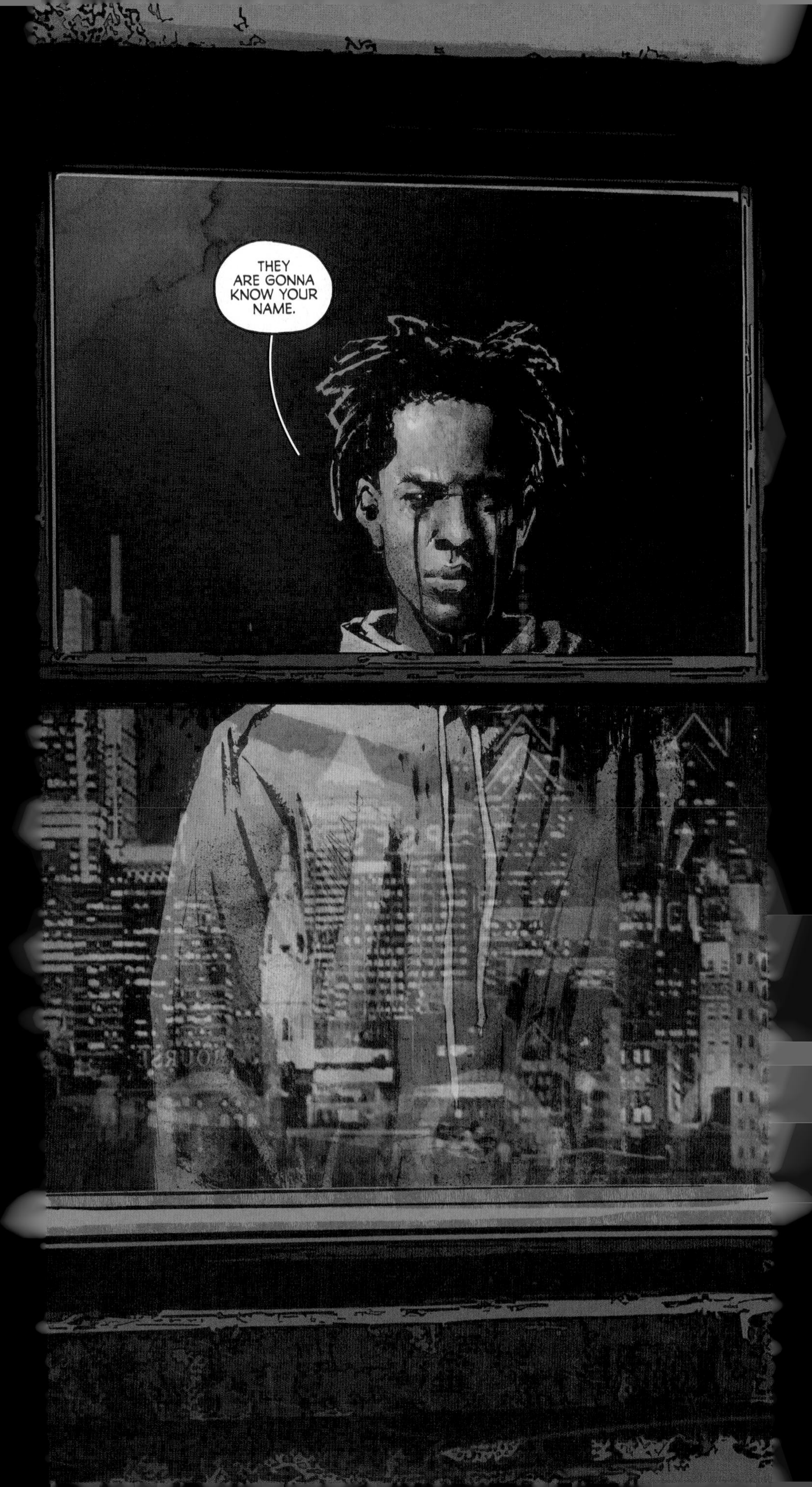
THEY ARE GONNA KNOW YOUR NAME.

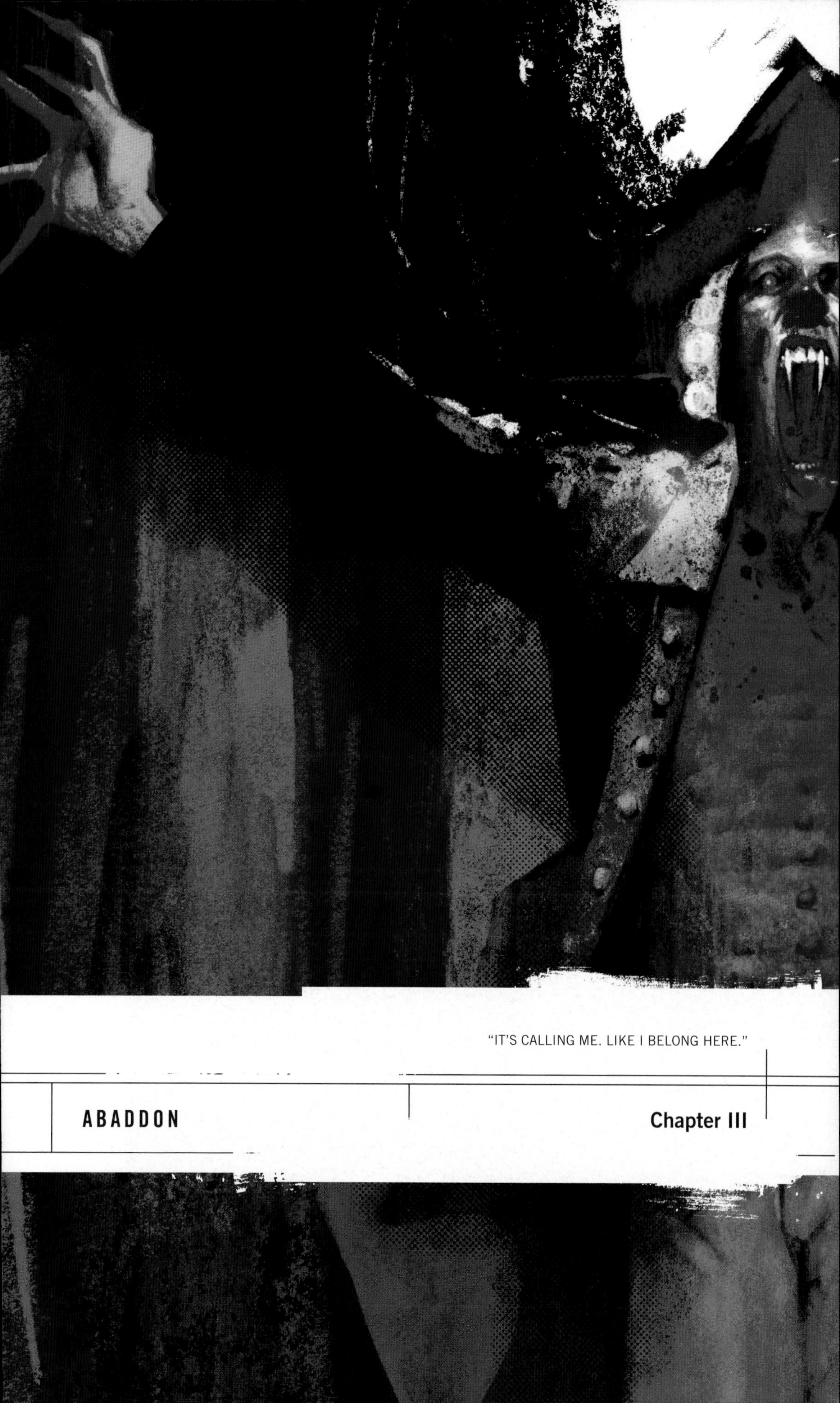

"IT'S CALLING ME. LIKE I BELONG HERE."

ABADDON

Chapter III

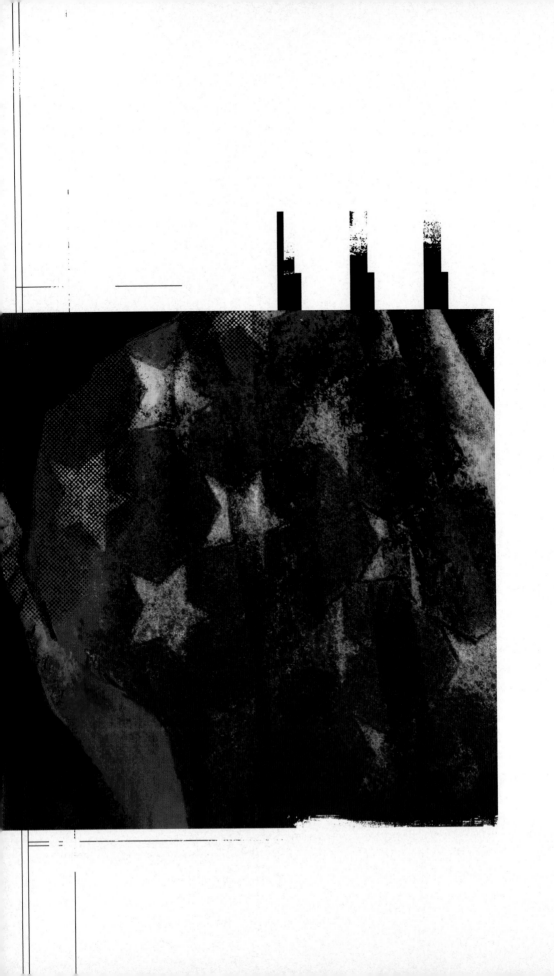

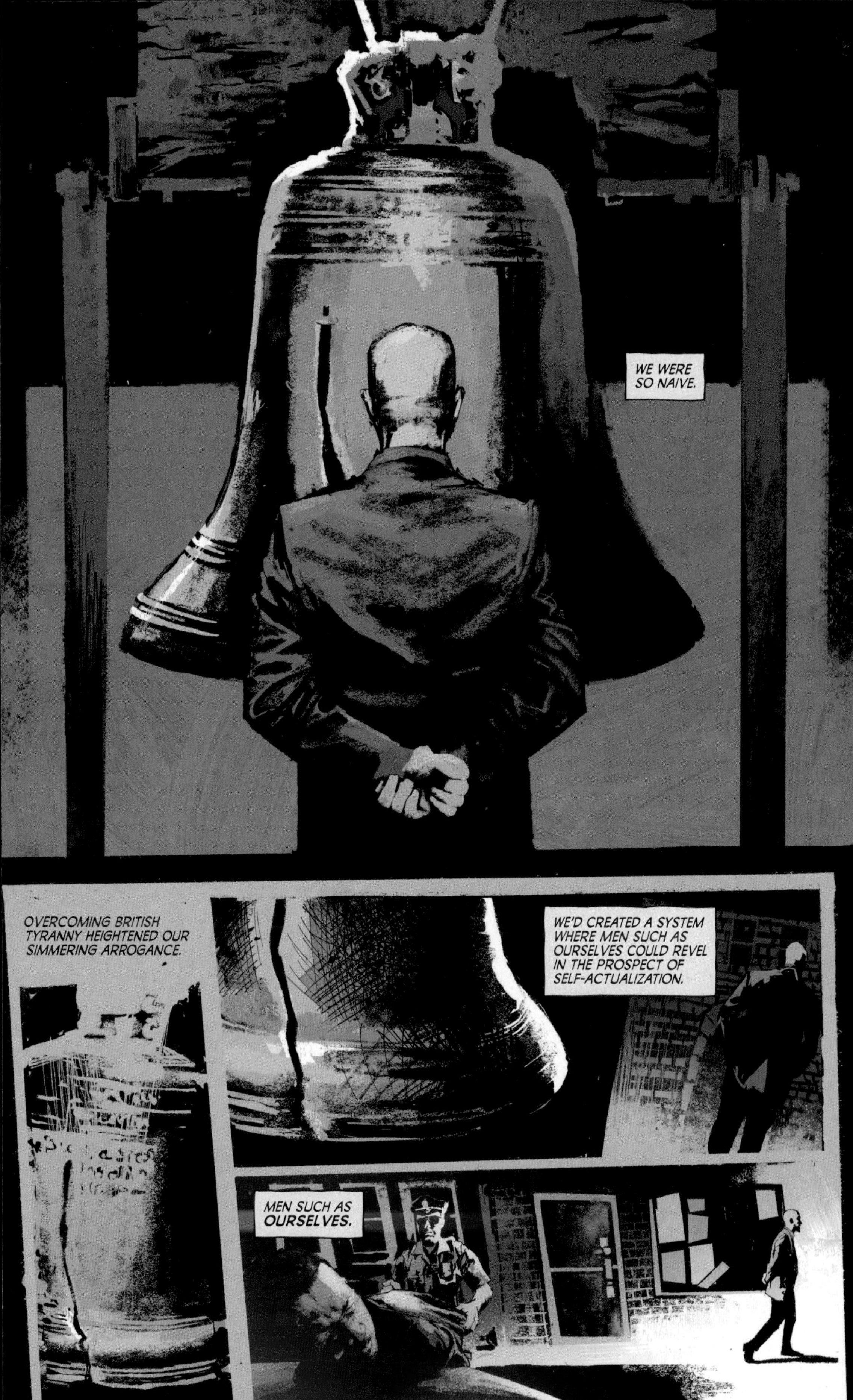
WE WERE SO NAIVE.
OVERCOMING BRITISH TYRANNY HEIGHTENED OUR SIMMERING ARROGANCE.
WE'D CREATED A SYSTEM WHERE MEN SUCH AS OURSELVES COULD REVEL IN THE PROSPECT OF SELF-ACTUALIZATION.
MEN SUCH AS OURSELVES.

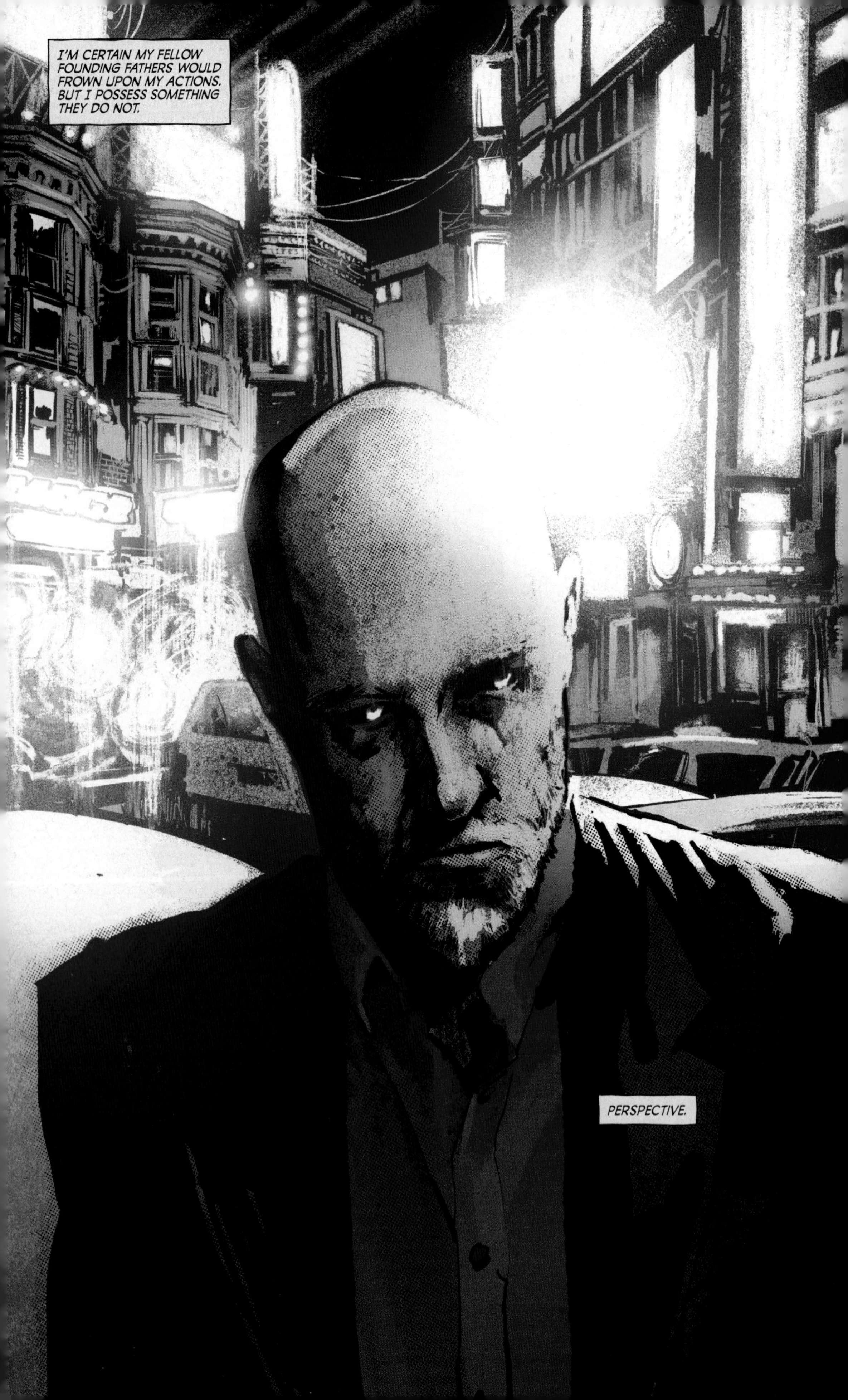
I'M CERTAIN MY FELLOW FOUNDING FATHERS WOULD FROWN UPON MY ACTIONS. BUT I POSSESS SOMETHING THEY DO NOT.
PERSPECTIVE.

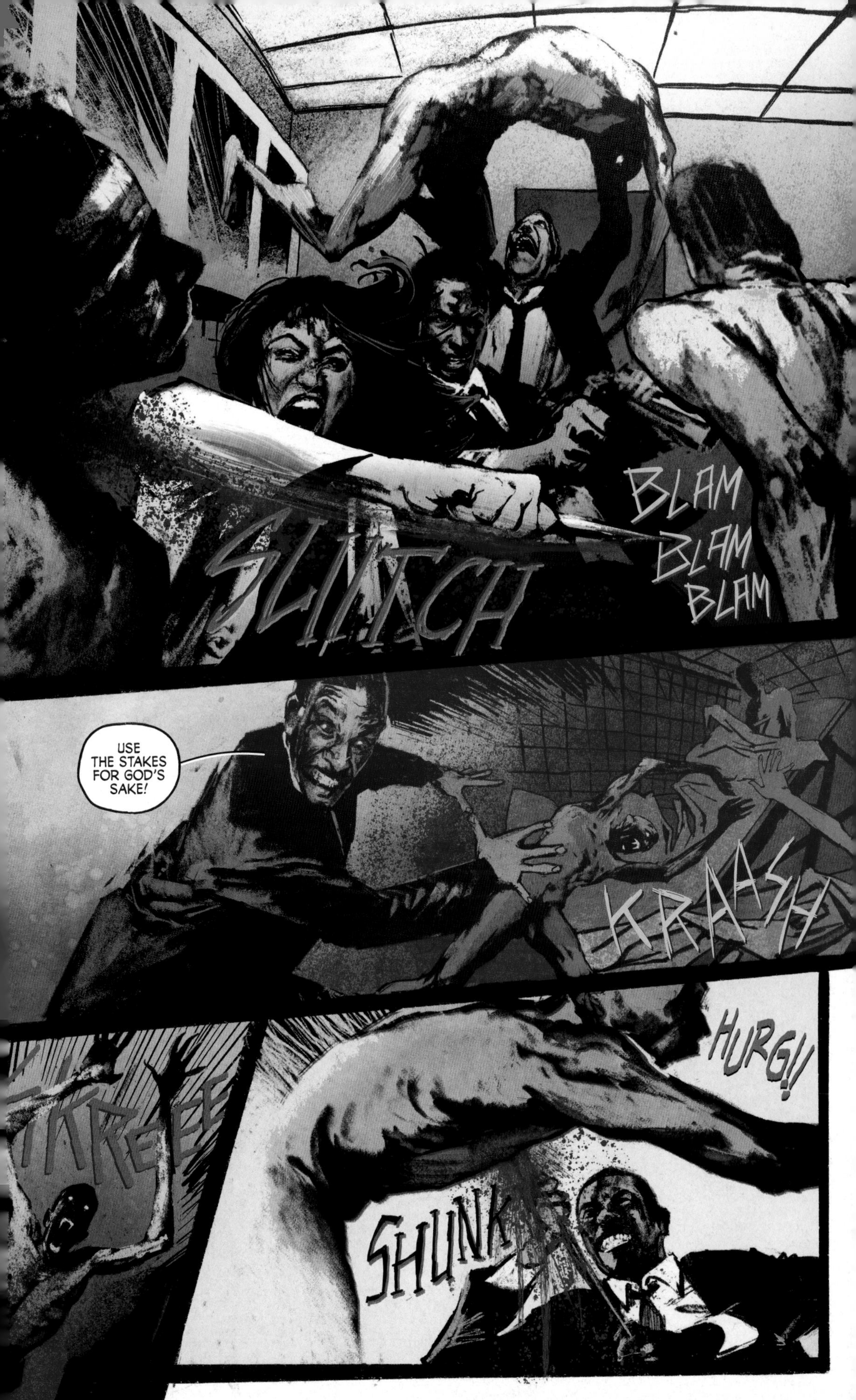
SLIIIICH
BLAM
BLAM
BLAM
USE THE STAKES FOR GOD'S SAKE!
KRAASH
KREEEE
HURG!!
SHUNK

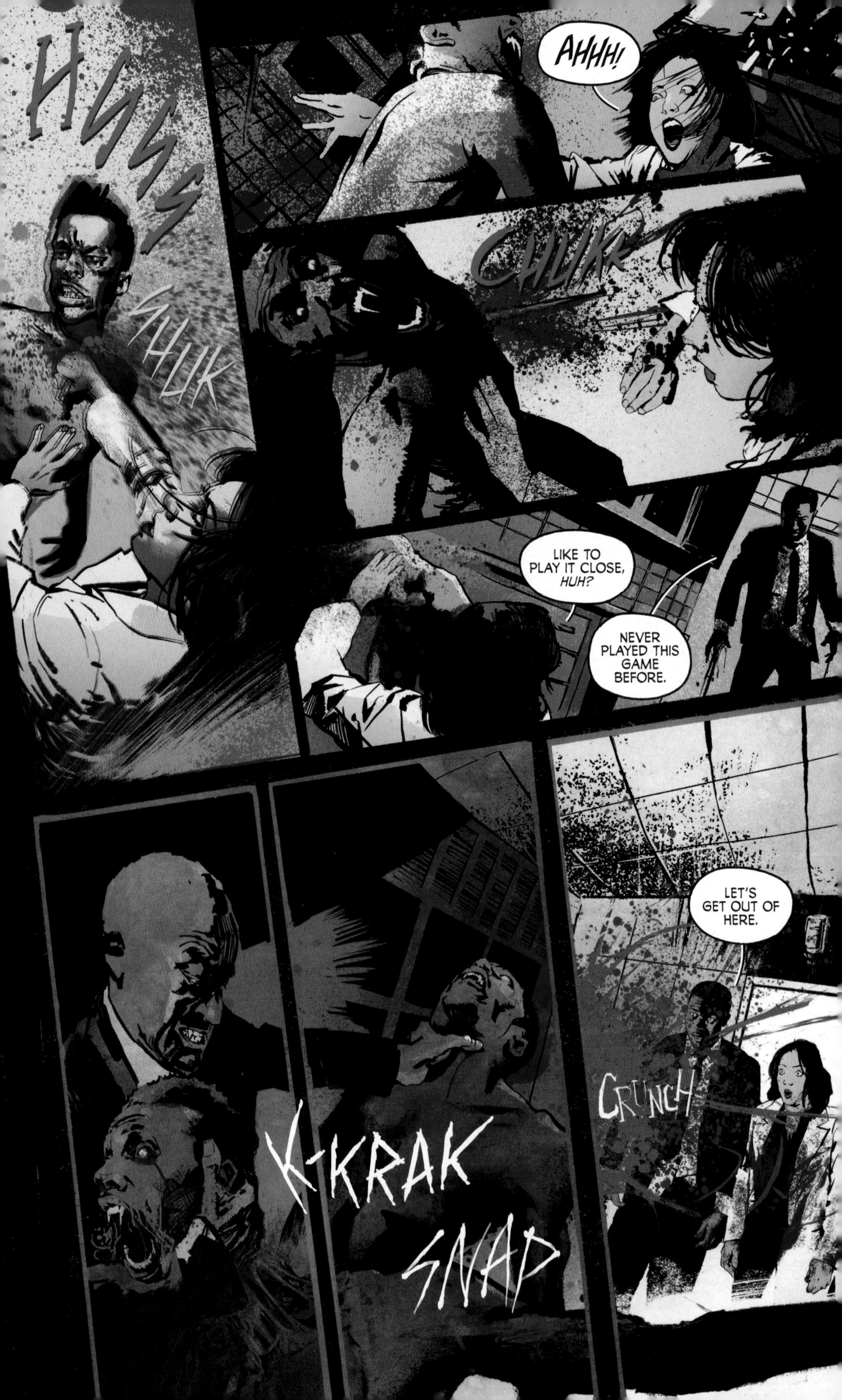

HNNNS
AHHH!
SHUK
CHUKK
LIKE TO PLAY IT CLOSE, *HUH?*
NEVER PLAYED THIS GAME BEFORE.
K-KRAK
SNAP
LET'S GET OUT OF HERE.
CRUNCH

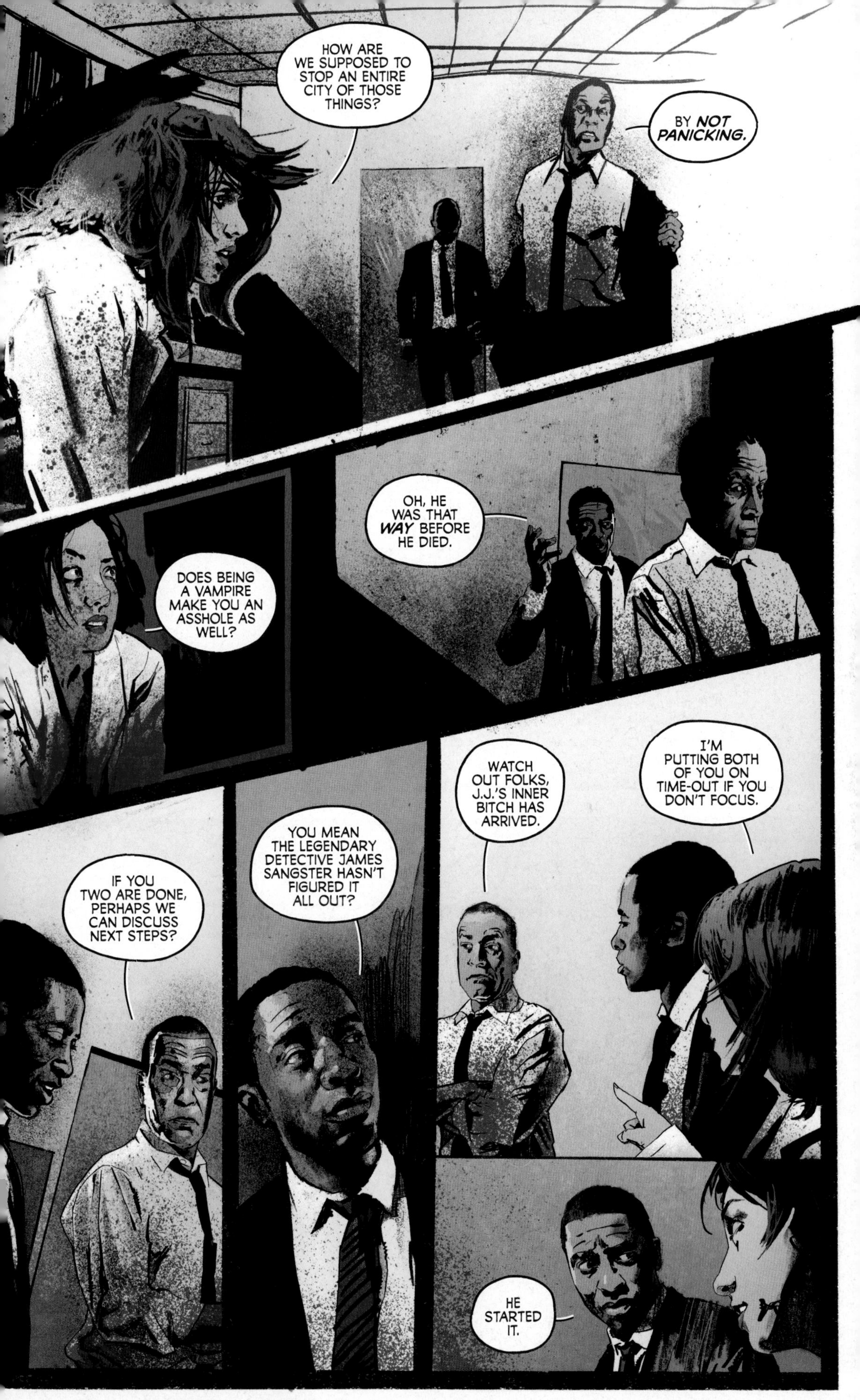
HOW ARE WE SUPPOSED TO STOP AN ENTIRE CITY OF THOSE THINGS?
BY *NOT PANICKING.*
DOES BEING A VAMPIRE MAKE YOU AN ASSHOLE AS WELL?
OH, HE WAS THAT *WAY* BEFORE HE DIED.
IF YOU TWO ARE DONE, PERHAPS WE CAN DISCUSS NEXT STEPS?
YOU MEAN THE LEGENDARY DETECTIVE JAMES SANGSTER HASN'T FIGURED IT ALL OUT?
WATCH OUT FOLKS, J.J.'S INNER BITCH HAS ARRIVED.
I'M PUTTING BOTH OF YOU ON TIME-OUT IF YOU DON'T FOCUS.
HE STARTED IT.

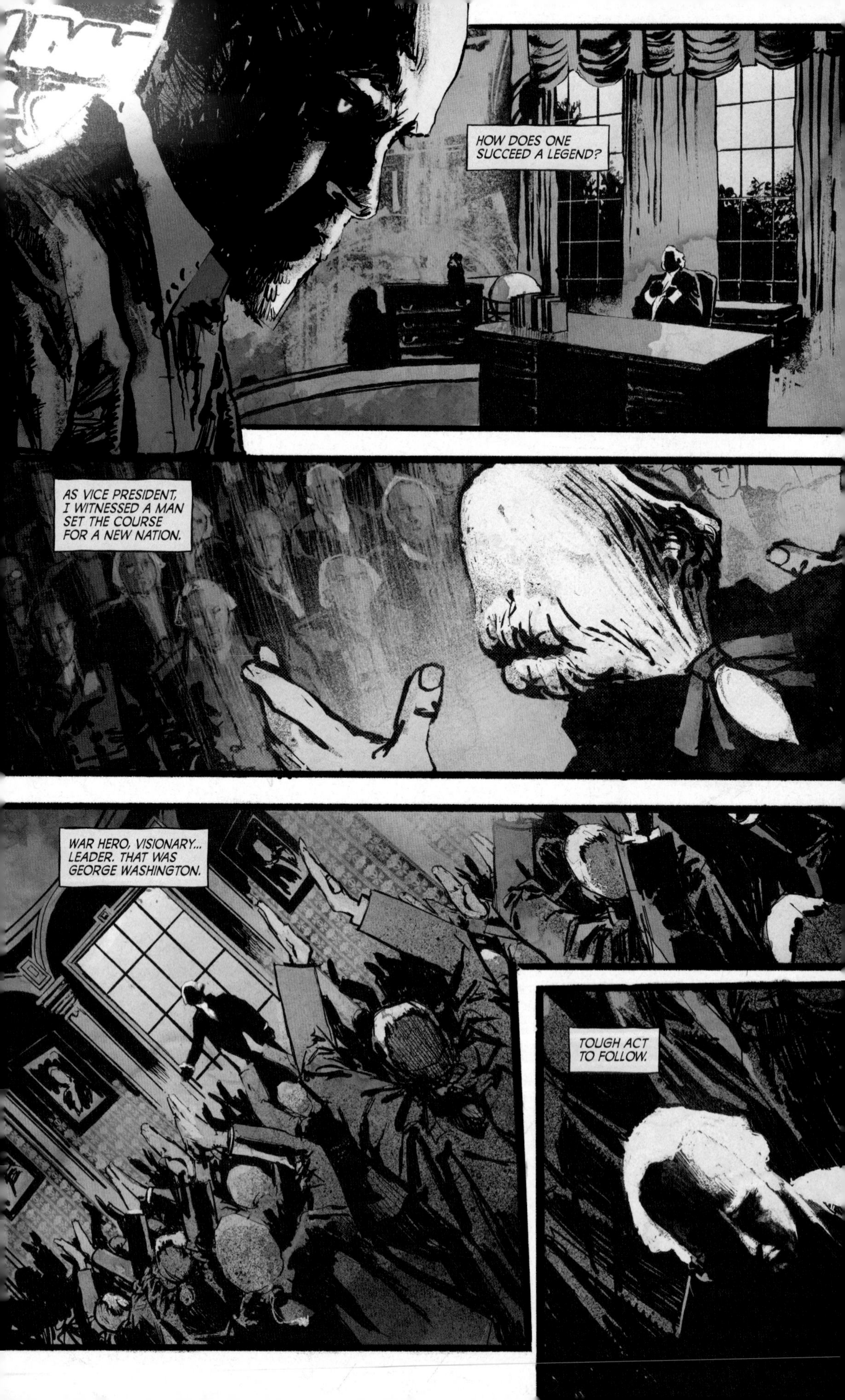
HOW DOES ONE SUCCEED A LEGEND?
AS VICE PRESIDENT, I WITNESSED A MAN SET THE COURSE FOR A NEW NATION.
WAR HERO, VISIONARY... LEADER. THAT WAS GEORGE WASHINGTON.
TOUGH ACT TO FOLLOW.

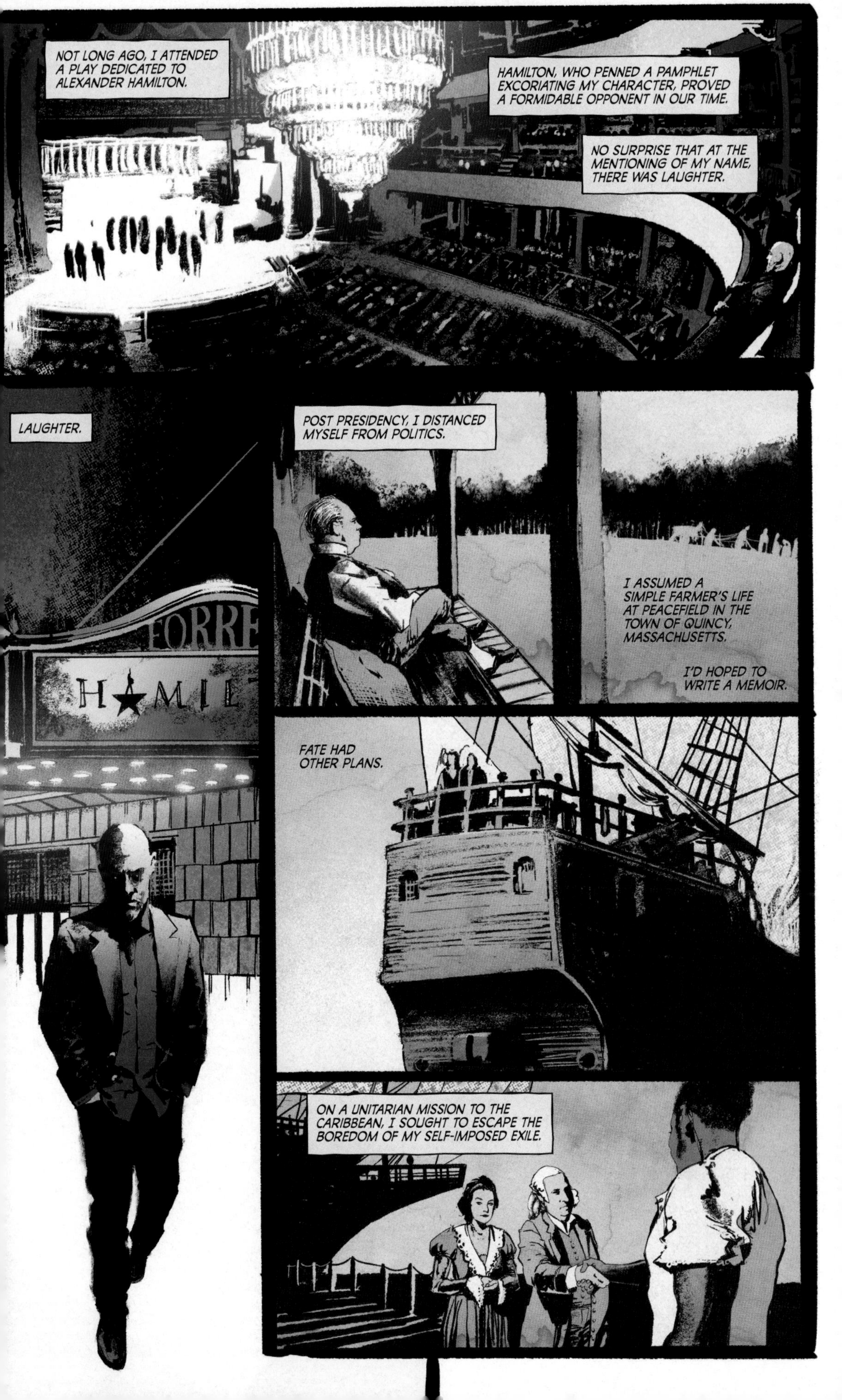
NOT LONG AGO, I ATTENDED A PLAY DEDICATED TO ALEXANDER HAMILTON.
HAMILTON, WHO PENNED A PAMPHLET EXCORIATING MY CHARACTER, PROVED A FORMIDABLE OPPONENT IN OUR TIME.
NO SURPRISE THAT AT THE MENTIONING OF MY NAME, THERE WAS LAUGHTER.
LAUGHTER.
FORRE
H★MIL
POST PRESIDENCY, I DISTANCED MYSELF FROM POLITICS.
I ASSUMED A SIMPLE FARMER'S LIFE AT PEACEFIELD IN THE TOWN OF QUINCY, MASSACHUSETTS.
I'D HOPED TO WRITE A MEMOIR.
FATE HAD OTHER PLANS.
ON A UNITARIAN MISSION TO THE CARIBBEAN, I SOUGHT TO ESCAPE THE BOREDOM OF MY SELF-IMPOSED EXILE.

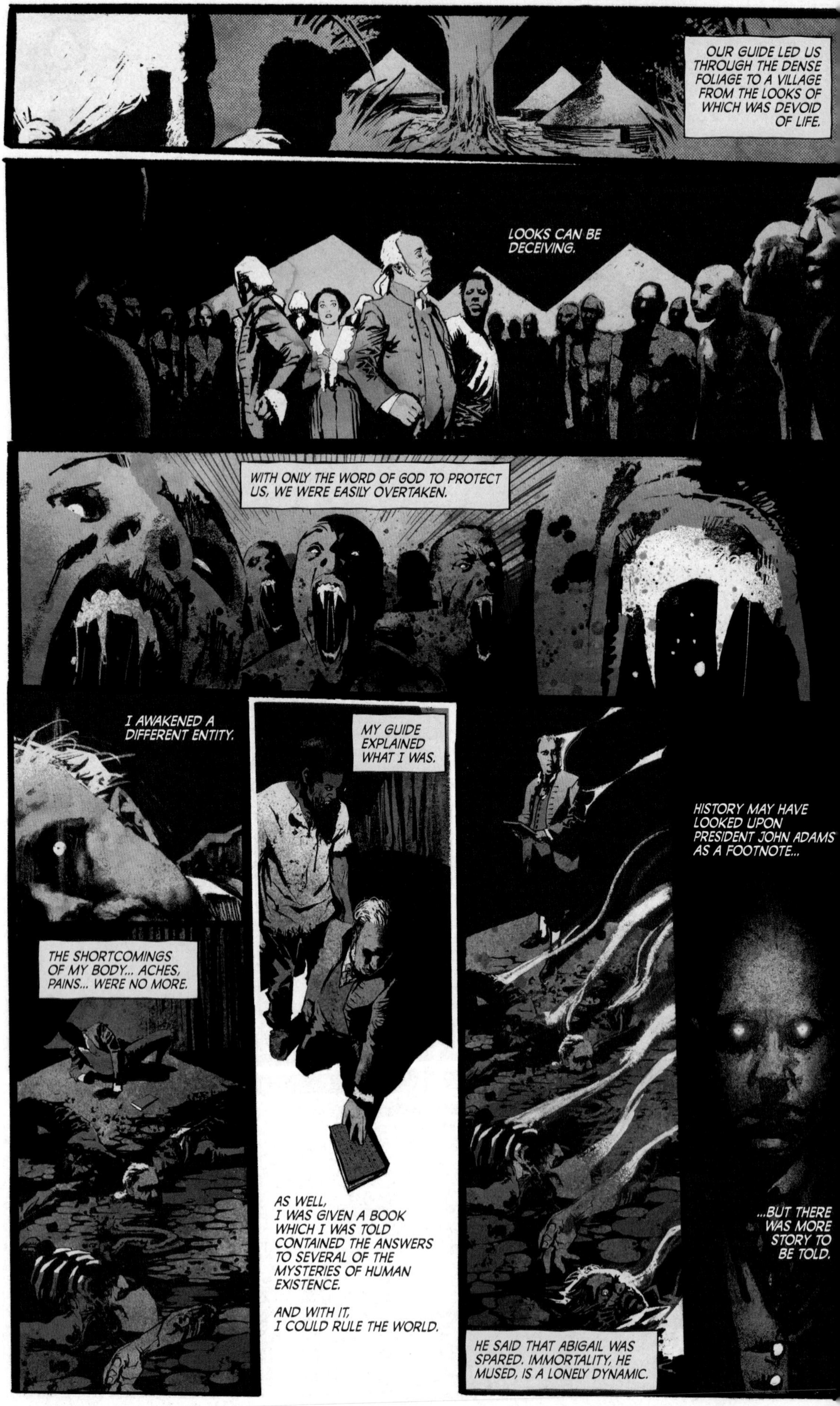
OUR GUIDE LED US THROUGH THE DENSE FOLIAGE TO A VILLAGE FROM THE LOOKS OF WHICH WAS DEVOID OF LIFE.
LOOKS CAN BE DECEIVING.
WITH ONLY THE WORD OF GOD TO PROTECT US, WE WERE EASILY OVERTAKEN.
I AWAKENED A DIFFERENT ENTITY.
THE SHORTCOMINGS OF MY BODY... ACHES, PAINS... WERE NO MORE.
MY GUIDE EXPLAINED WHAT I WAS.
AS WELL, I WAS GIVEN A BOOK WHICH I WAS TOLD CONTAINED THE ANSWERS TO SEVERAL OF THE MYSTERIES OF HUMAN EXISTENCE.
AND WITH IT, I COULD RULE THE WORLD.
HE SAID THAT ABIGAIL WAS SPARED. IMMORTALITY, HE MUSED, IS A LONELY DYNAMIC.
HISTORY MAY HAVE LOOKED UPON PRESIDENT JOHN ADAMS AS A FOOTNOTE...
...BUT THERE WAS MORE STORY TO BE TOLD.

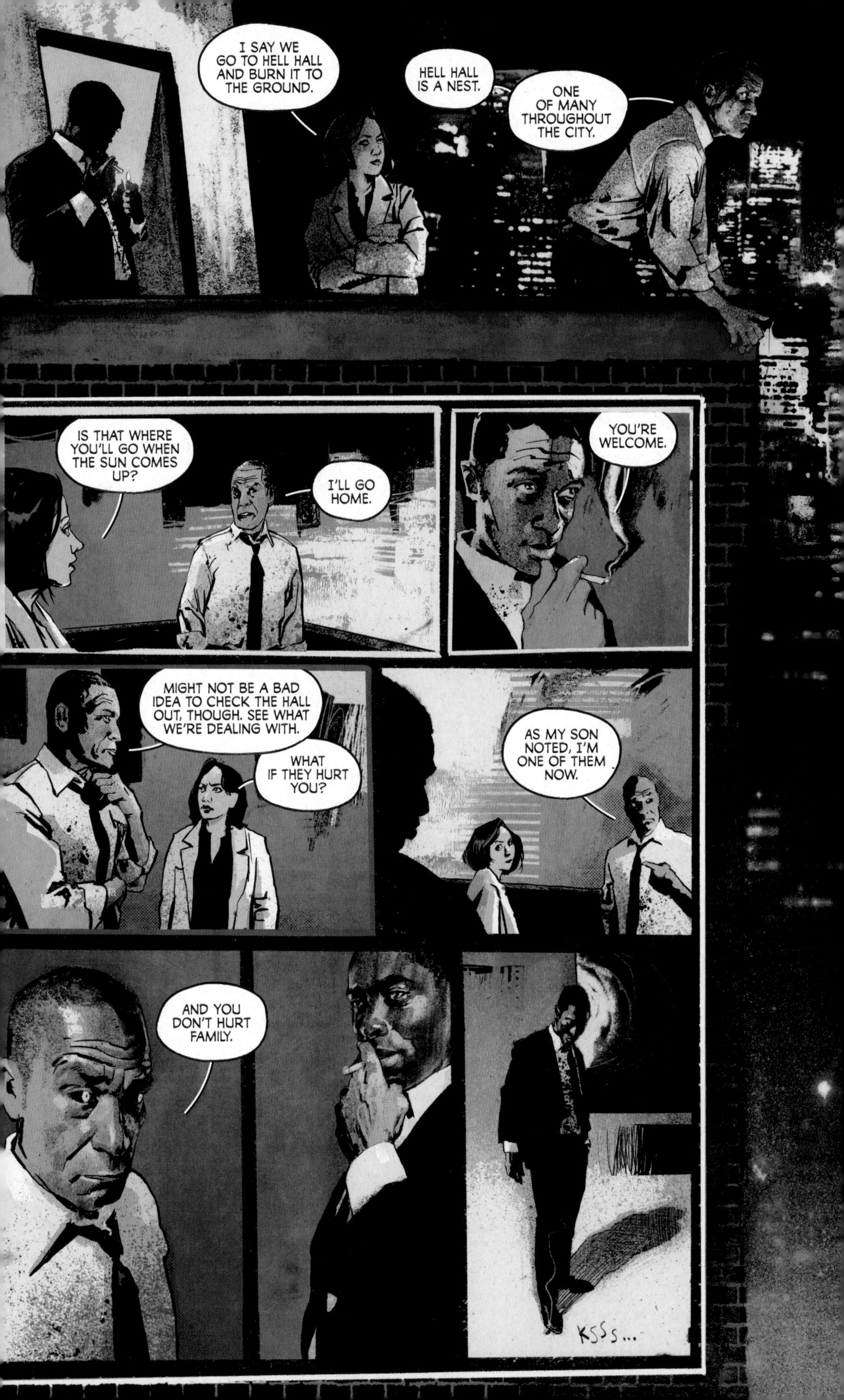
I SAY WE GO TO HELL HALL AND BURN IT TO THE GROUND.
HELL HALL IS A NEST.
ONE OF MANY THROUGHOUT THE CITY.
IS THAT WHERE YOU'LL GO WHEN THE SUN COMES UP?
I'LL GO HOME.
YOU'RE WELCOME.
MIGHT NOT BE A BAD IDEA TO CHECK THE HALL OUT, THOUGH. SEE WHAT WE'RE DEALING WITH.
WHAT IF THEY HURT YOU?
AS MY SON NOTED, I'M ONE OF THEM NOW.
AND YOU DON'T HURT FAMILY.
KSSS...

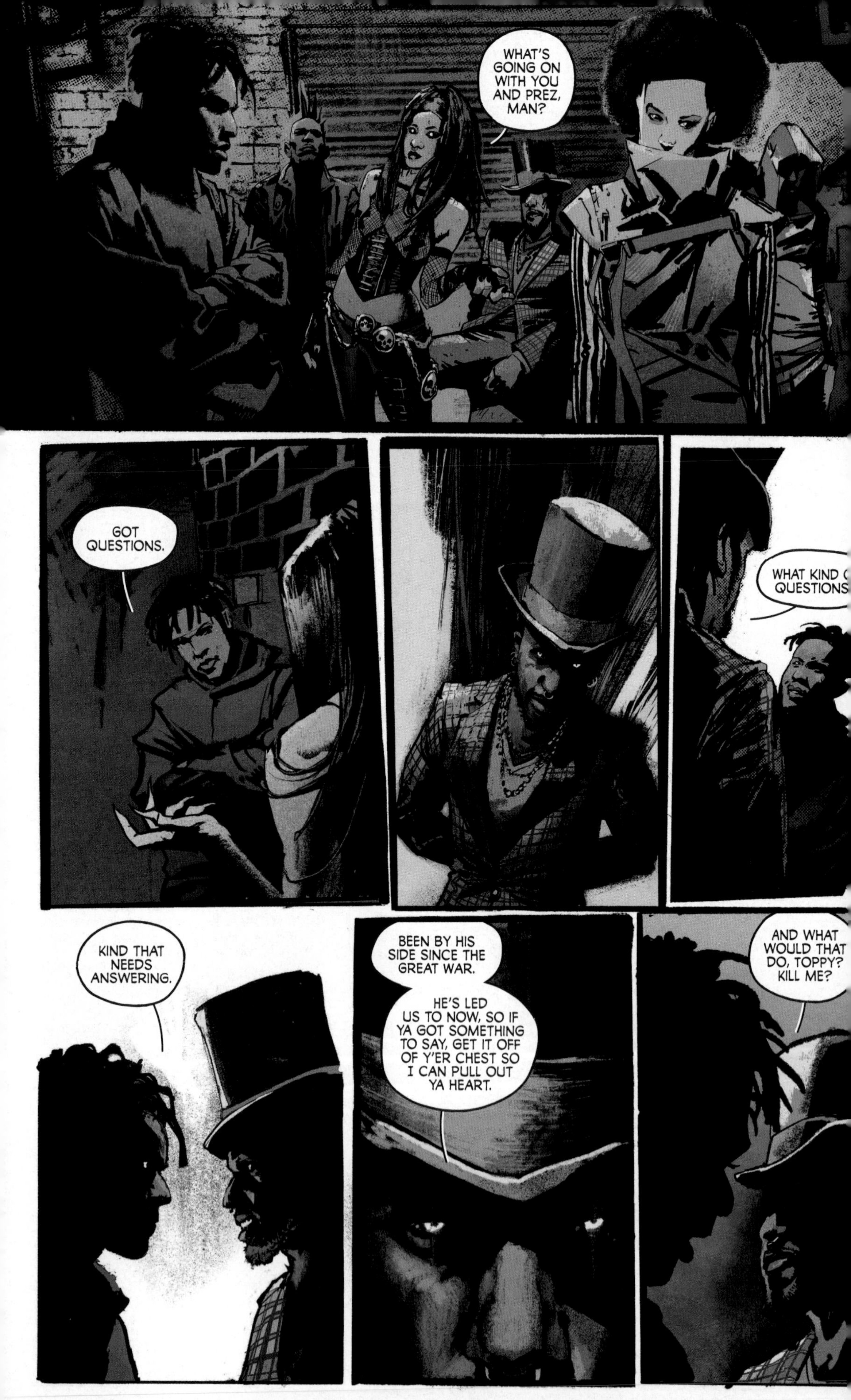
WHAT'S GOING ON WITH YOU AND PREZ, MAN?
GOT QUESTIONS.
WHAT KIND QUESTIONS
KIND THAT NEEDS ANSWERING.
BEEN BY HIS SIDE SINCE THE GREAT WAR.
HE'S LED US TO NOW, SO IF YA GOT SOMETHING TO SAY, GET IT OFF OF Y'ER CHEST SO I CAN PULL OUT YA HEART.
AND WHAT WOULD THAT DO, TOPPY? KILL ME?

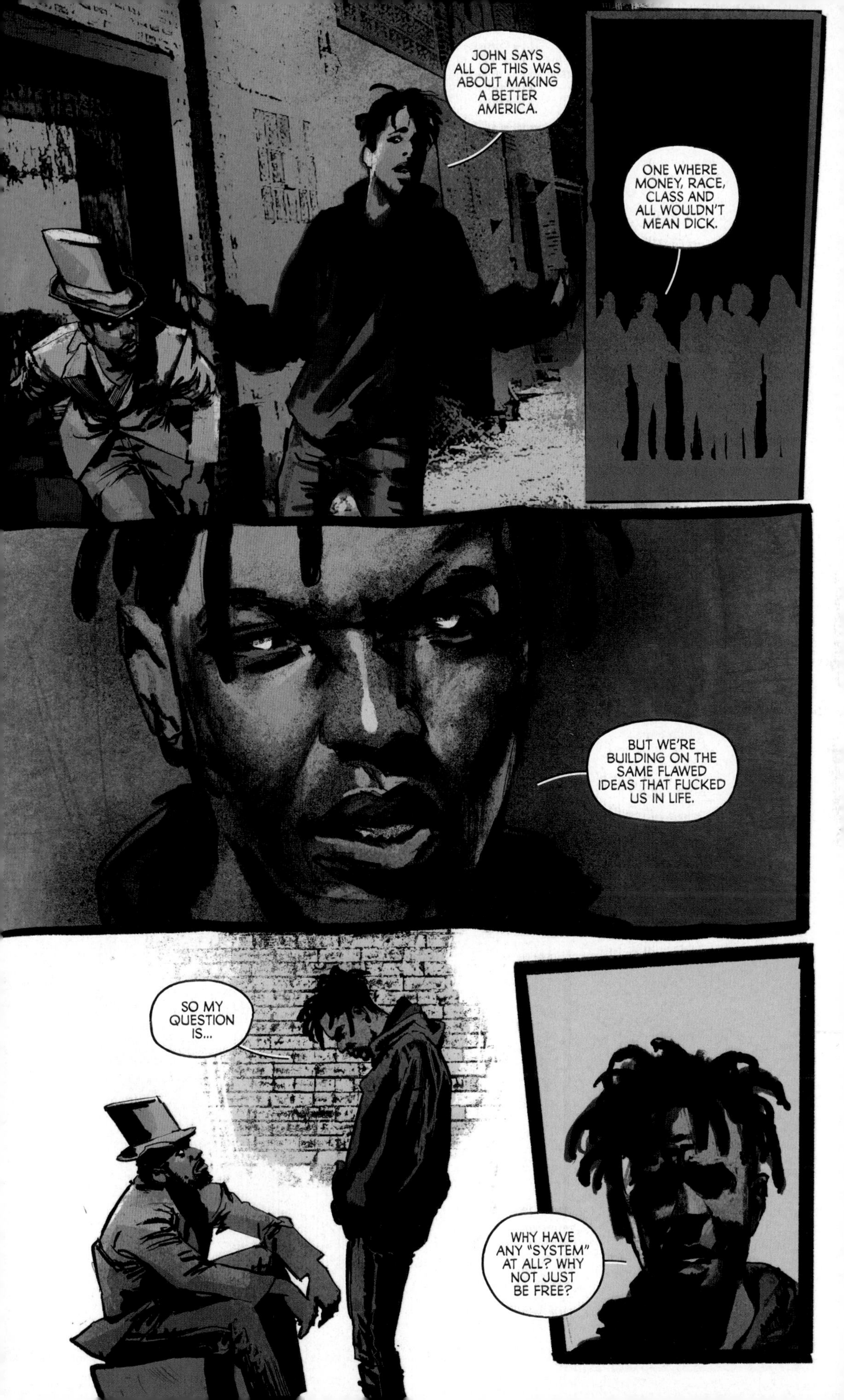
JOHN SAYS ALL OF THIS WAS ABOUT MAKING A BETTER AMERICA.
ONE WHERE MONEY, RACE, CLASS AND ALL WOULDN'T MEAN DICK.
BUT WE'RE BUILDING ON THE SAME FLAWED IDEAS THAT FUCKED US IN LIFE.
SO MY QUESTION IS...
WHY HAVE ANY "SYSTEM" AT ALL? WHY NOT JUST BE FREE?

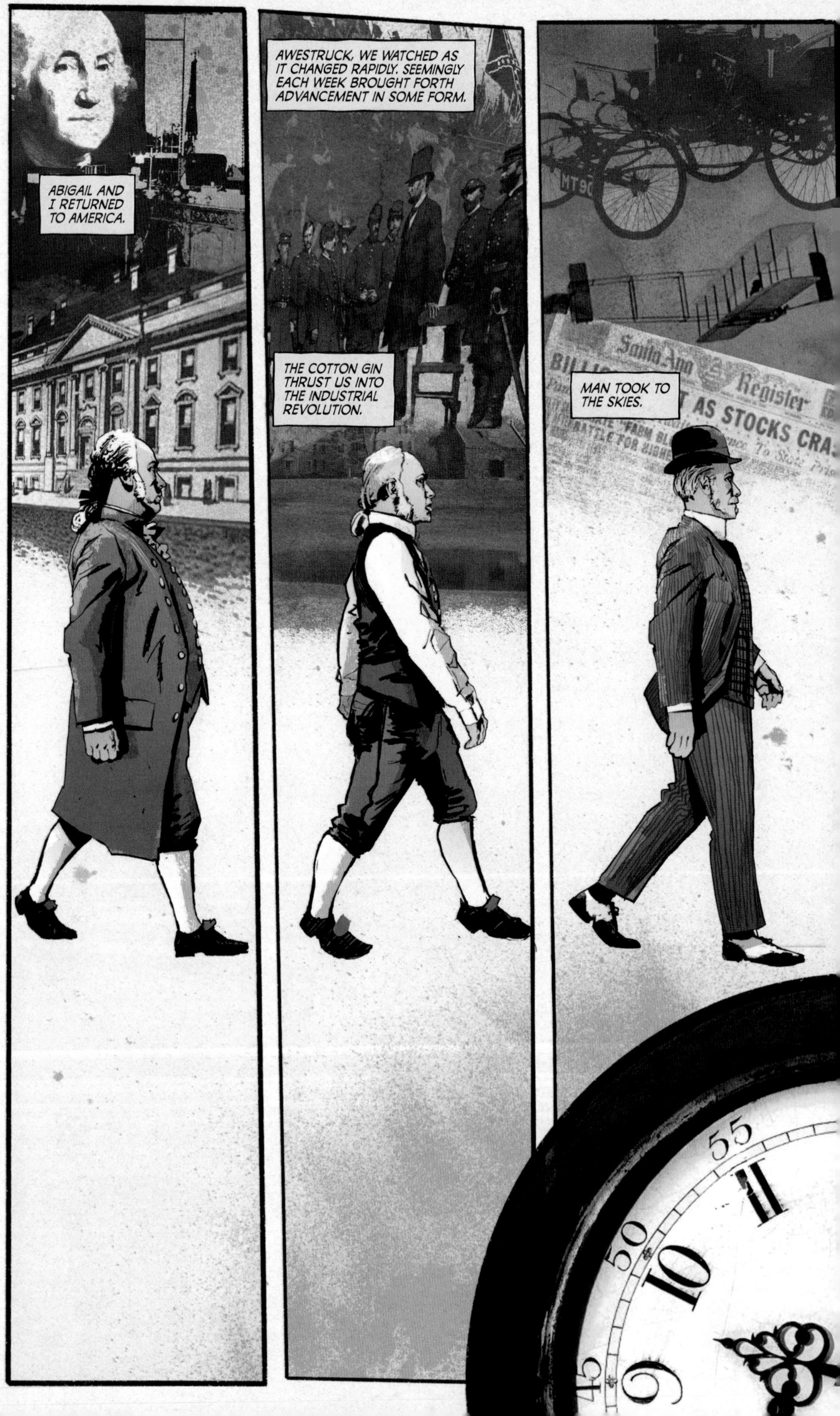
ABIGAIL AND I RETURNED TO AMERICA.
AWESTRUCK, WE WATCHED AS IT CHANGED RAPIDLY. SEEMINGLY EACH WEEK BROUGHT FORTH ADVANCEMENT IN SOME FORM.
THE COTTON GIN THRUST US INTO THE INDUSTRIAL REVOLUTION.
MAN TOOK TO THE SKIES.

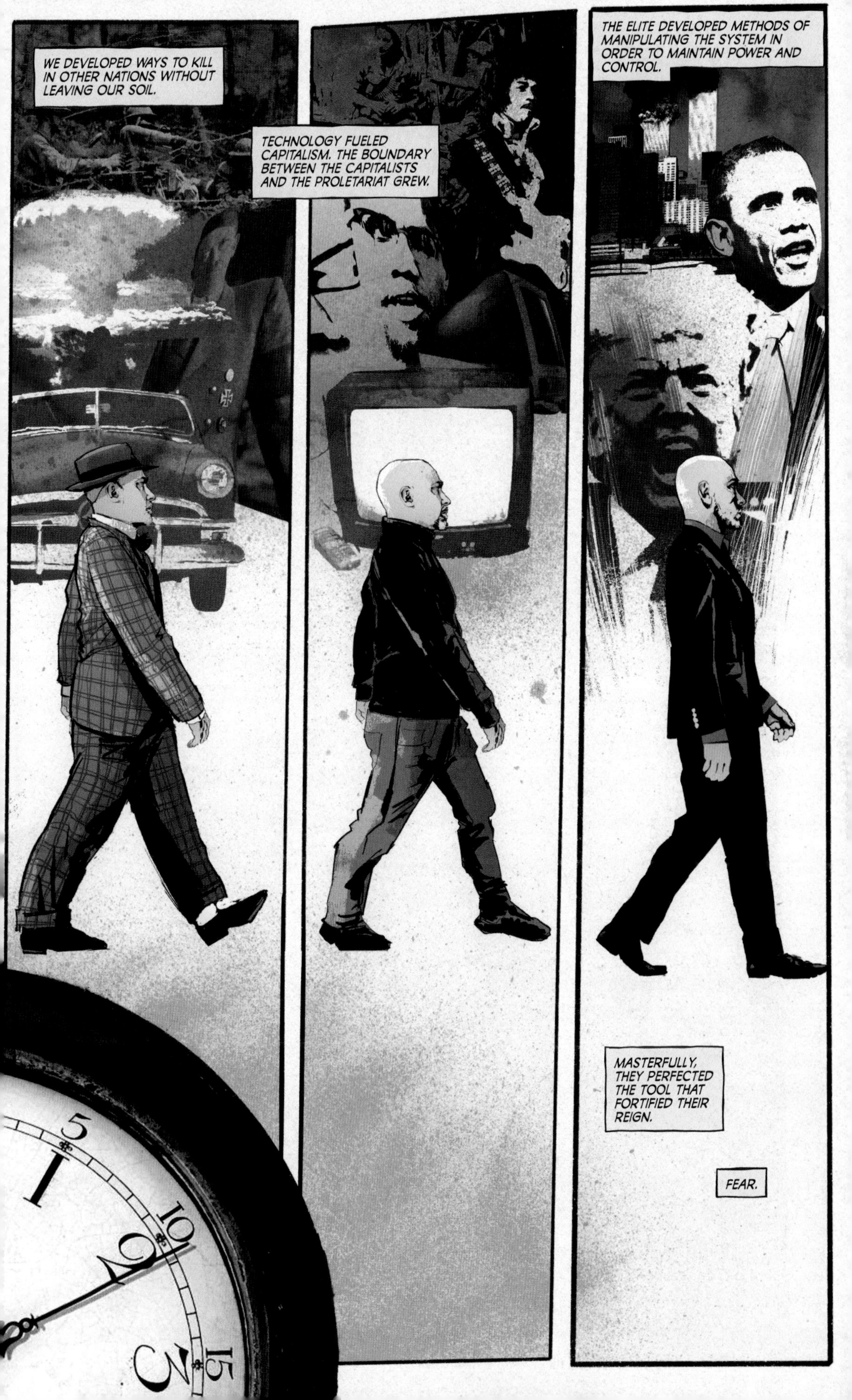
WE DEVELOPED WAYS TO KILL IN OTHER NATIONS WITHOUT LEAVING OUR SOIL.
TECHNOLOGY FUELED CAPITALISM. THE BOUNDARY BETWEEN THE CAPITALISTS AND THE PROLETARIAT GREW.
THE ELITE DEVELOPED METHODS OF MANIPULATING THE SYSTEM IN ORDER TO MAINTAIN POWER AND CONTROL.
MASTERFULLY, THEY PERFECTED THE TOOL THAT FORTIFIED THEIR REIGN.
FEAR.

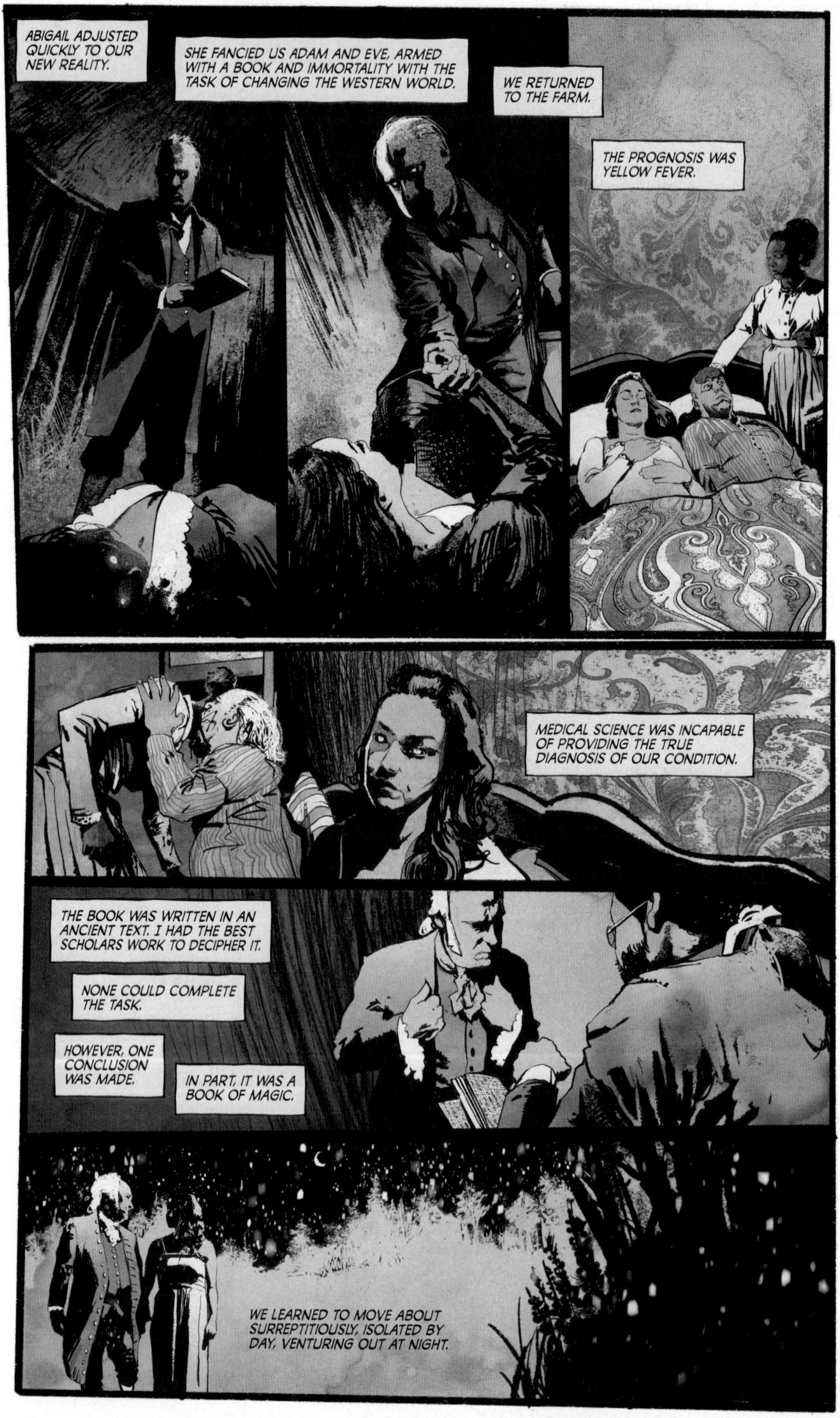
ABIGAIL ADJUSTED QUICKLY TO OUR NEW REALITY.
SHE FANCIED US ADAM AND EVE, ARMED WITH A BOOK AND IMMORTALITY WITH THE TASK OF CHANGING THE WESTERN WORLD.
WE RETURNED TO THE FARM.
THE PROGNOSIS WAS YELLOW FEVER.
MEDICAL SCIENCE WAS INCAPABLE OF PROVIDING THE TRUE DIAGNOSIS OF OUR CONDITION.
THE BOOK WAS WRITTEN IN AN ANCIENT TEXT. I HAD THE BEST SCHOLARS WORK TO DECIPHER IT.
NONE COULD COMPLETE THE TASK.
HOWEVER, ONE CONCLUSION WAS MADE.
IN PART, IT WAS A BOOK OF MAGIC.
WE LEARNED TO MOVE ABOUT SURREPTITIOUSLY, ISOLATED BY DAY, VENTURING OUT AT NIGHT.

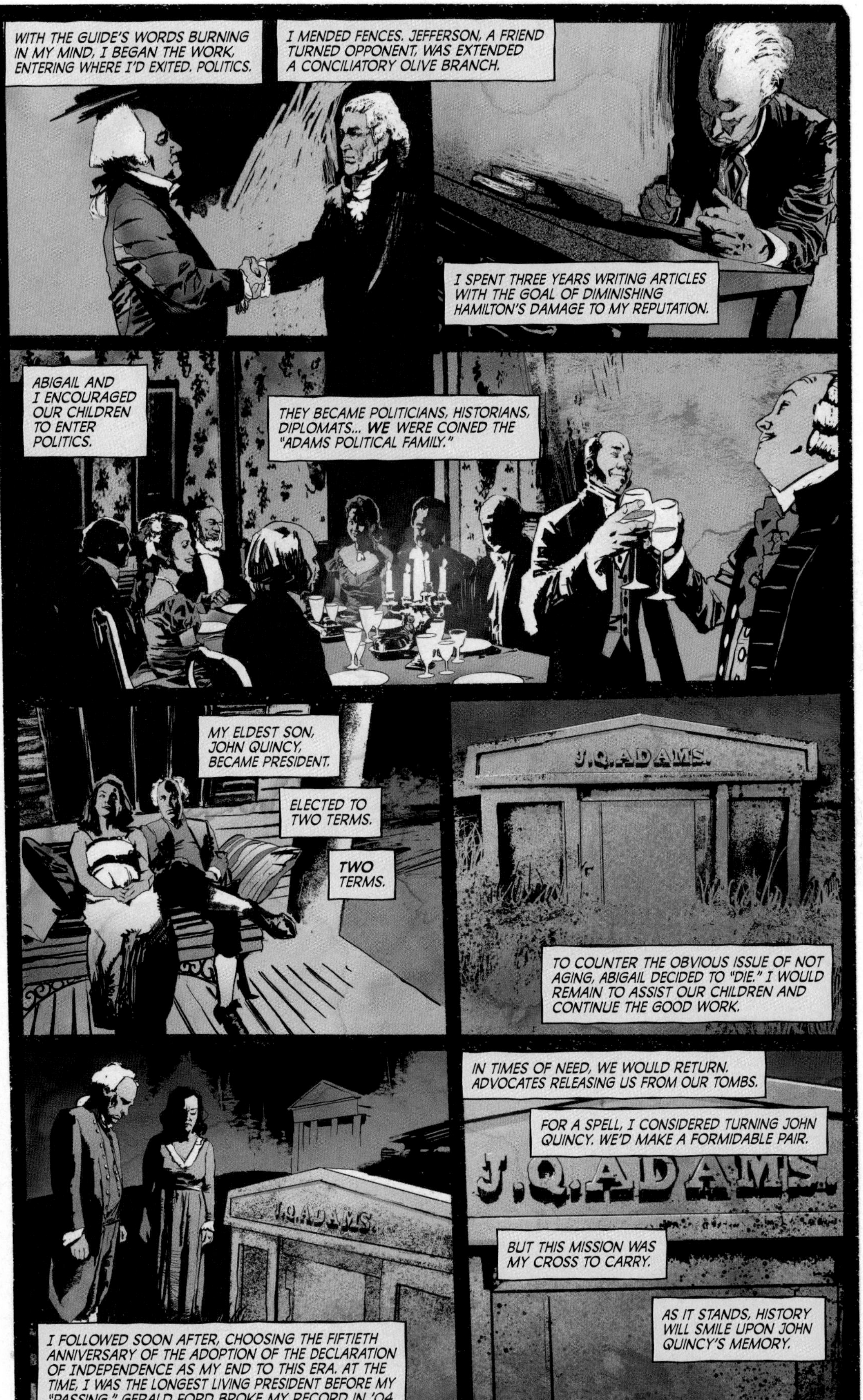
WITH THE GUIDE'S WORDS BURNING IN MY MIND, I BEGAN THE WORK, ENTERING WHERE I'D EXITED. POLITICS.
I MENDED FENCES. JEFFERSON, A FRIEND TURNED OPPONENT, WAS EXTENDED A CONCILIATORY OLIVE BRANCH.
I SPENT THREE YEARS WRITING ARTICLES WITH THE GOAL OF DIMINISHING HAMILTON'S DAMAGE TO MY REPUTATION.
ABIGAIL AND I ENCOURAGED OUR CHILDREN TO ENTER POLITICS.
THEY BECAME POLITICIANS, HISTORIANS, DIPLOMATS... **WE** WERE COINED THE "ADAMS POLITICAL FAMILY."
MY ELDEST SON, JOHN QUINCY, BECAME PRESIDENT.
ELECTED TO TWO TERMS.
TWO TERMS.
J.Q.ADAMS.
TO COUNTER THE OBVIOUS ISSUE OF NOT AGING, ABIGAIL DECIDED TO "DIE." I WOULD REMAIN TO ASSIST OUR CHILDREN AND CONTINUE THE GOOD WORK.
J.Q.ADAMS.
I FOLLOWED SOON AFTER, CHOOSING THE FIFTIETH ANNIVERSARY OF THE ADOPTION OF THE DECLARATION OF INDEPENDENCE AS MY END TO THIS ERA. AT THE TIME, I WAS THE LONGEST LIVING PRESIDENT BEFORE MY "PASSING." GERALD FORD BROKE MY RECORD IN '04.
IN TIMES OF NEED, WE WOULD RETURN. ADVOCATES RELEASING US FROM OUR TOMBS.
FOR A SPELL, I CONSIDERED TURNING JOHN QUINCY. WE'D MAKE A FORMIDABLE PAIR.
J.Q.ADAMS.
BUT THIS MISSION WAS MY CROSS TO CARRY.
AS IT STANDS, HISTORY WILL SMILE UPON JOHN QUINCY'S MEMORY.

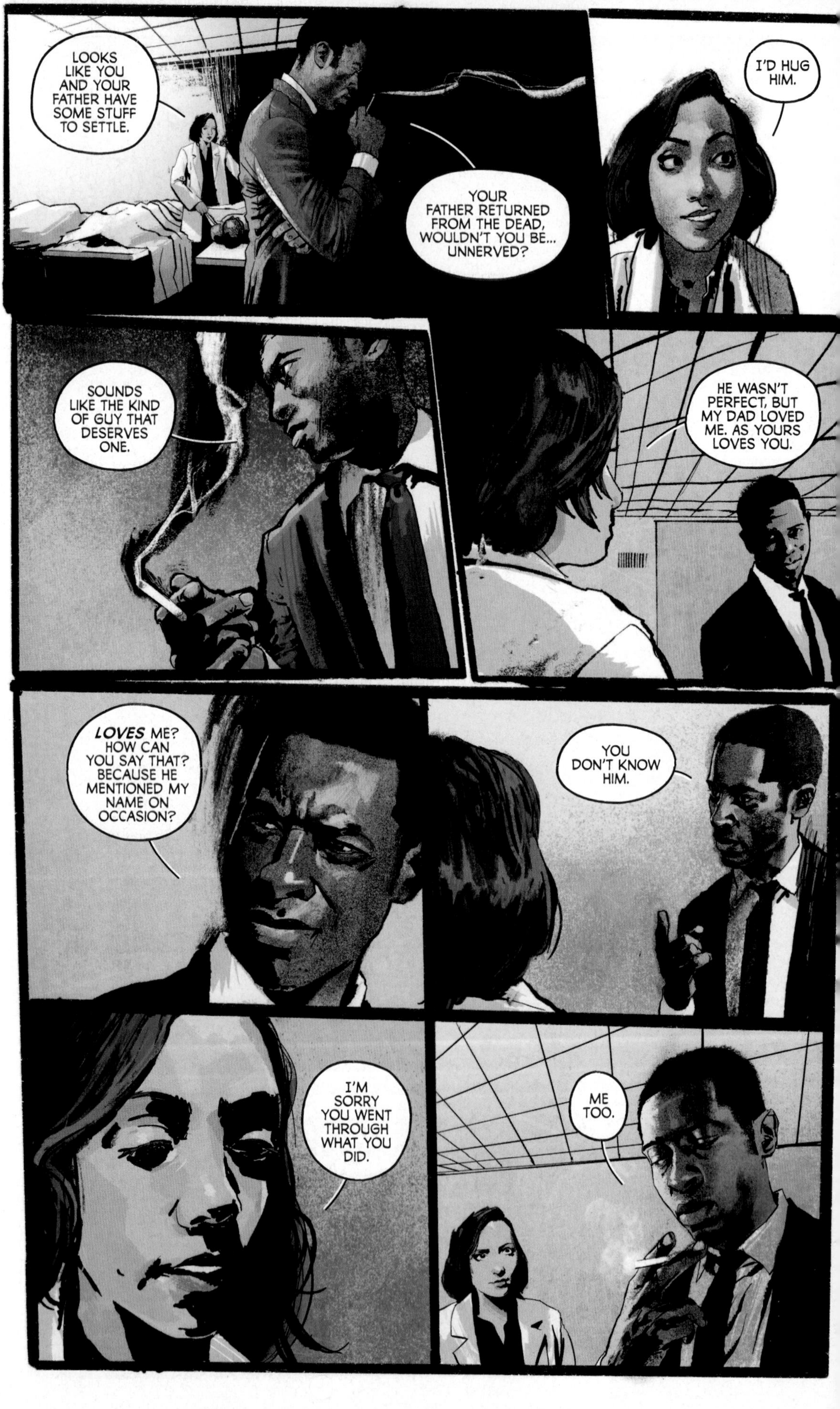
LOOKS LIKE YOU AND YOUR FATHER HAVE SOME STUFF TO SETTLE.
YOUR FATHER RETURNED FROM THE DEAD, WOULDN'T YOU BE... UNNERVED?
I'D HUG HIM.
SOUNDS LIKE THE KIND OF GUY THAT DESERVES ONE.
HE WASN'T PERFECT, BUT MY DAD LOVED ME. AS YOURS LOVES YOU.
LOVES ME? HOW CAN YOU SAY THAT? BECAUSE HE MENTIONED MY NAME ON OCCASION?
YOU DON'T KNOW HIM.
I'M SORRY YOU WENT THROUGH WHAT YOU DID.
ME TOO.

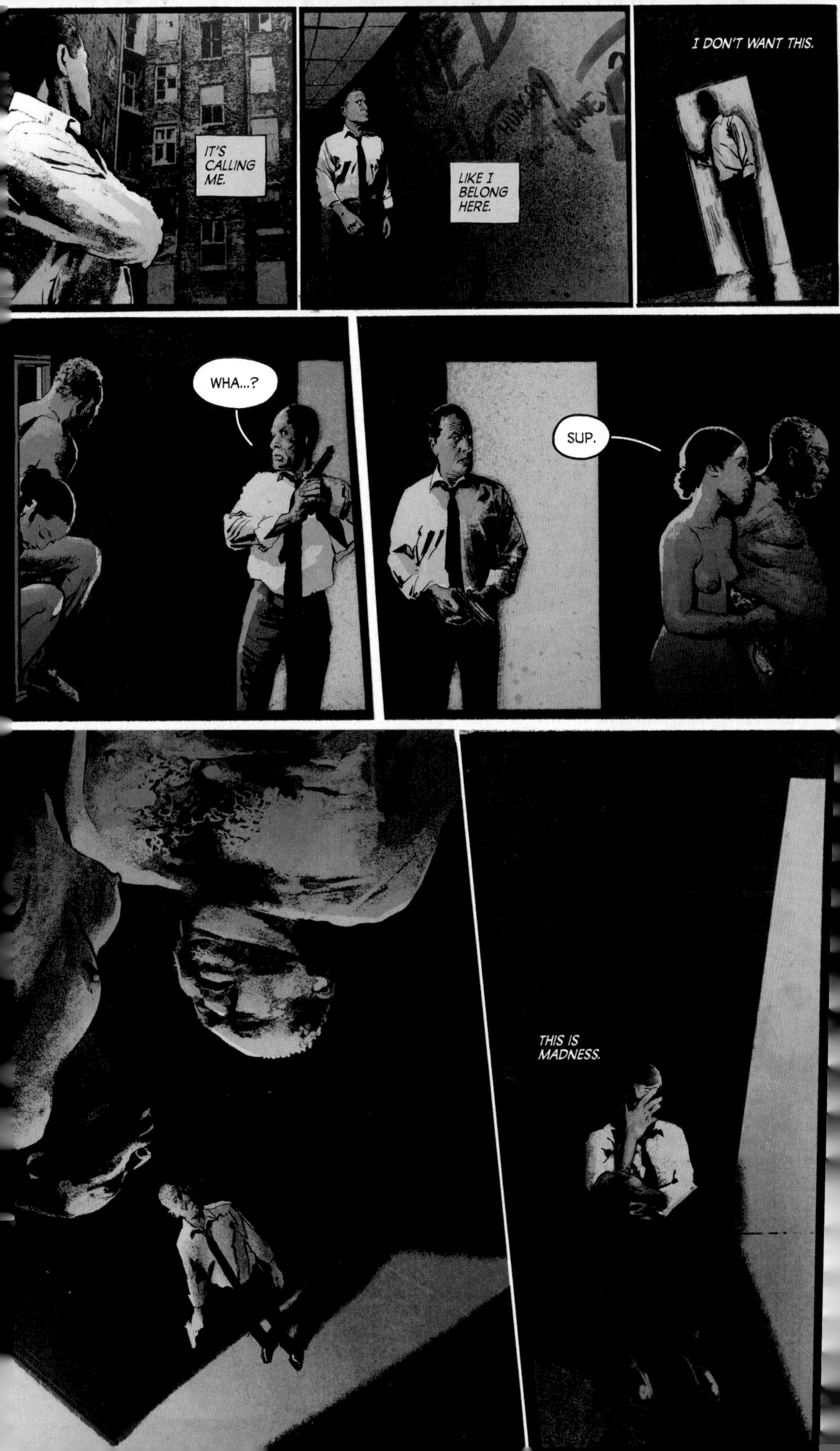
IT'S CALLING ME.
LIKE I BELONG HERE.
I DON'T WANT THIS.
WHA...?
SUP.
THIS IS MADNESS.

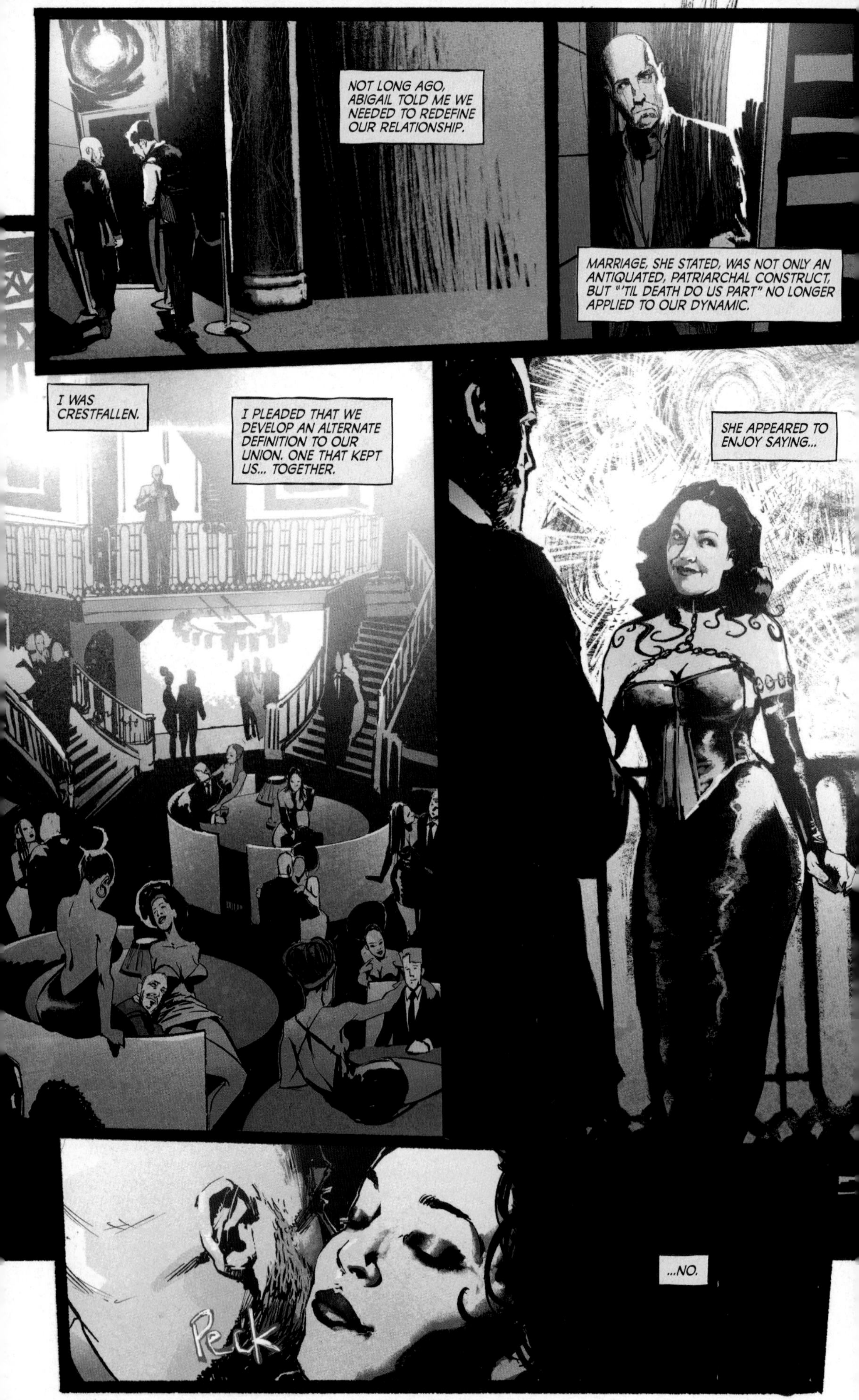
NOT LONG AGO, ABIGAIL TOLD ME WE NEEDED TO REDEFINE OUR RELATIONSHIP.
MARRIAGE, SHE STATED, WAS NOT ONLY AN ANTIQUATED, PATRIARCHAL CONSTRUCT, BUT "'TIL DEATH DO US PART" NO LONGER APPLIED TO OUR DYNAMIC.
I WAS CRESTFALLEN.
I PLEADED THAT WE DEVELOP AN ALTERNATE DEFINITION TO OUR UNION. ONE THAT KEPT US... TOGETHER.
SHE APPEARED TO ENJOY SAYING...
...NO.
PECK

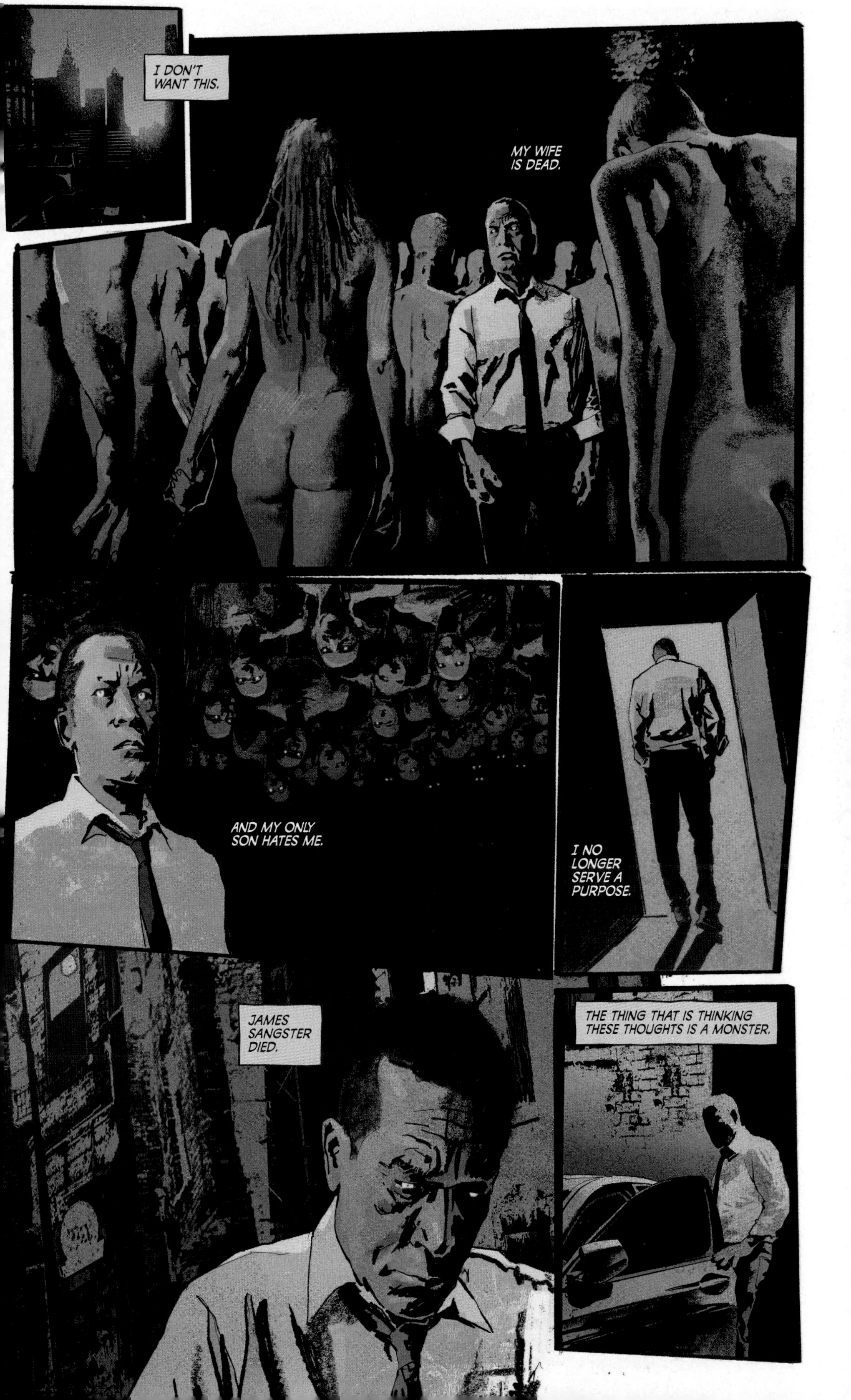
I DON'T WANT THIS.
MY WIFE IS DEAD.
AND MY ONLY SON HATES ME.
I NO LONGER SERVE A PURPOSE.
JAMES SANGSTER DIED.
THE THING THAT IS THINKING THESE THOUGHTS IS A MONSTER.

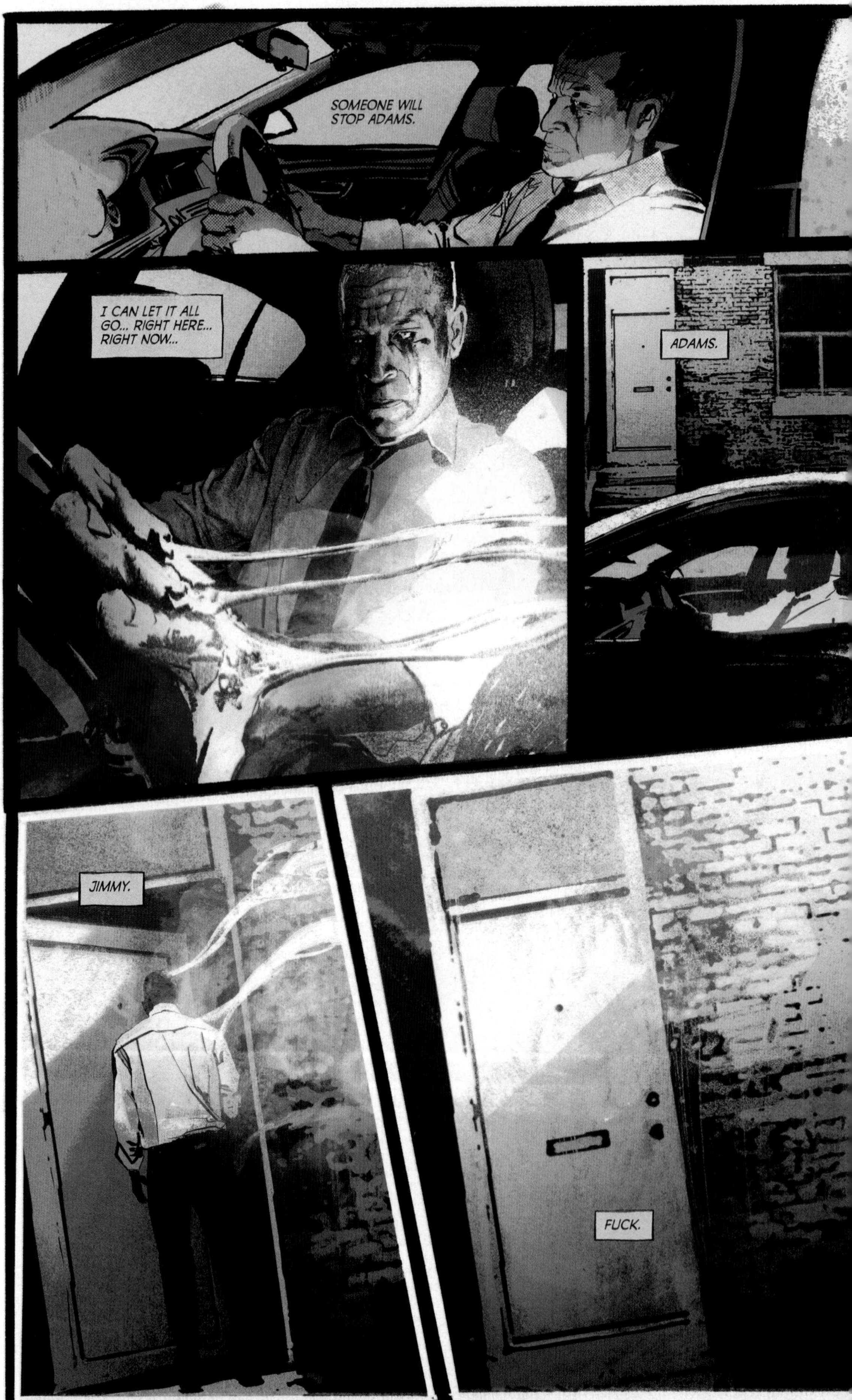
SOMEONE WILL STOP ADAMS.
I CAN LET IT ALL GO... RIGHT HERE... RIGHT NOW...
ADAMS.
JIMMY.
FUCK.

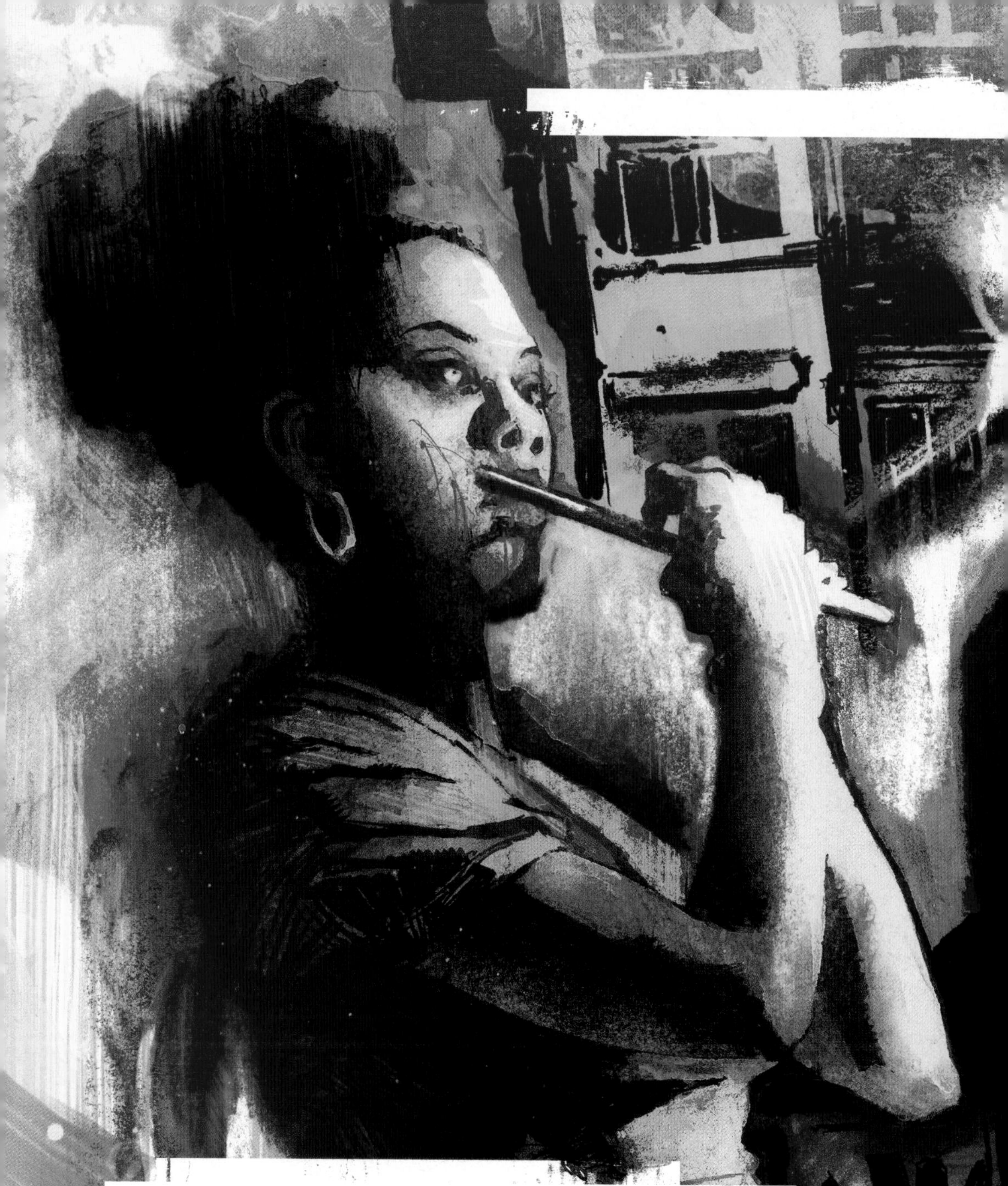

"THIS CITY DIED A LONG TIME AGO. JUST NOBODY HAD THE GUTS TO BURY IT."

...CRY OUT FOR REVOLUTION! Chapter IV

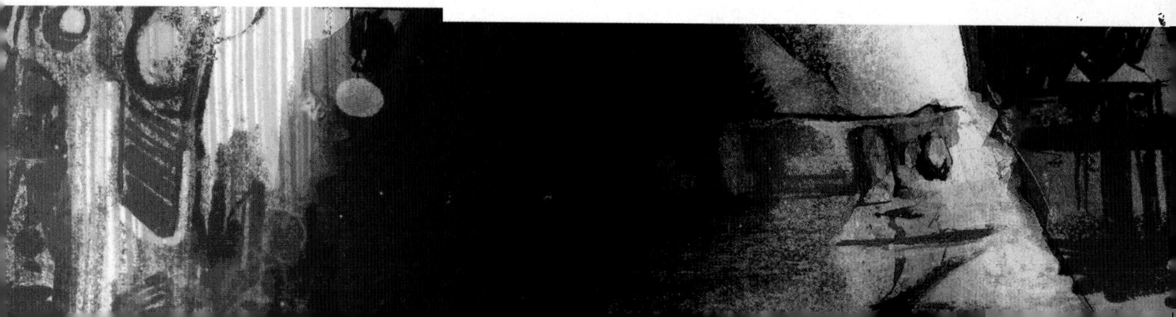

IV

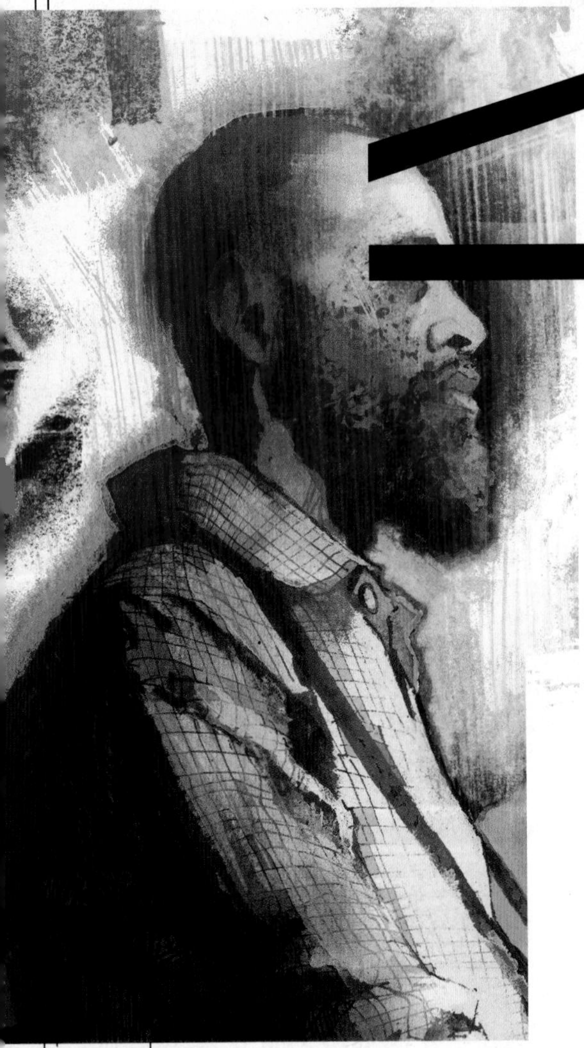

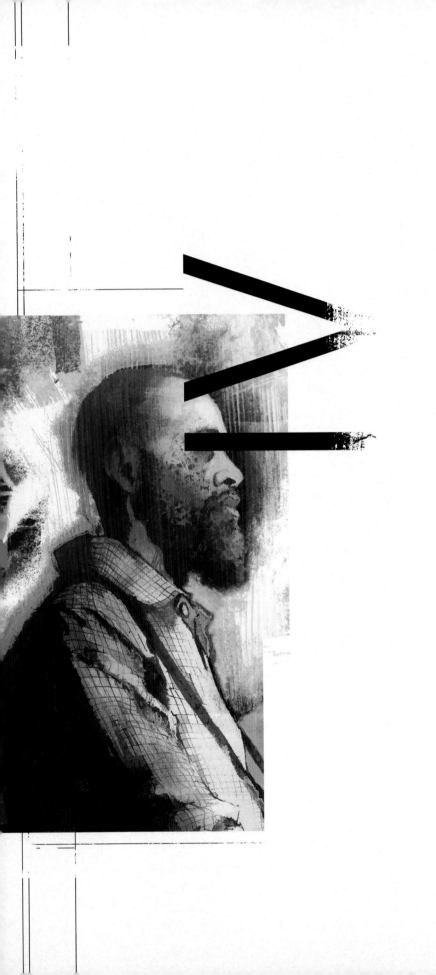

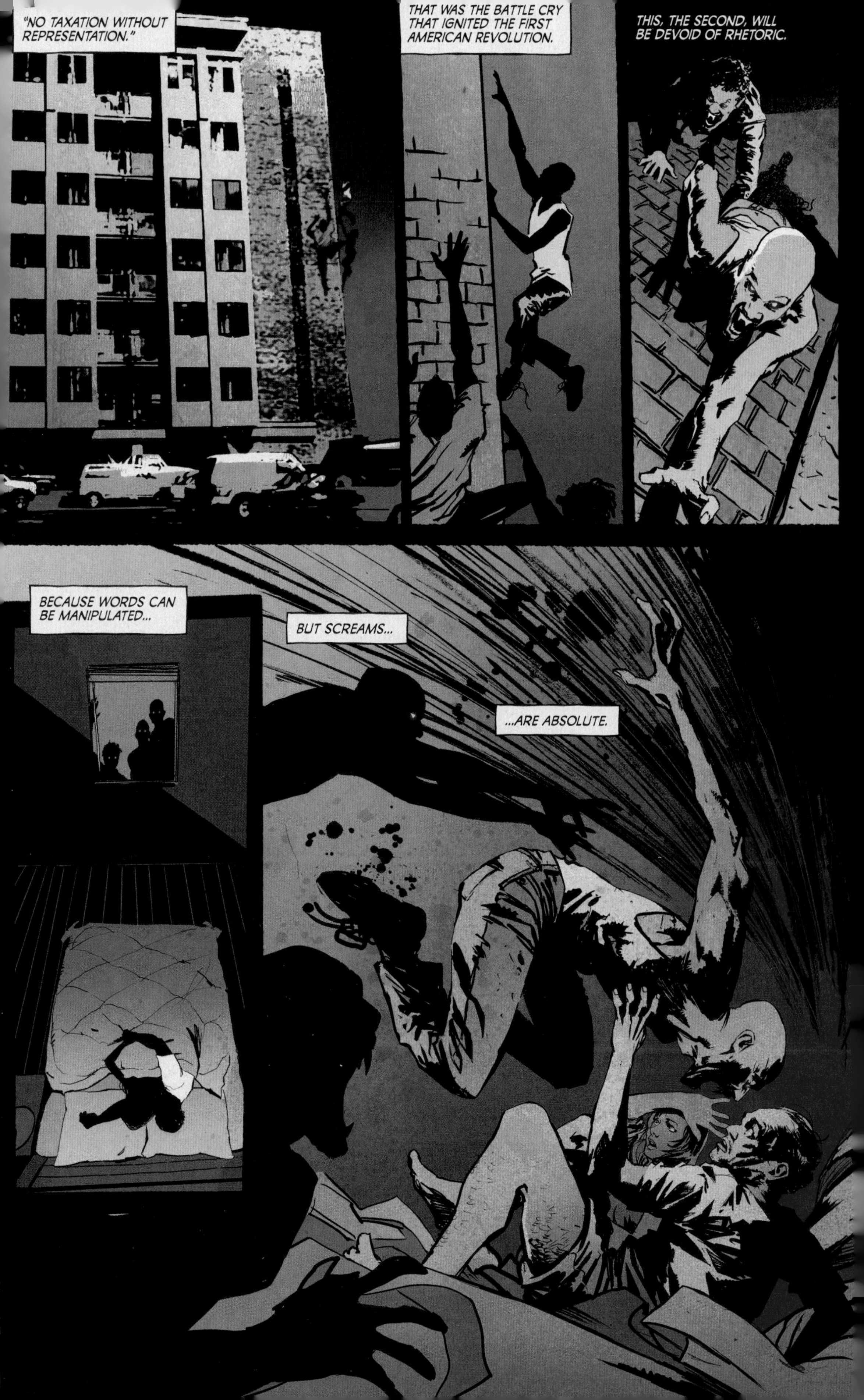
"NO TAXATION WITHOUT REPRESENTATION."
THAT WAS THE BATTLE CRY THAT IGNITED THE FIRST AMERICAN REVOLUTION.
THIS, THE SECOND, WILL BE DEVOID OF RHETORIC.
BECAUSE WORDS CAN BE MANIPULATED...
BUT SCREAMS...
...ARE ABSOLUTE.

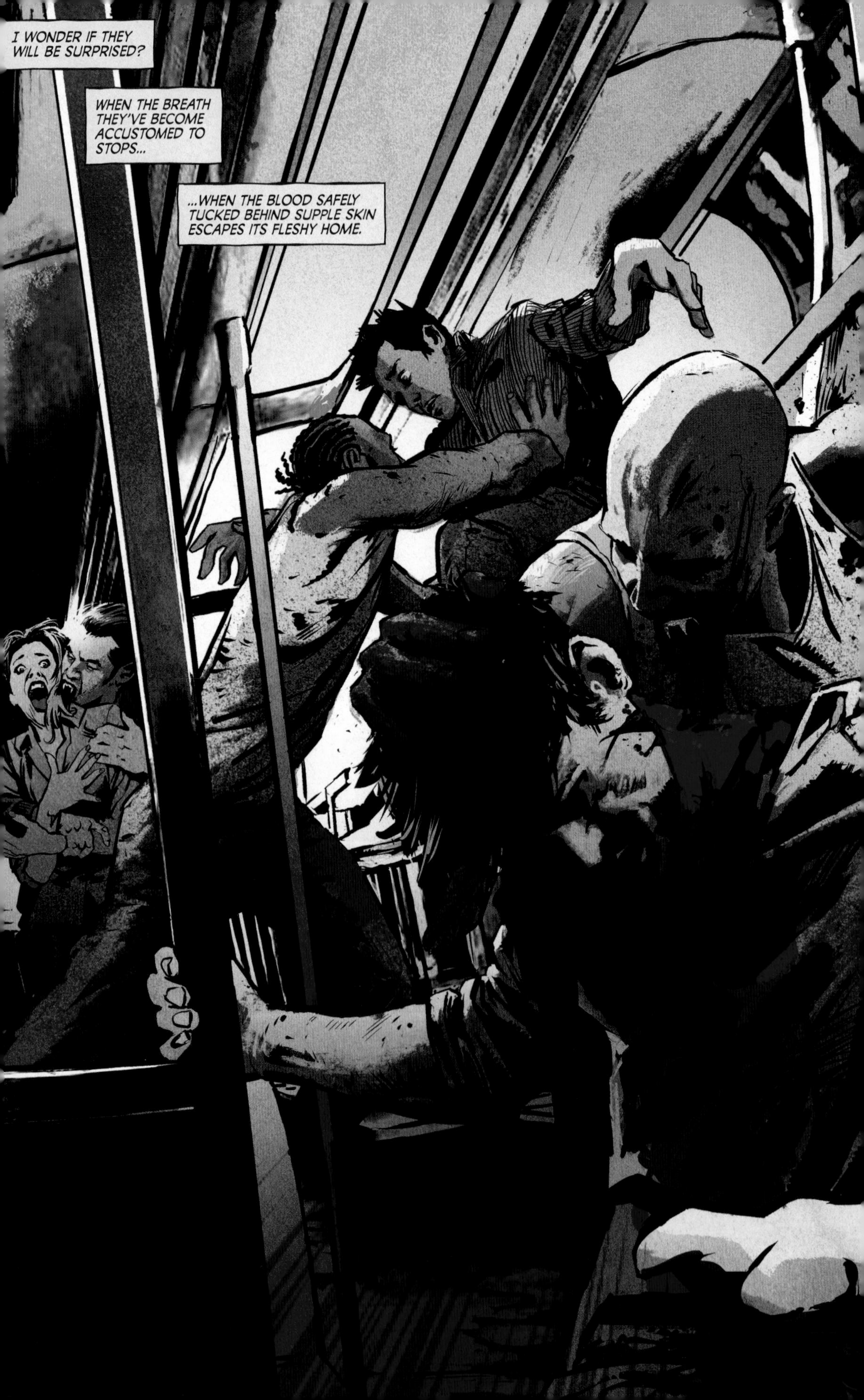
I WONDER IF THEY WILL BE SURPRISED?
WHEN THE BREATH THEY'VE BECOME ACCUSTOMED TO STOPS...
...WHEN THE BLOOD SAFELY TUCKED BEHIND SUPPLE SKIN ESCAPES ITS FLESHY HOME.

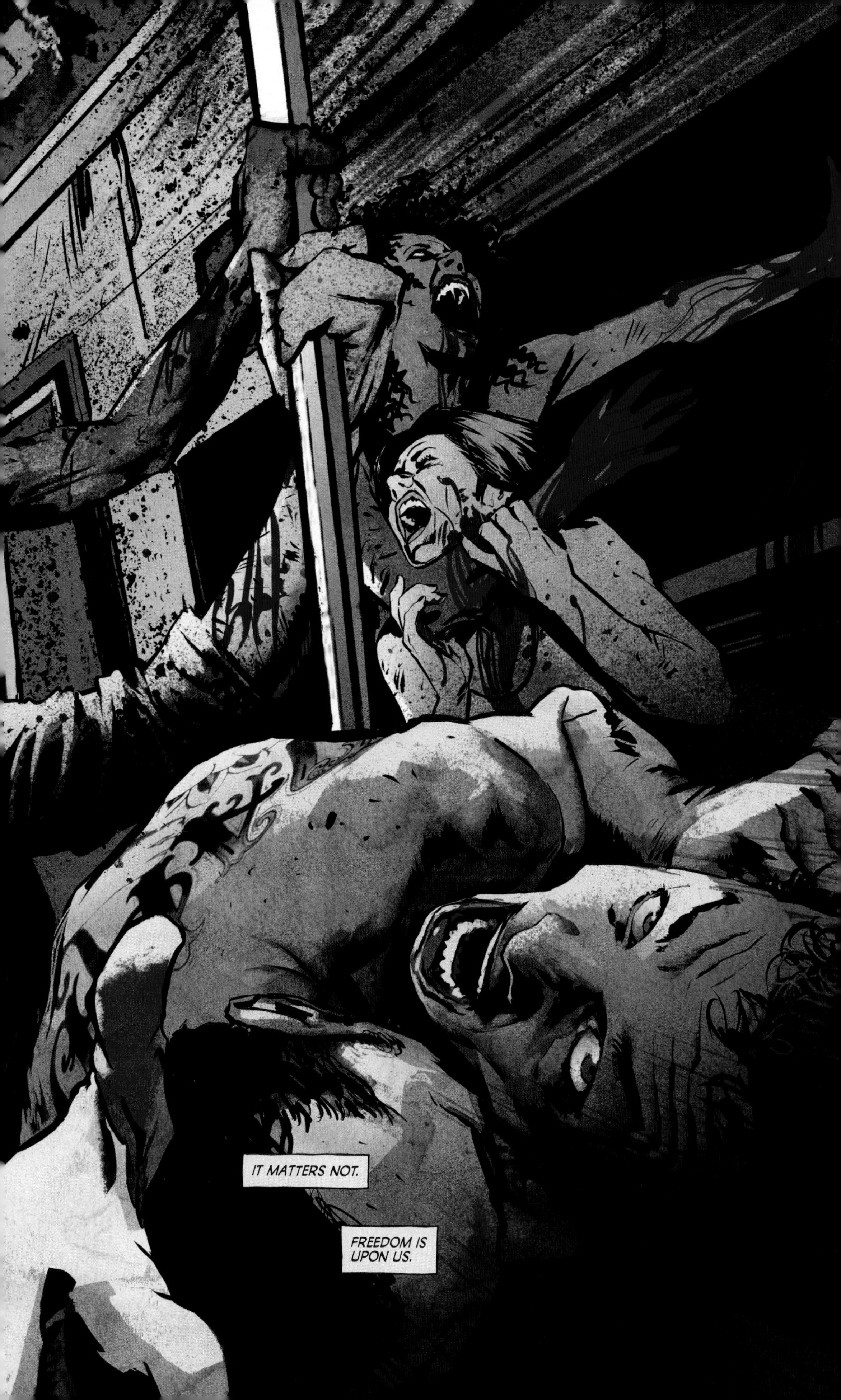
IT MATTERS NOT.
FREEDOM IS UPON US.

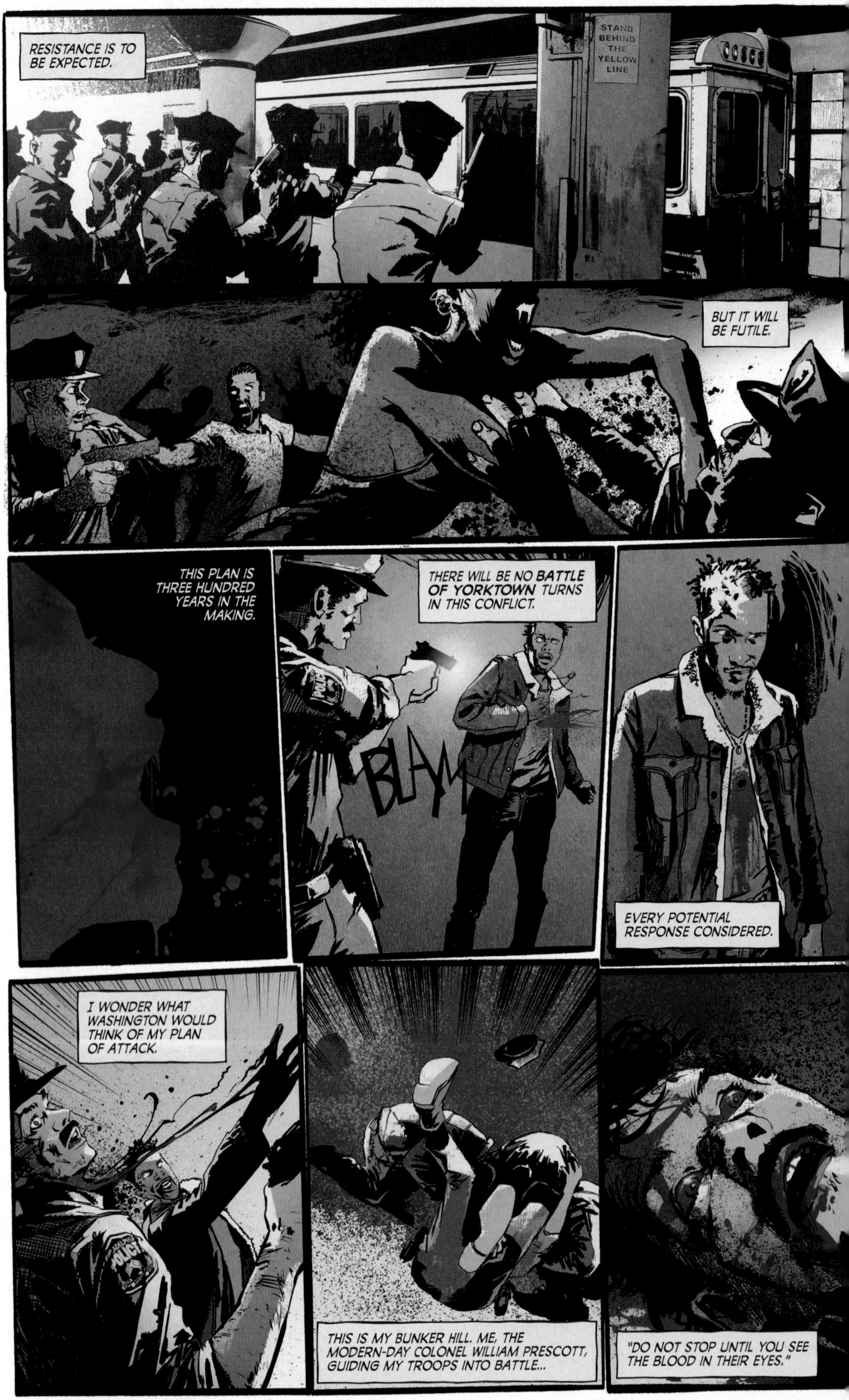
RESISTANCE IS TO BE EXPECTED.
STAND BEHIND THE YELLOW LINE
BUT IT WILL BE FUTILE.
THIS PLAN IS THREE HUNDRED YEARS IN THE MAKING.
THERE WILL BE NO BATTLE OF YORKTOWN TURNS IN THIS CONFLICT.
POLICE
BLAM
EVERY POTENTIAL RESPONSE CONSIDERED.
I WONDER WHAT WASHINGTON WOULD THINK OF MY PLAN OF ATTACK.
POLICE
THIS IS MY BUNKER HILL. ME, THE MODERN-DAY COLONEL WILLIAM PRESCOTT, GUIDING MY TROOPS INTO BATTLE...
"DO NOT STOP UNTIL YOU SEE THE BLOOD IN THEIR EYES."

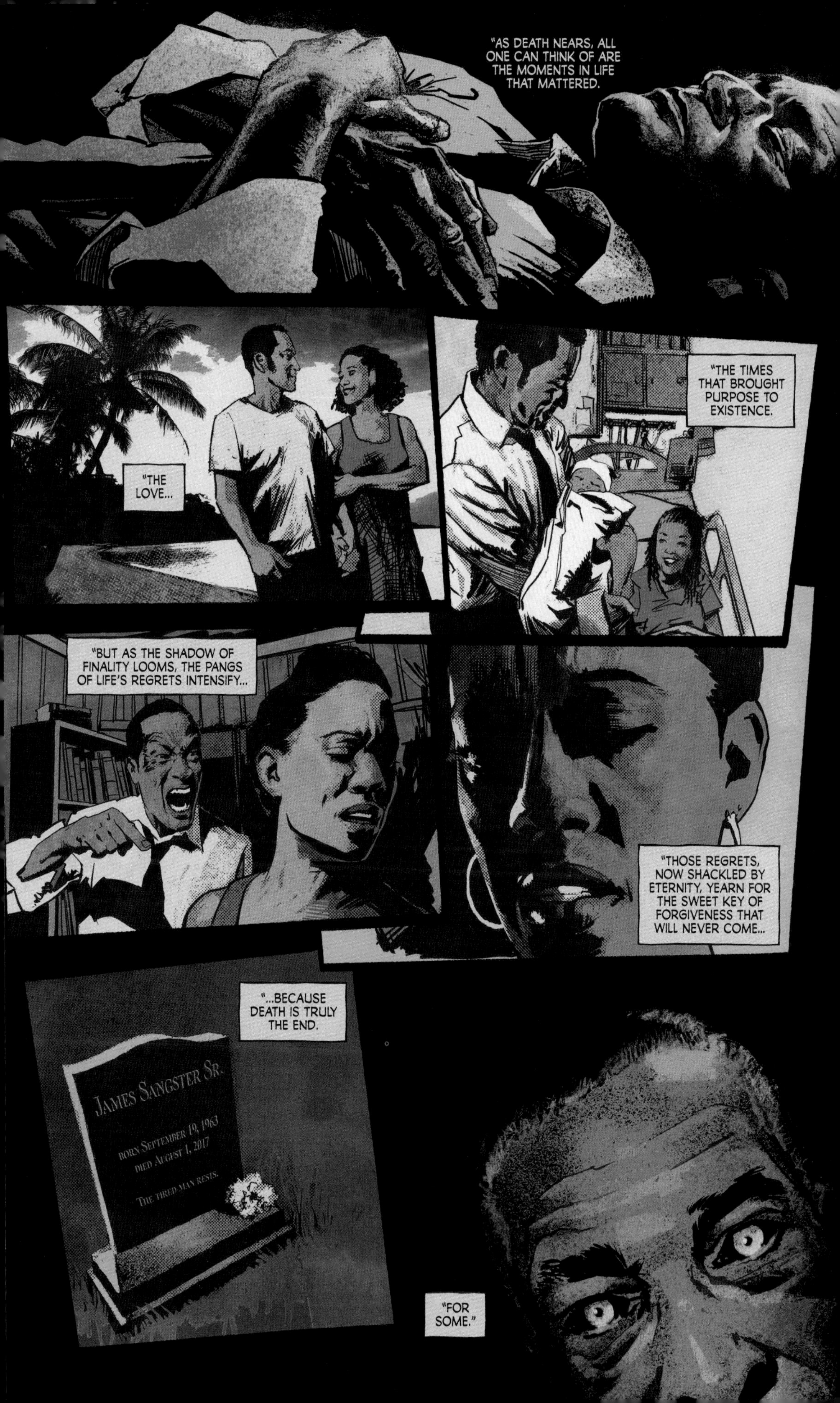
"AS DEATH NEARS, ALL ONE CAN THINK OF ARE THE MOMENTS IN LIFE THAT MATTERED.
"THE LOVE...
"THE TIMES THAT BROUGHT PURPOSE TO EXISTENCE.
"BUT AS THE SHADOW OF FINALITY LOOMS, THE PANGS OF LIFE'S REGRETS INTENSIFY...
"THOSE REGRETS, NOW SHACKLED BY ETERNITY, YEARN FOR THE SWEET KEY OF FORGIVENESS THAT WILL NEVER COME...
"...BECAUSE DEATH IS TRULY THE END.
JAMES SANGSTER SR.
BORN SEPTEMBER 19, 1963
DIED AUGUST 1, 2017
THE TIRED MAN RESTS.
"FOR SOME."

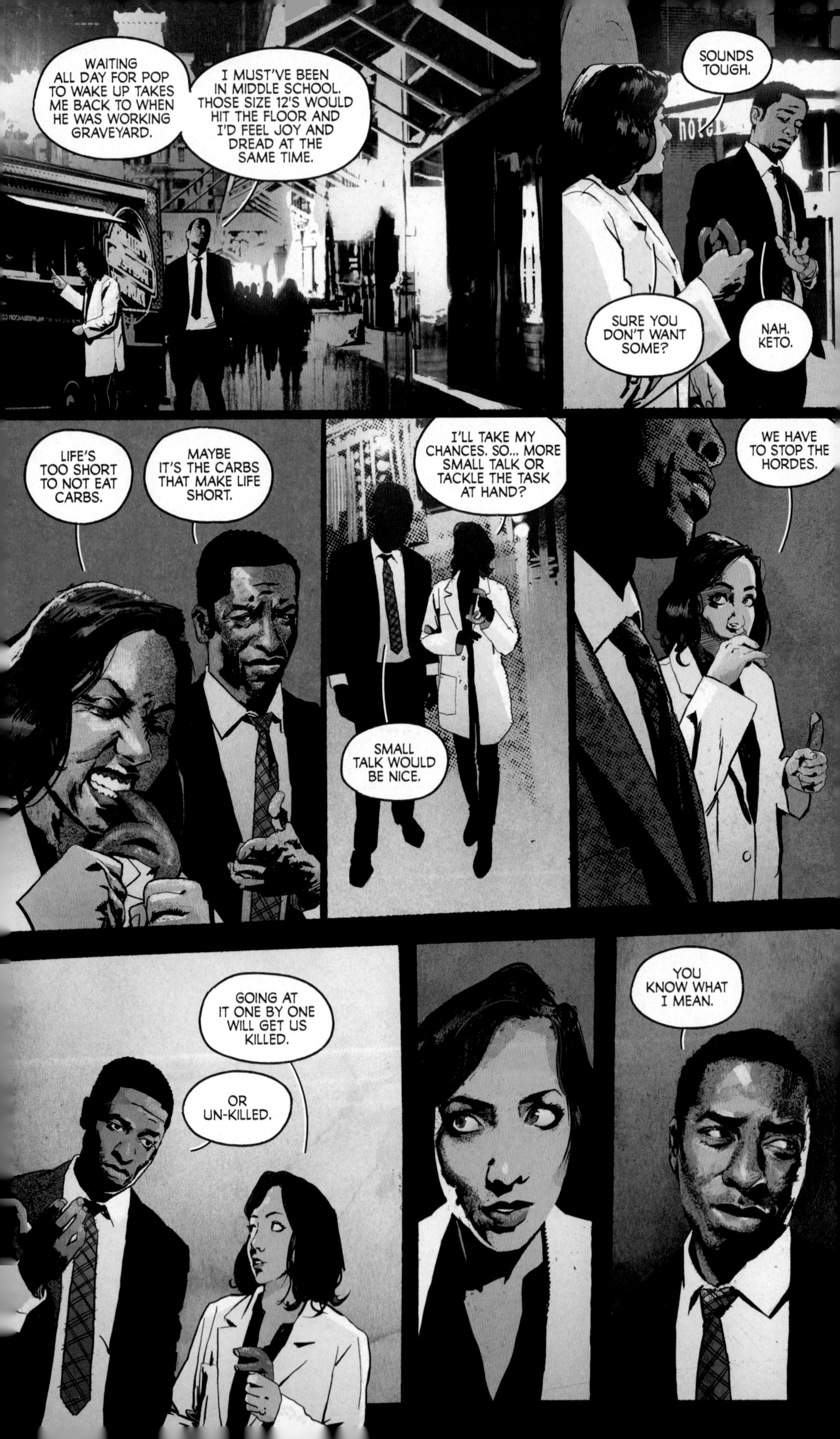
WAITING ALL DAY FOR POP TO WAKE UP TAKES ME BACK TO WHEN HE WAS WORKING GRAVEYARD.
I MUST'VE BEEN IN MIDDLE SCHOOL. THOSE SIZE 12'S WOULD HIT THE FLOOR AND I'D FEEL JOY AND DREAD AT THE SAME TIME.
SOUNDS TOUGH.
SURE YOU DON'T WANT SOME?
NAH. KETO.
LIFE'S TOO SHORT TO NOT EAT CARBS.
MAYBE IT'S THE CARBS THAT MAKE LIFE SHORT.
I'LL TAKE MY CHANCES. SO... MORE SMALL TALK OR TACKLE THE TASK AT HAND?
SMALL TALK WOULD BE NICE.
WE HAVE TO STOP THE HORDES.
GOING AT IT ONE BY ONE WILL GET US KILLED.
OR UN-KILLED.
YOU KNOW WHAT I MEAN.

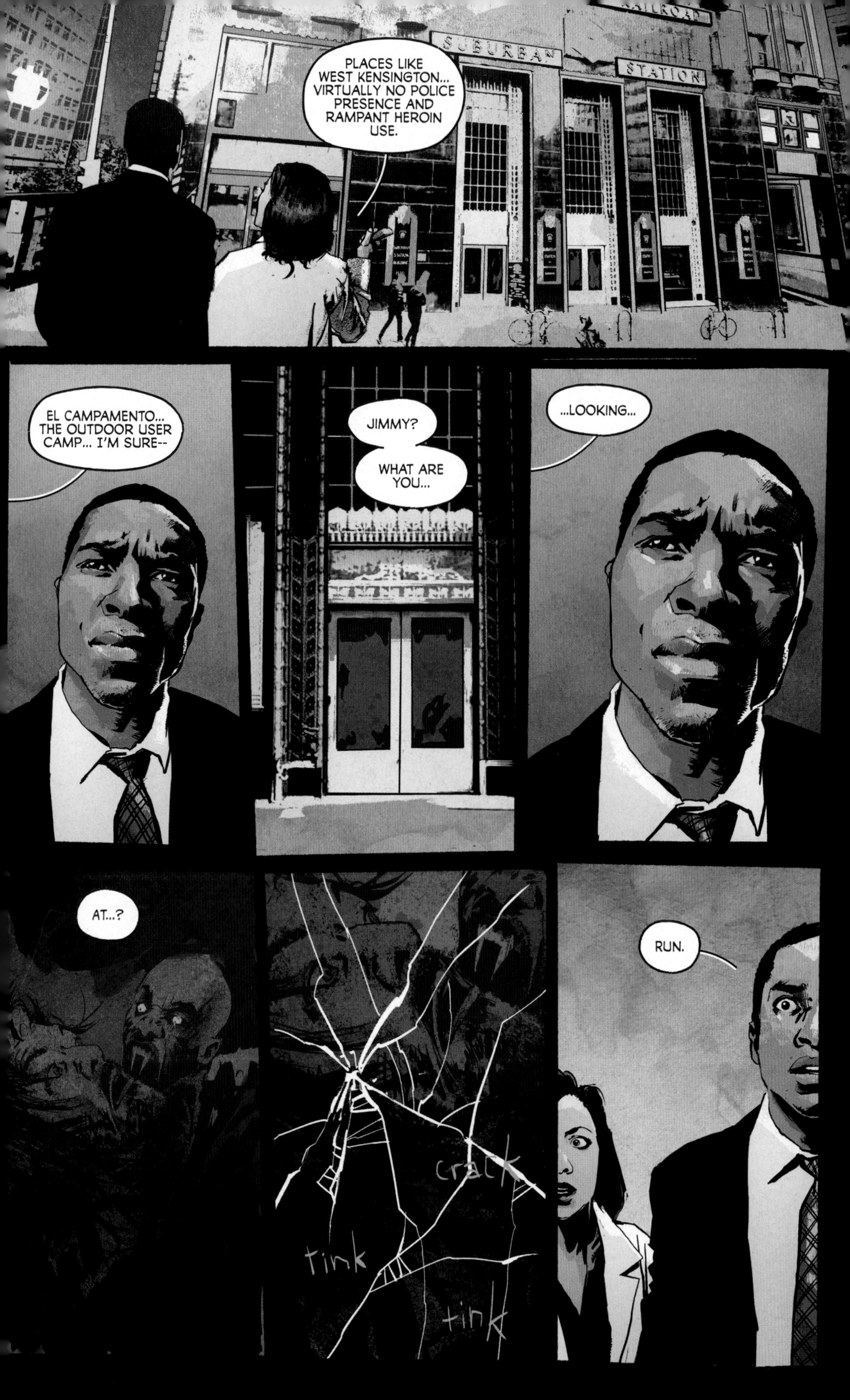
RAILROAD
SUBURBAN
STATION
PLACES LIKE WEST KENSINGTON... VIRTUALLY NO POLICE PRESENCE AND RAMPANT HEROIN USE.
EL CAMPAMENTO... THE OUTDOOR USER CAMP... I'M SURE--
JIMMY?
WHAT ARE YOU...
...LOOKING...
AT...?
crack
tink
tink
RUN.

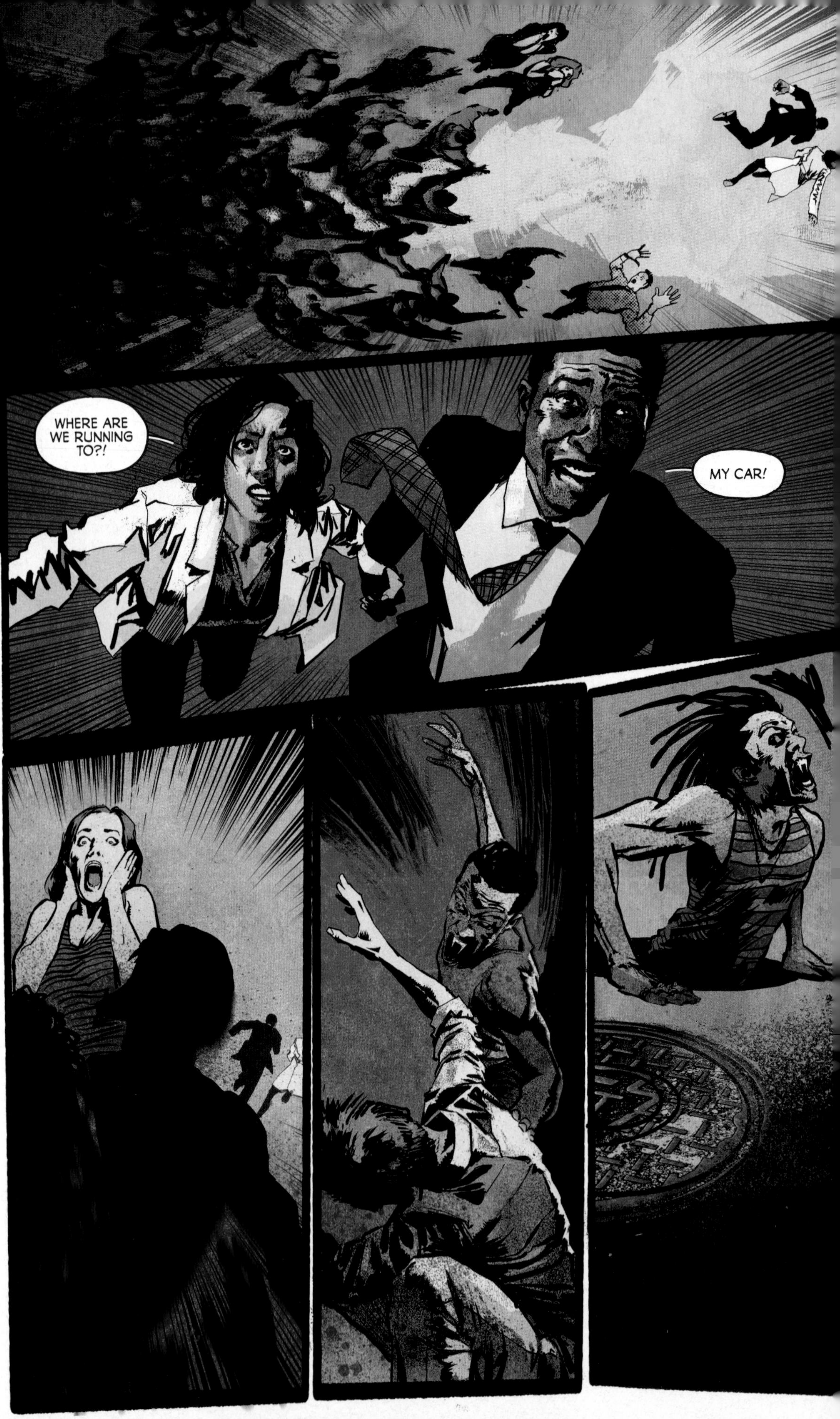
WHERE ARE WE RUNNING TO?!
MY CAR!

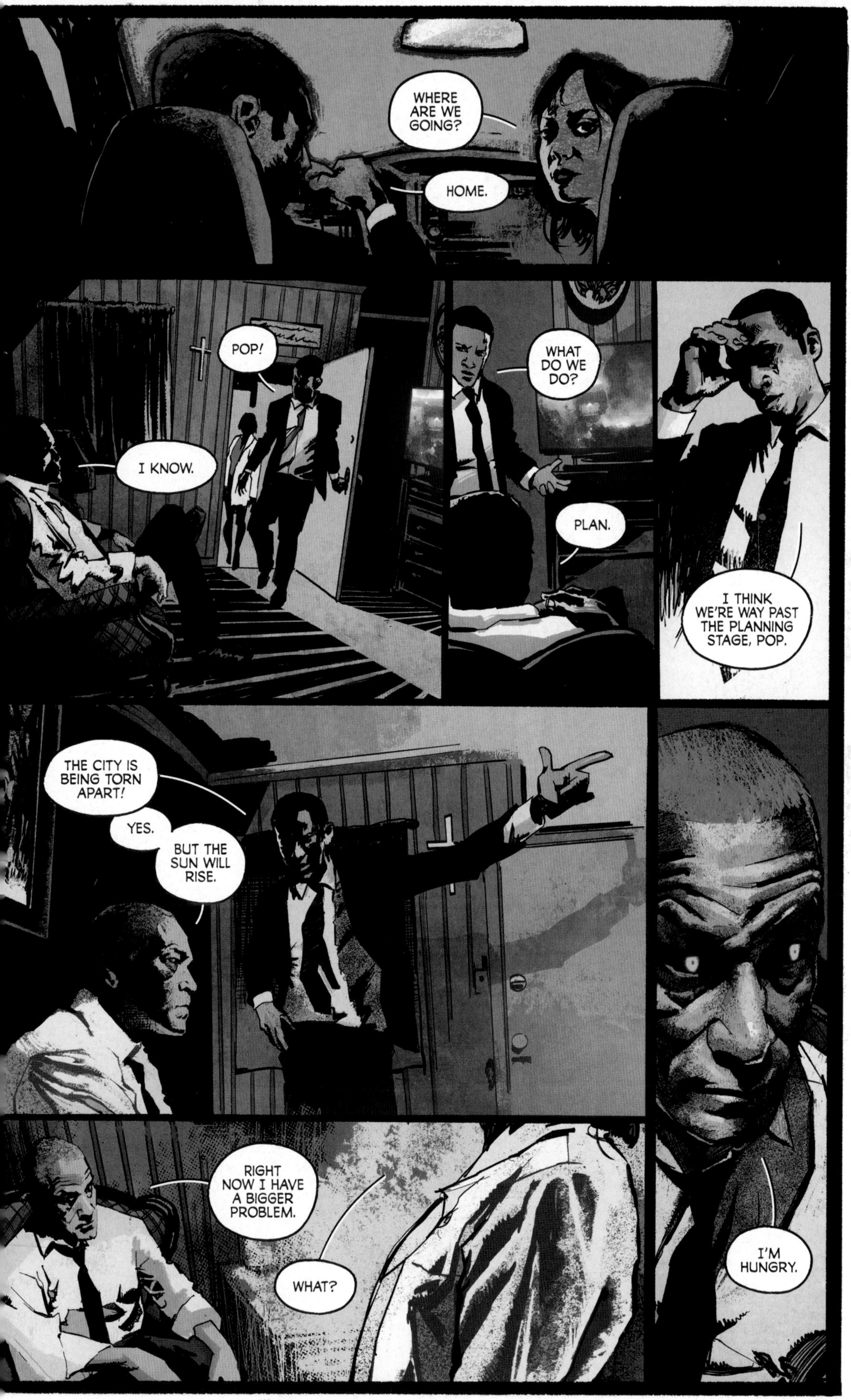

WHERE ARE WE GOING?
HOME.
POP!
I KNOW.
WHAT DO WE DO?
PLAN.
I THINK WE'RE WAY PAST THE PLANNING STAGE, POP.
THE CITY IS BEING TORN APART!
YES.
BUT THE SUN WILL RISE.
RIGHT NOW I HAVE A BIGGER PROBLEM.
WHAT?
I'M HUNGRY.

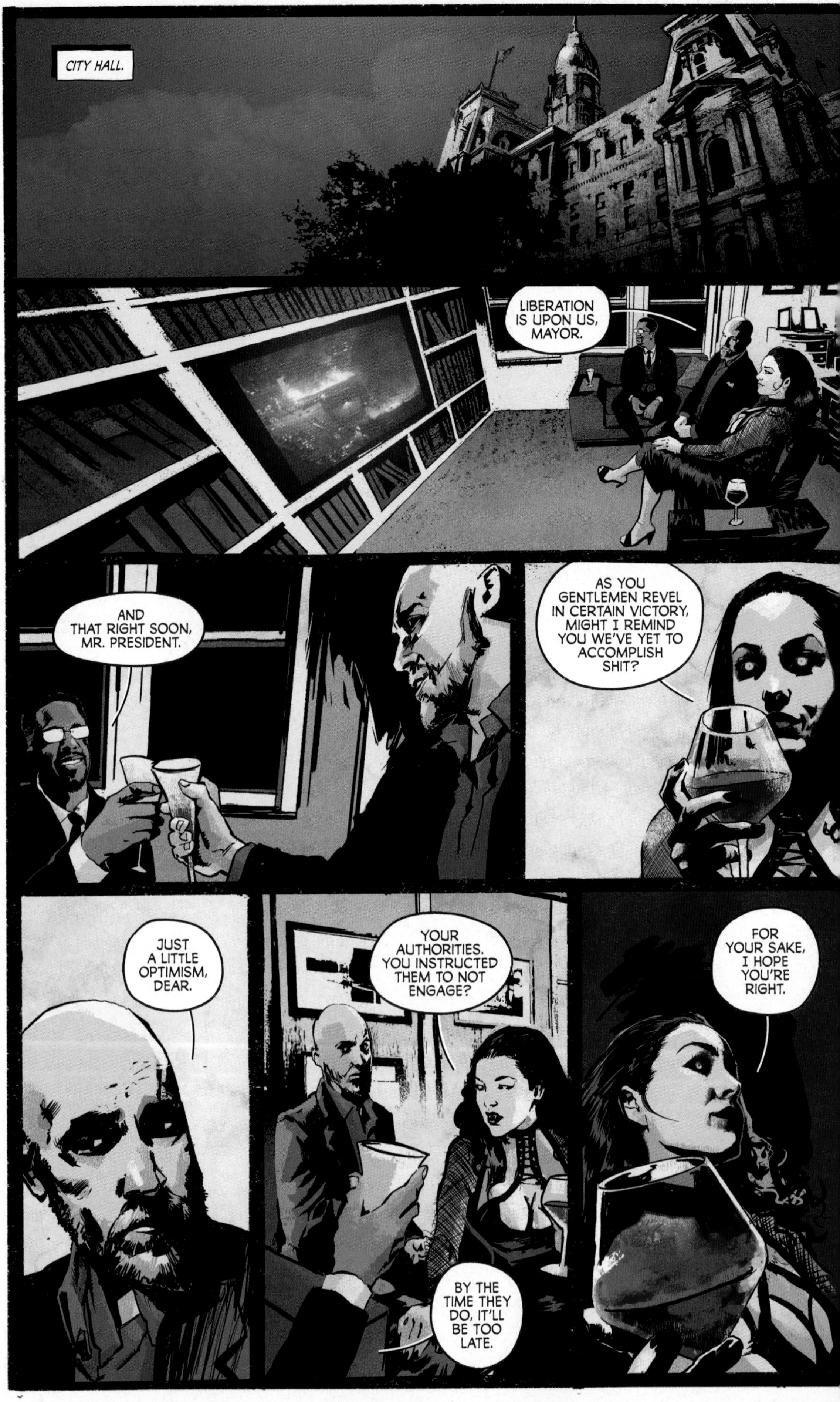
CITY HALL.
LIBERATION IS UPON US, MAYOR.
AND THAT RIGHT SOON, MR. PRESIDENT.
AS YOU GENTLEMEN REVEL IN CERTAIN VICTORY, MIGHT I REMIND YOU WE'VE YET TO ACCOMPLISH SHIT?
JUST A LITTLE OPTIMISM, DEAR.
YOUR AUTHORITIES. YOU INSTRUCTED THEM TO NOT ENGAGE?
BY THE TIME THEY DO, IT'LL BE TOO LATE.
FOR YOUR SAKE, I HOPE YOU'RE RIGHT.

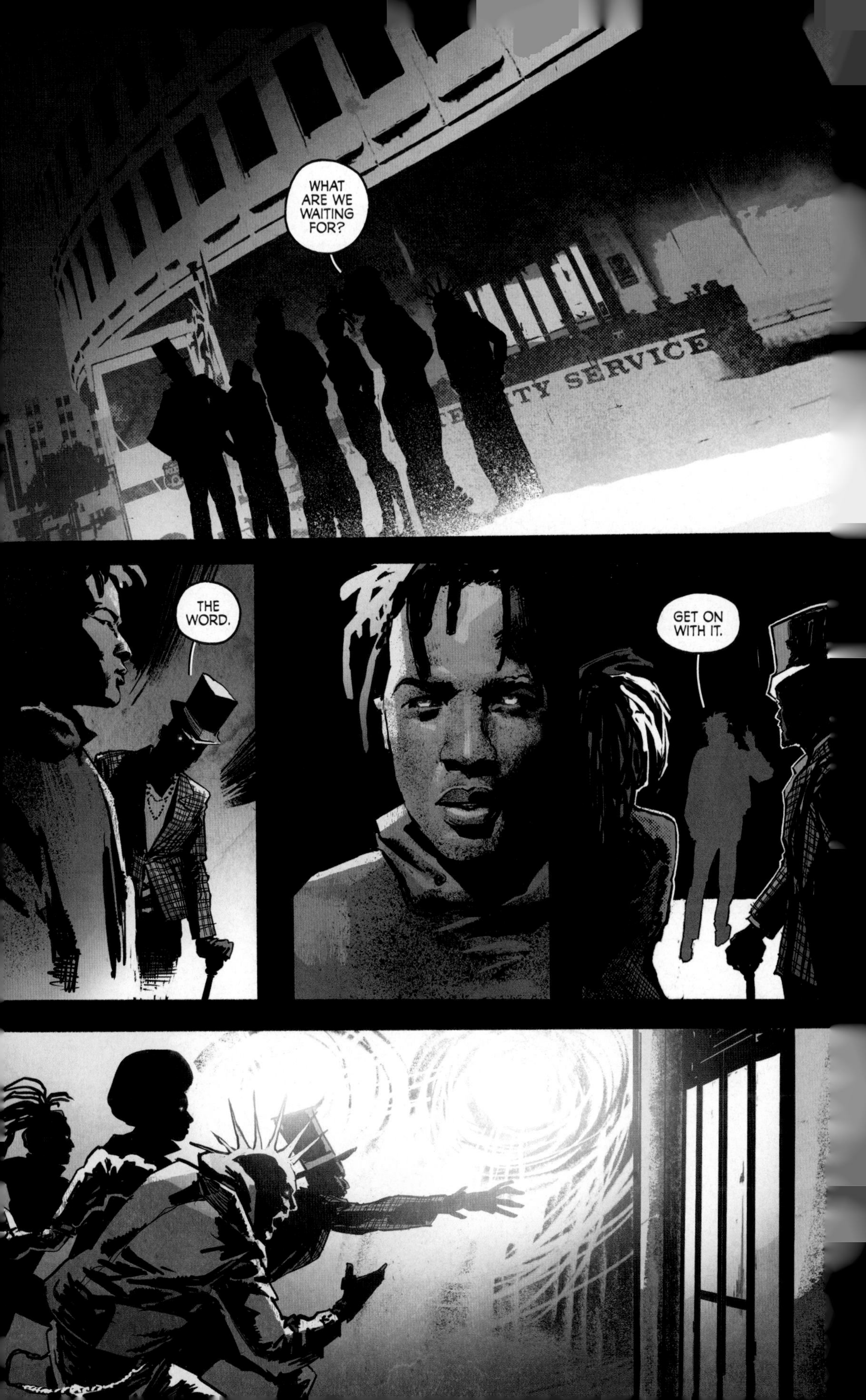
WHAT ARE WE WAITING FOR?
TY SERVICE
THE WORD.
GET ON WITH IT.

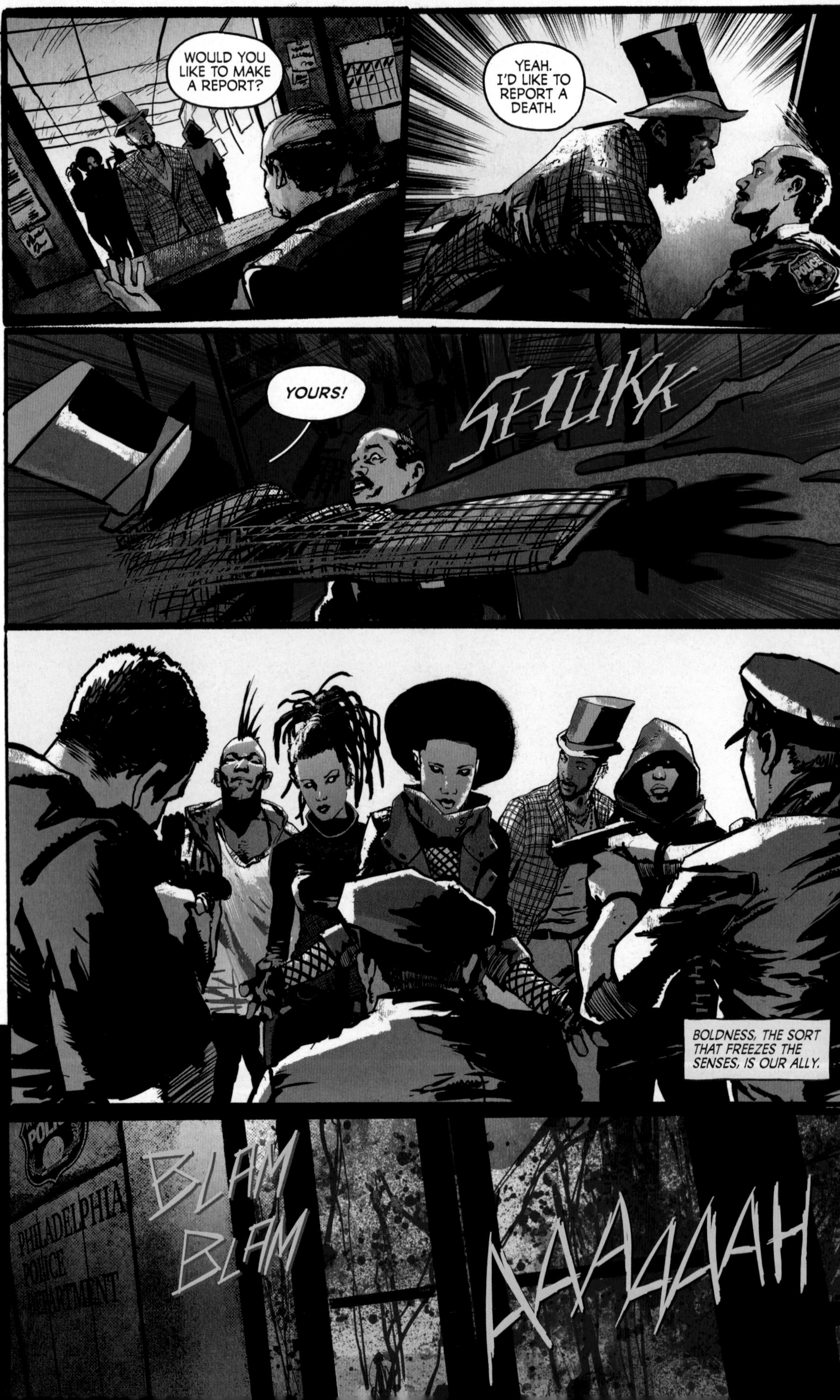
WOULD YOU LIKE TO MAKE A REPORT?
YEAH. I'D LIKE TO REPORT A DEATH.
YOURS!
SHUKK
BOLDNESS, THE SORT THAT FREEZES THE SENSES, IS OUR ALLY.
PHILADELPHIA POLICE DEPARTMENT
BLAM BLAM
AAAAAAH

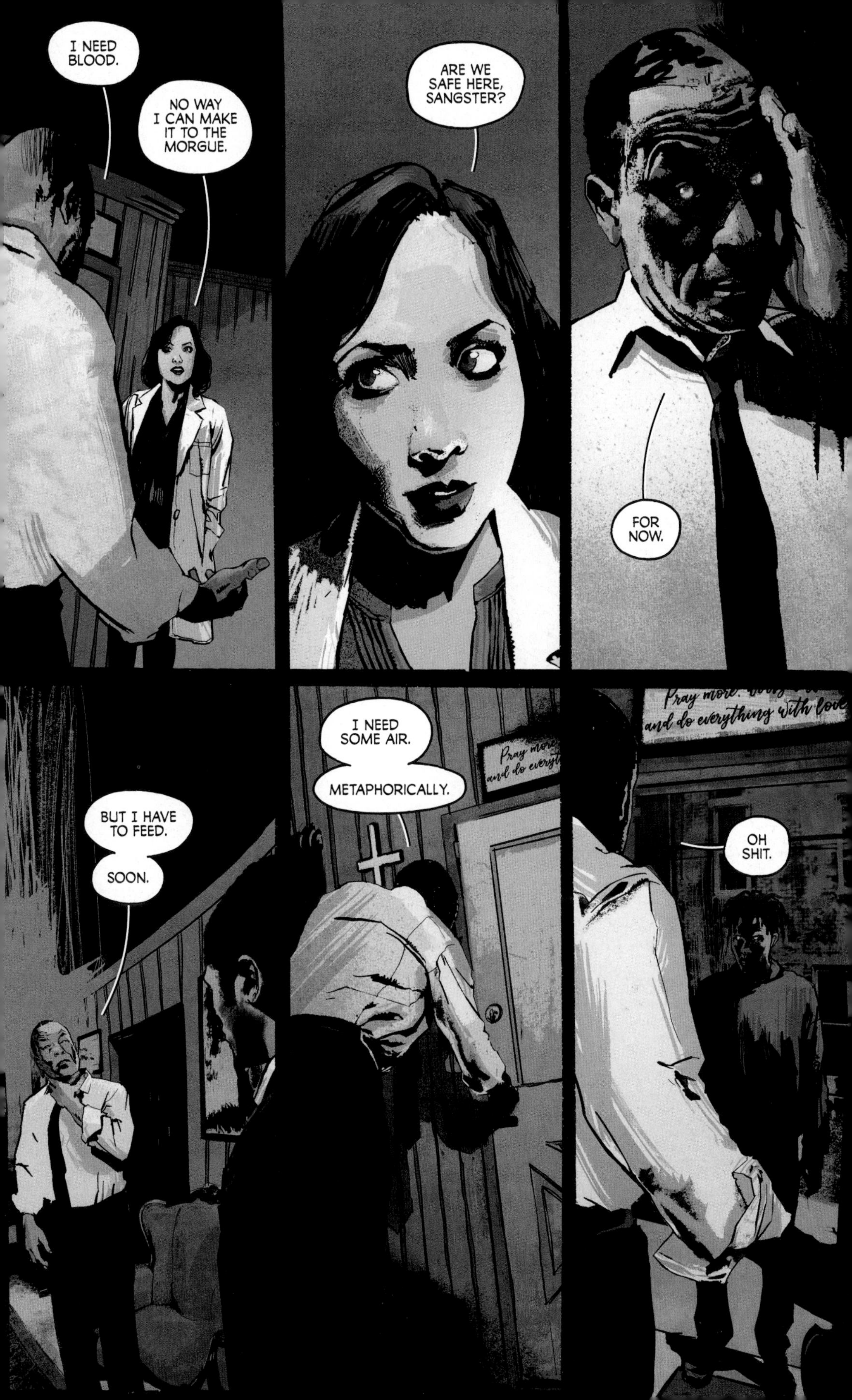
I NEED BLOOD.
NO WAY I CAN MAKE IT TO THE MORGUE.
ARE WE SAFE HERE, SANGSTER?
FOR NOW.
BUT I HAVE TO FEED.
SOON.
I NEED SOME AIR.
METAPHORICALLY.
OH SHIT.

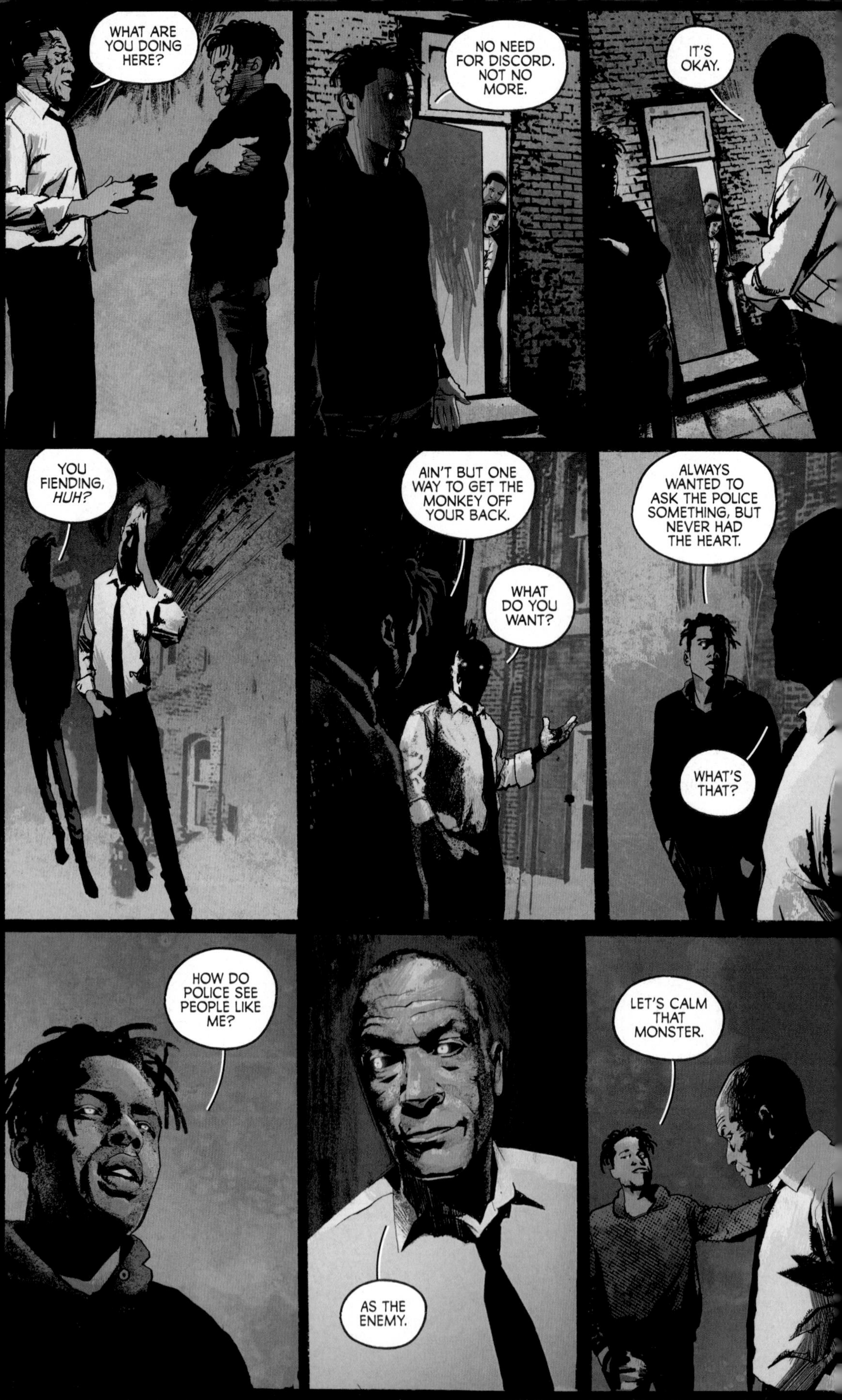
WHAT ARE YOU DOING HERE?
NO NEED FOR DISCORD. NOT NO MORE.
IT'S OKAY.
YOU FIENDING, *HUH?*
AIN'T BUT ONE WAY TO GET THE MONKEY OFF YOUR BACK.
WHAT DO YOU WANT?
ALWAYS WANTED TO ASK THE POLICE SOMETHING, BUT NEVER HAD THE HEART.
WHAT'S THAT?
HOW DO POLICE SEE PEOPLE LIKE ME?
AS THE ENEMY.
LET'S CALM THAT MONSTER.

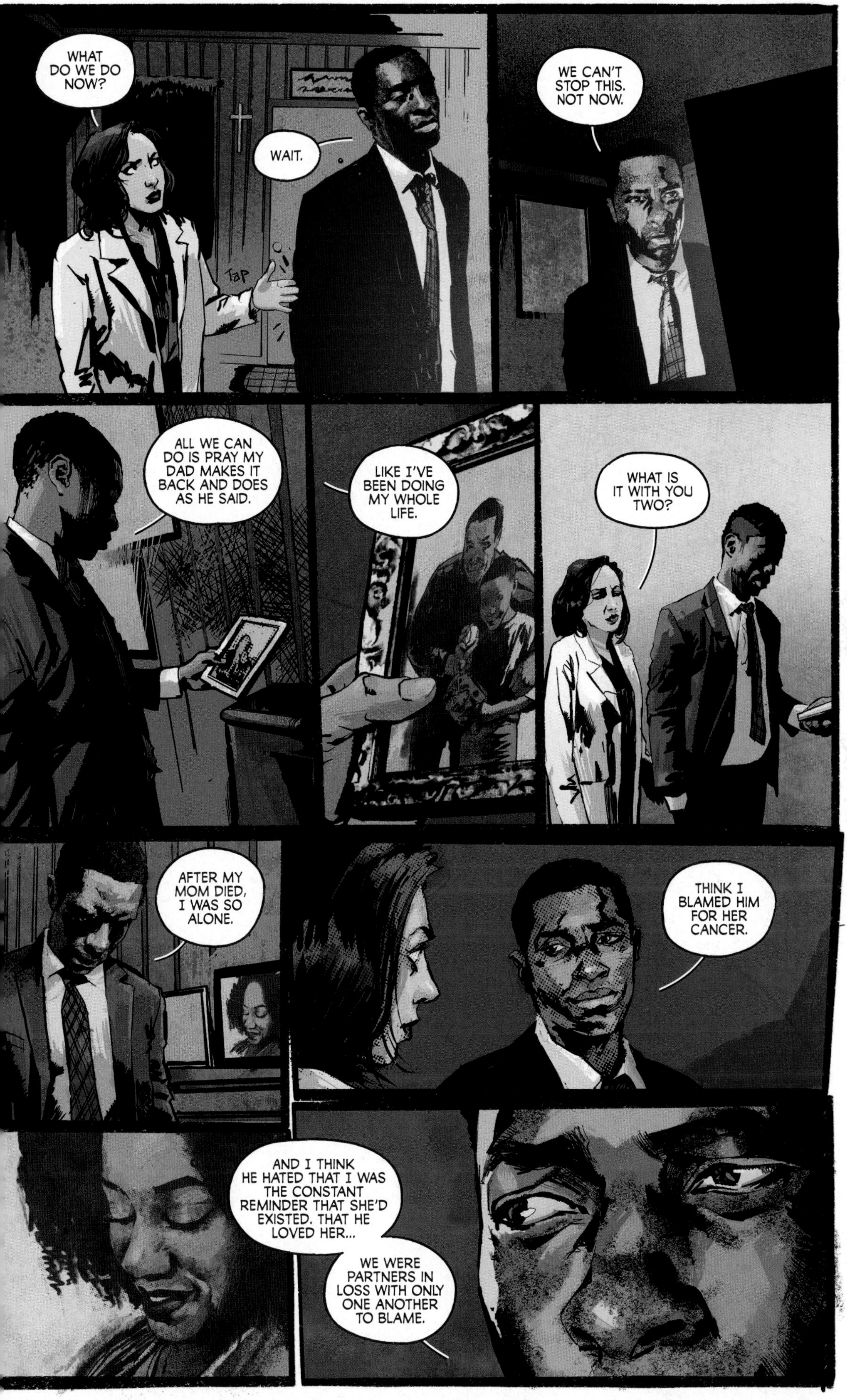
WHAT DO WE DO NOW?
WAIT.
TAP
WE CAN'T STOP THIS. NOT NOW.
ALL WE CAN DO IS PRAY MY DAD MAKES IT BACK AND DOES AS HE SAID.
LIKE I'VE BEEN DOING MY WHOLE LIFE.
WHAT IS IT WITH YOU TWO?
AFTER MY MOM DIED, I WAS SO ALONE.
THINK I BLAMED HIM FOR HER CANCER.
AND I THINK HE HATED THAT I WAS THE CONSTANT REMINDER THAT SHE'D EXISTED. THAT HE LOVED HER...
WE WERE PARTNERS IN LOSS WITH ONLY ONE ANOTHER TO BLAME.

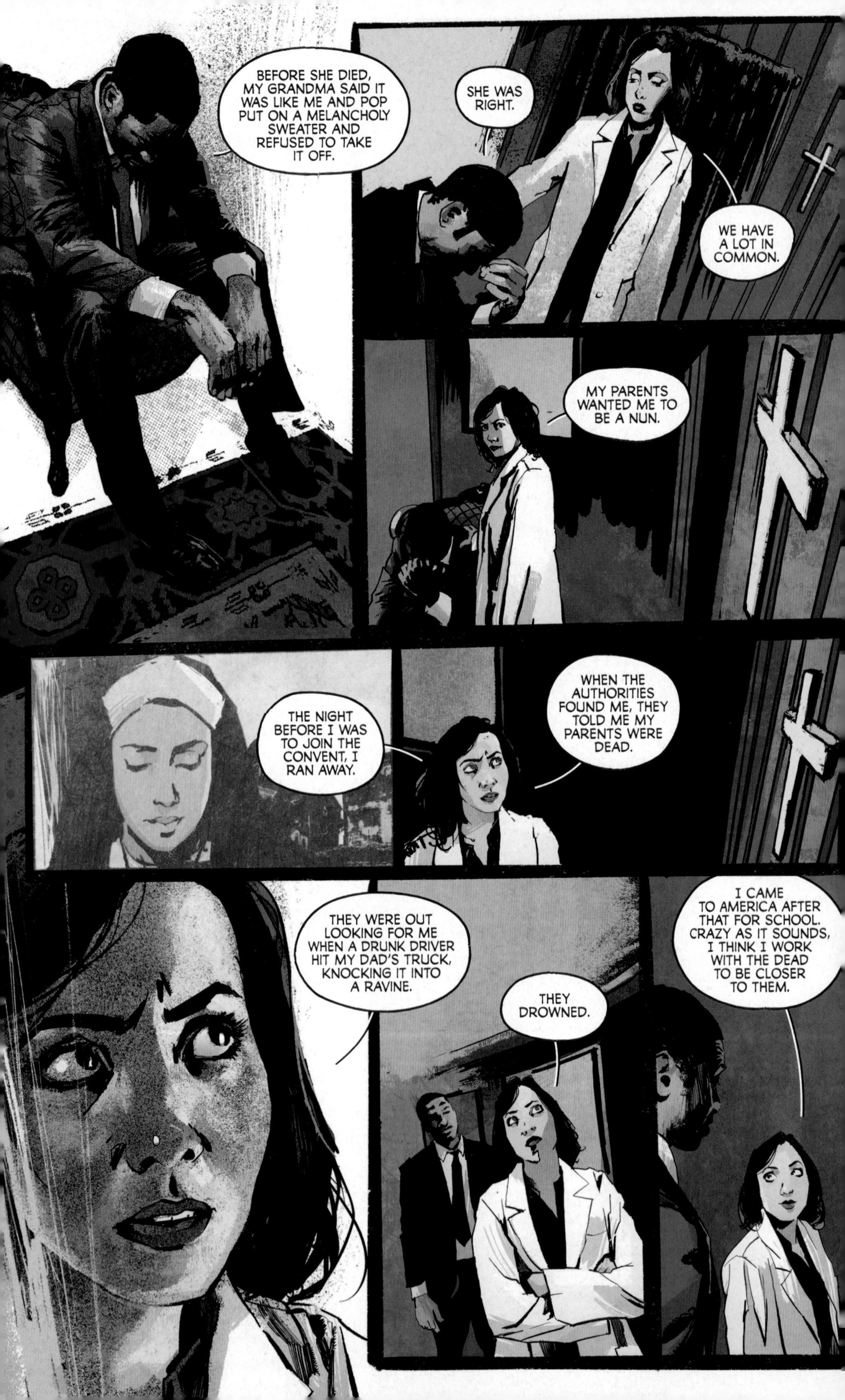
BEFORE SHE DIED, MY GRANDMA SAID IT WAS LIKE ME AND POP PUT ON A MELANCHOLY SWEATER AND REFUSED TO TAKE IT OFF.
SHE WAS RIGHT.
WE HAVE A LOT IN COMMON.
MY PARENTS WANTED ME TO BE A NUN.
THE NIGHT BEFORE I WAS TO JOIN THE CONVENT, I RAN AWAY.
WHEN THE AUTHORITIES FOUND ME, THEY TOLD ME MY PARENTS WERE DEAD.
THEY WERE OUT LOOKING FOR ME WHEN A DRUNK DRIVER HIT MY DAD'S TRUCK, KNOCKING IT INTO A RAVINE.
THEY DROWNED.
I CAME TO AMERICA AFTER THAT FOR SCHOOL. CRAZY AS IT SOUNDS, I THINK I WORK WITH THE DEAD TO BE CLOSER TO THEM.

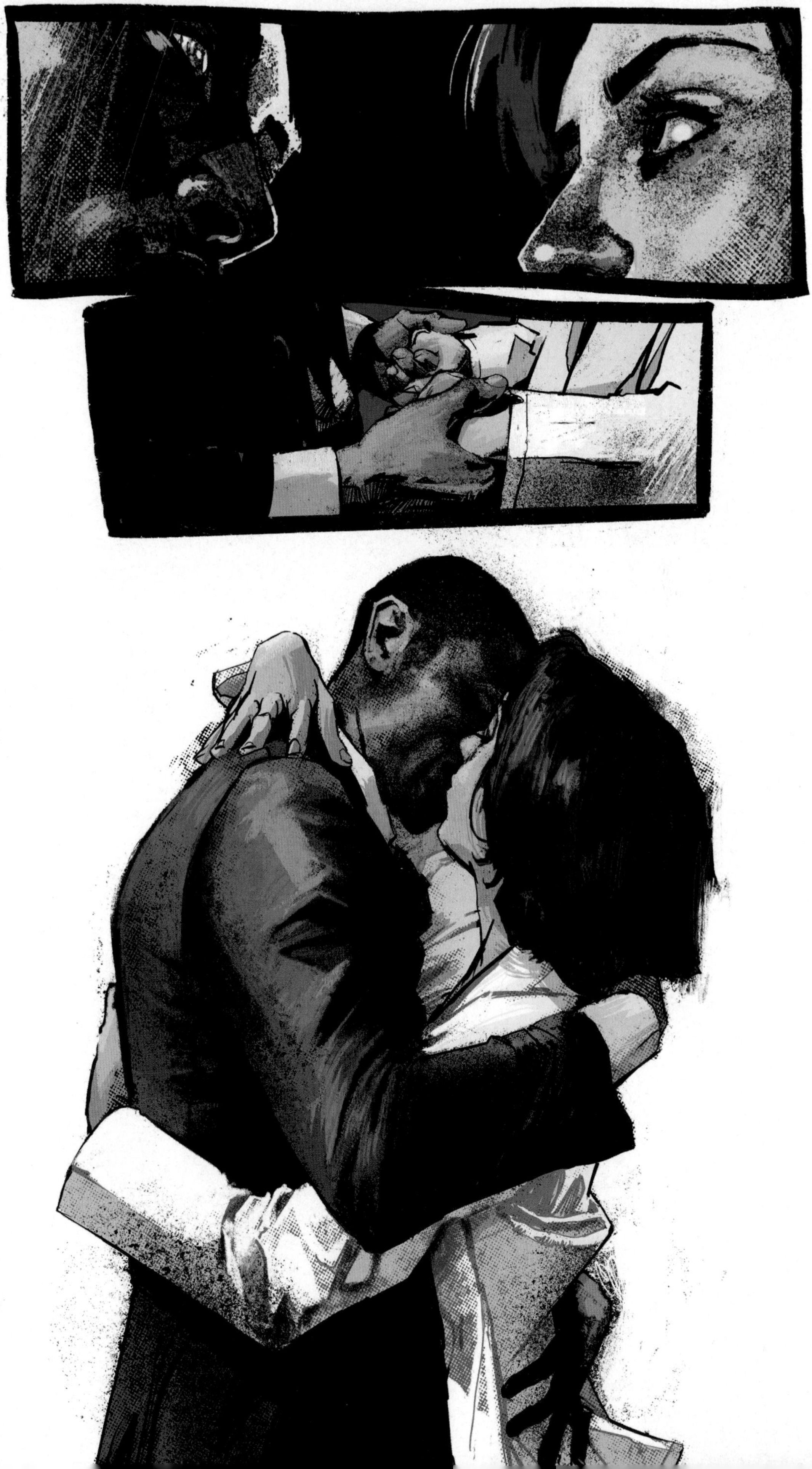

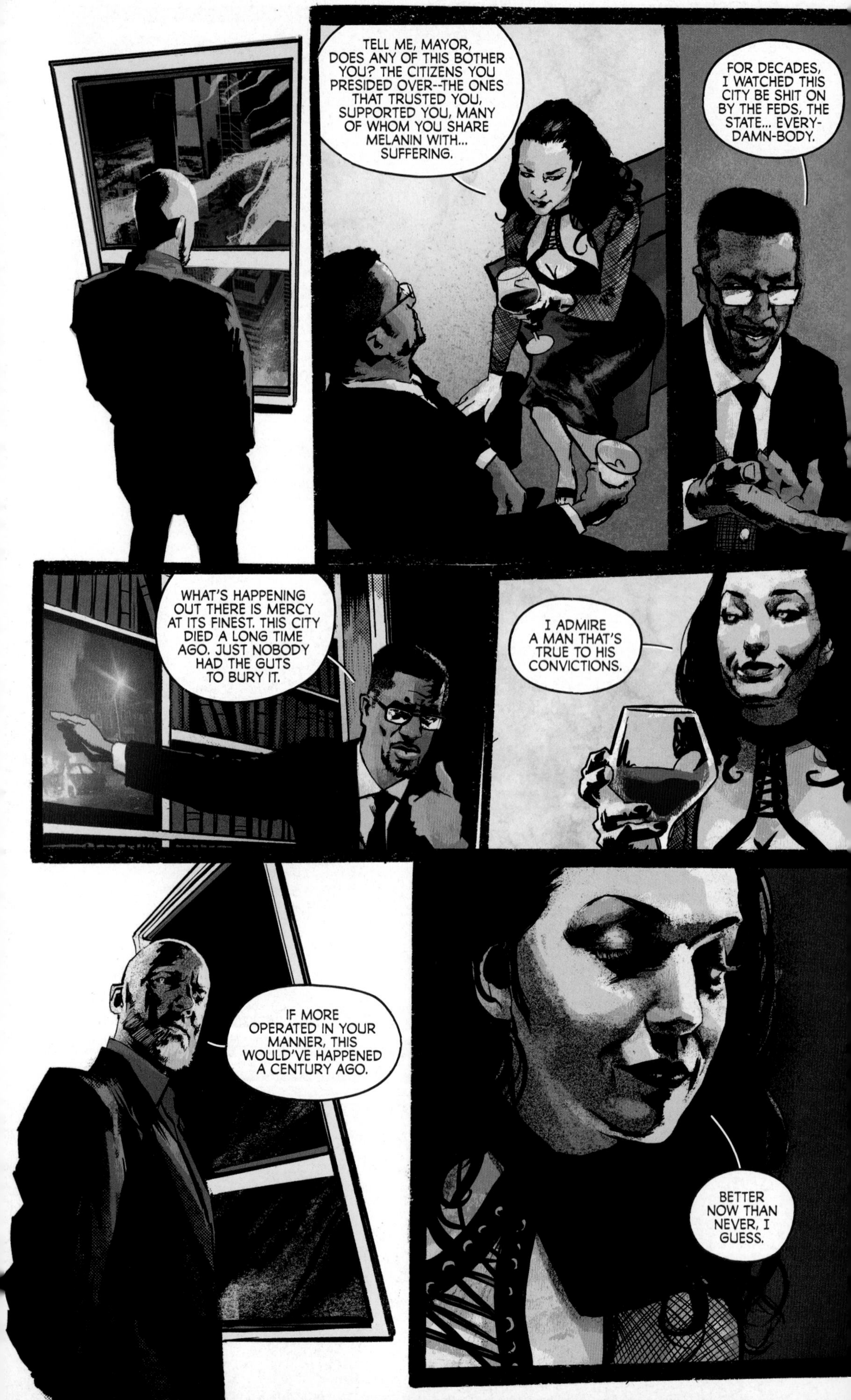

TELL ME, MAYOR, DOES ANY OF THIS BOTHER YOU? THE CITIZENS YOU PRESIDED OVER--THE ONES THAT TRUSTED YOU, SUPPORTED YOU, MANY OF WHOM YOU SHARE MELANIN WITH... SUFFERING.
FOR DECADES, I WATCHED THIS CITY BE SHIT ON BY THE FEDS, THE STATE... EVERY-DAMN-BODY.
WHAT'S HAPPENING OUT THERE IS MERCY AT ITS FINEST. THIS CITY DIED A LONG TIME AGO. JUST NOBODY HAD THE GUTS TO BURY IT.
I ADMIRE A MAN THAT'S TRUE TO HIS CONVICTIONS.
IF MORE OPERATED IN YOUR MANNER, THIS WOULD'VE HAPPENED A CENTURY AGO.
BETTER NOW THAN NEVER, I GUESS.

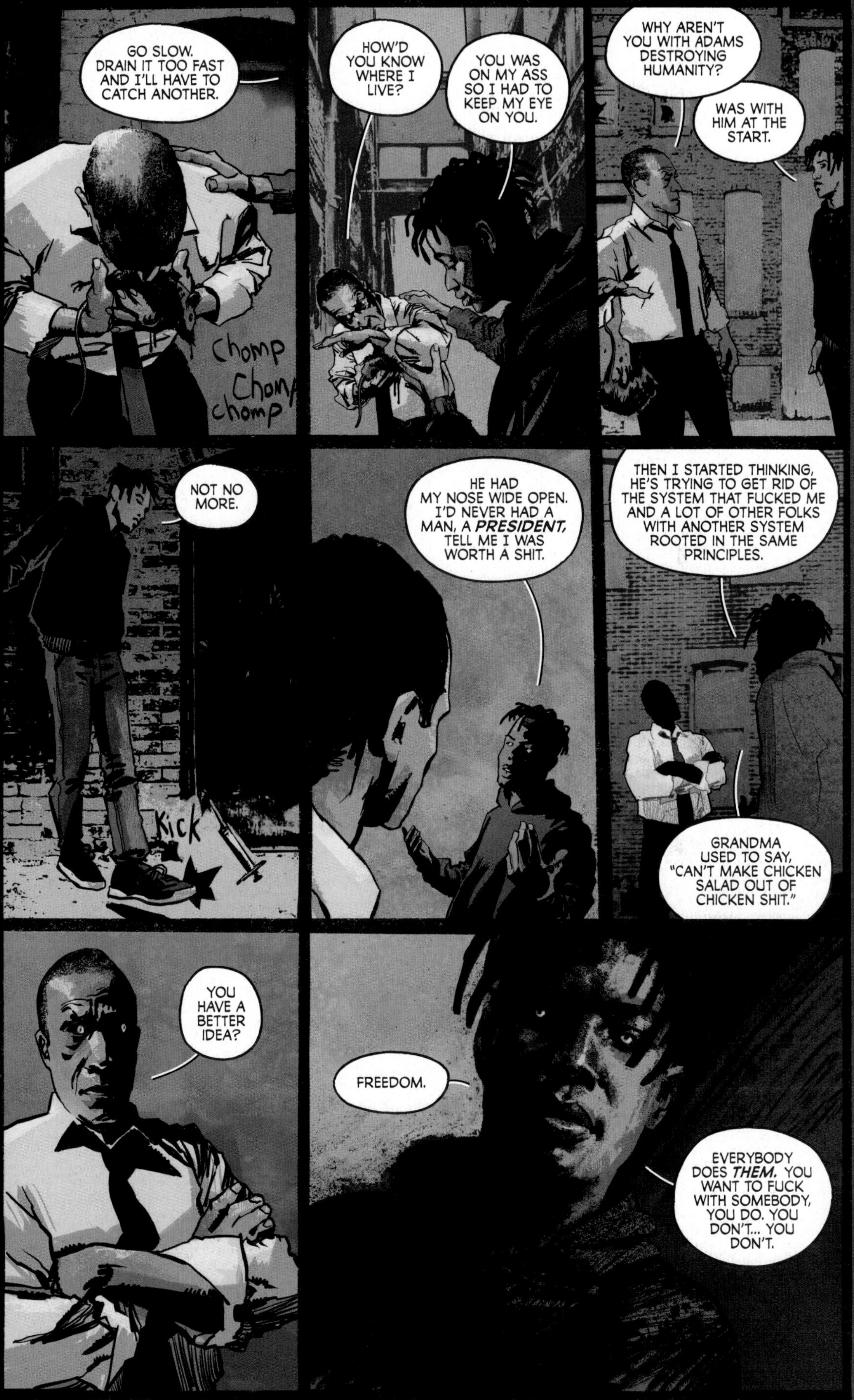
GO SLOW. DRAIN IT TOO FAST AND I'LL HAVE TO CATCH ANOTHER.
Chomp Chomp chomp
HOW'D YOU KNOW WHERE I LIVE?
YOU WAS ON MY ASS SO I HAD TO KEEP MY EYE ON YOU.
WHY AREN'T YOU WITH ADAMS DESTROYING HUMANITY?
WAS WITH HIM AT THE START.
NOT NO MORE.
KICK
HE HAD MY NOSE WIDE OPEN. I'D NEVER HAD A MAN, A *PRESIDENT,* TELL ME I WAS WORTH A SHIT.
THEN I STARTED THINKING, HE'S TRYING TO GET RID OF THE SYSTEM THAT FUCKED ME AND A LOT OF OTHER FOLKS WITH ANOTHER SYSTEM ROOTED IN THE SAME PRINCIPLES.
GRANDMA USED TO SAY, "CAN'T MAKE CHICKEN SALAD OUT OF CHICKEN SHIT."
YOU HAVE A BETTER IDEA?
FREEDOM.
EVERYBODY DOES *THEM.* YOU WANT TO FUCK WITH SOMEBODY, YOU DO. YOU DON'T... YOU DON'T.

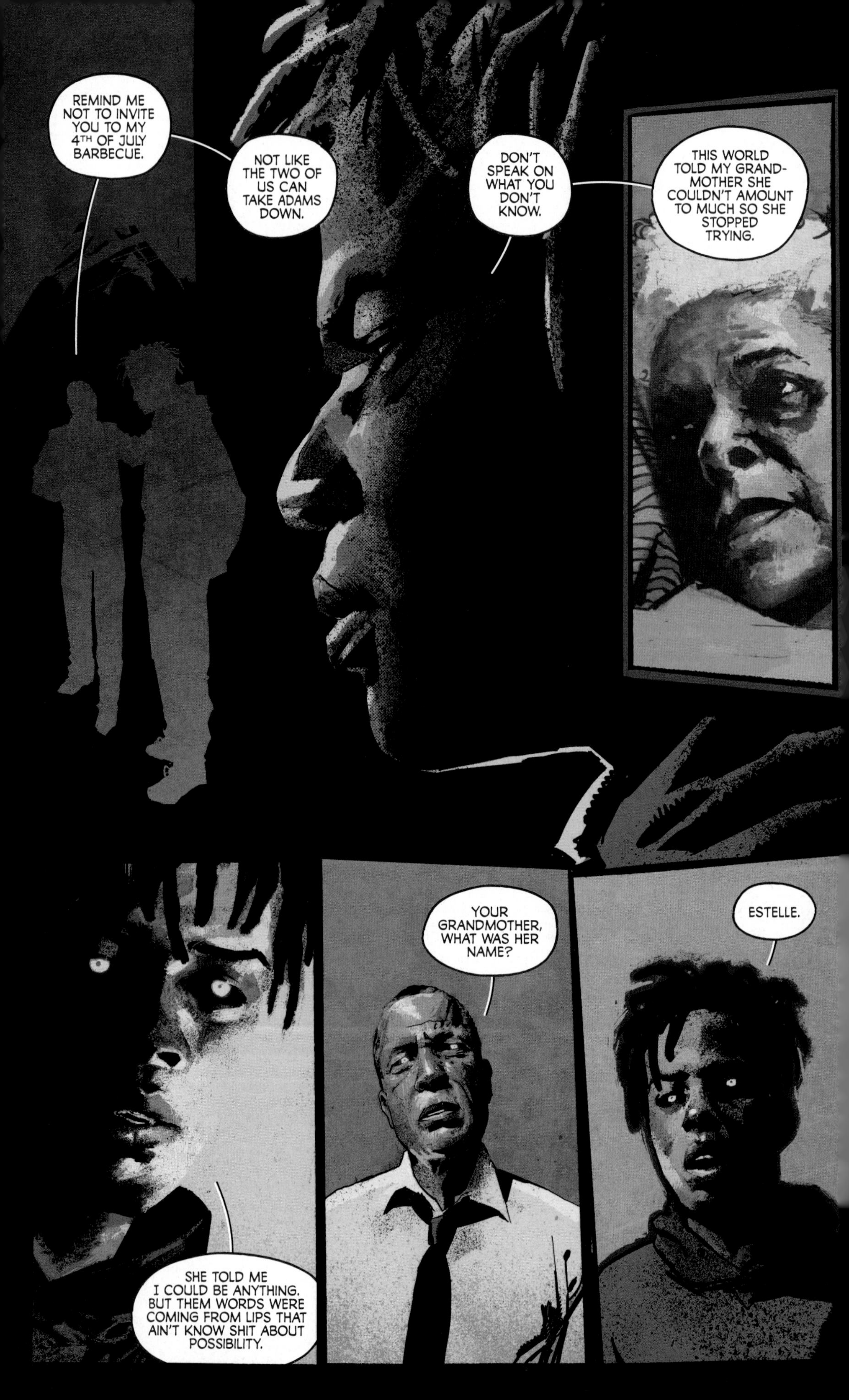
REMIND ME NOT TO INVITE YOU TO MY 4TH OF JULY BARBECUE.
NOT LIKE THE TWO OF US CAN TAKE ADAMS DOWN.
DON'T SPEAK ON WHAT YOU DON'T KNOW.
THIS WORLD TOLD MY GRAND-MOTHER SHE COULDN'T AMOUNT TO MUCH SO SHE STOPPED TRYING.
SHE TOLD ME I COULD BE ANYTHING. BUT THEM WORDS WERE COMING FROM LIPS THAT AIN'T KNOW SHIT ABOUT POSSIBILITY.
YOUR GRANDMOTHER, WHAT WAS HER NAME?
ESTELLE.

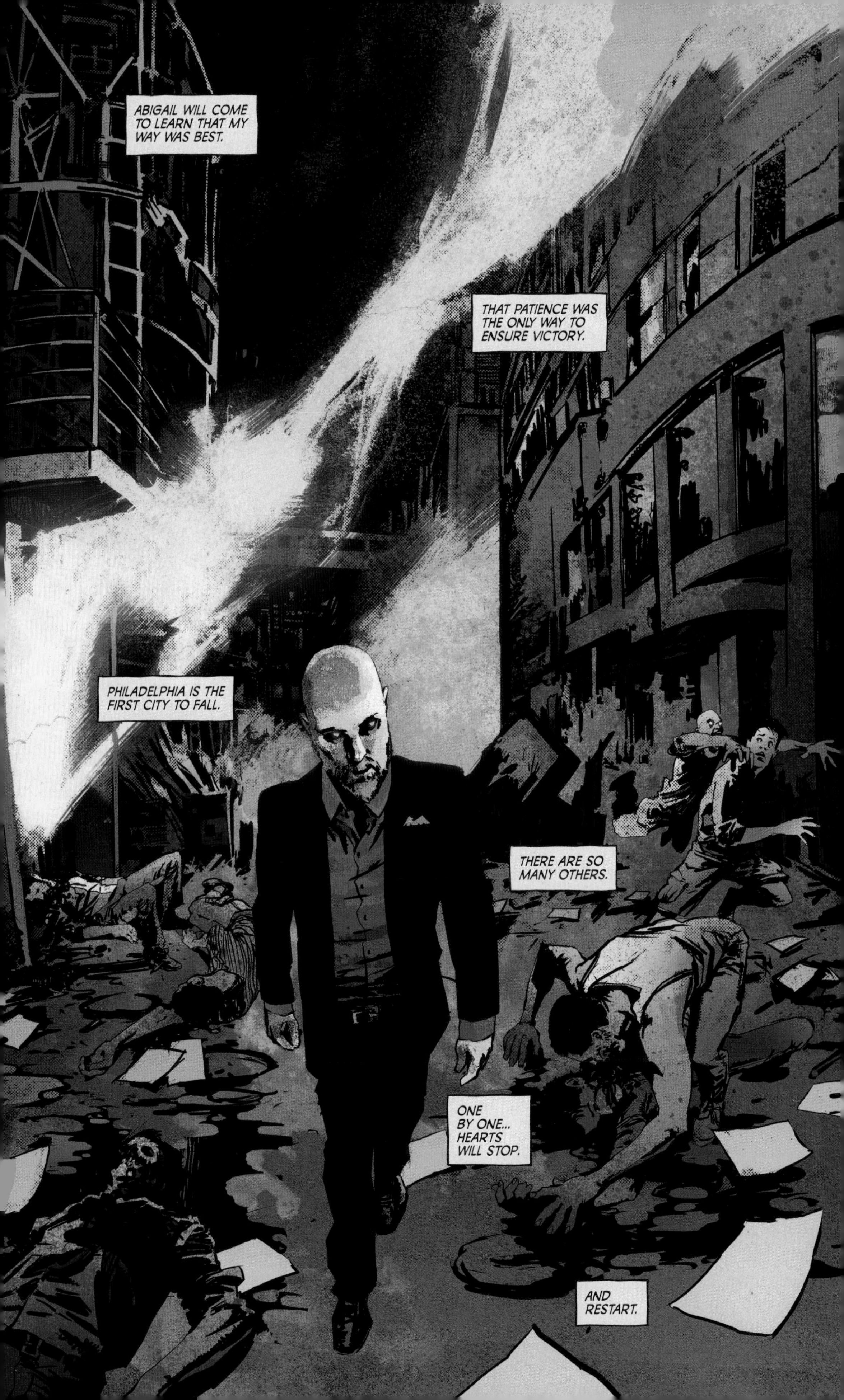
ABIGAIL WILL COME TO LEARN THAT MY WAY WAS BEST.
THAT PATIENCE WAS THE ONLY WAY TO ENSURE VICTORY.
PHILADELPHIA IS THE FIRST CITY TO FALL.
THERE ARE SO MANY OTHERS.
ONE BY ONE... HEARTS WILL STOP.
AND RESTART.

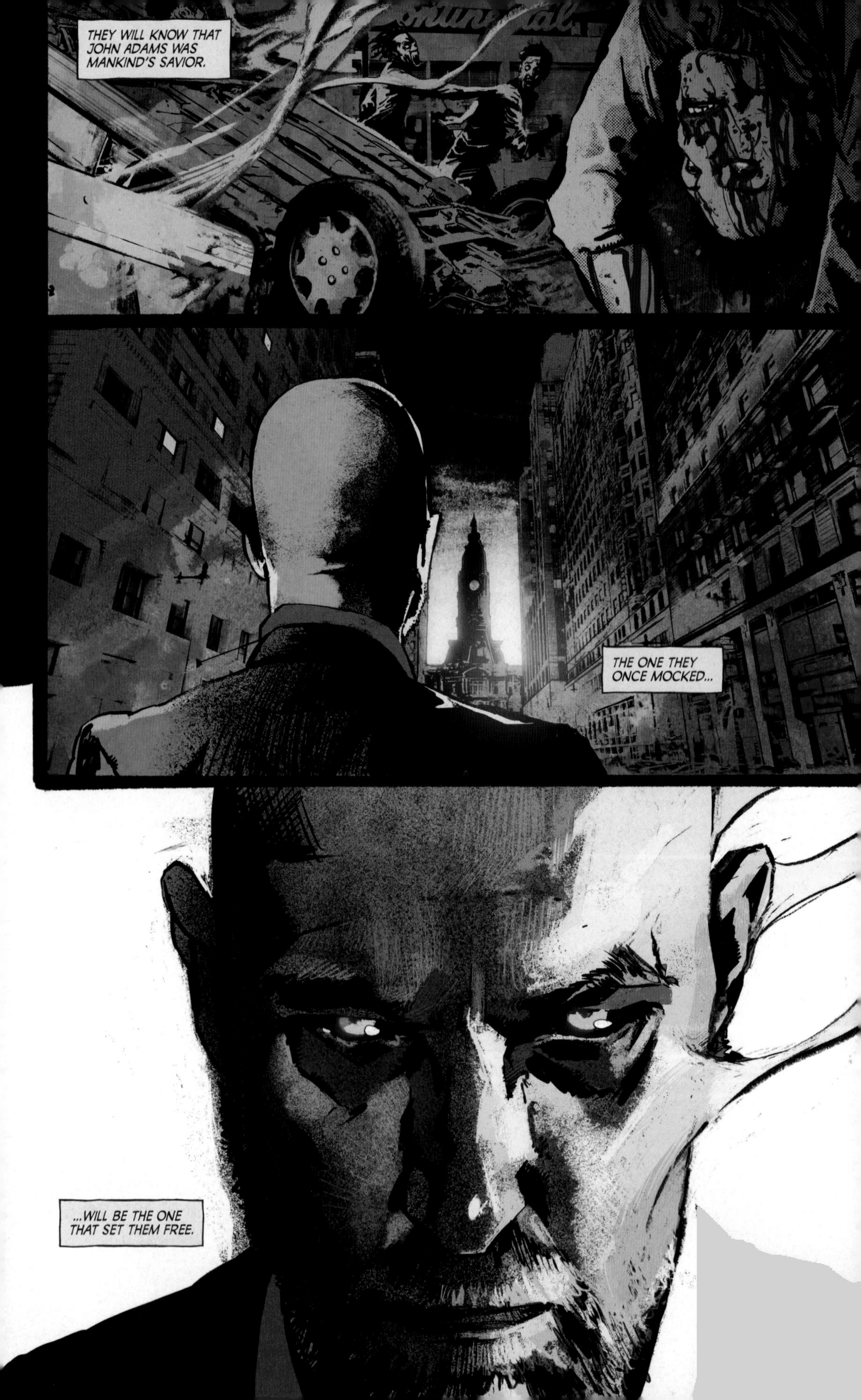
THEY WILL KNOW THAT JOHN ADAMS WAS MANKIND'S SAVIOR.
THE ONE THEY ONCE MOCKED...
...WILL BE THE ONE THAT SET THEM FREE.

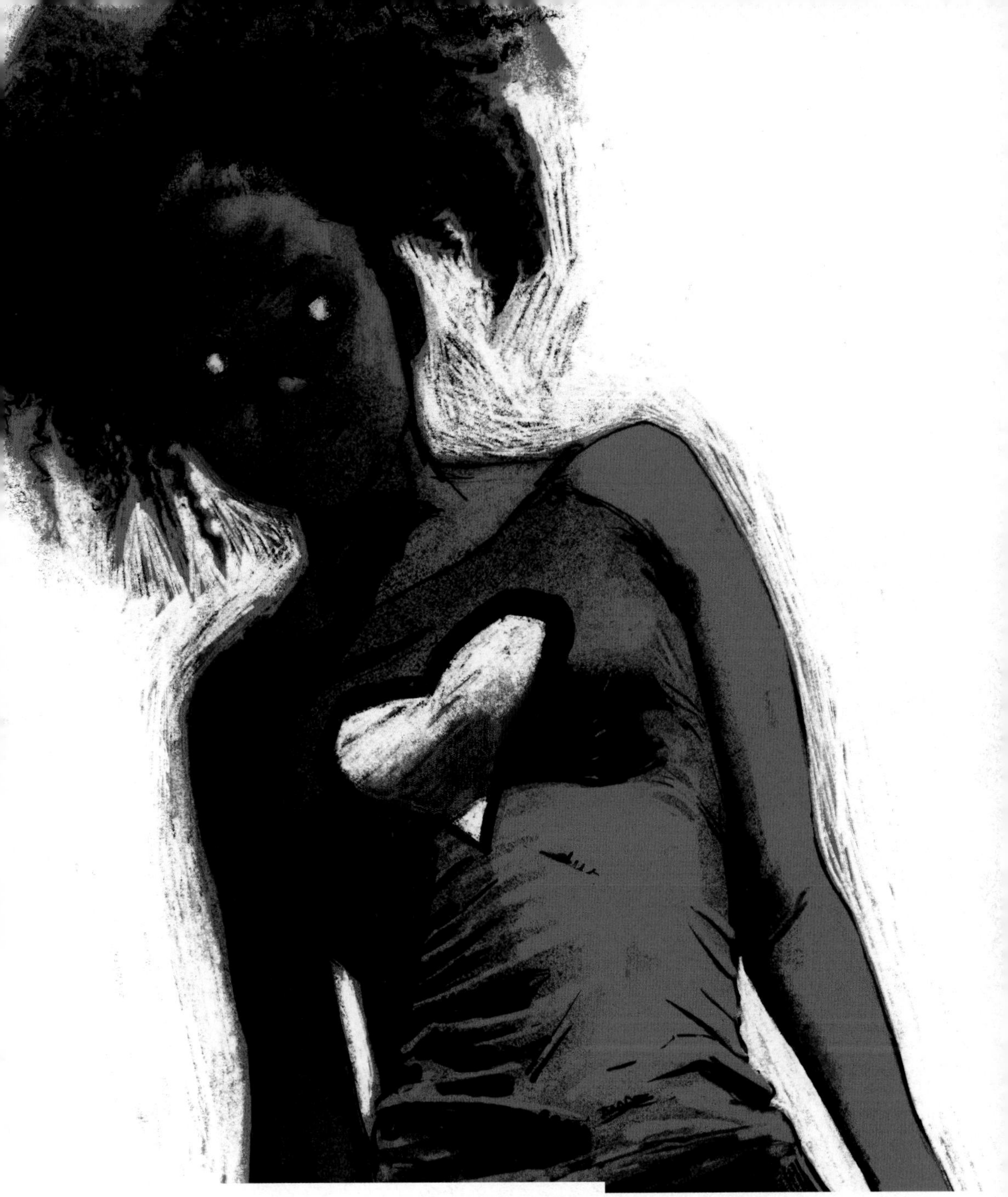

"I WANT TO FEEL THE SUN ON MY FACE. EVEN IF THAT MEANS THAT ONE DAY I'LL DIE."

THE SUN WILL RISE

Chapter V

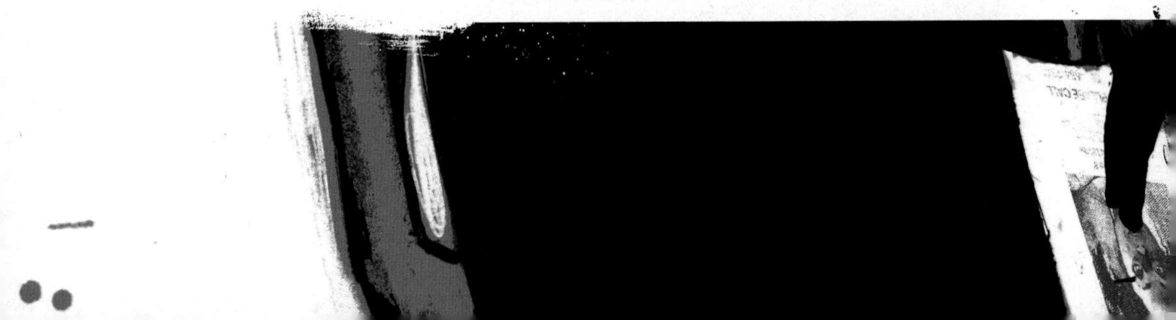

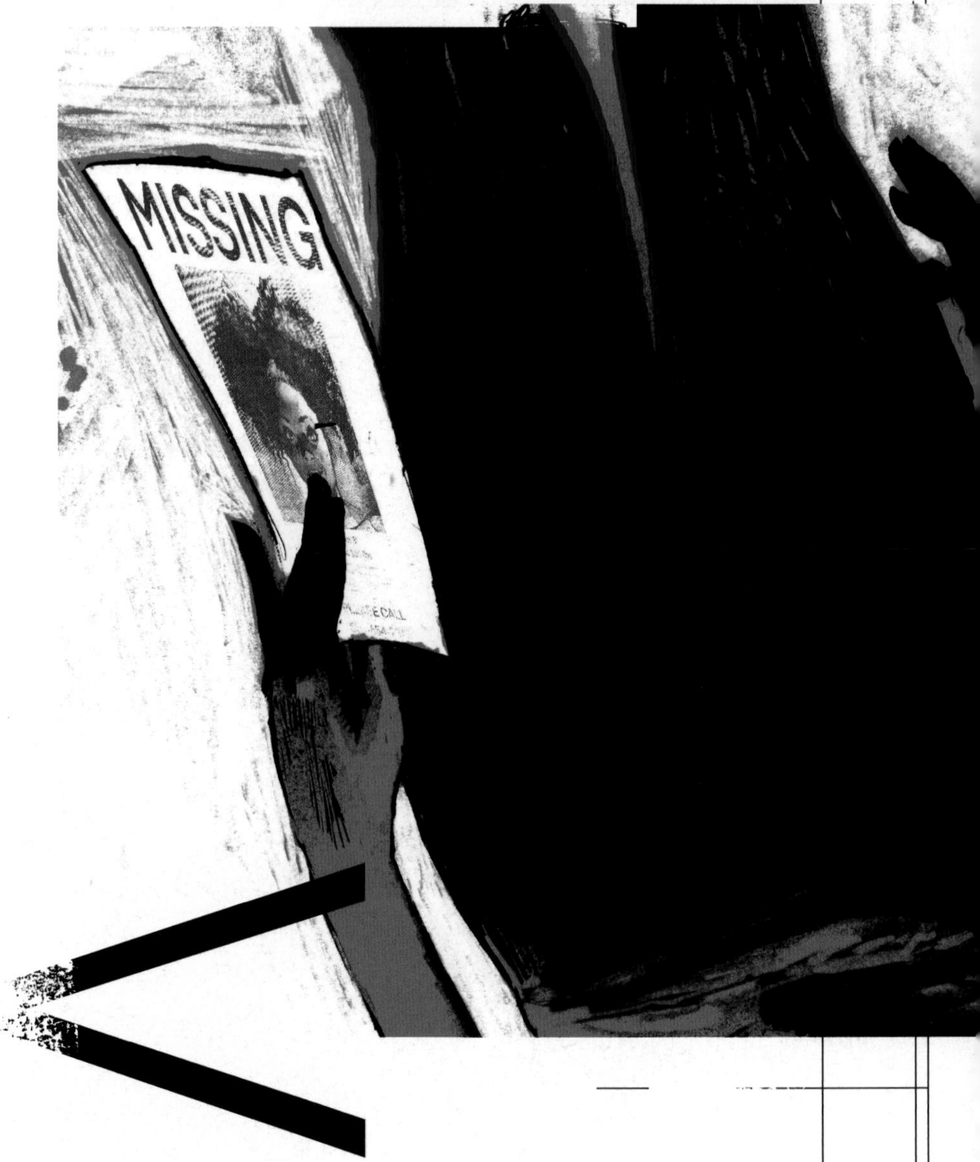
MISSING

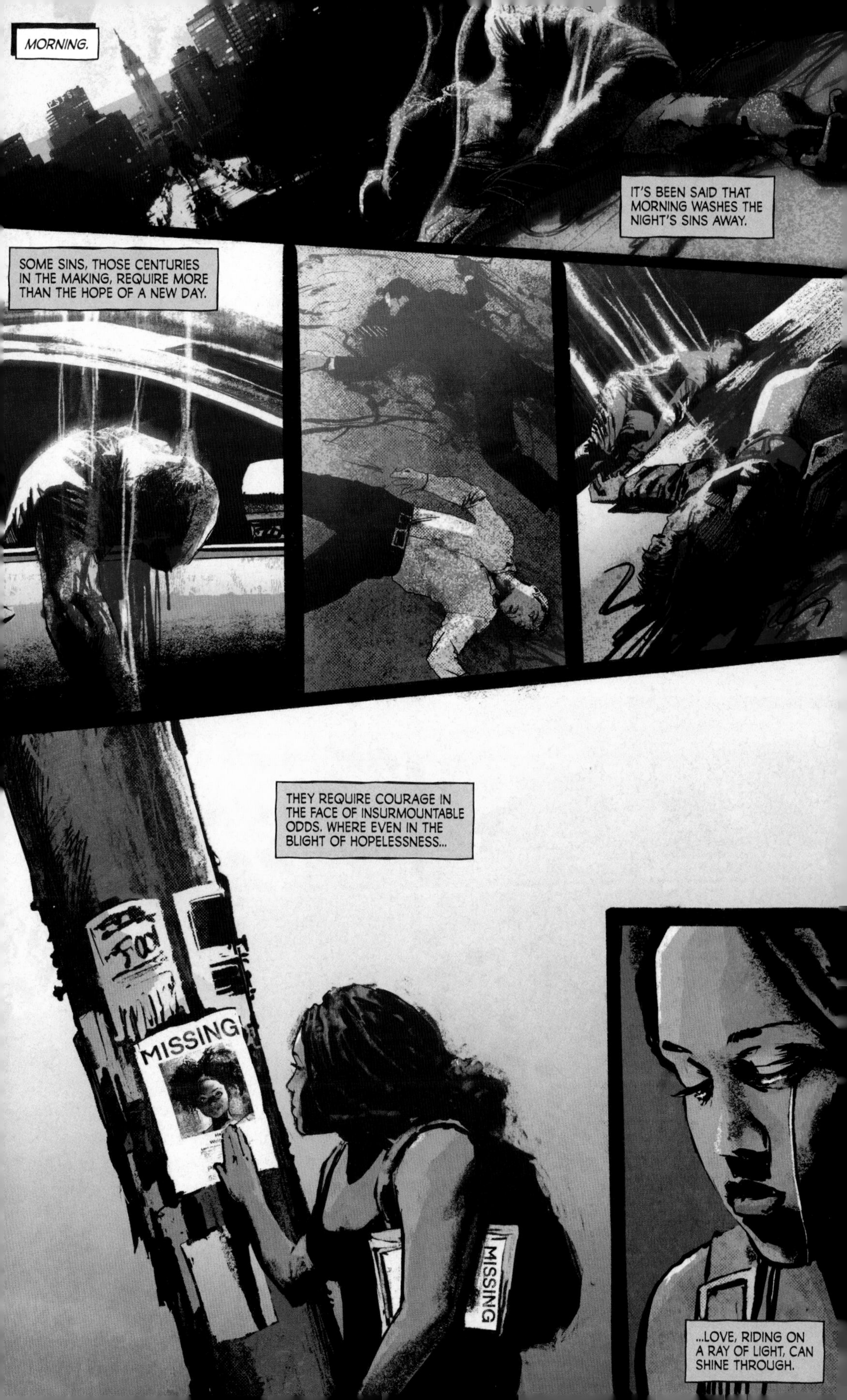
MORNING.
IT'S BEEN SAID THAT MORNING WASHES THE NIGHT'S SINS AWAY.
SOME SINS, THOSE CENTURIES IN THE MAKING, REQUIRE MORE THAN THE HOPE OF A NEW DAY.
THEY REQUIRE COURAGE IN THE FACE OF INSURMOUNTABLE ODDS. WHERE EVEN IN THE BLIGHT OF HOPELESSNESS...
MISSING
MISSING
...LOVE, RIDING ON A RAY OF LIGHT, CAN SHINE THROUGH.

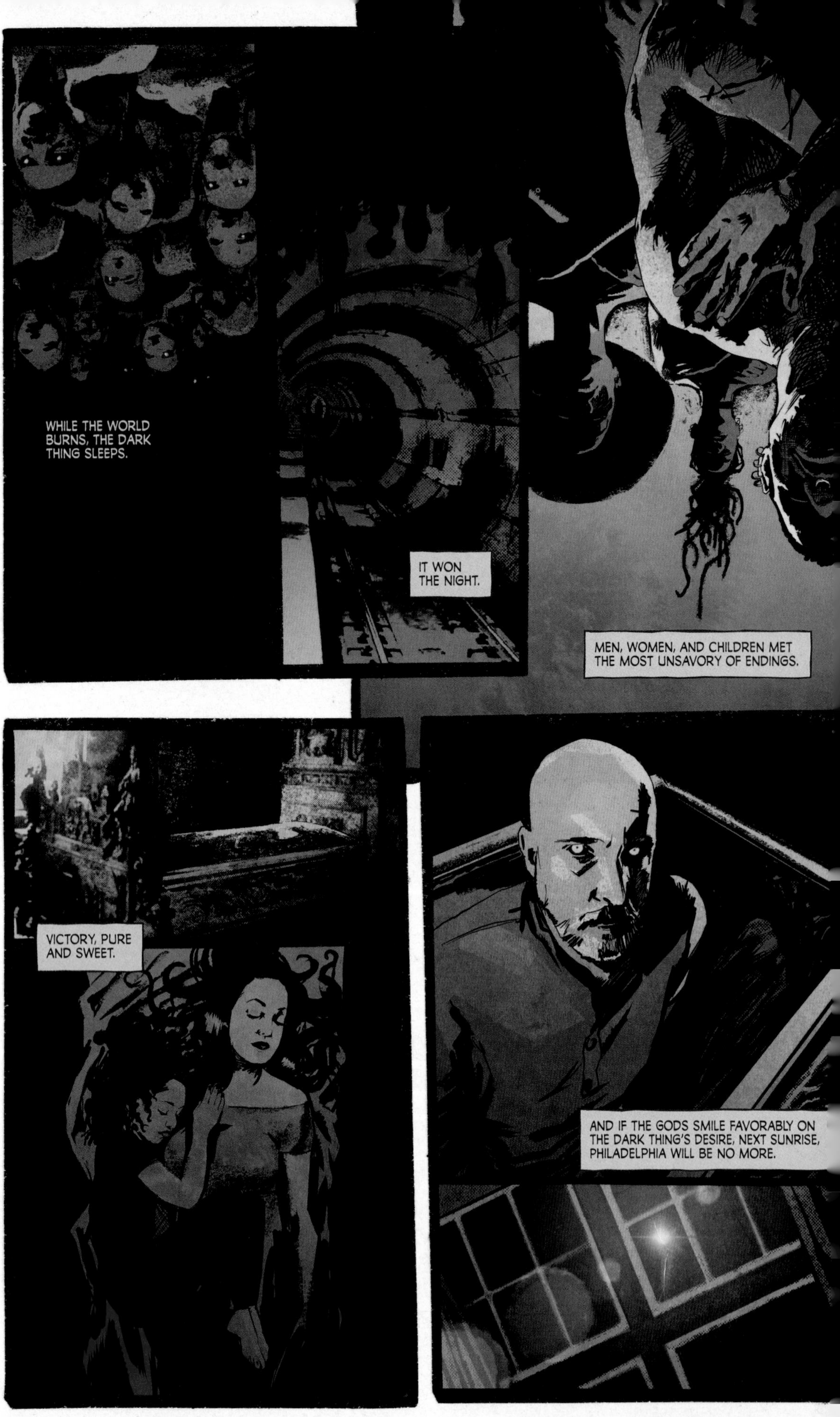
WHILE THE WORLD BURNS, THE DARK THING SLEEPS.
IT WON THE NIGHT.
MEN, WOMEN, AND CHILDREN MET THE MOST UNSAVORY OF ENDINGS.
VICTORY, PURE AND SWEET.
AND IF THE GODS SMILE FAVORABLY ON THE DARK THING'S DESIRE, NEXT SUNRISE, PHILADELPHIA WILL BE NO MORE.

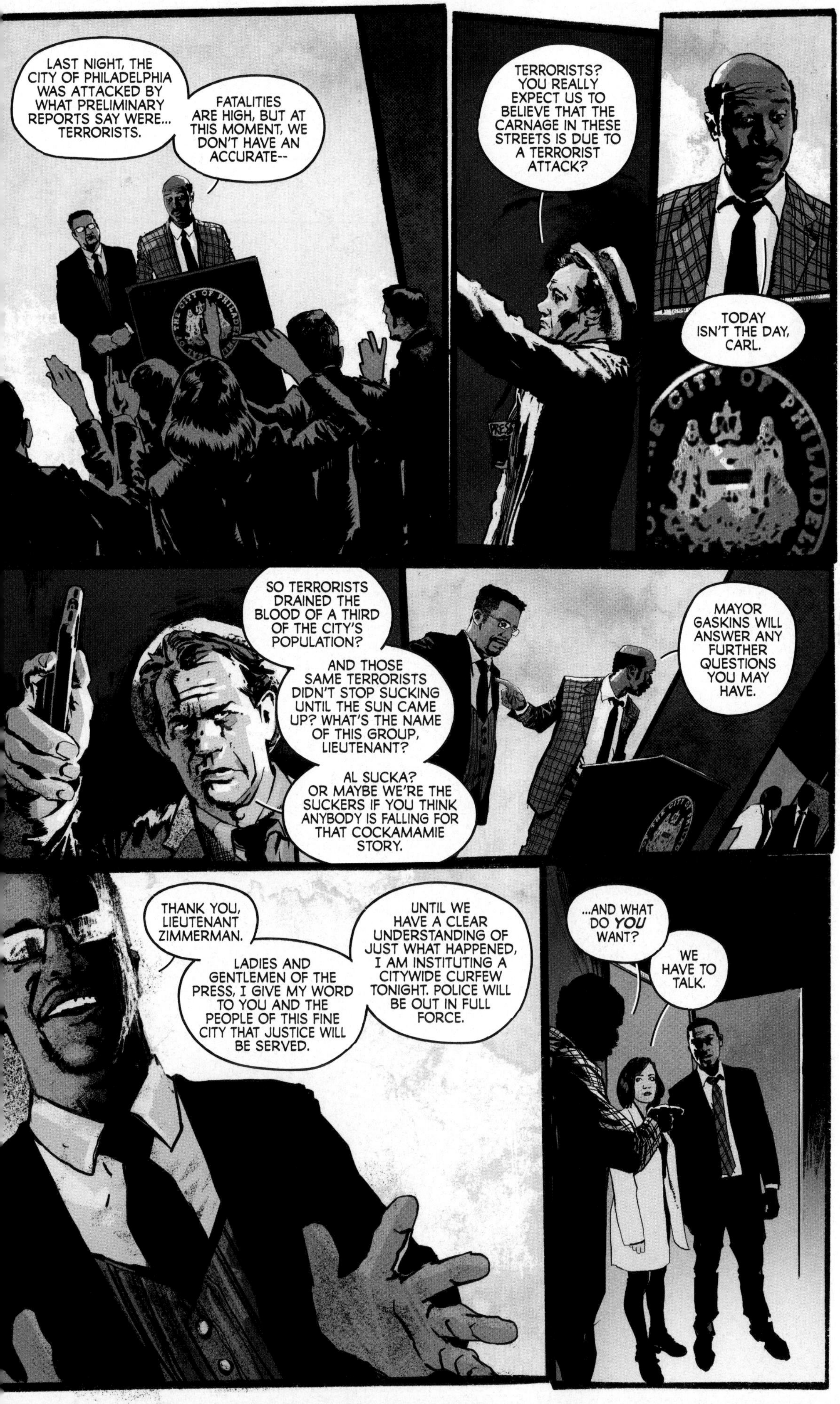
LAST NIGHT, THE CITY OF PHILADELPHIA WAS ATTACKED BY WHAT PRELIMINARY REPORTS SAY WERE... TERRORISTS.
FATALITIES ARE HIGH, BUT AT THIS MOMENT, WE DON'T HAVE AN ACCURATE--
TERRORISTS? YOU REALLY EXPECT US TO BELIEVE THAT THE CARNAGE IN THESE STREETS IS DUE TO A TERRORIST ATTACK?
TODAY ISN'T THE DAY, CARL.
SO TERRORISTS DRAINED THE BLOOD OF A THIRD OF THE CITY'S POPULATION?
AND THOSE SAME TERRORISTS DIDN'T STOP SUCKING UNTIL THE SUN CAME UP? WHAT'S THE NAME OF THIS GROUP, LIEUTENANT?
AL SUCKA? OR MAYBE WE'RE THE SUCKERS IF YOU THINK ANYBODY IS FALLING FOR THAT COCKAMAMIE STORY.
MAYOR GASKINS WILL ANSWER ANY FURTHER QUESTIONS YOU MAY HAVE.
THANK YOU, LIEUTENANT ZIMMERMAN.
LADIES AND GENTLEMEN OF THE PRESS, I GIVE MY WORD TO YOU AND THE PEOPLE OF THIS FINE CITY THAT JUSTICE WILL BE SERVED.
UNTIL WE HAVE A CLEAR UNDERSTANDING OF JUST WHAT HAPPENED, I AM INSTITUTING A CITYWIDE CURFEW TONIGHT. POLICE WILL BE OUT IN FULL FORCE.
...AND WHAT DO *YOU* WANT?
WE HAVE TO TALK.

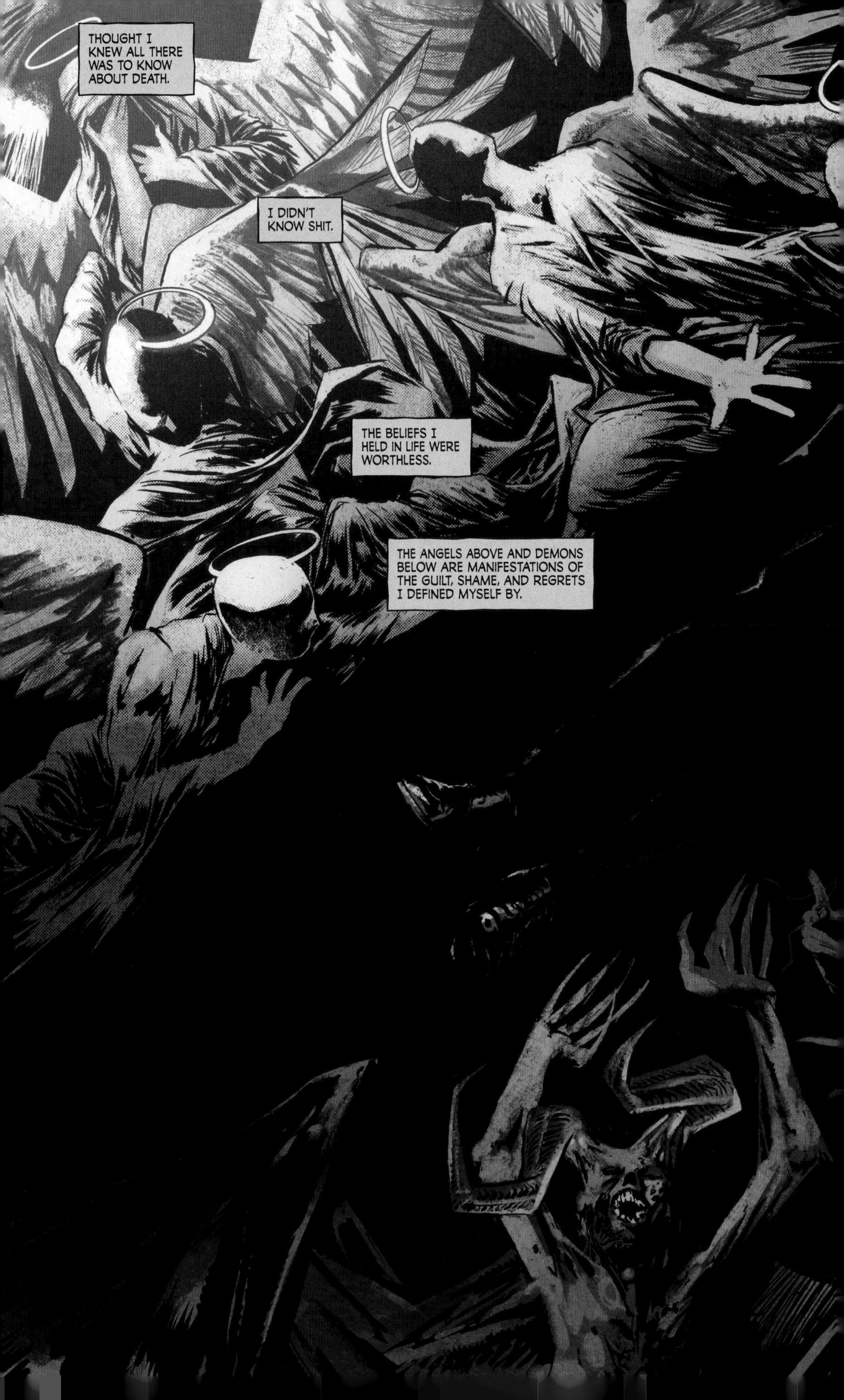
THOUGHT I KNEW ALL THERE WAS TO KNOW ABOUT DEATH.
I DIDN'T KNOW SHIT.
THE BELIEFS I HELD IN LIFE WERE WORTHLESS.
THE ANGELS ABOVE AND DEMONS BELOW ARE MANIFESTATIONS OF THE GUILT, SHAME, AND REGRETS I DEFINED MYSELF BY.

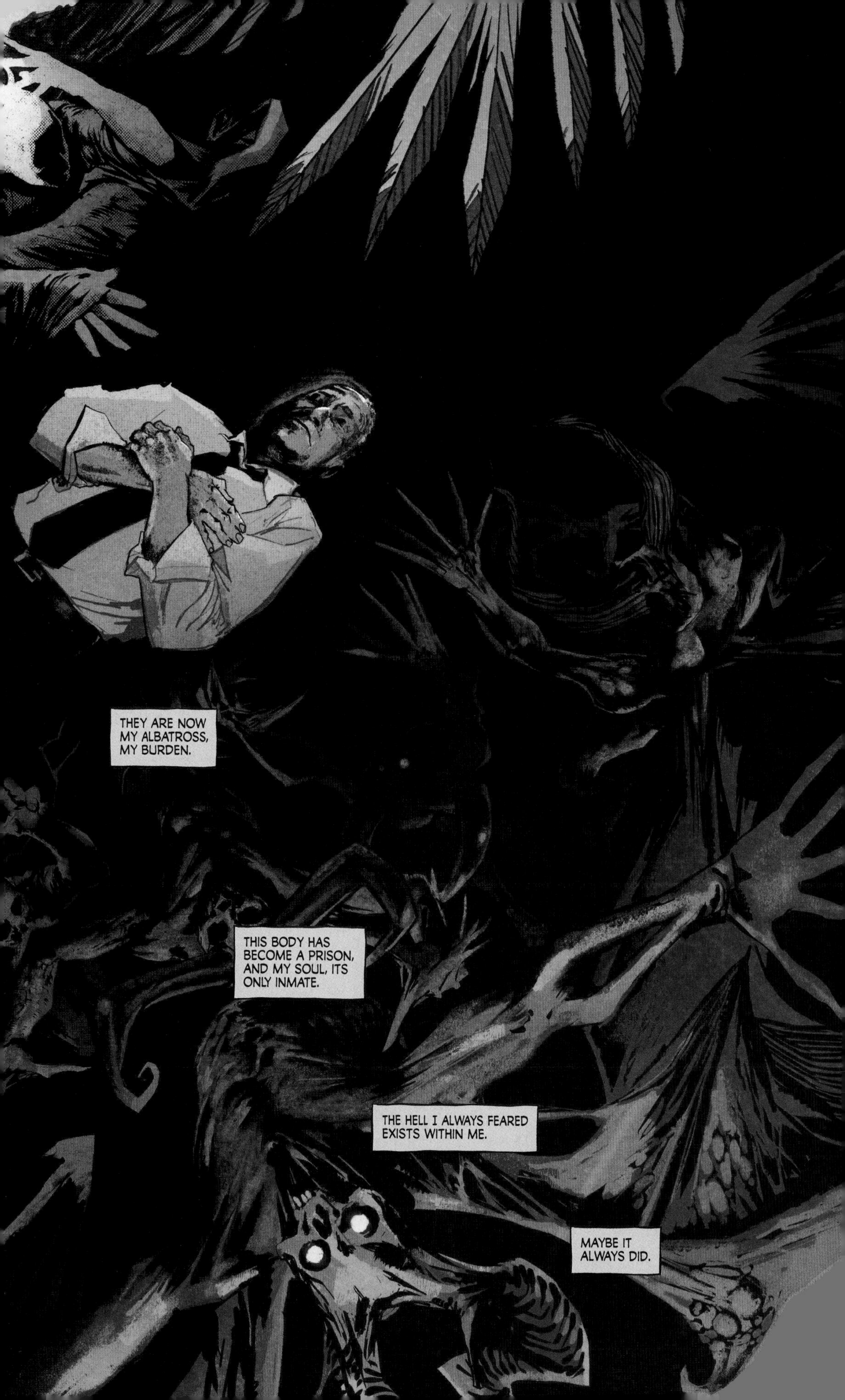
THEY ARE NOW MY ALBATROSS, MY BURDEN.
THIS BODY HAS BECOME A PRISON, AND MY SOUL, ITS ONLY INMATE.
THE HELL I ALWAYS FEARED EXISTS WITHIN ME.
MAYBE IT ALWAYS DID.

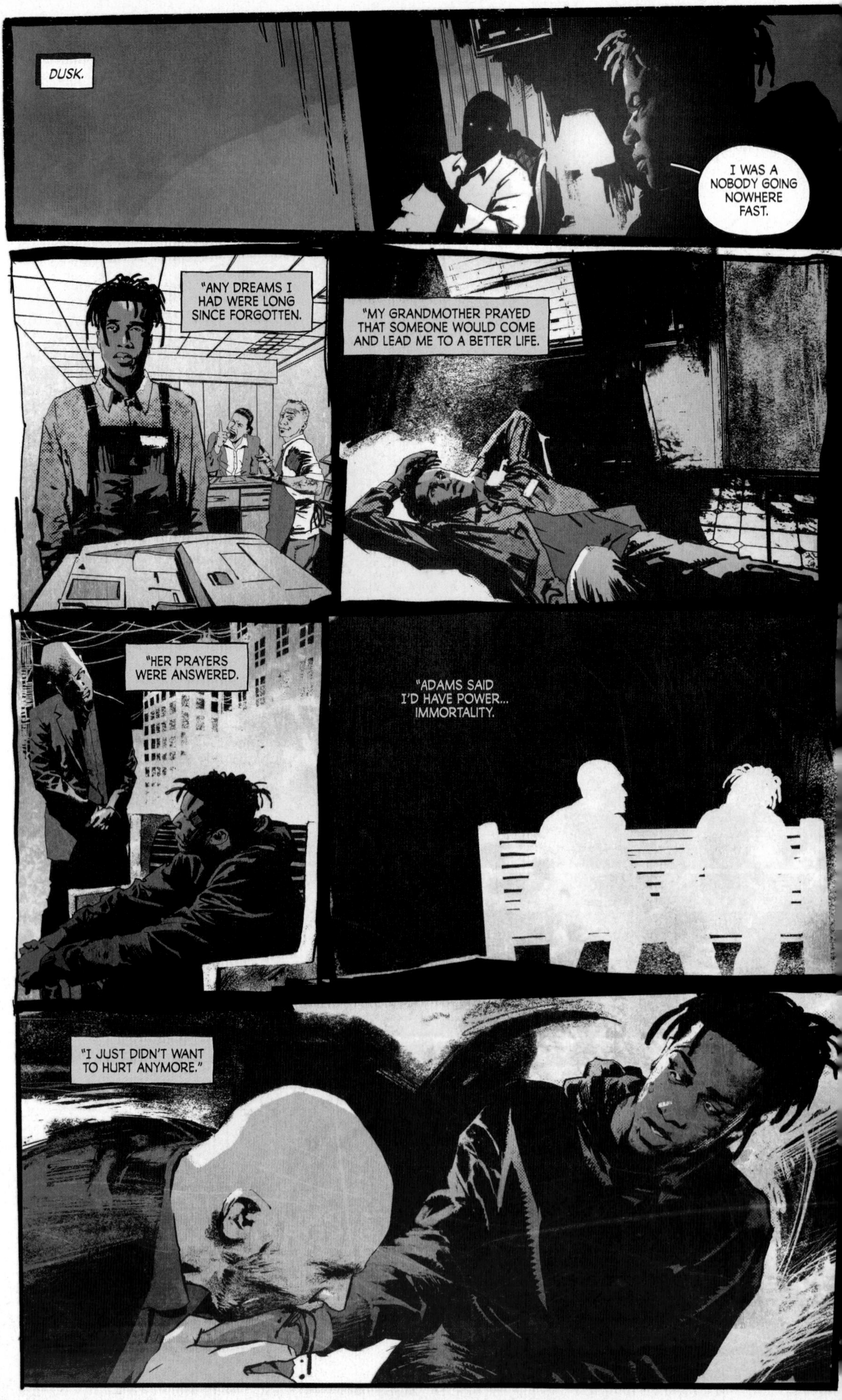
DUSK.
I WAS A NOBODY GOING NOWHERE FAST.
"ANY DREAMS I HAD WERE LONG SINCE FORGOTTEN.
"MY GRANDMOTHER PRAYED THAT SOMEONE WOULD COME AND LEAD ME TO A BETTER LIFE.
"HER PRAYERS WERE ANSWERED.
"ADAMS SAID I'D HAVE POWER... IMMORTALITY.
"I JUST DIDN'T WANT TO HURT ANYMORE."

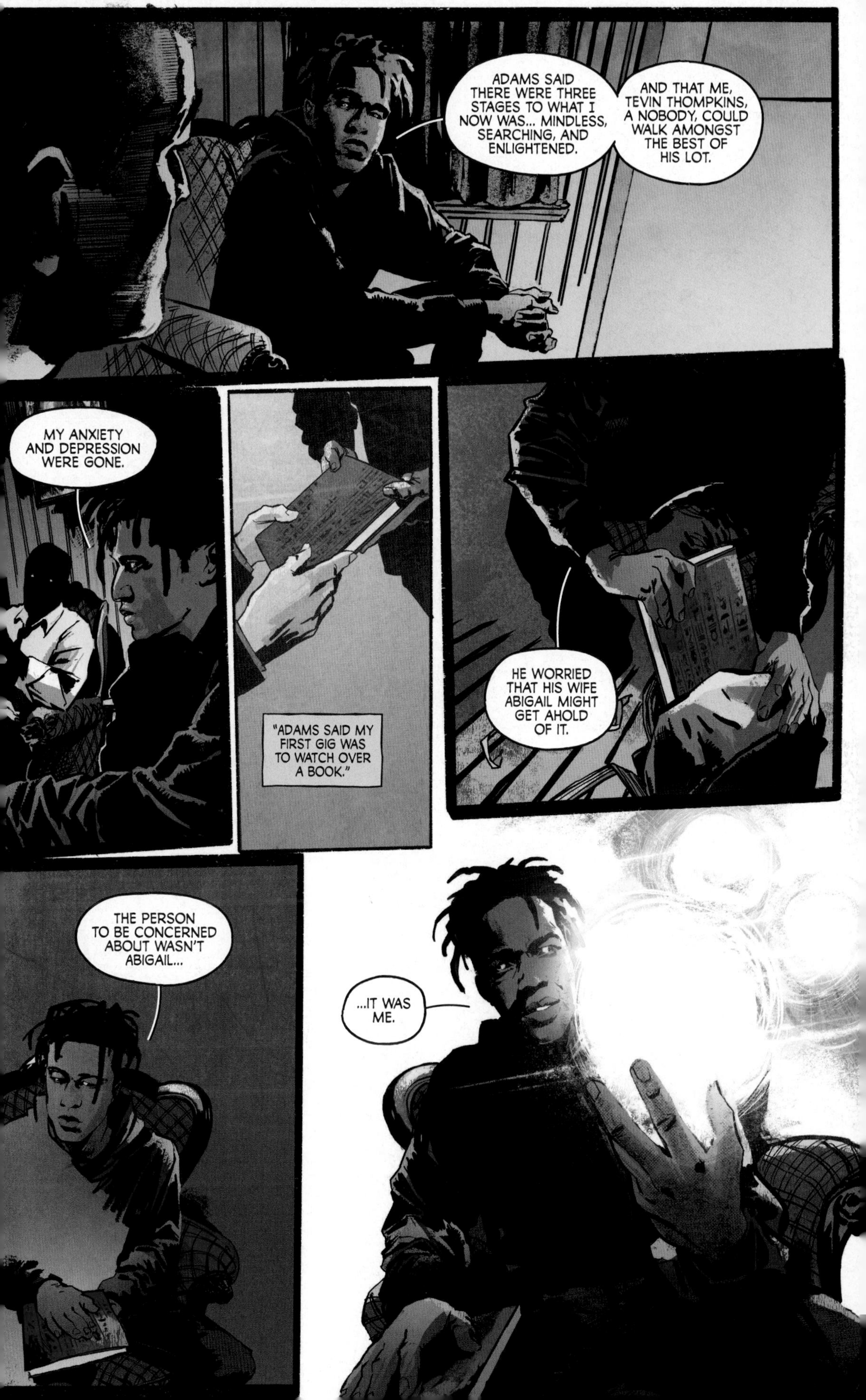
ADAMS SAID THERE WERE THREE STAGES TO WHAT I NOW WAS... MINDLESS, SEARCHING, AND ENLIGHTENED.
AND THAT ME, TEVIN THOMPKINS, A NOBODY, COULD WALK AMONGST THE BEST OF HIS LOT.
MY ANXIETY AND DEPRESSION WERE GONE.
"ADAMS SAID MY FIRST GIG WAS TO WATCH OVER A BOOK."
HE WORRIED THAT HIS WIFE ABIGAIL MIGHT GET AHOLD OF IT.
THE PERSON TO BE CONCERNED ABOUT WASN'T ABIGAIL...
...IT WAS ME.

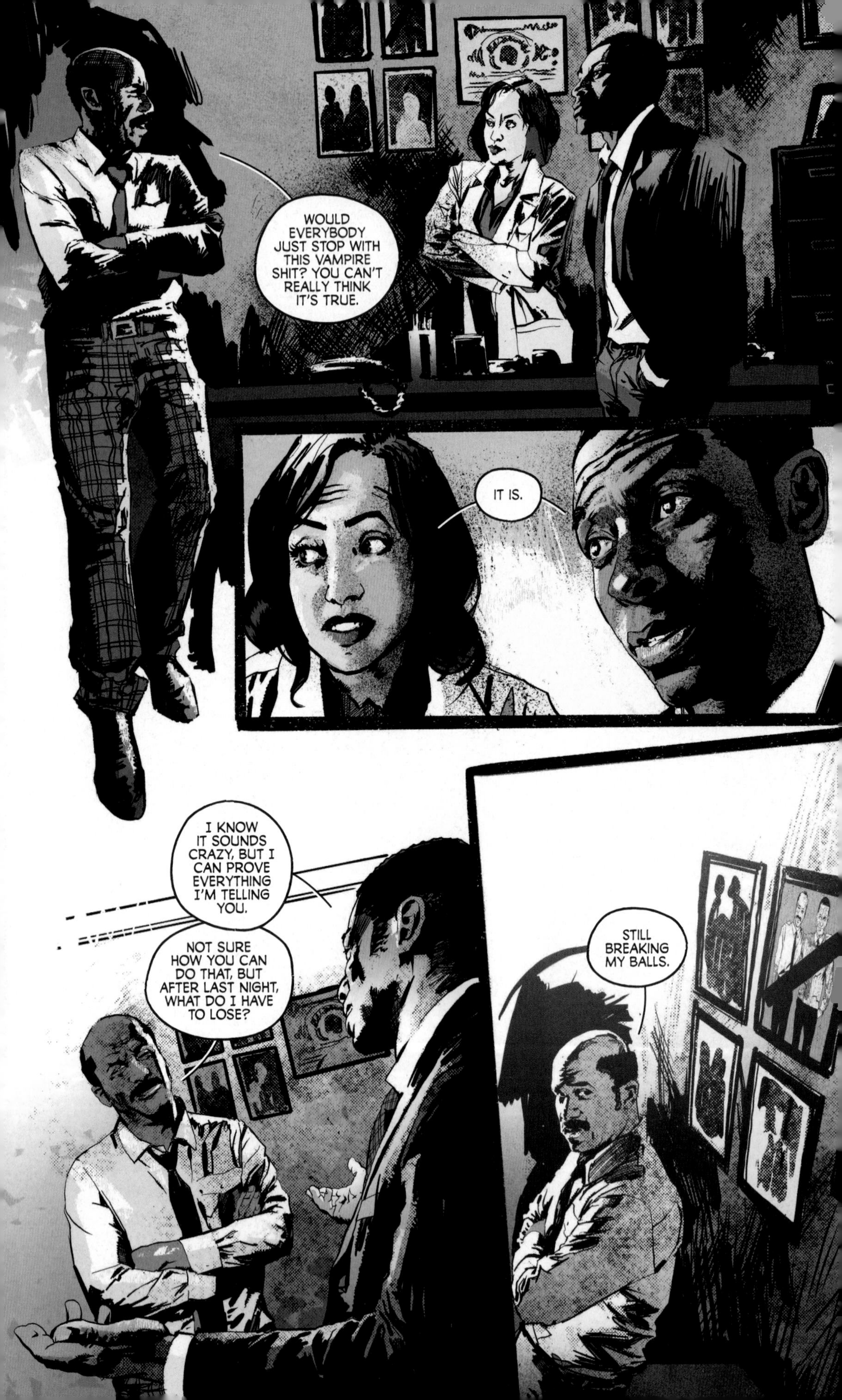
WOULD EVERYBODY JUST STOP WITH THIS VAMPIRE SHIT? YOU CAN'T REALLY THINK IT'S TRUE.
IT IS.
I KNOW IT SOUNDS CRAZY, BUT I CAN PROVE EVERYTHING I'M TELLING YOU.
NOT SURE HOW YOU CAN DO THAT, BUT AFTER LAST NIGHT, WHAT DO I HAVE TO LOSE?
STILL BREAKING MY BALLS.

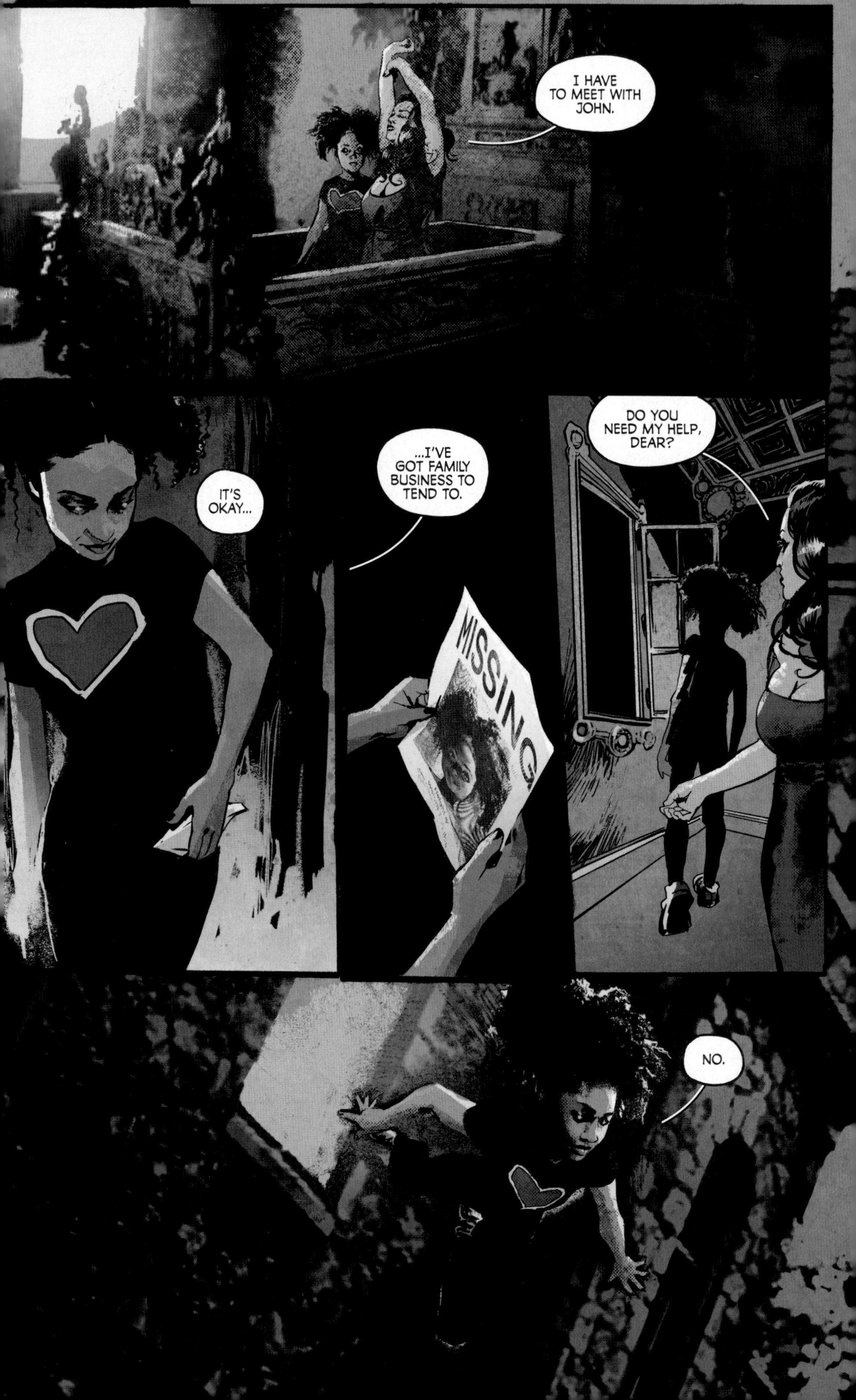
I HAVE TO MEET WITH JOHN.
IT'S OKAY...
...I'VE GOT FAMILY BUSINESS TO TEND TO.
MISSING
DO YOU NEED MY HELP, DEAR?
NO.

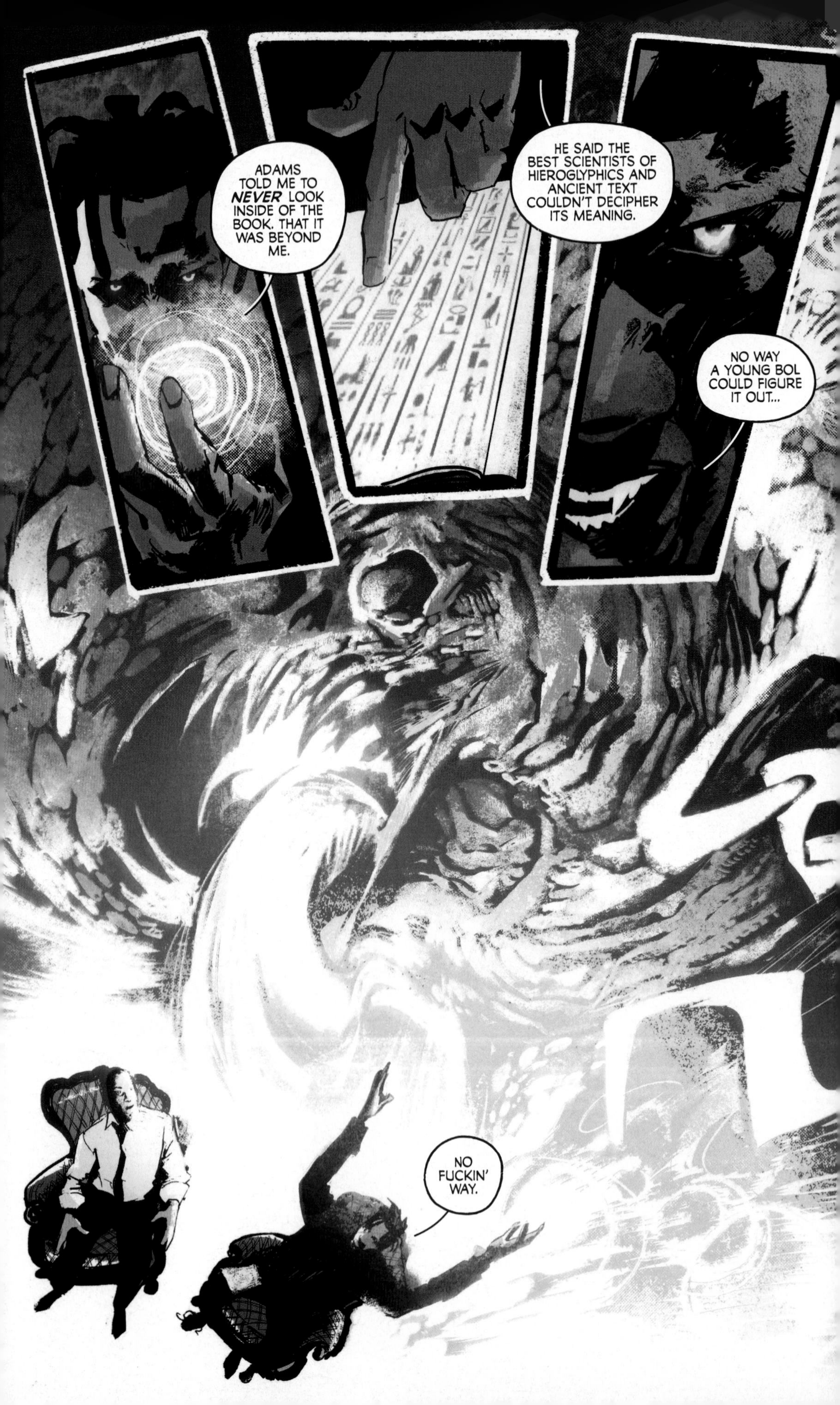
ADAMS TOLD ME TO NEVER LOOK INSIDE OF THE BOOK. THAT IT WAS BEYOND ME.
HE SAID THE BEST SCIENTISTS OF HIEROGLYPHICS AND ANCIENT TEXT COULDN'T DECIPHER ITS MEANING.
NO WAY A YOUNG BOL COULD FIGURE IT OUT...
NO FUCKIN' WAY.

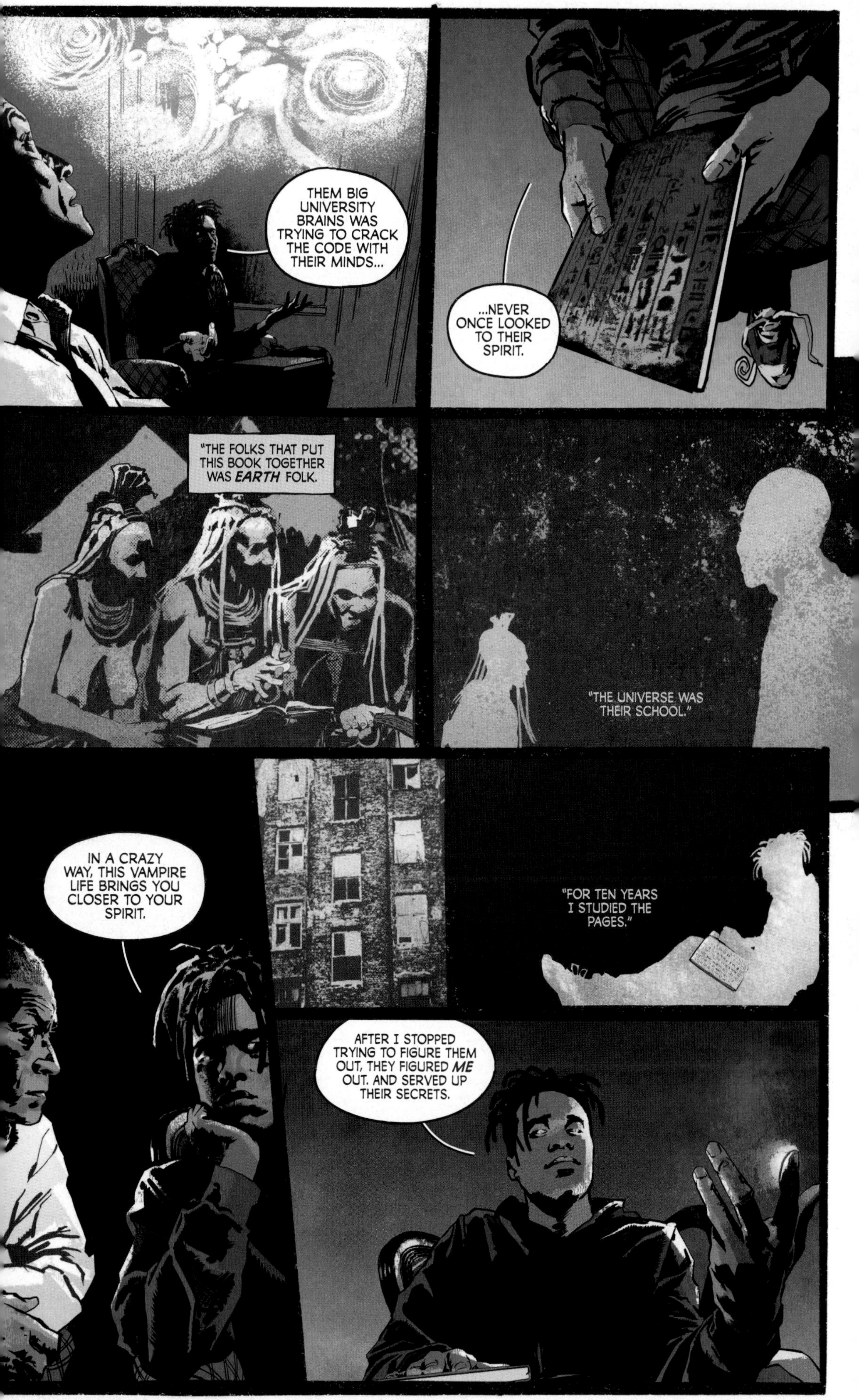
THEM BIG UNIVERSITY BRAINS WAS TRYING TO CRACK THE CODE WITH THEIR MINDS...
...NEVER ONCE LOOKED TO THEIR SPIRIT.
"THE FOLKS THAT PUT THIS BOOK TOGETHER WAS *EARTH* FOLK.
"THE UNIVERSE WAS THEIR SCHOOL."
IN A CRAZY WAY, THIS VAMPIRE LIFE BRINGS YOU CLOSER TO YOUR SPIRIT.
"FOR TEN YEARS I STUDIED THE PAGES."
AFTER I STOPPED TRYING TO FIGURE THEM OUT, THEY FIGURED *ME* OUT. AND SERVED UP THEIR SECRETS.

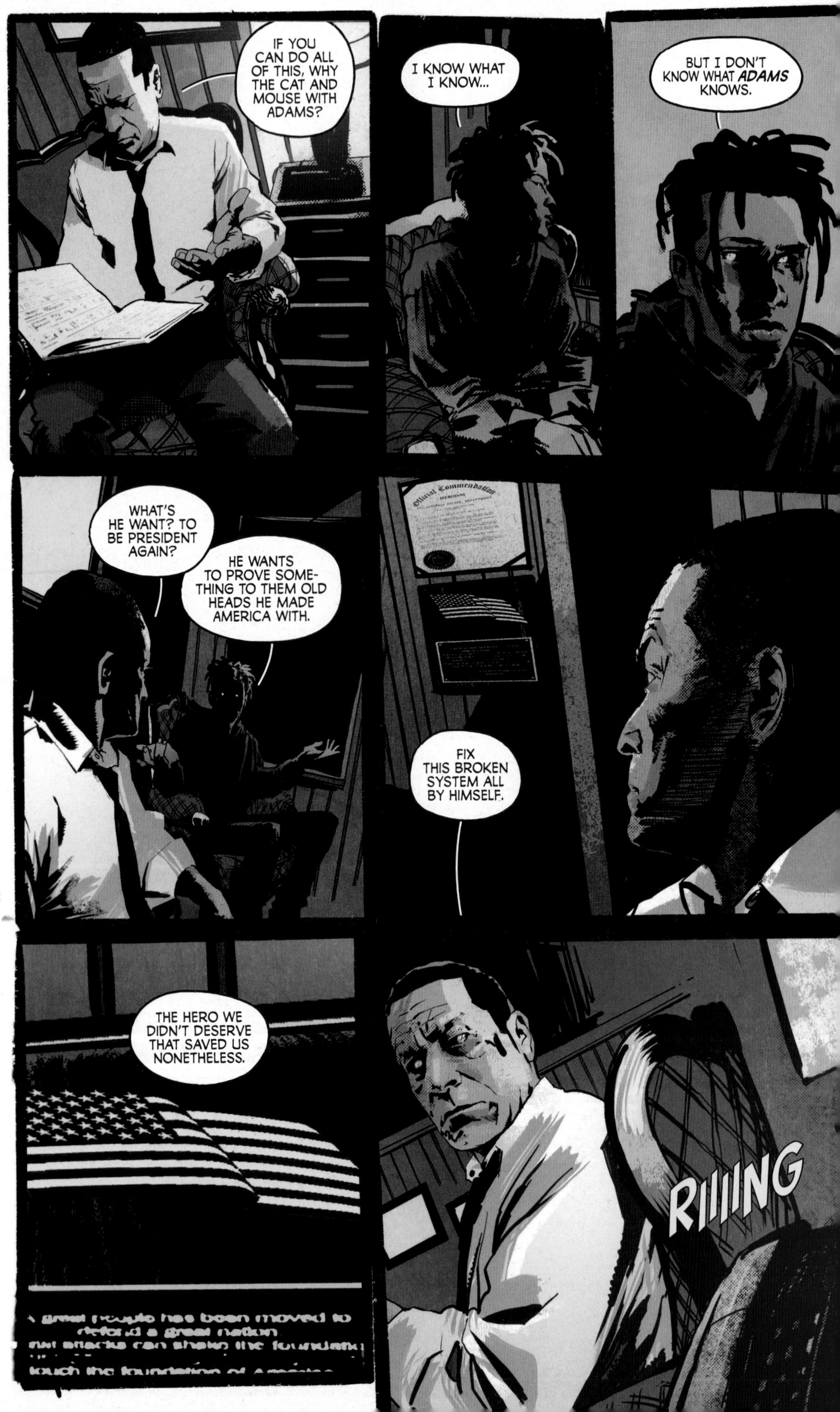
IF YOU CAN DO ALL OF THIS, WHY THE CAT AND MOUSE WITH ADAMS?
I KNOW WHAT I KNOW...
BUT I DON'T KNOW WHAT *ADAMS* KNOWS.
WHAT'S HE WANT? TO BE PRESIDENT AGAIN?
HE WANTS TO PROVE SOME-THING TO THEM OLD HEADS HE MADE AMERICA WITH.
Official Commendation
FIX THIS BROKEN SYSTEM ALL BY HIMSELF.
THE HERO WE DIDN'T DESERVE THAT SAVED US NONETHELESS.
RIIIING

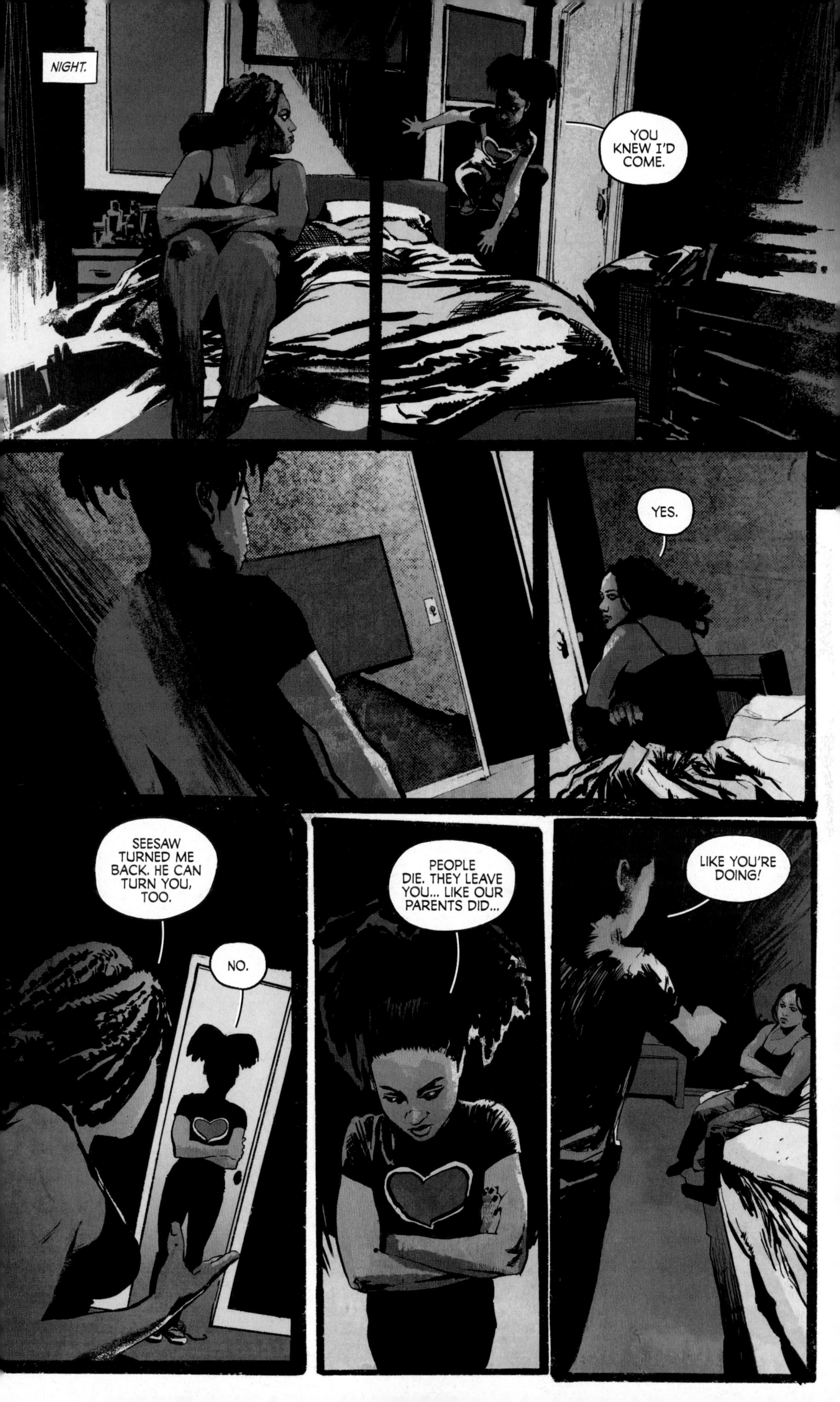
NIGHT.
YOU KNEW I'D COME.
YES.
SEESAW TURNED ME BACK. HE CAN TURN YOU, TOO.
NO.
PEOPLE DIE. THEY LEAVE YOU... LIKE OUR PARENTS DID...
LIKE YOU'RE DOING!

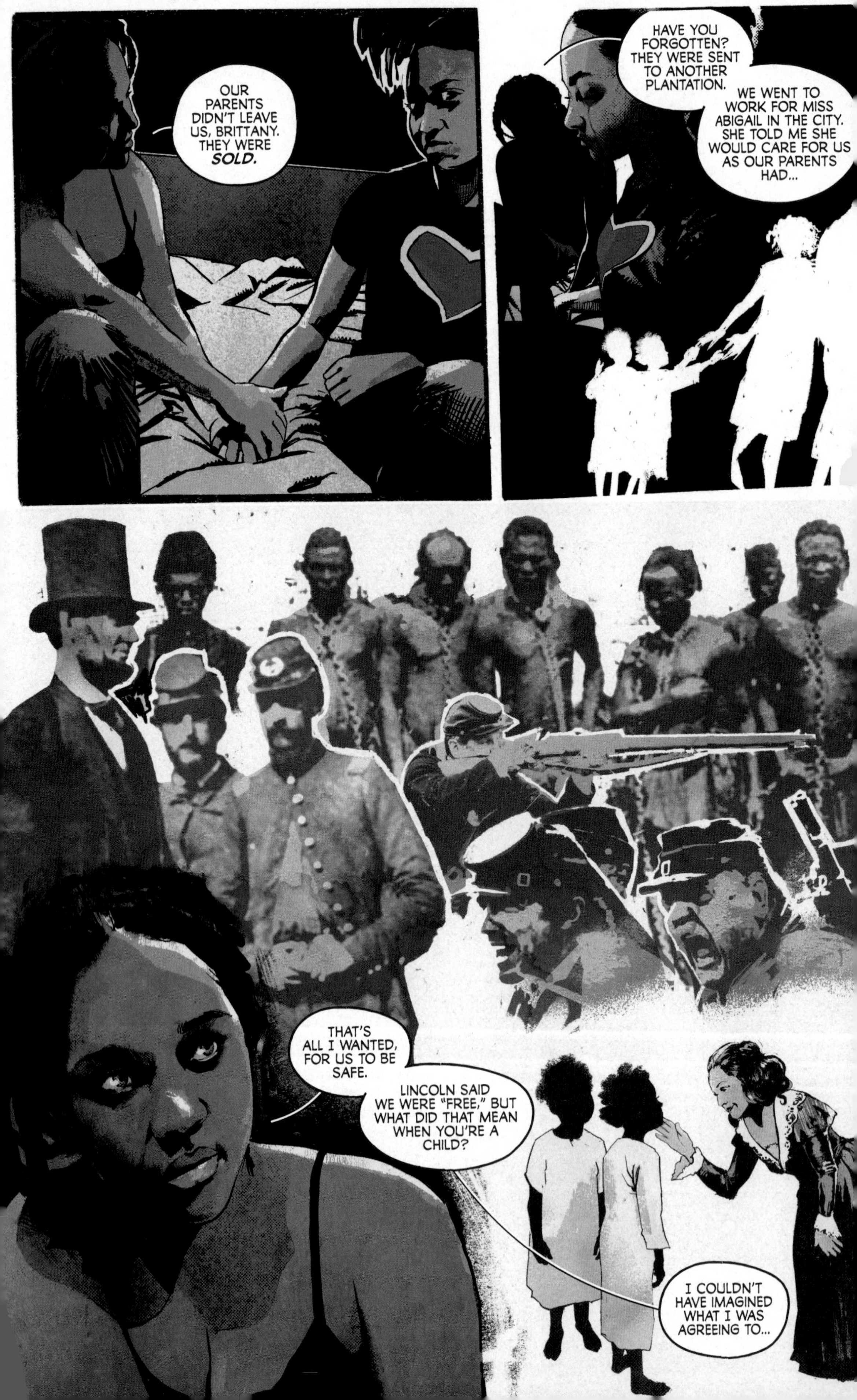
OUR PARENTS DIDN'T LEAVE US, BRITTANY. THEY WERE *SOLD.*
HAVE YOU FORGOTTEN? THEY WERE SENT TO ANOTHER PLANTATION.
WE WENT TO WORK FOR MISS ABIGAIL IN THE CITY. SHE TOLD ME SHE WOULD CARE FOR US AS OUR PARENTS HAD...
THAT'S ALL I WANTED, FOR US TO BE SAFE.
LINCOLN SAID WE WERE "FREE," BUT WHAT DID THAT MEAN WHEN YOU'RE A CHILD?
I COULDN'T HAVE IMAGINED WHAT I WAS AGREEING TO...

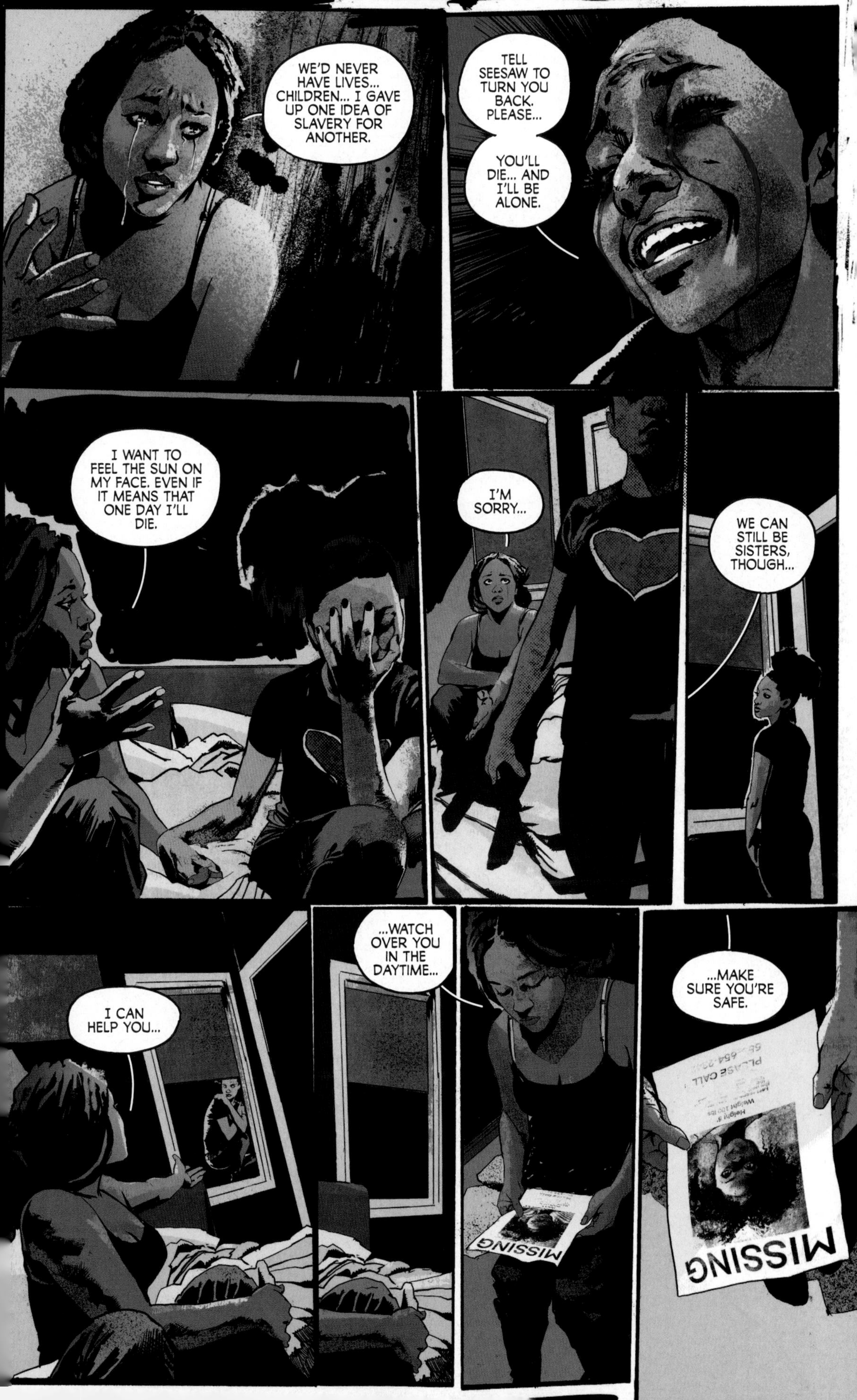
WE'D NEVER HAVE LIVES... CHILDREN... I GAVE UP ONE IDEA OF SLAVERY FOR ANOTHER.
TELL SEESAW TO TURN YOU BACK. PLEASE...
YOU'LL DIE... AND I'LL BE ALONE.
I WANT TO FEEL THE SUN ON MY FACE. EVEN IF IT MEANS THAT ONE DAY I'LL DIE.
I'M SORRY...
WE CAN STILL BE SISTERS, THOUGH...
I CAN HELP YOU...
...WATCH OVER YOU IN THE DAYTIME...
...MAKE SURE YOU'RE SAFE.
MISSING
PLEASE CALL
MISSING

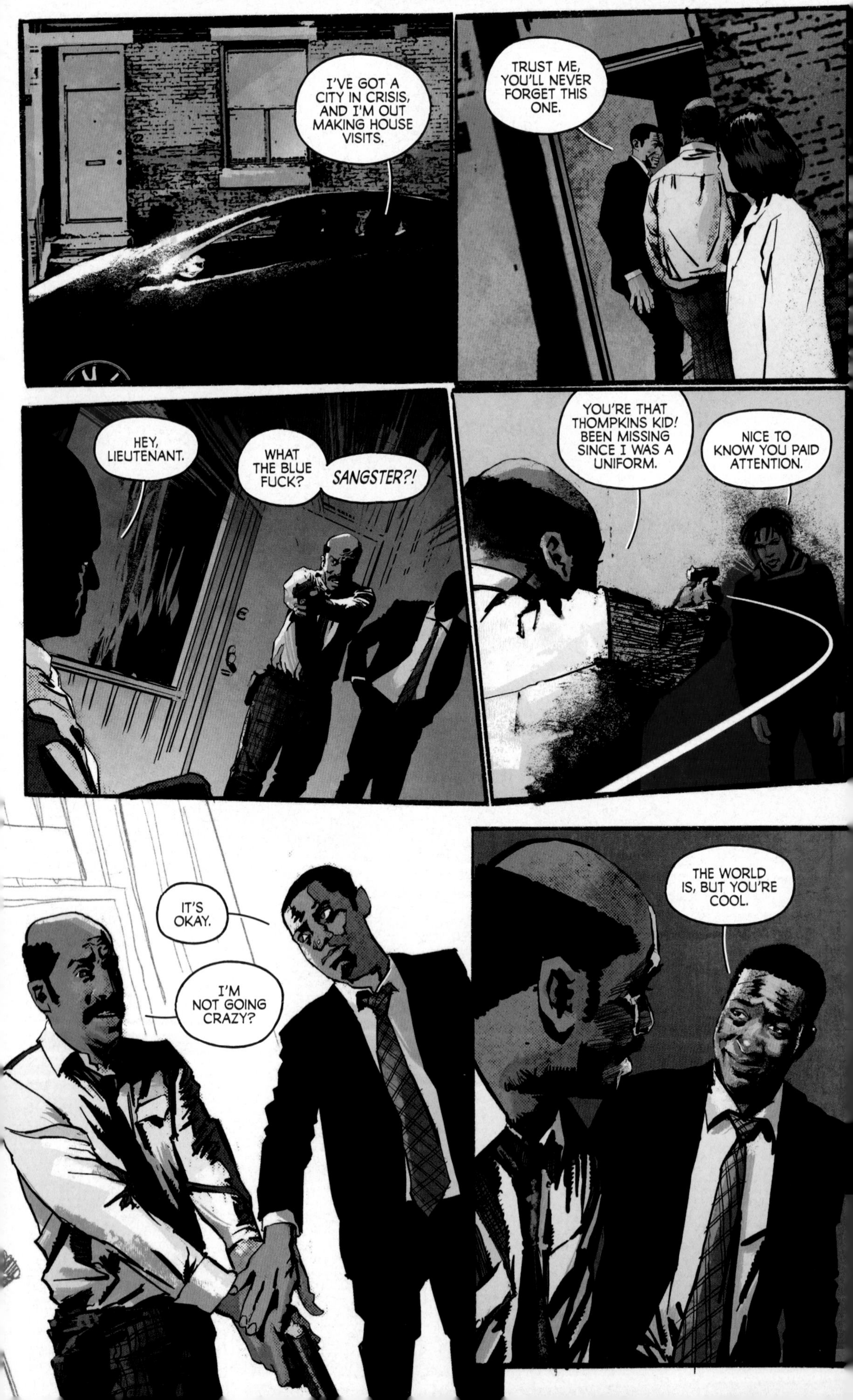
I'VE GOT A CITY IN CRISIS, AND I'M OUT MAKING HOUSE VISITS.
TRUST ME, YOU'LL NEVER FORGET THIS ONE.
HEY, LIEUTENANT.
WHAT THE BLUE FUCK?
SANGSTER?!
YOU'RE THAT THOMPKINS KID! BEEN MISSING SINCE I WAS A UNIFORM.
NICE TO KNOW YOU PAID ATTENTION.
IT'S OKAY.
I'M NOT GOING CRAZY?
THE WORLD IS, BUT YOU'RE COOL.

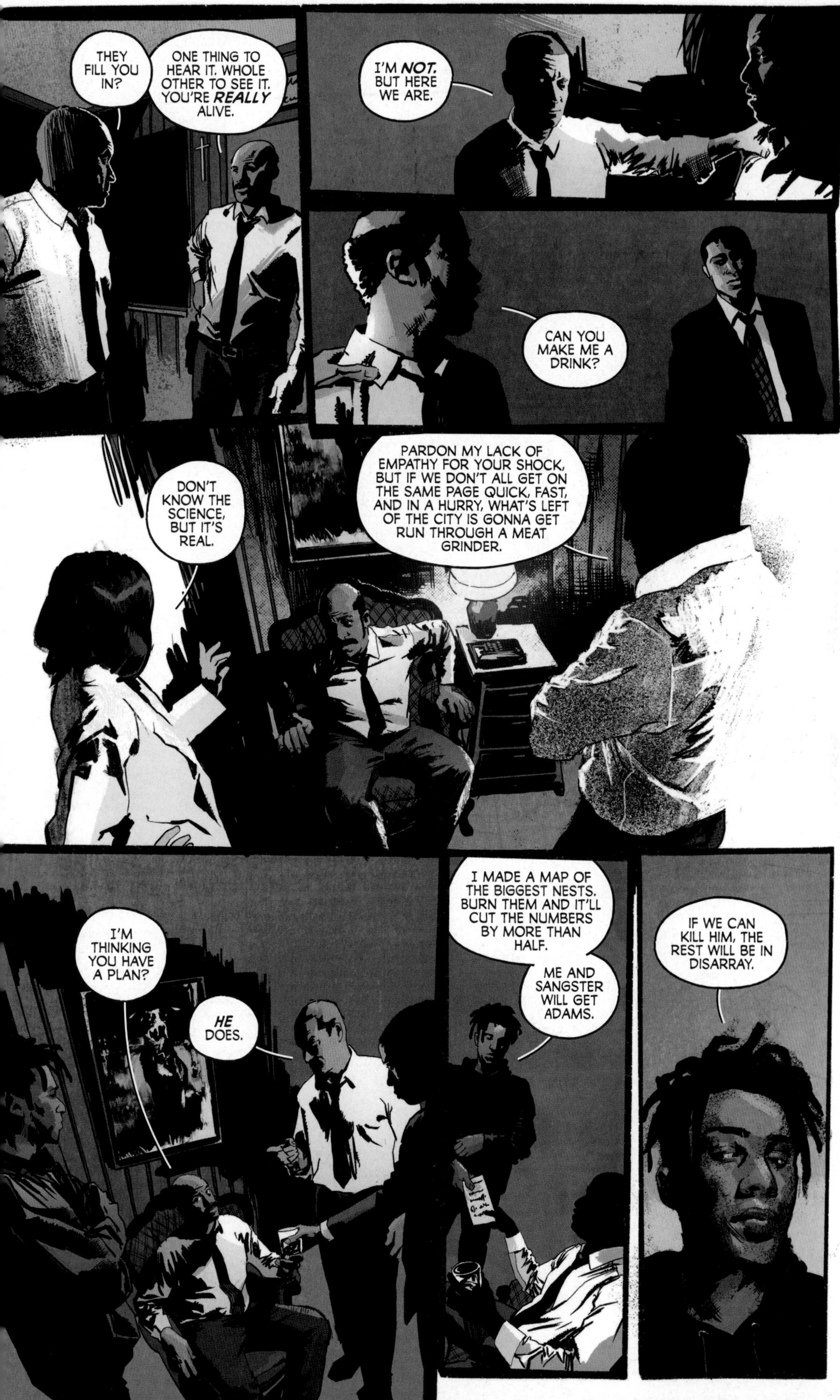

THEY FILL YOU IN?
ONE THING TO HEAR IT. WHOLE OTHER TO SEE IT. YOU'RE REALLY ALIVE.
I'M NOT. BUT HERE WE ARE.
CAN YOU MAKE ME A DRINK?
DON'T KNOW THE SCIENCE, BUT IT'S REAL.
PARDON MY LACK OF EMPATHY FOR YOUR SHOCK, BUT IF WE DON'T ALL GET ON THE SAME PAGE QUICK, FAST, AND IN A HURRY, WHAT'S LEFT OF THE CITY IS GONNA GET RUN THROUGH A MEAT GRINDER.
I'M THINKING YOU HAVE A PLAN?
HE DOES.
I MADE A MAP OF THE BIGGEST NESTS. BURN THEM AND IT'LL CUT THE NUMBERS BY MORE THAN HALF.
ME AND SANGSTER WILL GET ADAMS.
IF WE CAN KILL HIM, THE REST WILL BE IN DISARRAY.

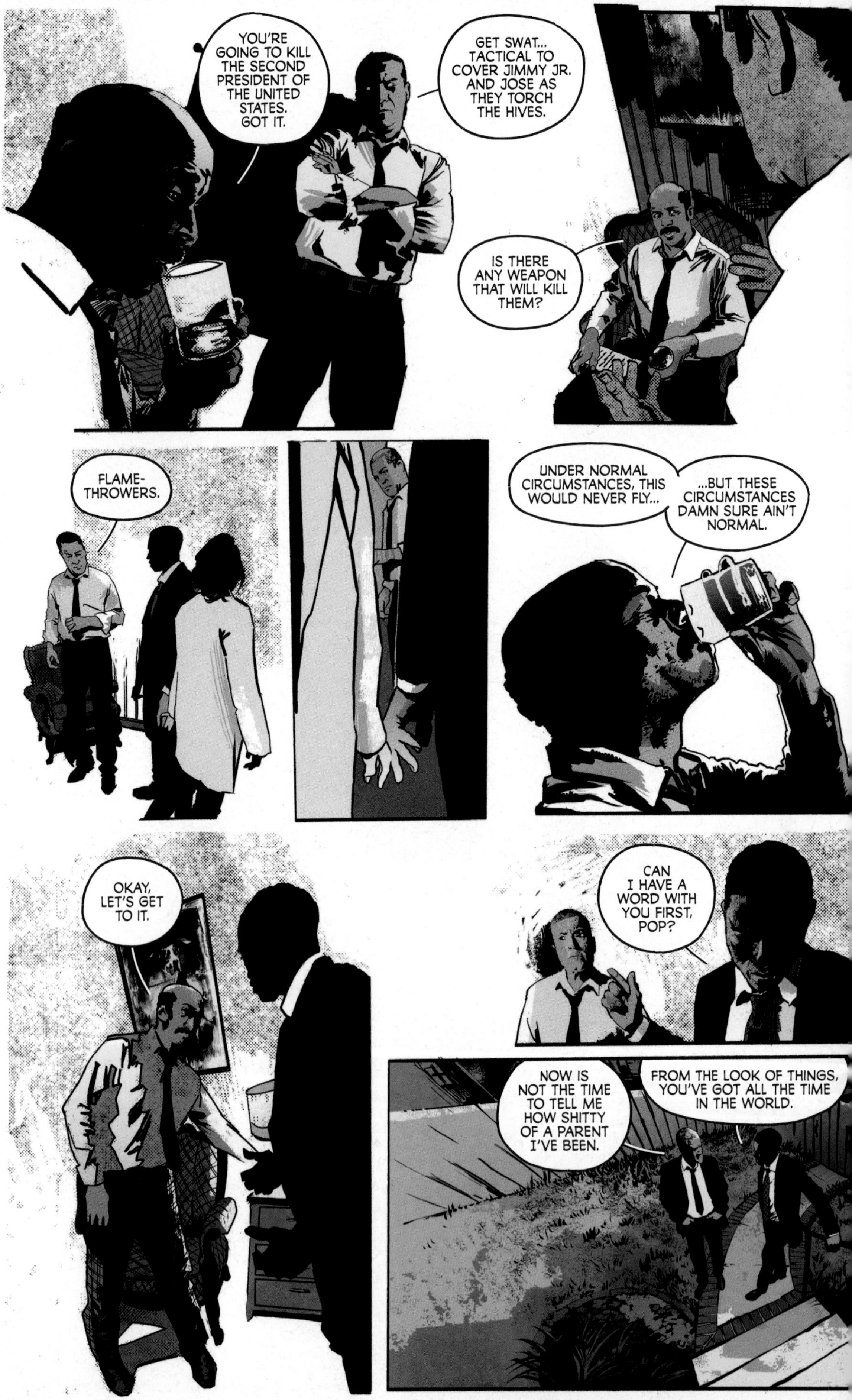
YOU'RE GOING TO KILL THE SECOND PRESIDENT OF THE UNITED STATES. GOT IT.
GET SWAT... TACTICAL TO COVER JIMMY JR. AND JOSE AS THEY TORCH THE HIVES.
IS THERE ANY WEAPON THAT WILL KILL THEM?
FLAME-THROWERS.
UNDER NORMAL CIRCUMSTANCES, THIS WOULD NEVER FLY...
...BUT THESE CIRCUMSTANCES DAMN SURE AIN'T NORMAL.
OKAY, LET'S GET TO IT.
CAN I HAVE A WORD WITH YOU FIRST, POP?
NOW IS NOT THE TIME TO TELL ME HOW SHITTY OF A PARENT I'VE BEEN.
FROM THE LOOK OF THINGS, YOU'VE GOT ALL THE TIME IN THE WORLD.

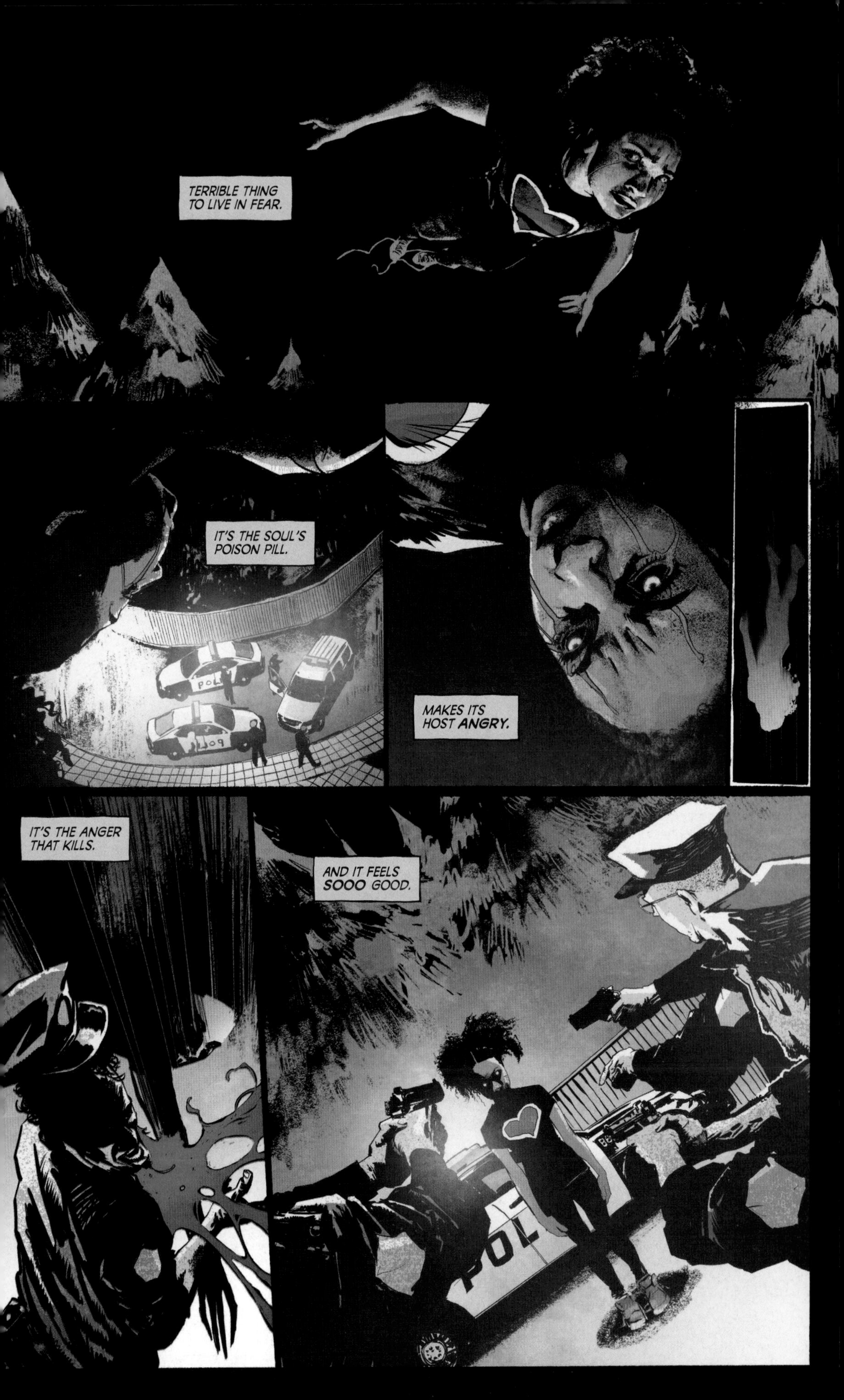

TERRIBLE THING TO LIVE IN FEAR.
IT'S THE SOUL'S POISON PILL.
MAKES ITS HOST ANGRY.
IT'S THE ANGER THAT KILLS.
AND IT FEELS SOOO GOOD.
POL

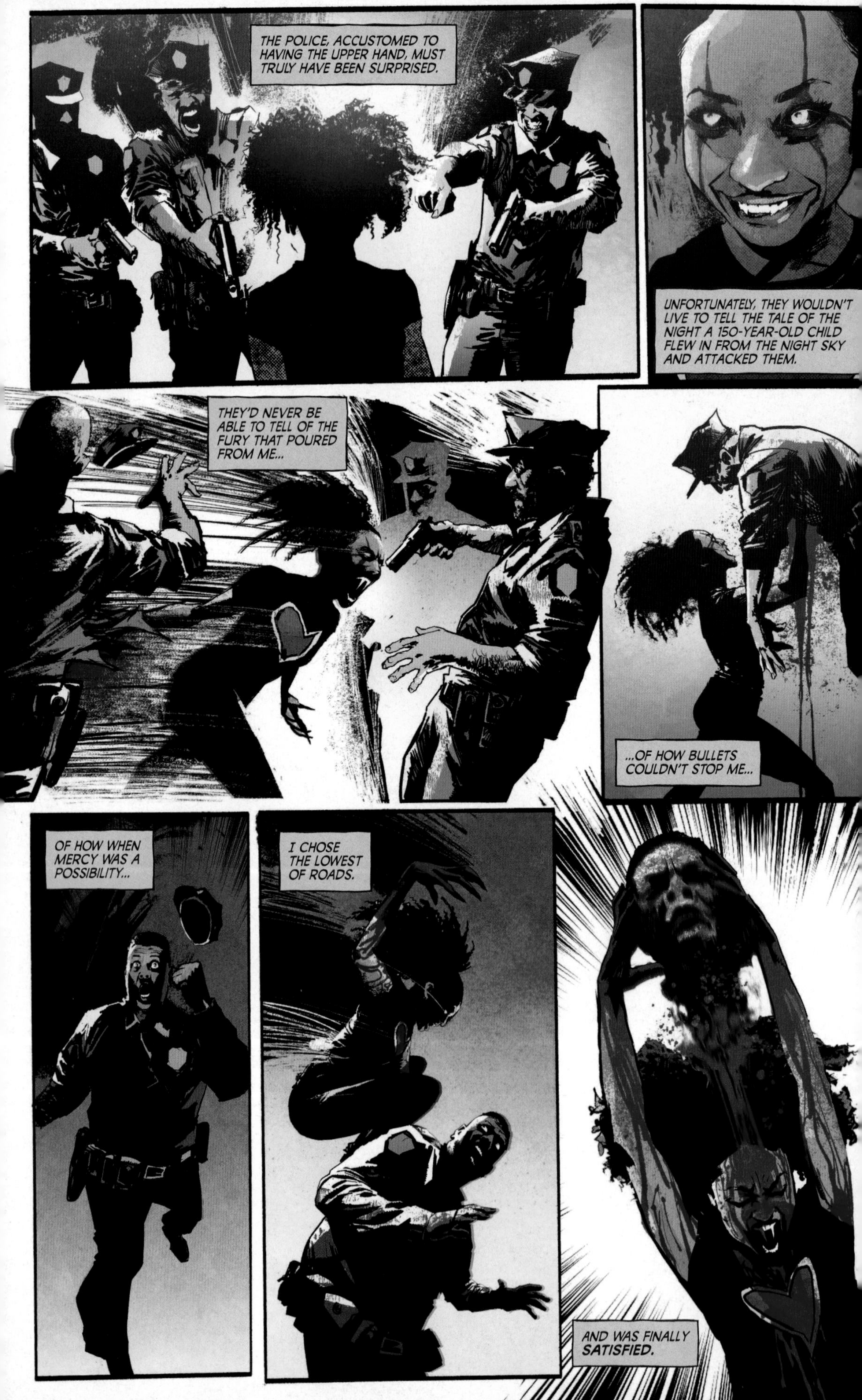
THE POLICE, ACCUSTOMED TO HAVING THE UPPER HAND, MUST TRULY HAVE BEEN SURPRISED.
UNFORTUNATELY, THEY WOULDN'T LIVE TO TELL THE TALE OF THE NIGHT A 150-YEAR-OLD CHILD FLEW IN FROM THE NIGHT SKY AND ATTACKED THEM.
THEY'D NEVER BE ABLE TO TELL OF THE FURY THAT POURED FROM ME...
...OF HOW BULLETS COULDN'T STOP ME...
OF HOW WHEN MERCY WAS A POSSIBILITY...
I CHOSE THE LOWEST OF ROADS.
AND WAS FINALLY SATISFIED.

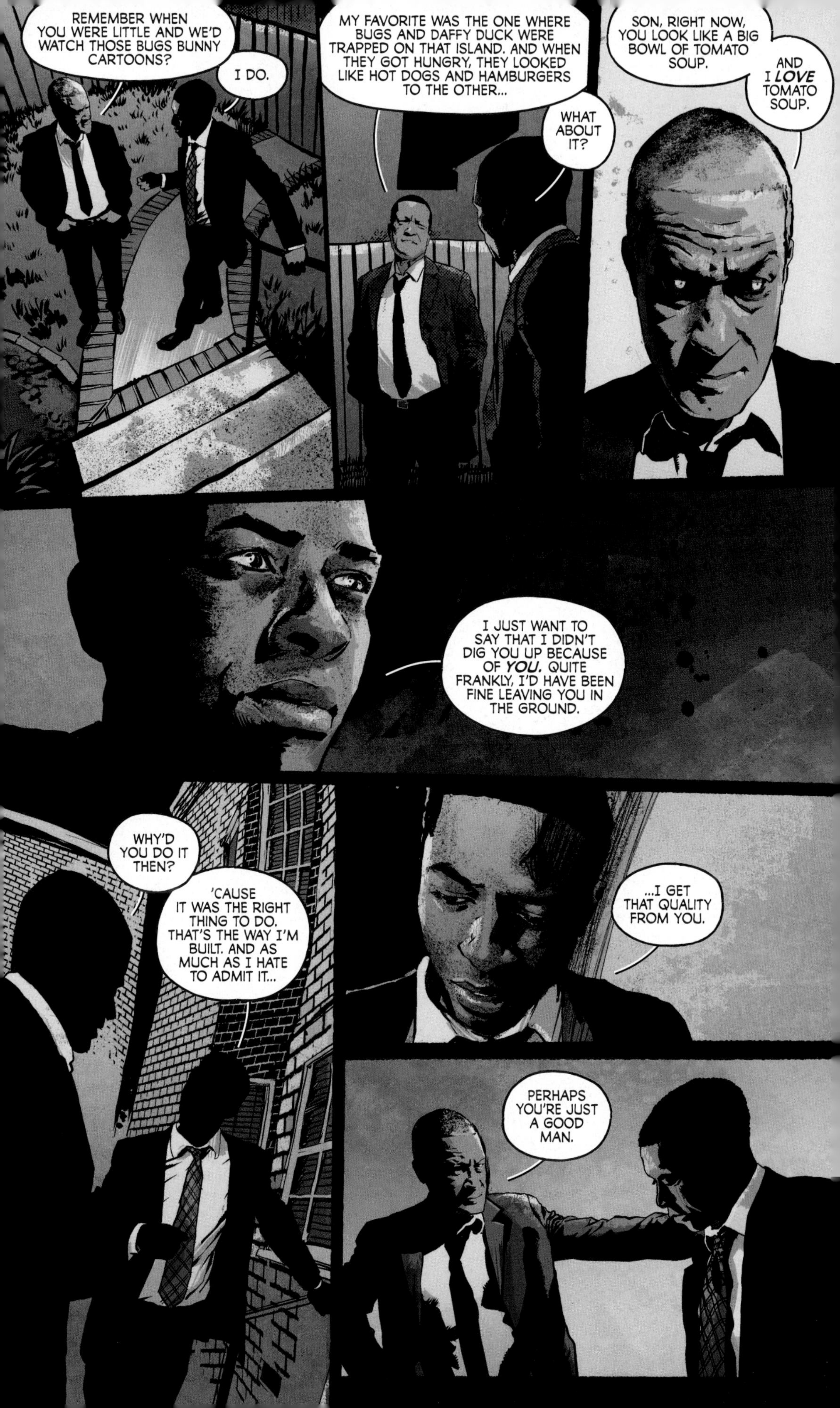
REMEMBER WHEN YOU WERE LITTLE AND WE'D WATCH THOSE BUGS BUNNY CARTOONS?
I DO.
MY FAVORITE WAS THE ONE WHERE BUGS AND DAFFY DUCK WERE TRAPPED ON THAT ISLAND. AND WHEN THEY GOT HUNGRY, THEY LOOKED LIKE HOT DOGS AND HAMBURGERS TO THE OTHER...
WHAT ABOUT IT?
SON, RIGHT NOW, YOU LOOK LIKE A BIG BOWL OF TOMATO SOUP.
AND I *LOVE* TOMATO SOUP.
I JUST WANT TO SAY THAT I DIDN'T DIG YOU UP BECAUSE OF *YOU.* QUITE FRANKLY, I'D HAVE BEEN FINE LEAVING YOU IN THE GROUND.
WHY'D YOU DO IT THEN?
'CAUSE IT WAS THE RIGHT THING TO DO. THAT'S THE WAY I'M BUILT. AND AS MUCH AS I HATE TO ADMIT IT...
...I GET THAT QUALITY FROM YOU.
PERHAPS YOU'RE JUST A GOOD MAN.

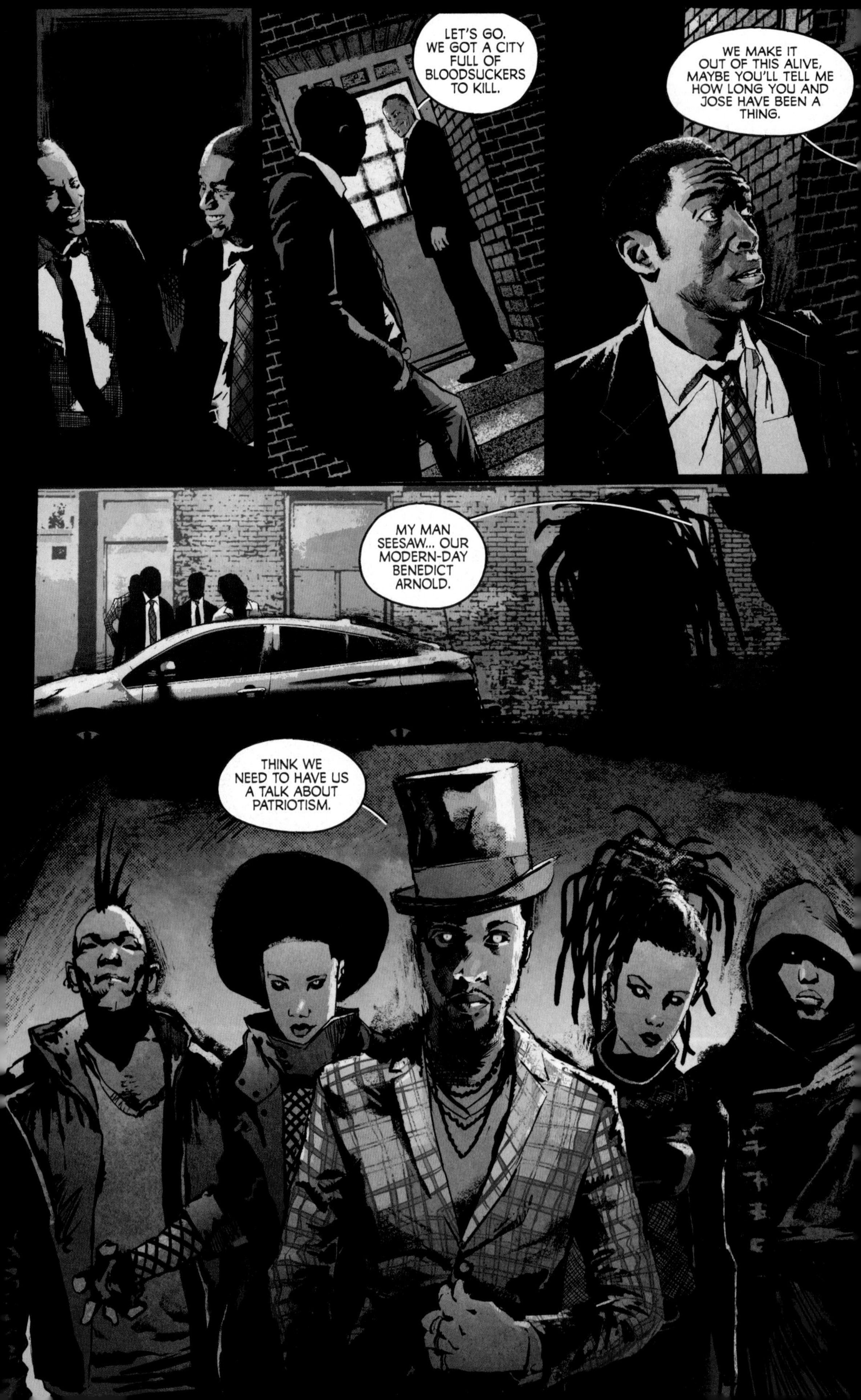
LET'S GO. WE GOT A CITY FULL OF BLOODSUCKERS TO KILL.
WE MAKE IT OUT OF THIS ALIVE, MAYBE YOU'LL TELL ME HOW LONG YOU AND JOSE HAVE BEEN A THING.
MY MAN SEESAW... OUR MODERN-DAY BENEDICT ARNOLD.
THINK WE NEED TO HAVE US A TALK ABOUT PATRIOTISM.

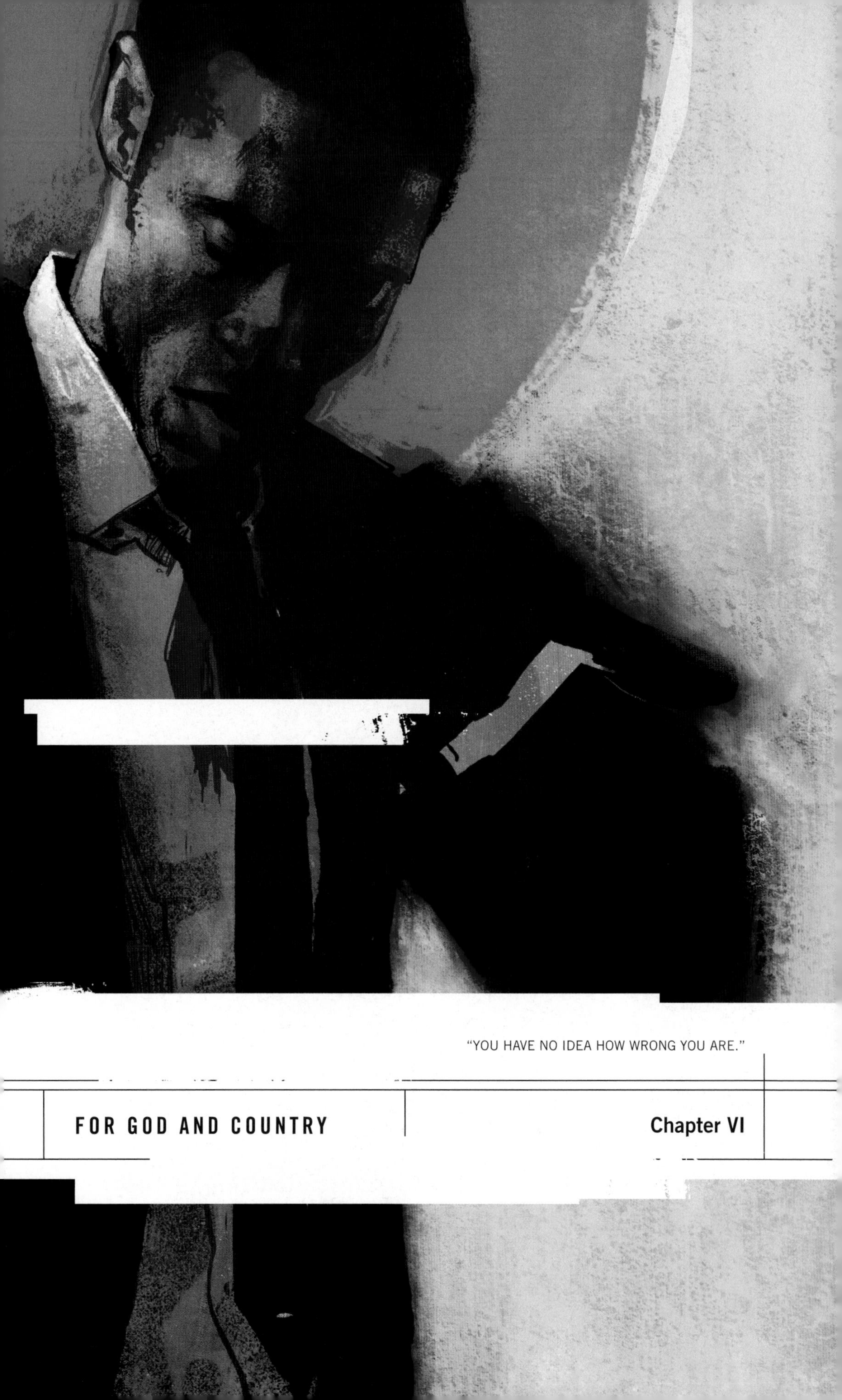

"YOU HAVE NO IDEA HOW WRONG YOU ARE."

FOR GOD AND COUNTRY

Chapter VI

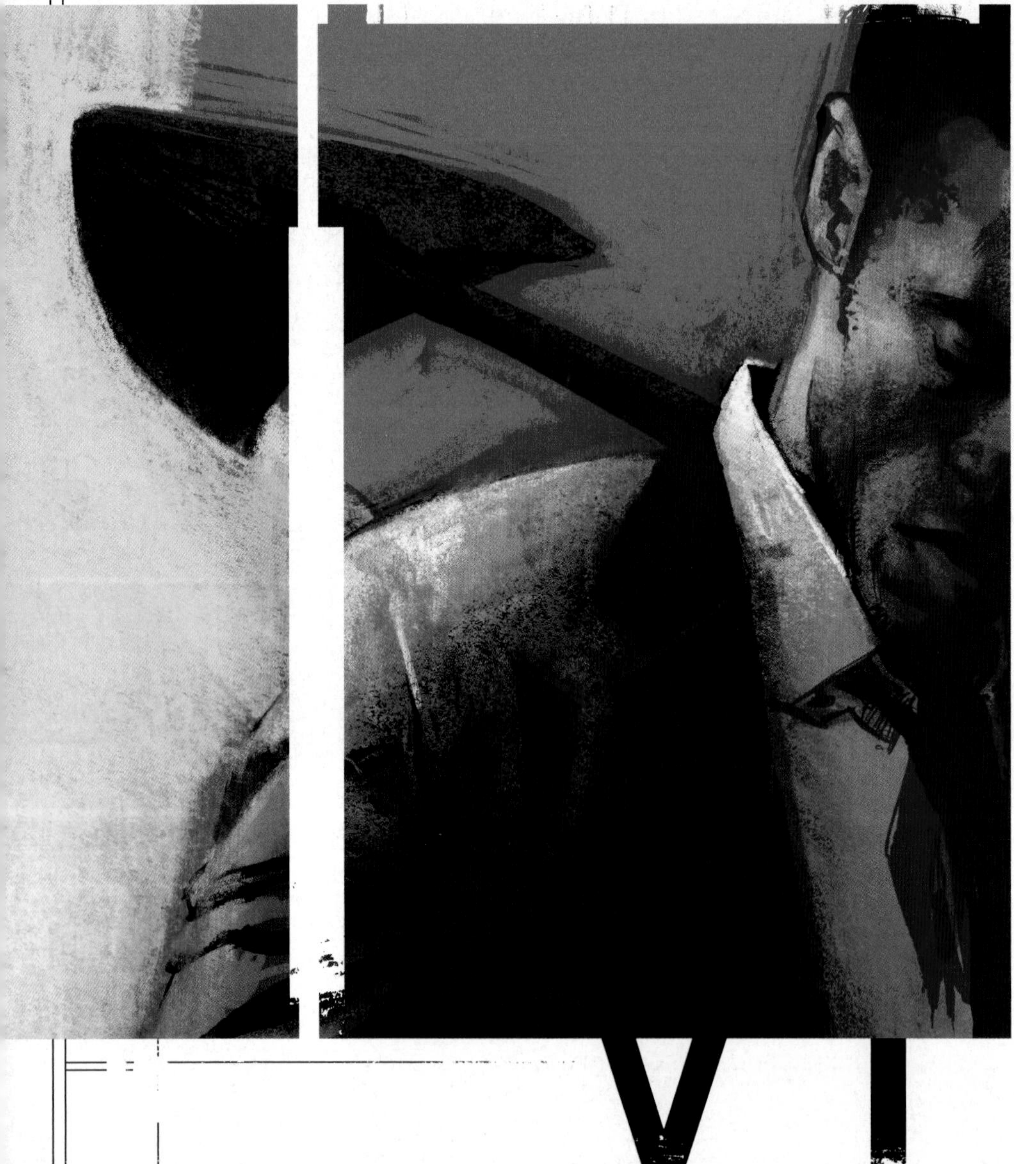

VI

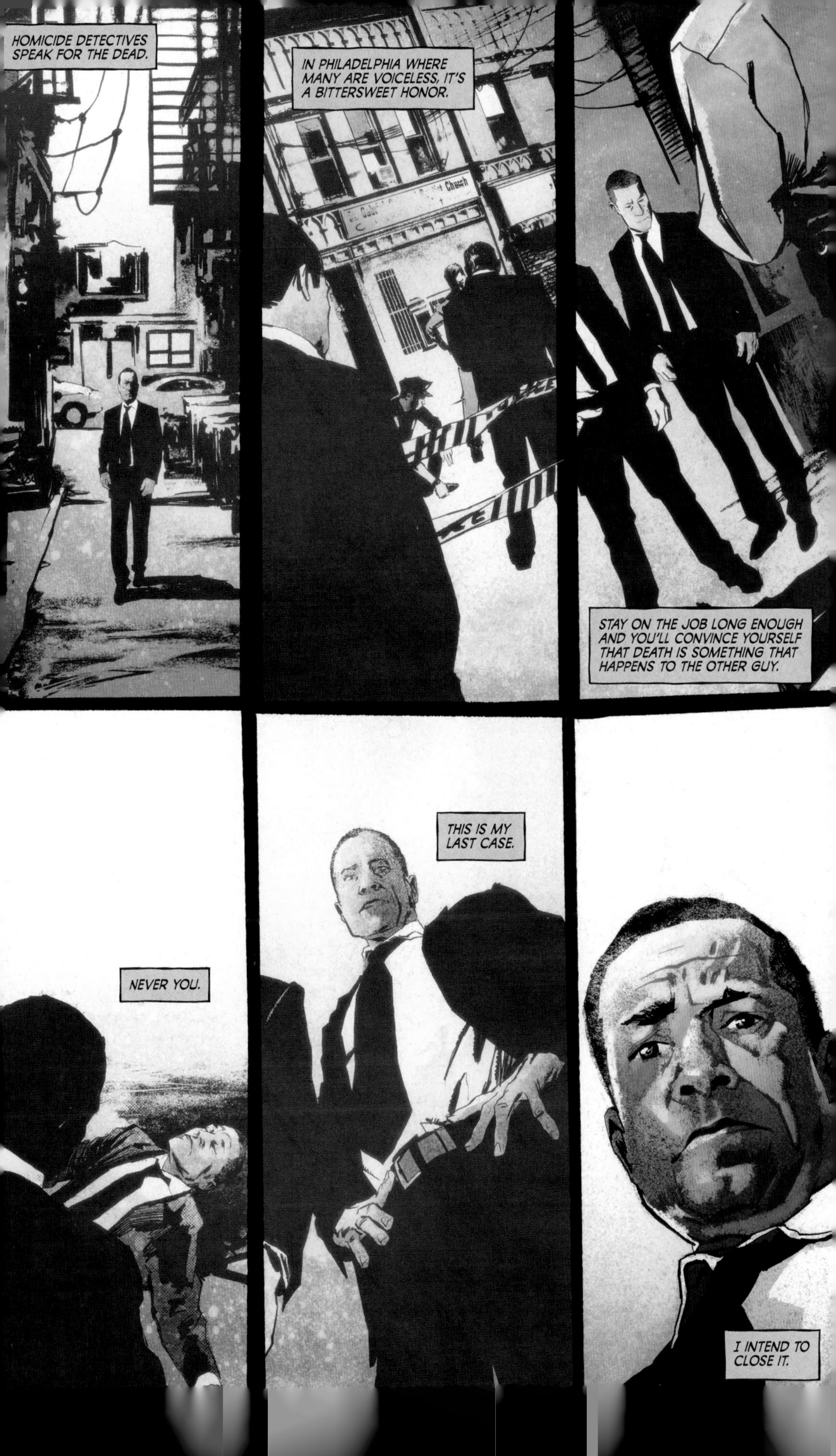
HOMICIDE DETECTIVES SPEAK FOR THE DEAD.
IN PHILADELPHIA WHERE MANY ARE VOICELESS, IT'S A BITTERSWEET HONOR.
STAY ON THE JOB LONG ENOUGH AND YOU'LL CONVINCE YOURSELF THAT DEATH IS SOMETHING THAT HAPPENS TO THE OTHER GUY.
NEVER YOU.
THIS IS MY LAST CASE.
I INTEND TO CLOSE IT.

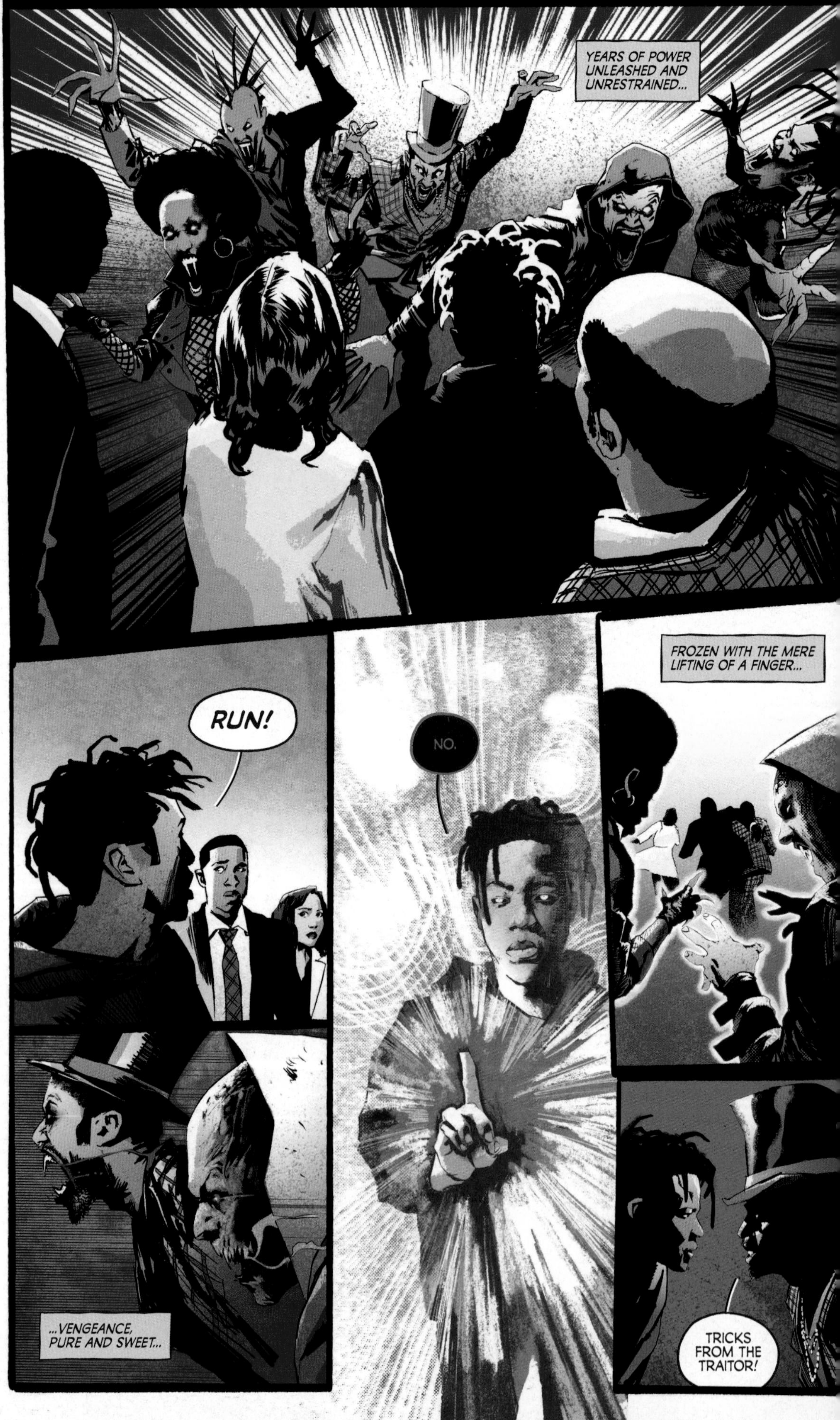
YEARS OF POWER UNLEASHED AND UNRESTRAINED...
RUN!
NO.
FROZEN WITH THE MERE LIFTING OF A FINGER...
...VENGEANCE, PURE AND SWEET...
TRICKS FROM THE TRAITOR!

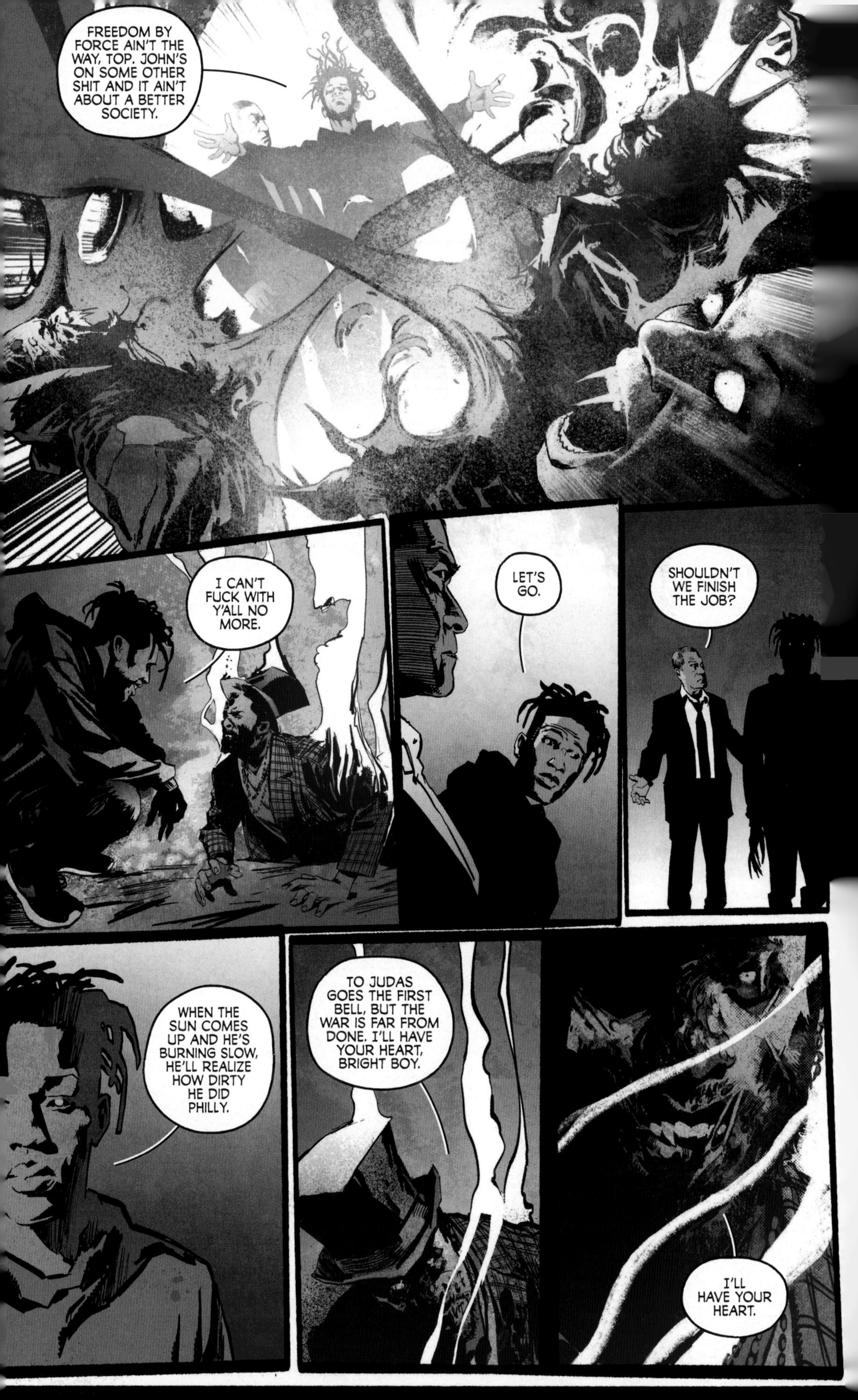
FREEDOM BY FORCE AIN'T THE WAY, TOP. JOHN'S ON SOME OTHER SHIT AND IT AIN'T ABOUT A BETTER SOCIETY.
I CAN'T FUCK WITH Y'ALL NO MORE.
LET'S GO.
SHOULDN'T WE FINISH THE JOB?
WHEN THE SUN COMES UP AND HE'S BURNING SLOW, HE'LL REALIZE HOW DIRTY HE DID PHILLY.
TO JUDAS GOES THE FIRST BELL, BUT THE WAR IS FAR FROM DONE. I'LL HAVE YOUR HEART, BRIGHT BOY.
I'LL HAVE YOUR HEART.

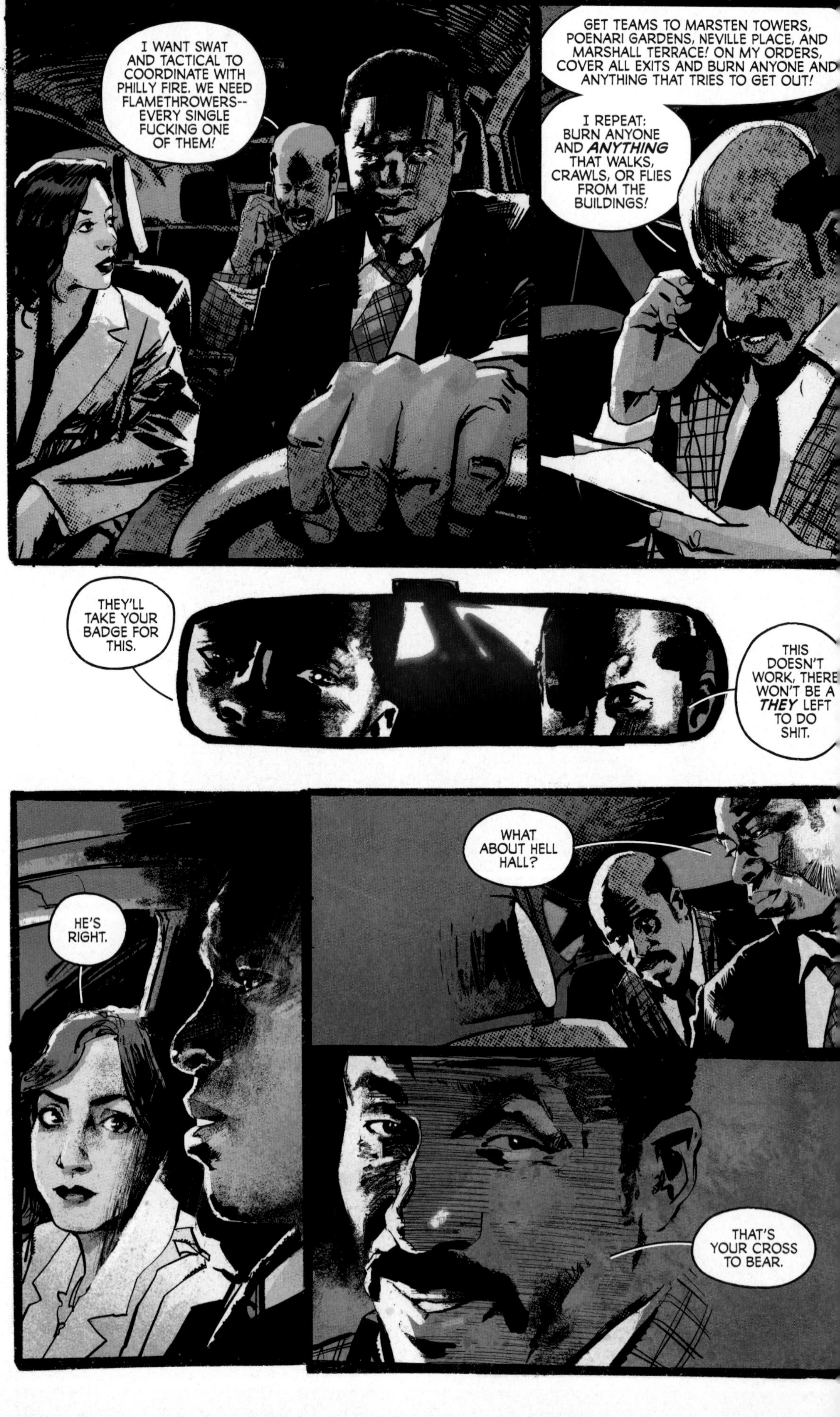
I WANT SWAT AND TACTICAL TO COORDINATE WITH PHILLY FIRE. WE NEED FLAMETHROWERS-- EVERY SINGLE FUCKING ONE OF THEM!
GET TEAMS TO MARSTEN TOWERS, POENARI GARDENS, NEVILLE PLACE, AND MARSHALL TERRACE! ON MY ORDERS, COVER ALL EXITS AND BURN ANYONE AND ANYTHING THAT TRIES TO GET OUT!
I REPEAT: BURN ANYONE AND ANYTHING THAT WALKS, CRAWLS, OR FLIES FROM THE BUILDINGS!
THEY'LL TAKE YOUR BADGE FOR THIS.
THIS DOESN'T WORK, THERE WON'T BE A THEY LEFT TO DO SHIT.
HE'S RIGHT.
WHAT ABOUT HELL HALL?
THAT'S YOUR CROSS TO BEAR.

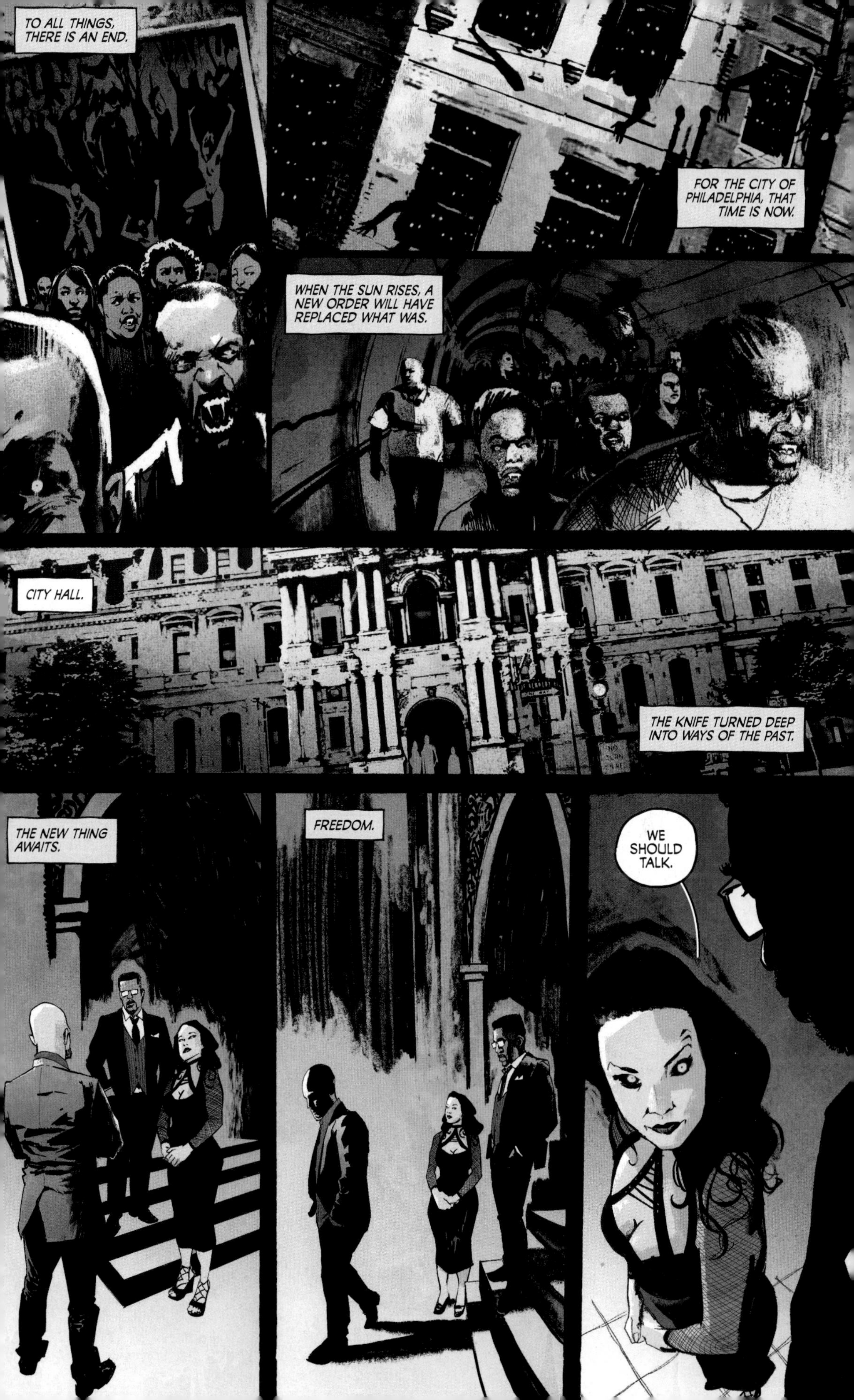

TO ALL THINGS, THERE IS AN END.
FOR THE CITY OF PHILADELPHIA, THAT TIME IS NOW.
WHEN THE SUN RISES, A NEW ORDER WILL HAVE REPLACED WHAT WAS.
CITY HALL.
THE KNIFE TURNED DEEP INTO WAYS OF THE PAST.
THE NEW THING AWAITS.
FREEDOM.
WE SHOULD TALK.

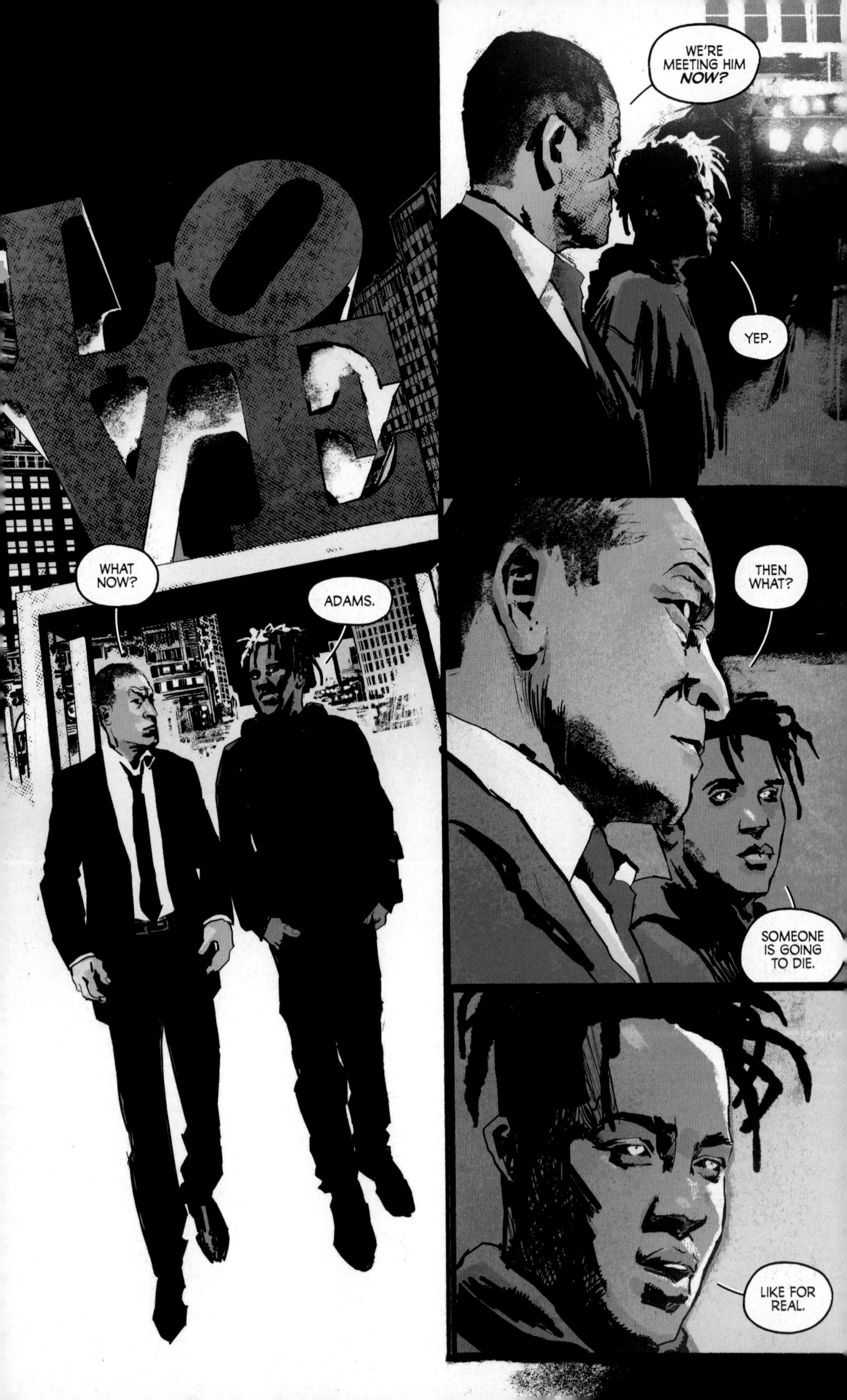
WHAT NOW?
ADAMS.
WE'RE MEETING HIM *NOW?*
YEP.
THEN WHAT?
SOMEONE IS GOING TO DIE.
LIKE FOR REAL.

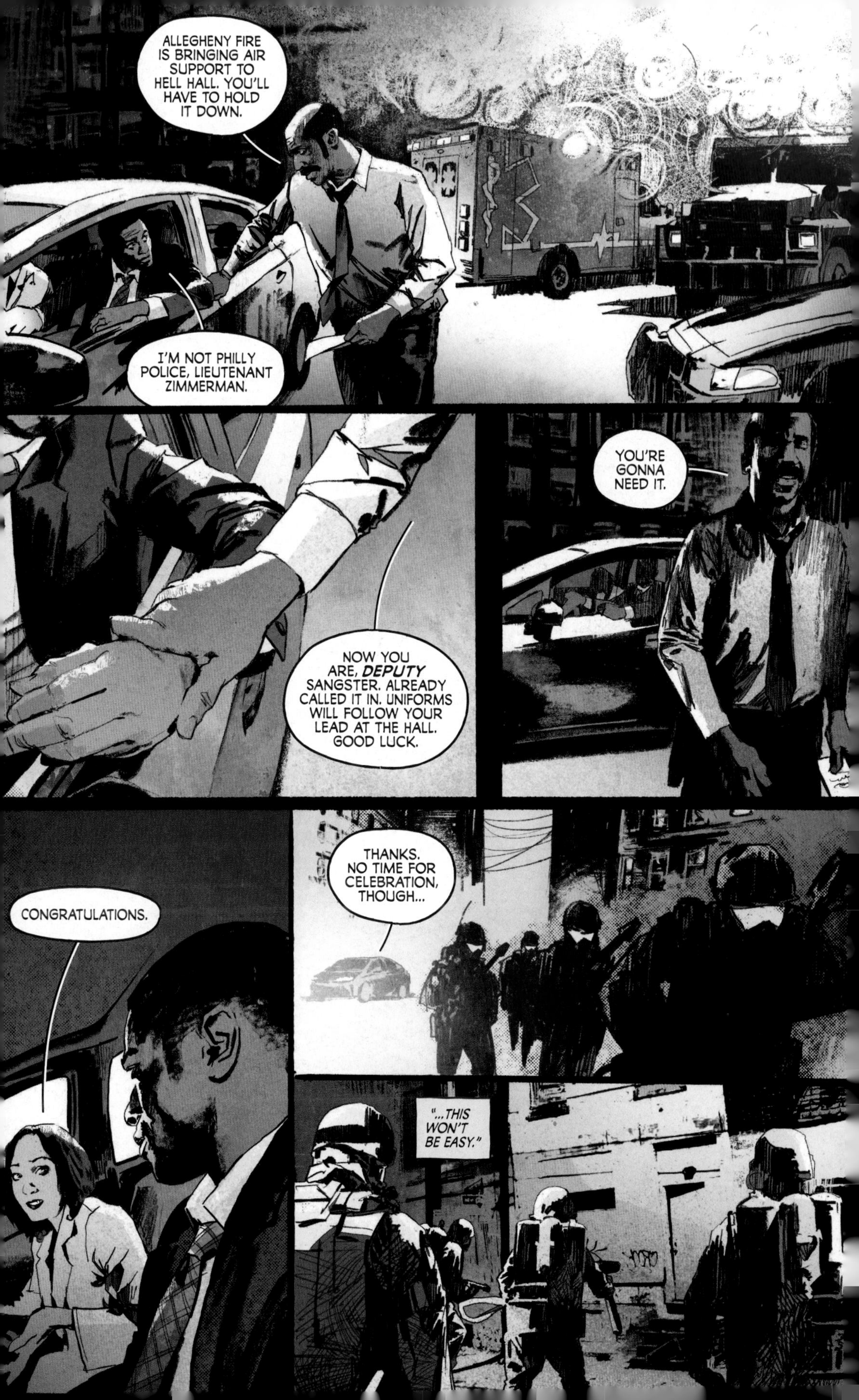
ALLEGHENY FIRE IS BRINGING AIR SUPPORT TO HELL HALL. YOU'LL HAVE TO HOLD IT DOWN.
I'M NOT PHILLY POLICE, LIEUTENANT ZIMMERMAN.
NOW YOU ARE, *DEPUTY* SANGSTER. ALREADY CALLED IT IN. UNIFORMS WILL FOLLOW YOUR LEAD AT THE HALL. GOOD LUCK.
YOU'RE GONNA NEED IT.
CONGRATULATIONS.
THANKS. NO TIME FOR CELEBRATION, THOUGH...
"...THIS WON'T BE EASY."

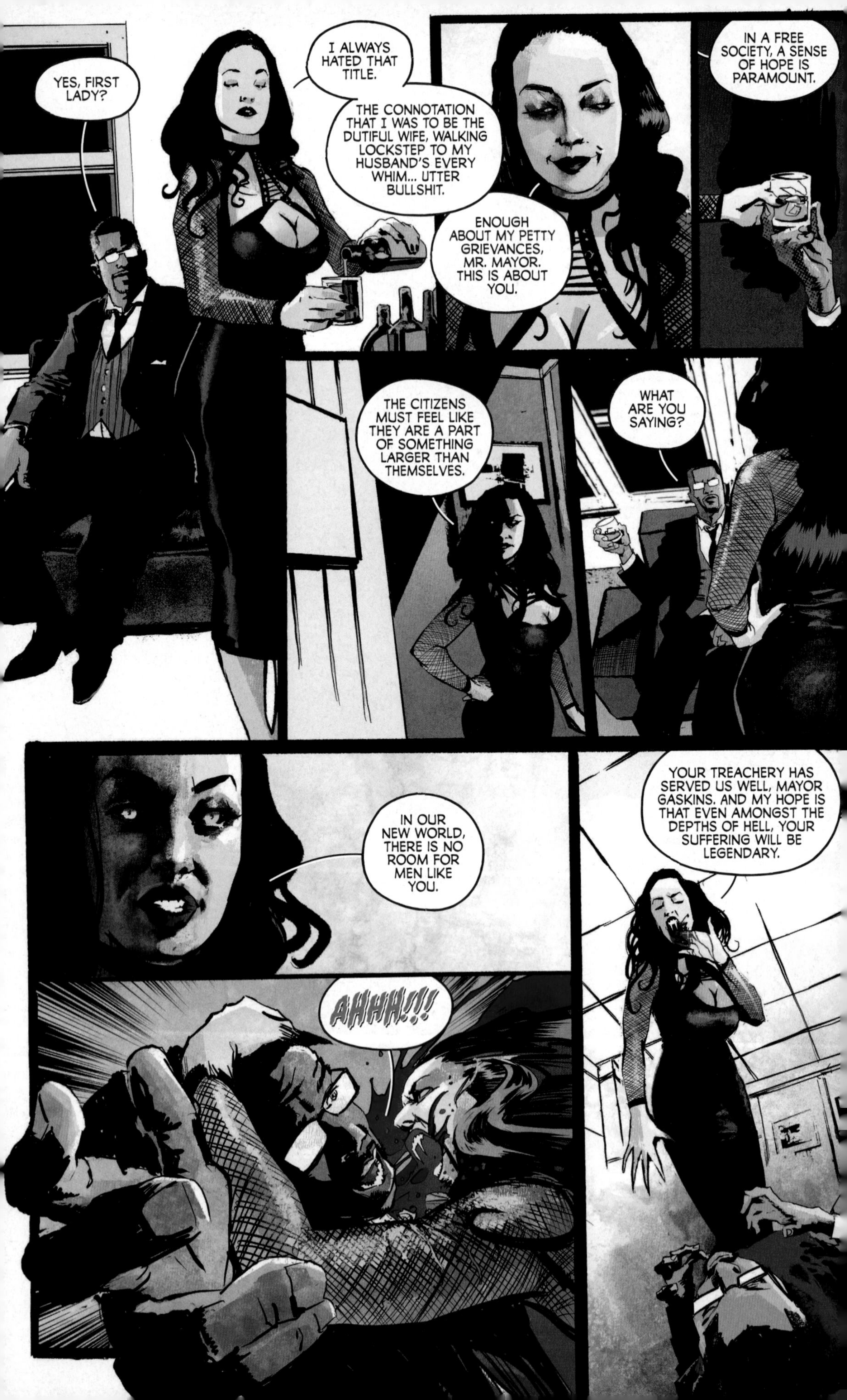
YES, FIRST LADY?
I ALWAYS HATED THAT TITLE.
THE CONNOTATION THAT I WAS TO BE THE DUTIFUL WIFE, WALKING LOCKSTEP TO MY HUSBAND'S EVERY WHIM... UTTER BULLSHIT.
ENOUGH ABOUT MY PETTY GRIEVANCES, MR. MAYOR. THIS IS ABOUT YOU.
IN A FREE SOCIETY, A SENSE OF HOPE IS PARAMOUNT.
THE CITIZENS MUST FEEL LIKE THEY ARE A PART OF SOMETHING LARGER THAN THEMSELVES.
WHAT ARE YOU SAYING?
IN OUR NEW WORLD, THERE IS NO ROOM FOR MEN LIKE YOU.
AHHH!!!
YOUR TREACHERY HAS SERVED US WELL, MAYOR GASKINS. AND MY HOPE IS THAT EVEN AMONGST THE DEPTHS OF HELL, YOUR SUFFERING WILL BE LEGENDARY.

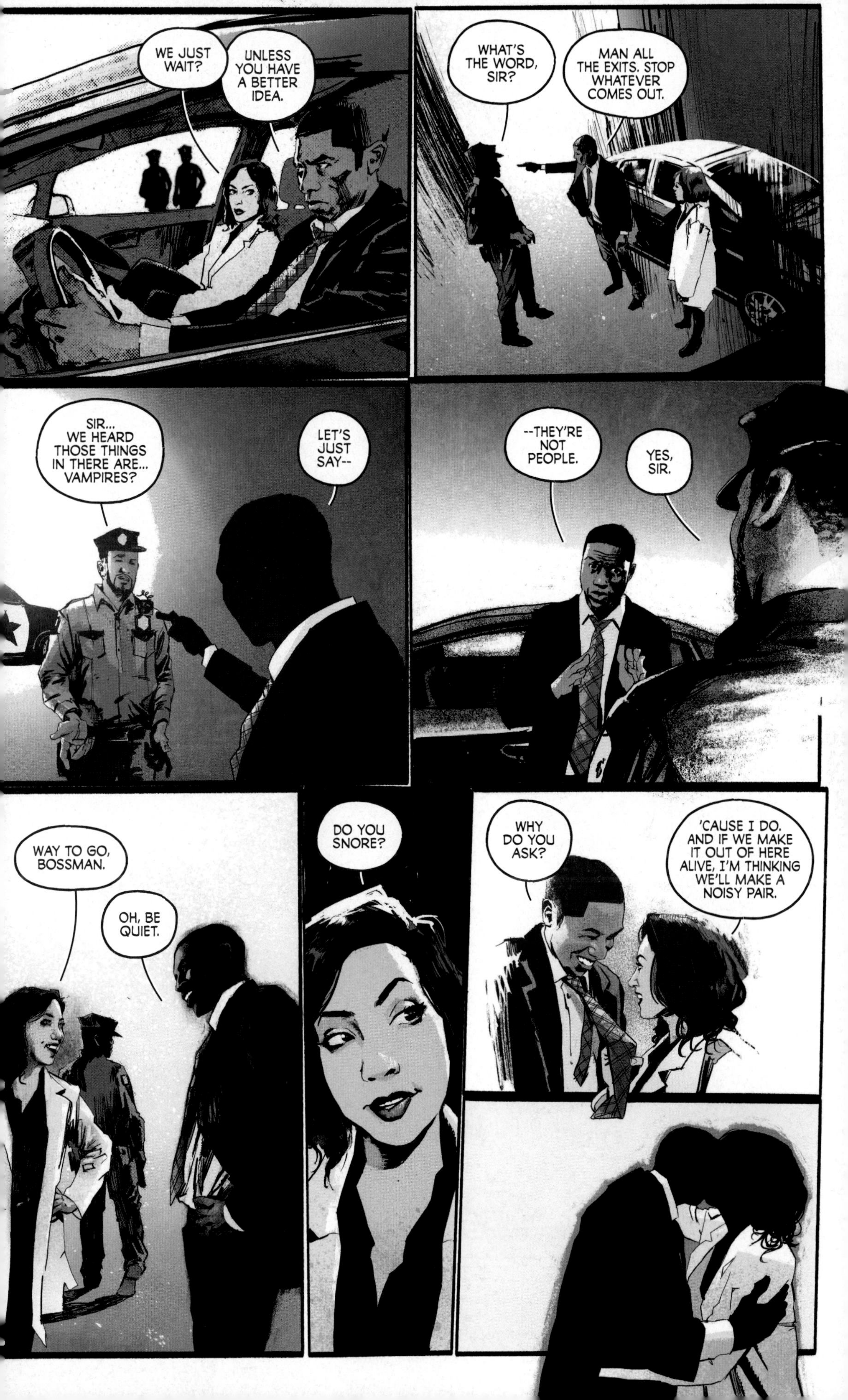
WE JUST WAIT?
UNLESS YOU HAVE A BETTER IDEA.
WHAT'S THE WORD, SIR?
MAN ALL THE EXITS. STOP WHATEVER COMES OUT.
SIR... WE HEARD THOSE THINGS IN THERE ARE... VAMPIRES?
LET'S JUST SAY--
--THEY'RE NOT PEOPLE.
YES, SIR.
WAY TO GO, BOSSMAN.
OH, BE QUIET.
DO YOU SNORE?
WHY DO YOU ASK?
'CAUSE I DO. AND IF WE MAKE IT OUT OF HERE ALIVE, I'M THINKING WE'LL MAKE A NOISY PAIR.

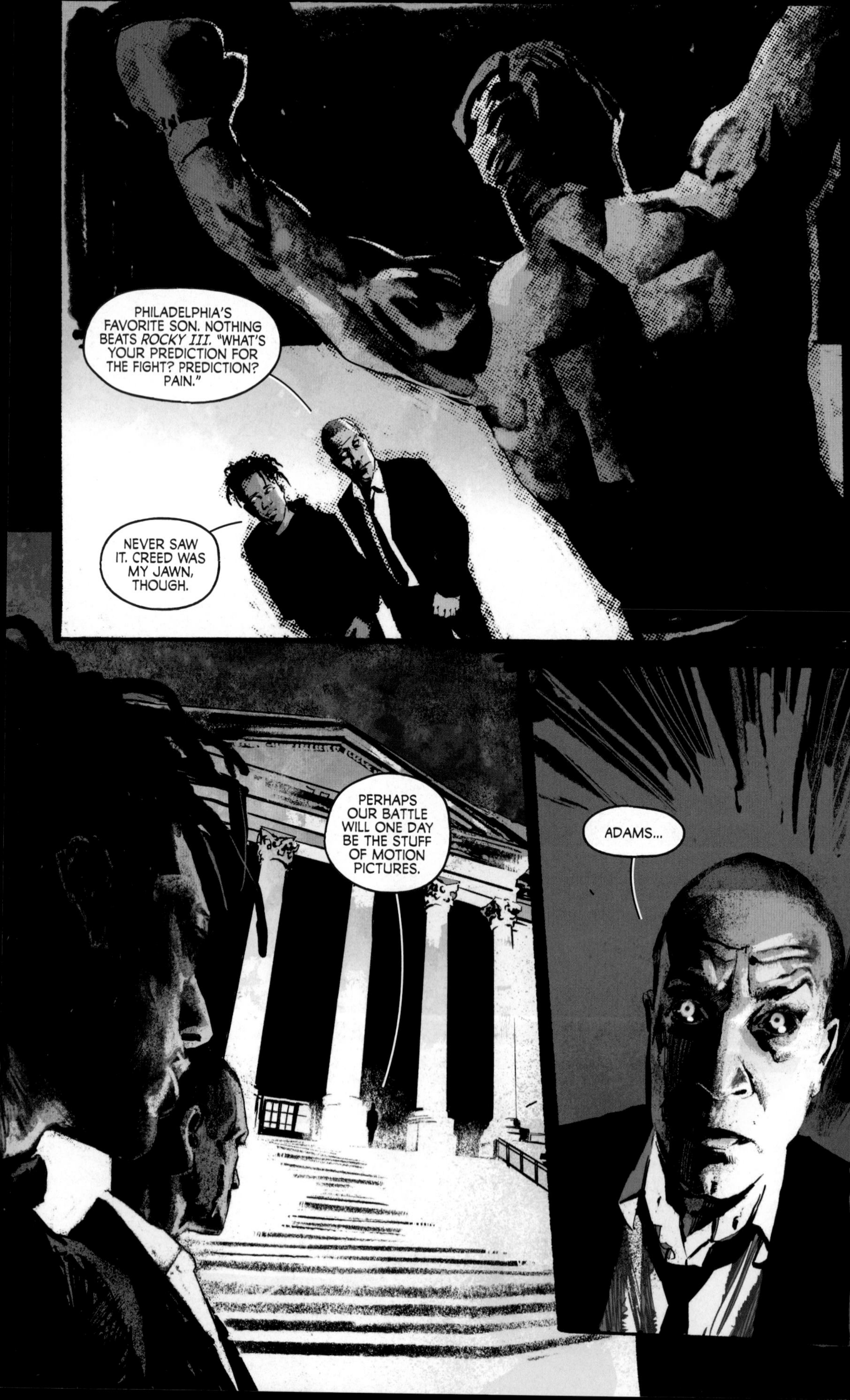
PHILADELPHIA'S FAVORITE SON. NOTHING BEATS *ROCKY III.* "WHAT'S YOUR PREDICTION FOR THE FIGHT? PREDICTION? PAIN."
NEVER SAW IT. CREED WAS MY JAWN, THOUGH.
PERHAPS OUR BATTLE WILL ONE DAY BE THE STUFF OF MOTION PICTURES.
ADAMS...

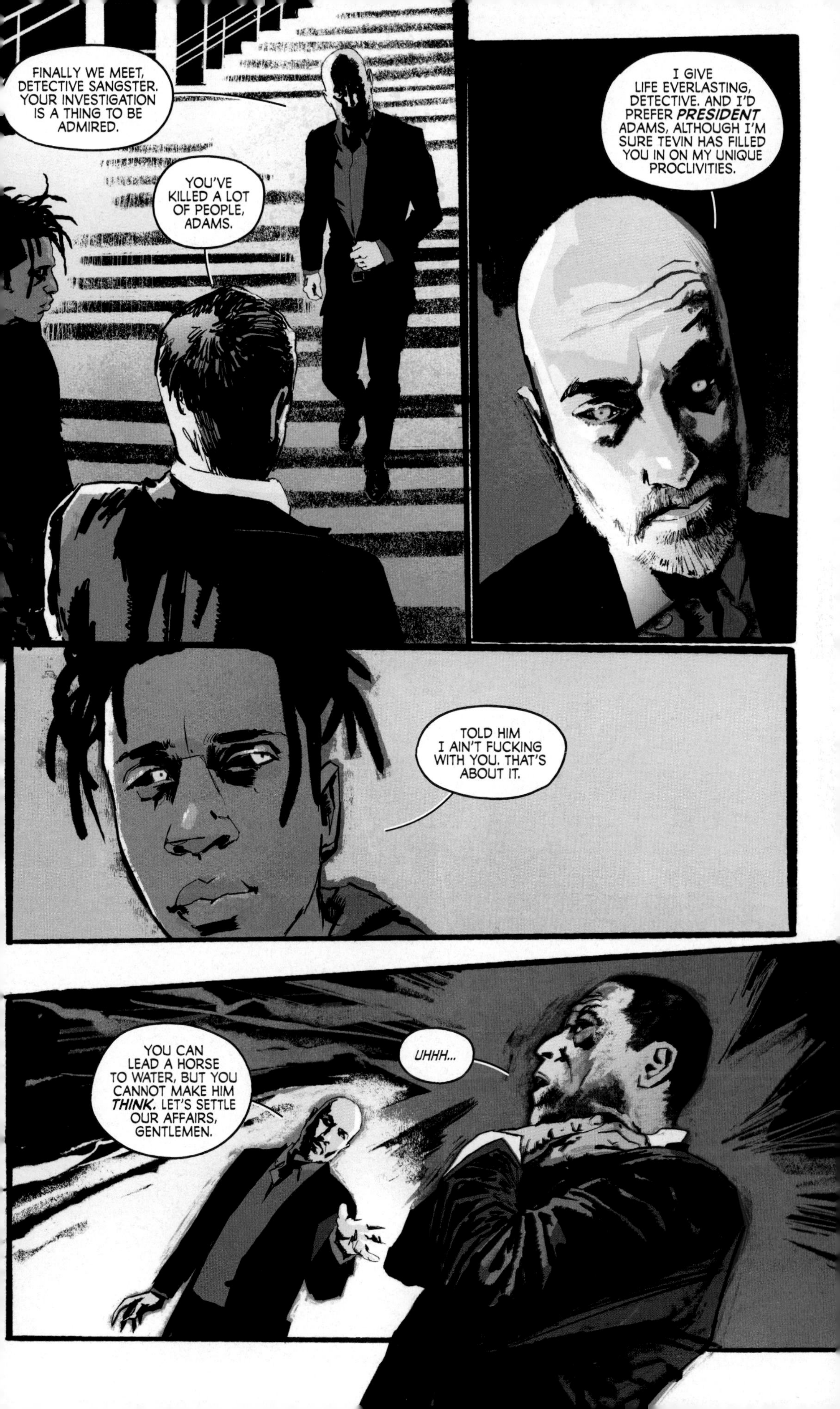
FINALLY WE MEET, DETECTIVE SANGSTER. YOUR INVESTIGATION IS A THING TO BE ADMIRED.
YOU'VE KILLED A LOT OF PEOPLE, ADAMS.
I GIVE LIFE EVERLASTING, DETECTIVE. AND I'D PREFER *PRESIDENT* ADAMS, ALTHOUGH I'M SURE TEVIN HAS FILLED YOU IN ON MY UNIQUE PROCLIVITIES.
TOLD HIM I AIN'T FUCKING WITH YOU. THAT'S ABOUT IT.
YOU CAN LEAD A HORSE TO WATER, BUT YOU CANNOT MAKE HIM *THINK*. LET'S SETTLE OUR AFFAIRS, GENTLEMEN.
UHHH...

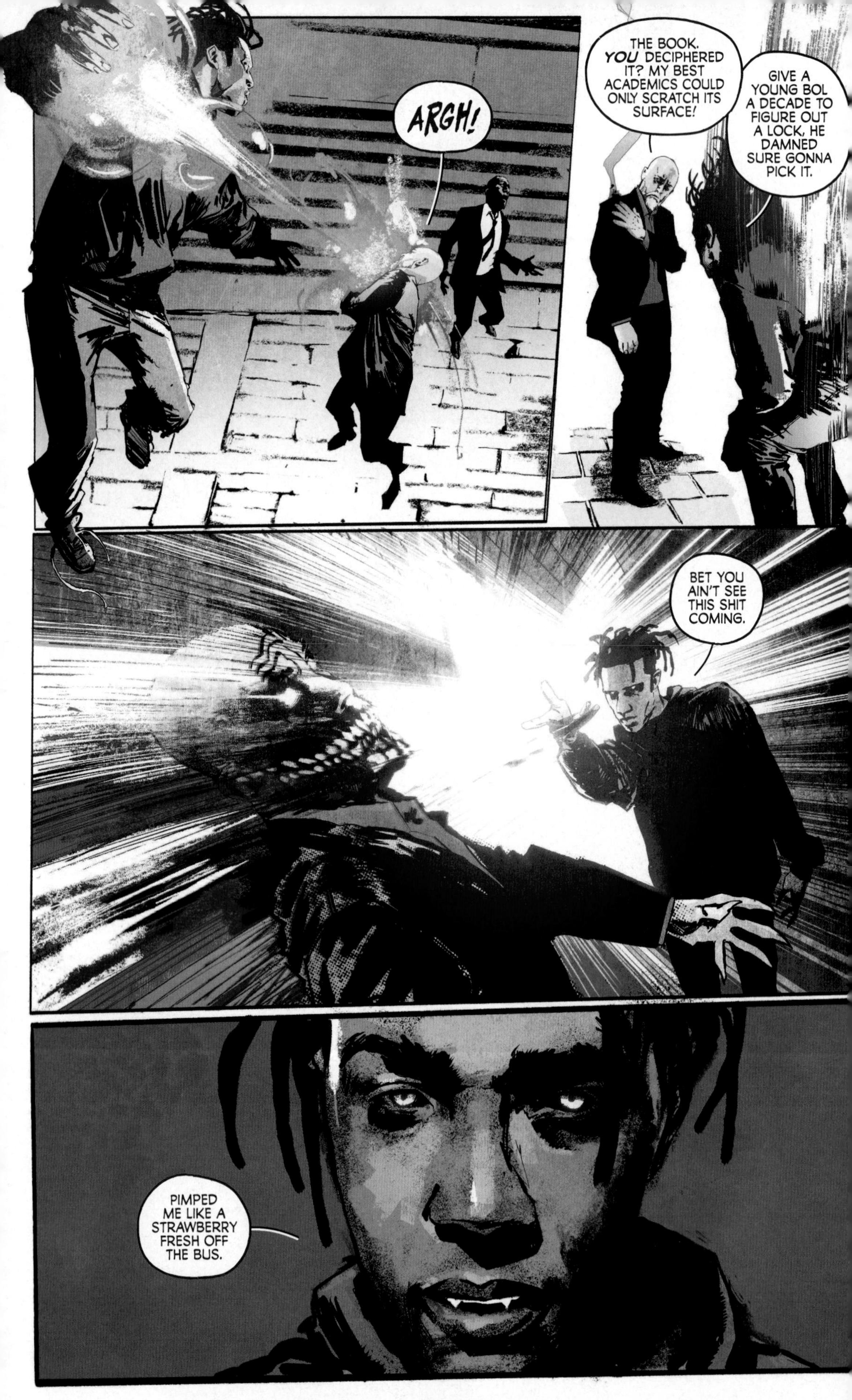
ARGH!
THE BOOK. YOU DECIPHERED IT? MY BEST ACADEMICS COULD ONLY SCRATCH ITS SURFACE!
GIVE A YOUNG BOL A DECADE TO FIGURE OUT A LOCK, HE DAMNED SURE GONNA PICK IT.
BET YOU AIN'T SEE THIS SHIT COMING.
PIMPED ME LIKE A STRAWBERRY FRESH OFF THE BUS.

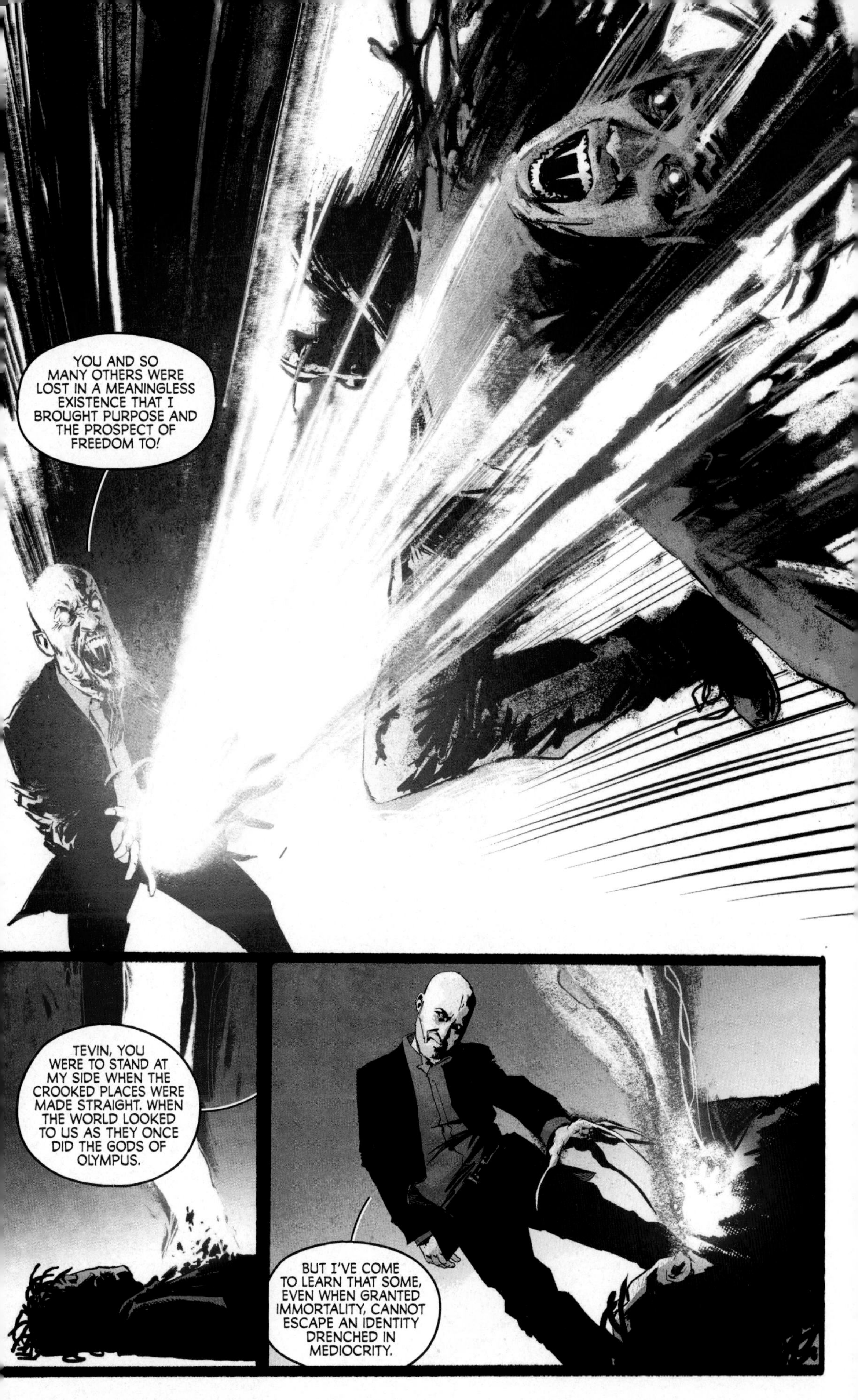
YOU AND SO MANY OTHERS WERE LOST IN A MEANINGLESS EXISTENCE THAT I BROUGHT PURPOSE AND THE PROSPECT OF FREEDOM TO!
TEVIN, YOU WERE TO STAND AT MY SIDE WHEN THE CROOKED PLACES WERE MADE STRAIGHT. WHEN THE WORLD LOOKED TO US AS THEY ONCE DID THE GODS OF OLYMPUS.
BUT I'VE COME TO LEARN THAT SOME, EVEN WHEN GRANTED IMMORTALITY, CANNOT ESCAPE AN IDENTITY DRENCHED IN MEDIOCRITY.

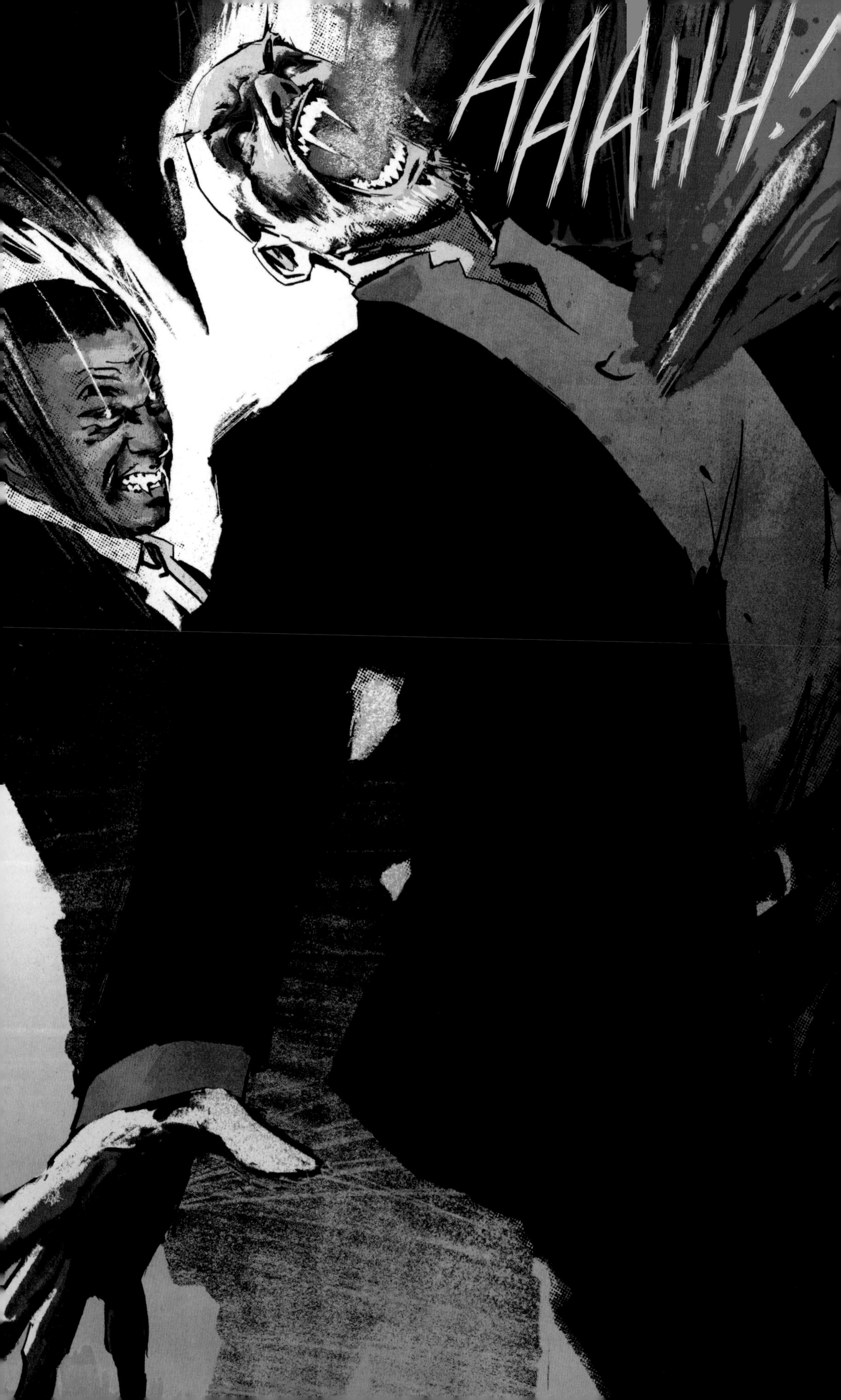
AAAHH!

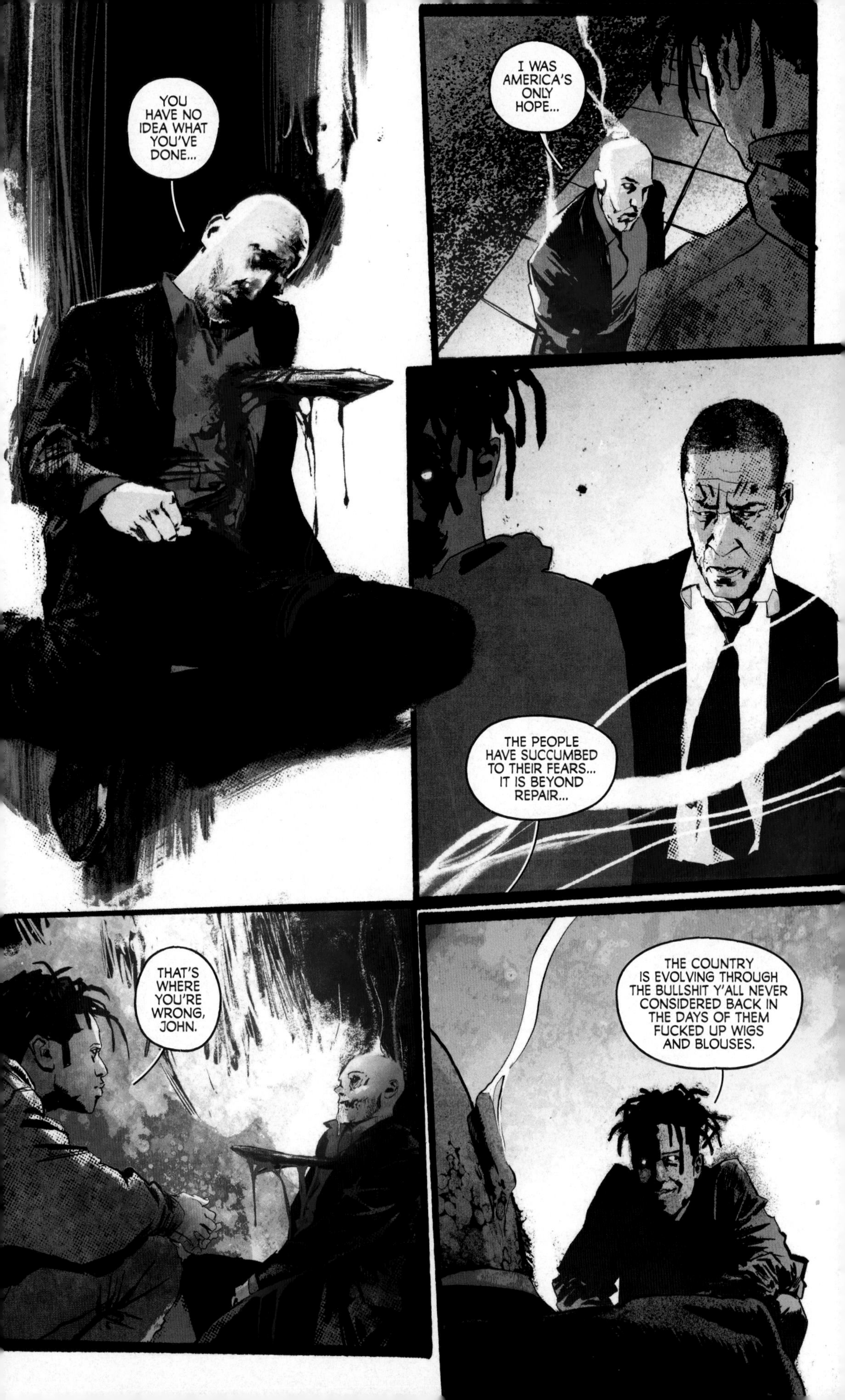
YOU HAVE NO IDEA WHAT YOU'VE DONE...
I WAS AMERICA'S ONLY HOPE...
THE PEOPLE HAVE SUCCUMBED TO THEIR FEARS... IT IS BEYOND REPAIR...
THAT'S WHERE YOU'RE WRONG, JOHN.
THE COUNTRY IS EVOLVING THROUGH THE BULLSHIT Y'ALL NEVER CONSIDERED BACK IN THE DAYS OF THEM FUCKED UP WIGS AND BLOUSES.

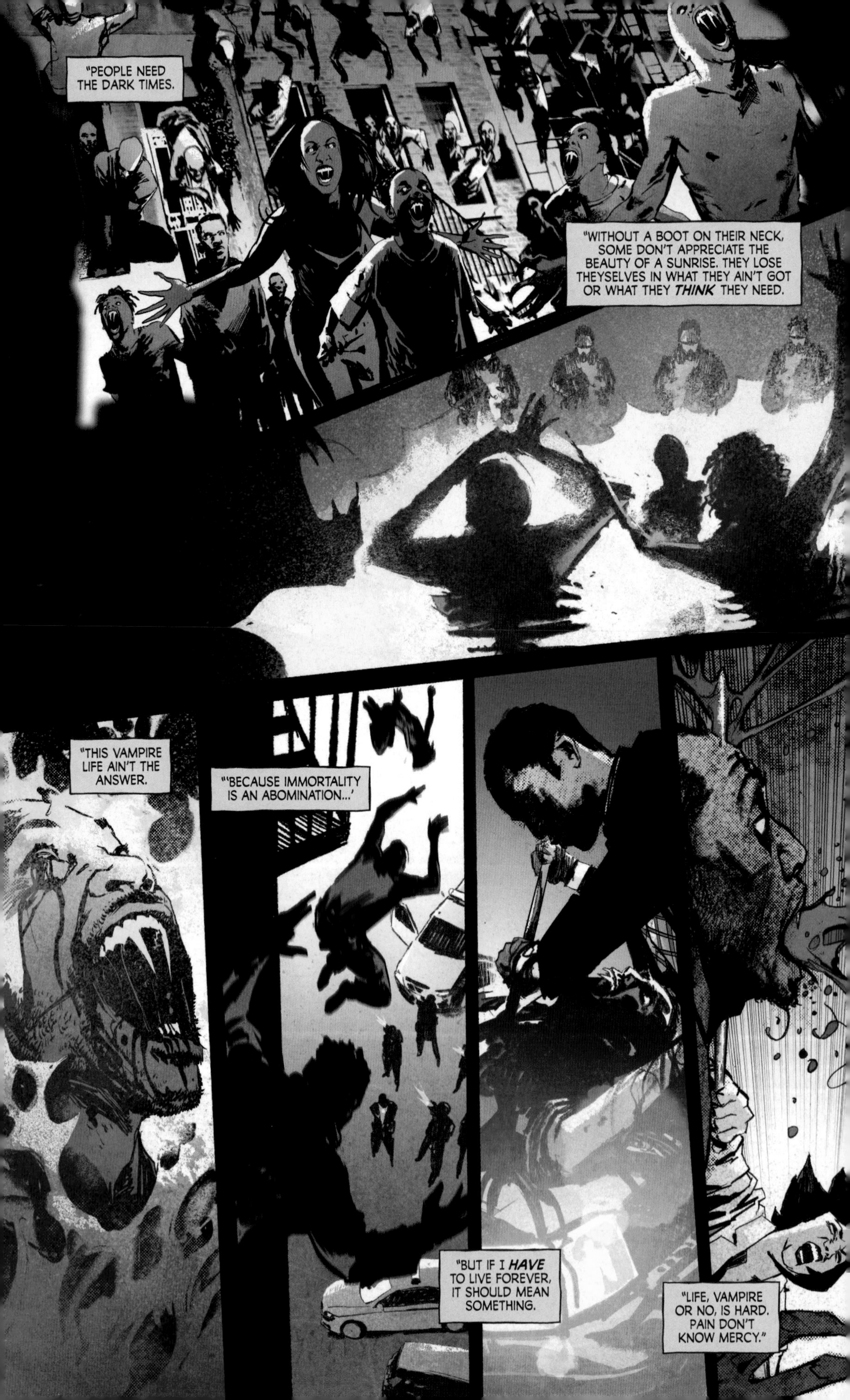
"PEOPLE NEED THE DARK TIMES.
"WITHOUT A BOOT ON THEIR NECK, SOME DON'T APPRECIATE THE BEAUTY OF A SUNRISE. THEY LOSE THEYSELVES IN WHAT THEY AIN'T GOT OR WHAT THEY *THINK* THEY NEED.
"THIS VAMPIRE LIFE AIN'T THE ANSWER.
"'BECAUSE IMMORTALITY IS AN ABOMINATION...'
"BUT IF I *HAVE* TO LIVE FOREVER, IT SHOULD MEAN SOMETHING.
"LIFE, VAMPIRE OR NO, IS HARD. PAIN DON'T KNOW MERCY."

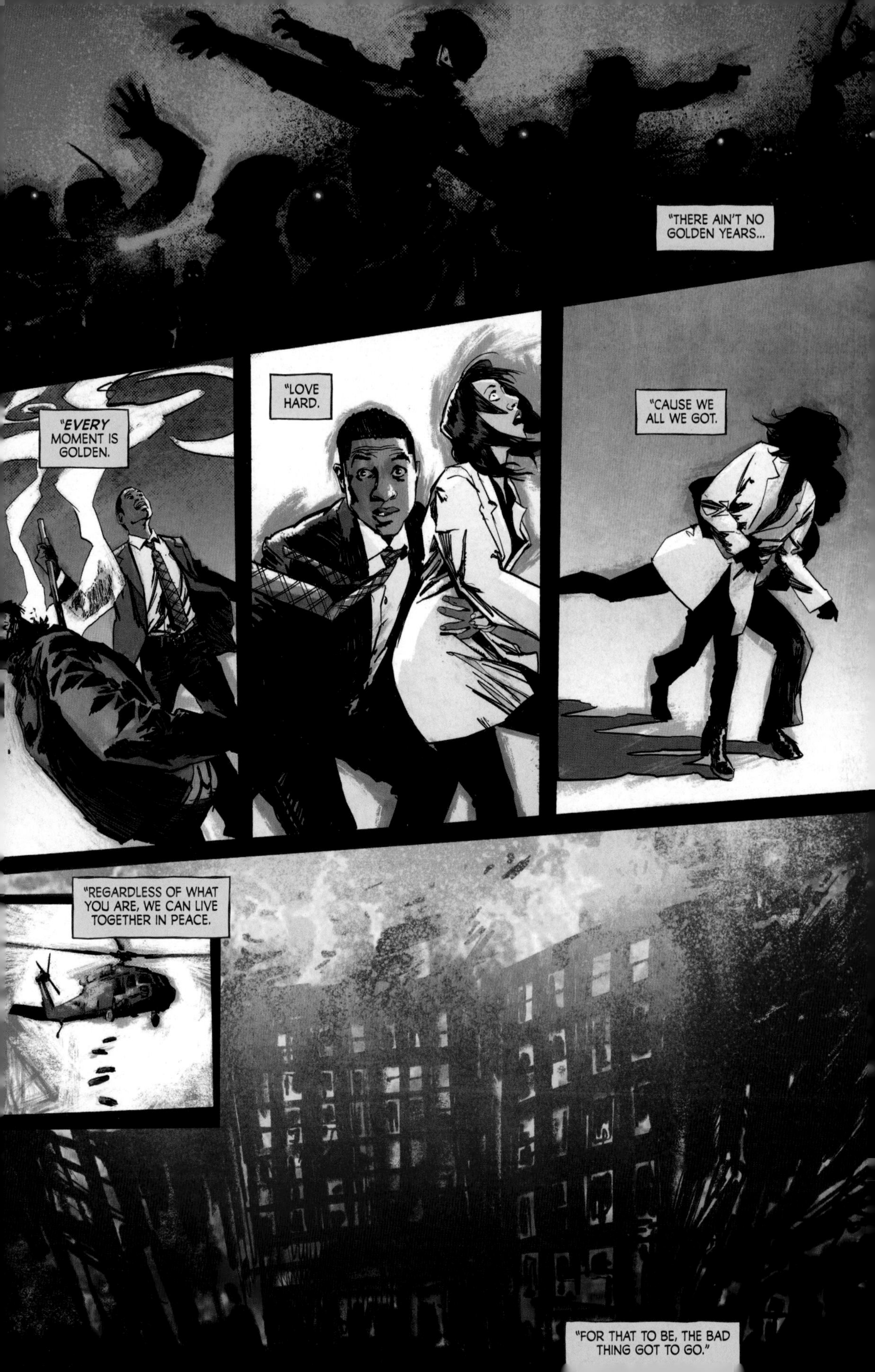
"THERE AIN'T NO GOLDEN YEARS...
"*EVERY* MOMENT IS GOLDEN.
"LOVE HARD.
"CAUSE WE ALL WE GOT.
"REGARDLESS OF WHAT YOU ARE, WE CAN LIVE TOGETHER IN PEACE.
"FOR THAT TO BE, THE BAD THING GOT TO GO."

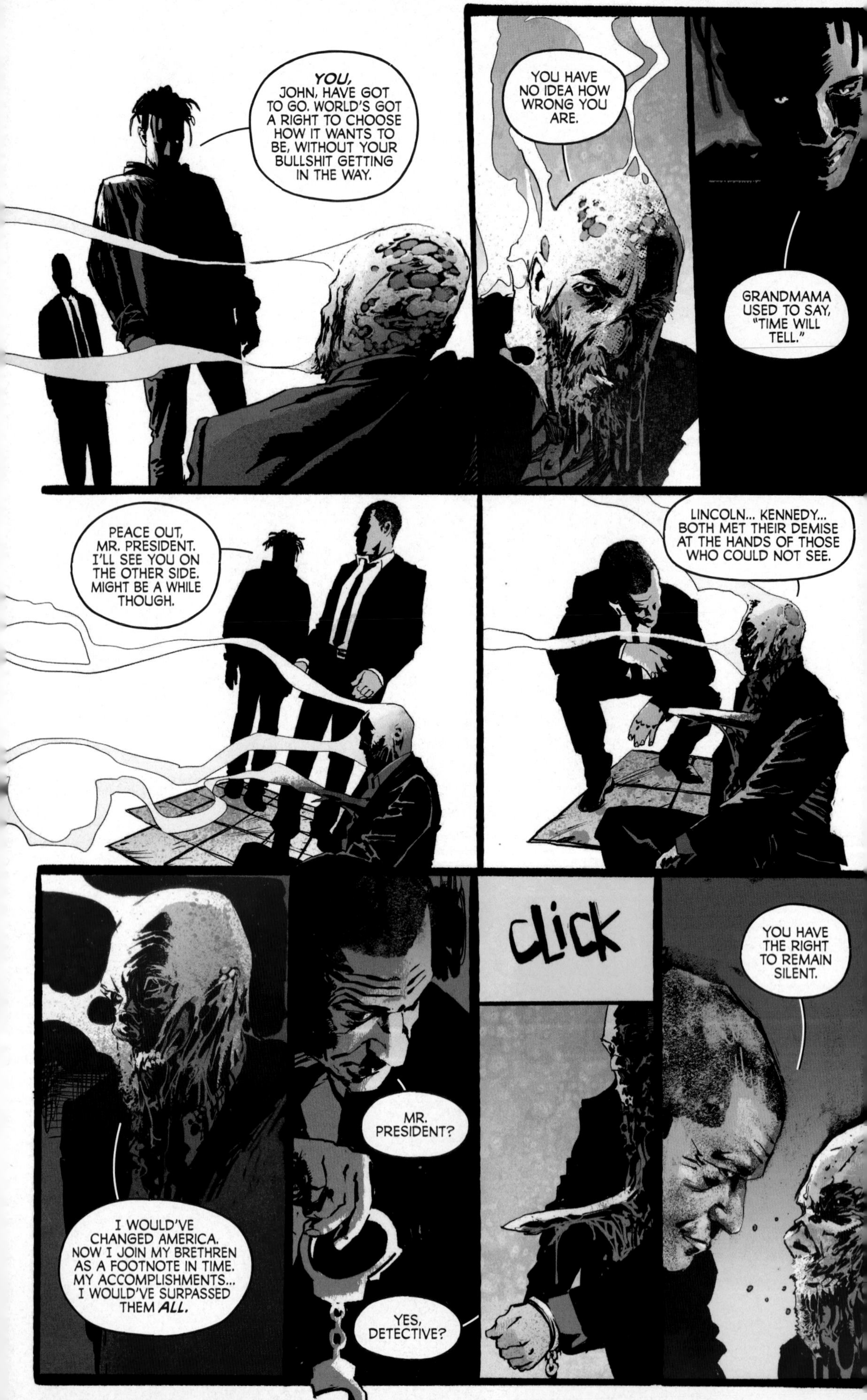
YOU, JOHN, HAVE GOT TO GO. WORLD'S GOT A RIGHT TO CHOOSE HOW IT WANTS TO BE, WITHOUT YOUR BULLSHIT GETTING IN THE WAY.
YOU HAVE NO IDEA HOW WRONG YOU ARE.
GRANDMAMA USED TO SAY, "TIME WILL TELL."
PEACE OUT, MR. PRESIDENT. I'LL SEE YOU ON THE OTHER SIDE. MIGHT BE A WHILE THOUGH.
LINCOLN... KENNEDY... BOTH MET THEIR DEMISE AT THE HANDS OF THOSE WHO COULD NOT SEE.
I WOULD'VE CHANGED AMERICA. NOW I JOIN MY BRETHREN AS A FOOTNOTE IN TIME. MY ACCOMPLISHMENTS... I WOULD'VE SURPASSED THEM ALL.
MR. PRESIDENT?
YES, DETECTIVE?
CLICK
YOU HAVE THE RIGHT TO REMAIN SILENT.

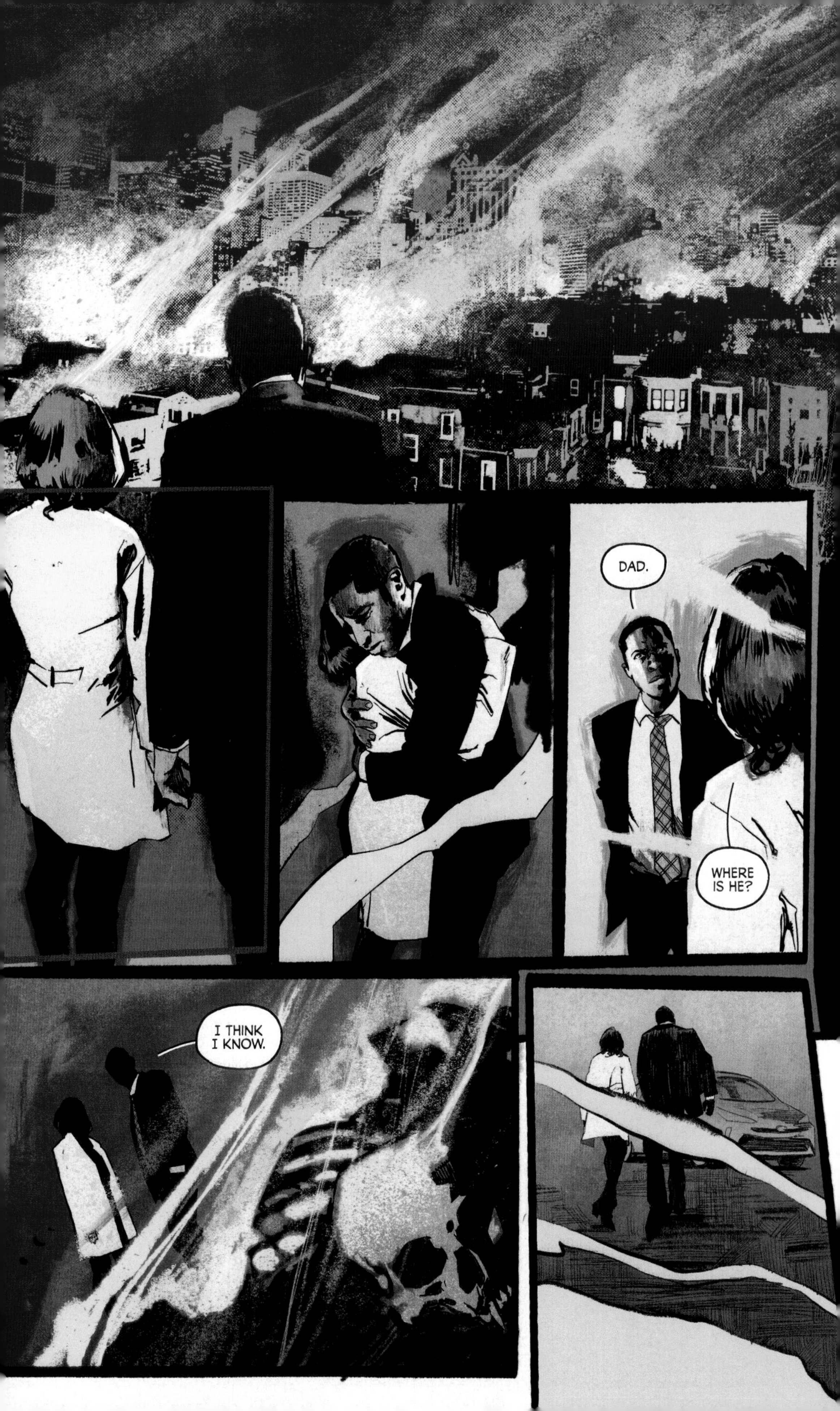
DAD.
WHERE IS HE?
I THINK I KNOW.

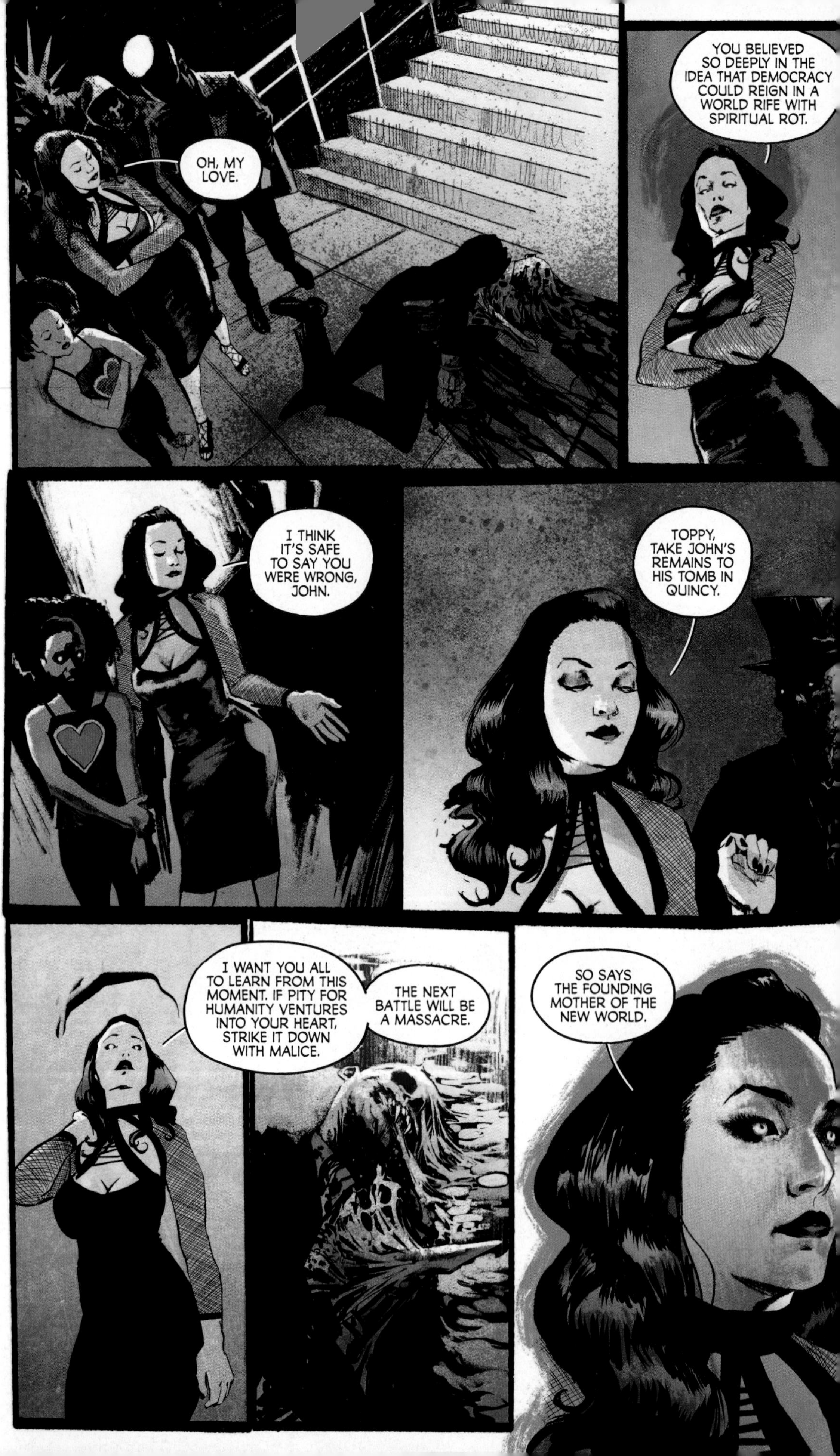
OH, MY LOVE.
YOU BELIEVED SO DEEPLY IN THE IDEA THAT DEMOCRACY COULD REIGN IN A WORLD RIFE WITH SPIRITUAL ROT.
I THINK IT'S SAFE TO SAY YOU WERE WRONG, JOHN.
TOPPY, TAKE JOHN'S REMAINS TO HIS TOMB IN QUINCY.
I WANT YOU ALL TO LEARN FROM THIS MOMENT. IF PITY FOR HUMANITY VENTURES INTO YOUR HEART, STRIKE IT DOWN WITH MALICE.
THE NEXT BATTLE WILL BE A MASSACRE.
SO SAYS THE FOUNDING MOTHER OF THE NEW WORLD.

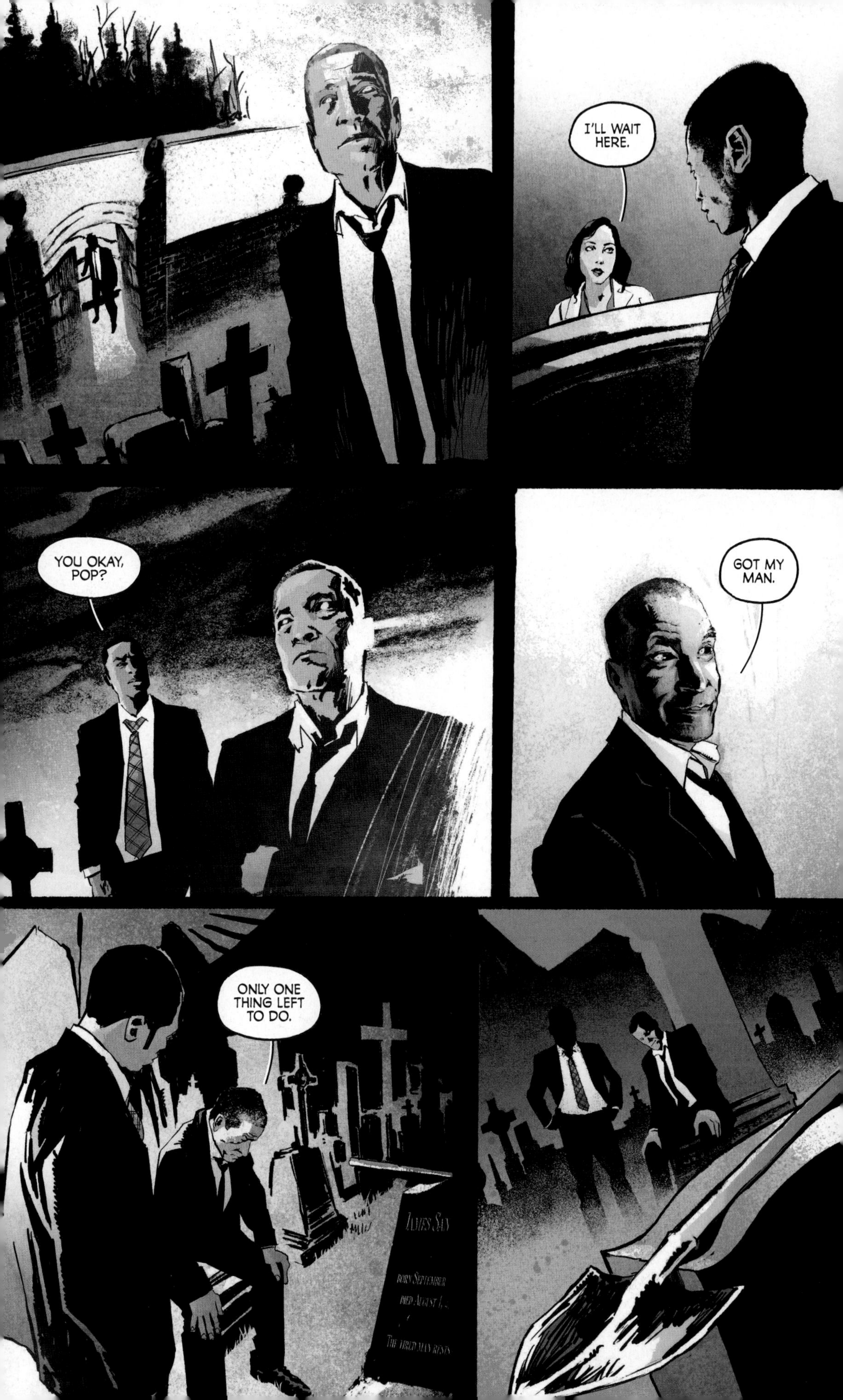
I'LL WAIT HERE.
YOU OKAY, POP?
GOT MY MAN.
ONLY ONE THING LEFT TO DO.

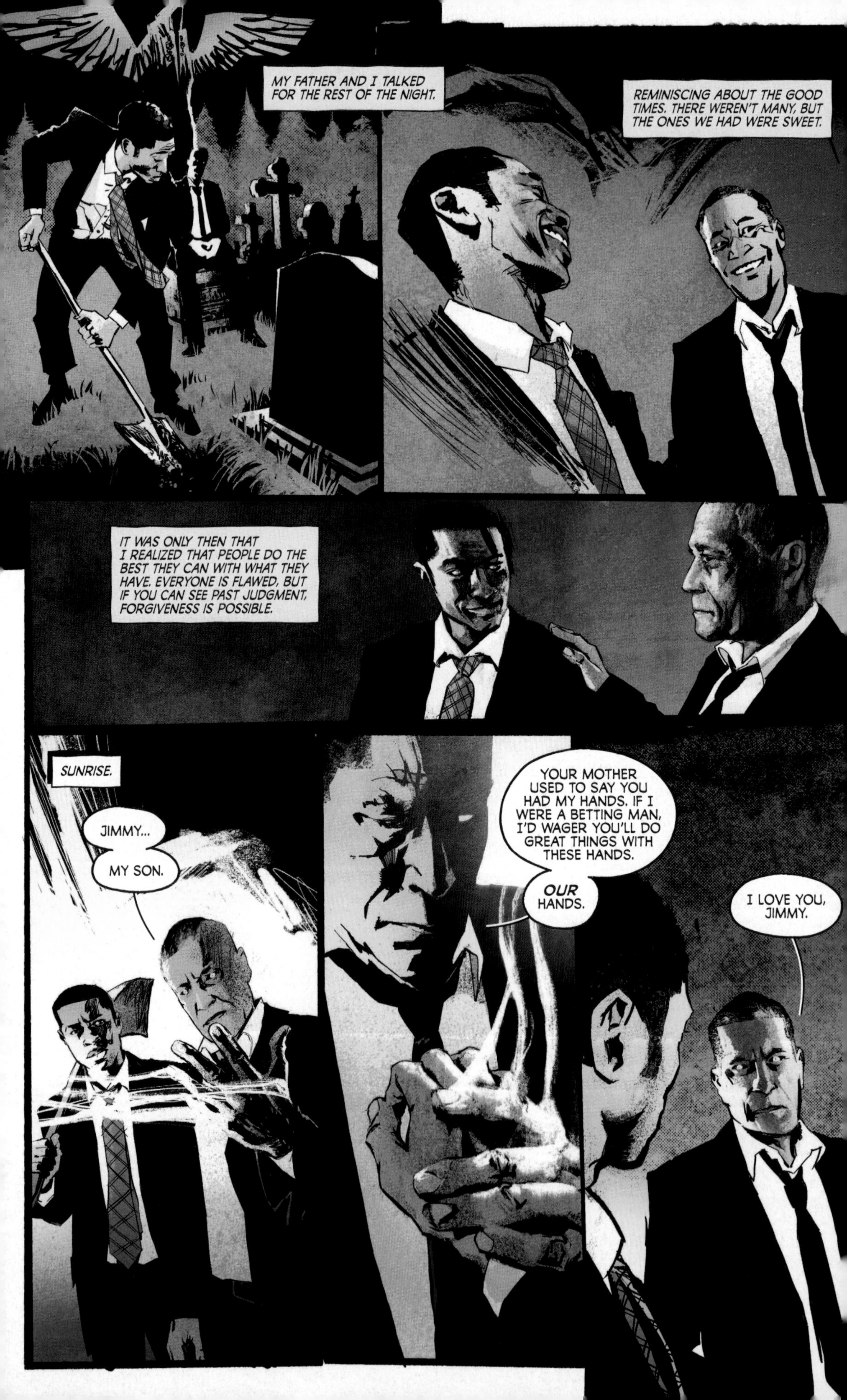
MY FATHER AND I TALKED FOR THE REST OF THE NIGHT.
REMINISCING ABOUT THE GOOD TIMES. THERE WEREN'T MANY, BUT THE ONES WE HAD WERE SWEET.
IT WAS ONLY THEN THAT I REALIZED THAT PEOPLE DO THE BEST THEY CAN WITH WHAT THEY HAVE. EVERYONE IS FLAWED, BUT IF YOU CAN SEE PAST JUDGMENT, FORGIVENESS IS POSSIBLE.
SUNRISE.
JIMMY...
MY SON.
YOUR MOTHER USED TO SAY YOU HAD MY HANDS. IF I WERE A BETTING MAN, I'D WAGER YOU'LL DO GREAT THINGS WITH THESE HANDS.
OUR HANDS.
I LOVE YOU, JIMMY.

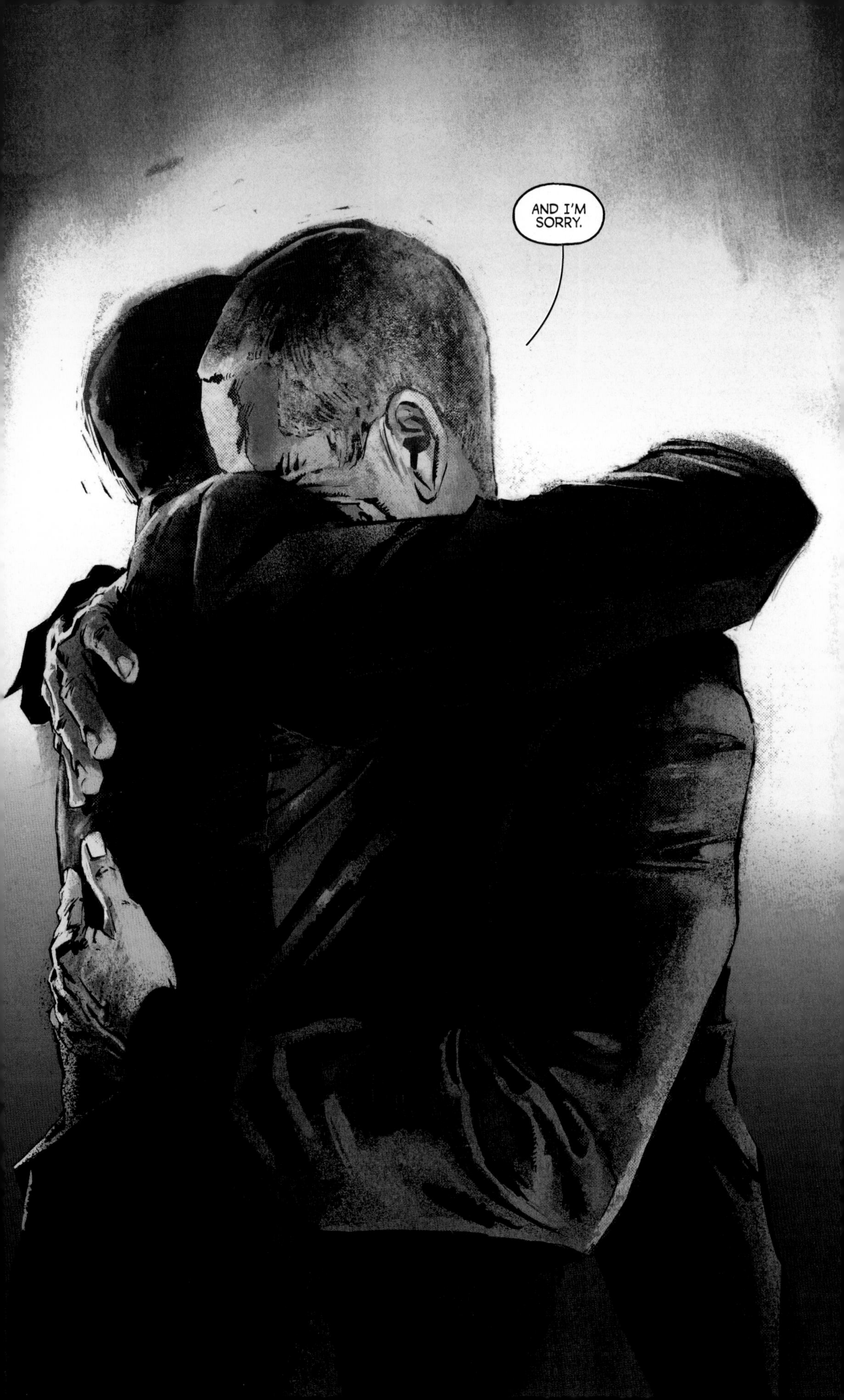
AND I'M SORRY.

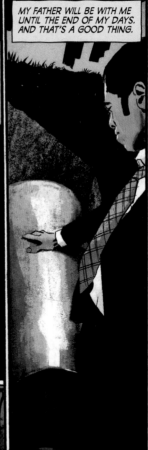

MY FATHER WILL BE WITH ME UNTIL THE END OF MY DAYS. AND THAT'S A GOOD THING.

I'M PROUD TO BE HIS SON.

JAMES SANGSTER SR.

BORN SEPTEMBER 19, 1963
DIED AUGUST 1, 2017

THE TIRED MAN RESTS.

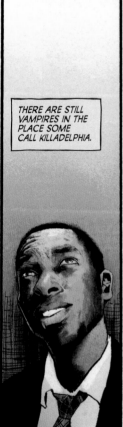

THERE ARE STILL VAMPIRES IN THE PLACE SOME CALL KILLADELPHIA.

SOMEONE WILL HAVE TO ENSURE THEY NEVER RISE UP.

JAMES SANGSTER JR. ACCEPTS THAT RESPONSIBILITY.

BECAUSE THAT'S WHAT MY FATHER WOULD DO.

THE END.

AFTERWORD

So that, my friends, is the end of the first story arc of *Killadelphia*. If you've been with us from the beginning, **thank you**. If you're just hopping on board, **thank you** as well! I wanted to take this time to answer a couple of frequently asked questions about the book as well as shout-out a few acknowledgements before the sun comes up and I have to pull down the shades.

WHY JOHN ADAMS?

The idea for this book had been swirling around my imagination since I was a kid. The television movies of the week and subsequent show *Kolchak: The Night Stalker* starring Darren McGavin (written by the late, great Richard Matheson) changed my life. The basic math of "vampire comes to the city and the cops try to stop it" was born.

But as I watched a number of vampire movies and read a bunch of books, I soon learned that a number of other writers had that math to their vampire-themed stories as well. So I needed a wild card, and on my sixth trip to the musical *Hamilton*, it hit me. "John Adams!" Now, a lot of folks have seen *Hamilton* and I doubt few have walked out thinking John Adams was a vampire.

But I did.

Of all the founding fathers, John seemed to get the least amount of appreciation from historians. What if he were alive today to see the degree of criticism he's received? What if he'd walked through time and watched America evolve from the idea of freedom (even though slavery existed in his day) to the polarized society we currently call home? What if he had the power to change the course of an America he helped design?

Those questions and more were the straws that stirred the idea. And although I'm biased, I think he made a fine vampire.

THE SANGSTER STORY—WHERE DID IT COME FROM?

My biological father wasn't a regular part of my upbringing, and my stepfather and I often did not see eye to eye. For a long time, I took the struggles in both relationships personally. It wasn't until I became a young parent that I realized we all do the best we can. My hope is that my children forgive me for my shortcomings as a father, and along that same train of thought, perhaps I should do the same for my parents.

So the Sangster story is a combination of my relationships with my fathers, my son, and several of my friends that struggle to find peace in their relationships with their parents. This, in part, is a tribute to them.

THANK YOU

First, Jason Shawn Alexander. My friend, my brother, and one of the greatest artists this industry has ever seen. Can't thank you enough for bringing this story to life and holding me accountable throughout the process. I look forward to many years of collaboration as this has been one of the best of my career. I apologize for always having to meet at Delmonico's and promise for the second arc's meetings we'll add some variety to our dinner meetings.

Luis NCT, Marshall Dillon, Greg Tumbarello, Shannon Bailey, and Brent Ashe—you guys are phenomenal! I can't imagine attempting to put this book together without your collective talents. Thank you. Thank you. Thank you.

As well, thank you Image Comics for your faith and support for *Killadelphia*.

My manager and friend Brian Dobbins, who has listened to me whine for years about "this vampire idea." As well, a big shout-out goes to Darrell Miller, my longtime attorney and friend. I appreciate both of your support not only in this process, but the one that's to come.

To Tory Metzger, Renee Witt, and the fine folks at Levantine Films, thank you for your passion and belief in *Killadelphia*. To my assistant Carlos Gutierrez, who is typing this and surprised to see his name, thank you for all of your hard work and patience.

To my family. You are my foundation and I love you with all of my heart. To you, the fans of *Killadelphia*, thank you! I promise there's more to come and I hope it's to your liking. Last, but not least, to the city of Philadelphia—a city that has a lot of heart and the spirit of a champion. Thank you for being you.

Rodney Barnes
Los Angeles, 2020

P.S. There are still vampires in Philadelphia. They hate the idea of losing (like the Sixers and Eagles) and vow to come back with a vengeance! And this time, they just might win… —RB

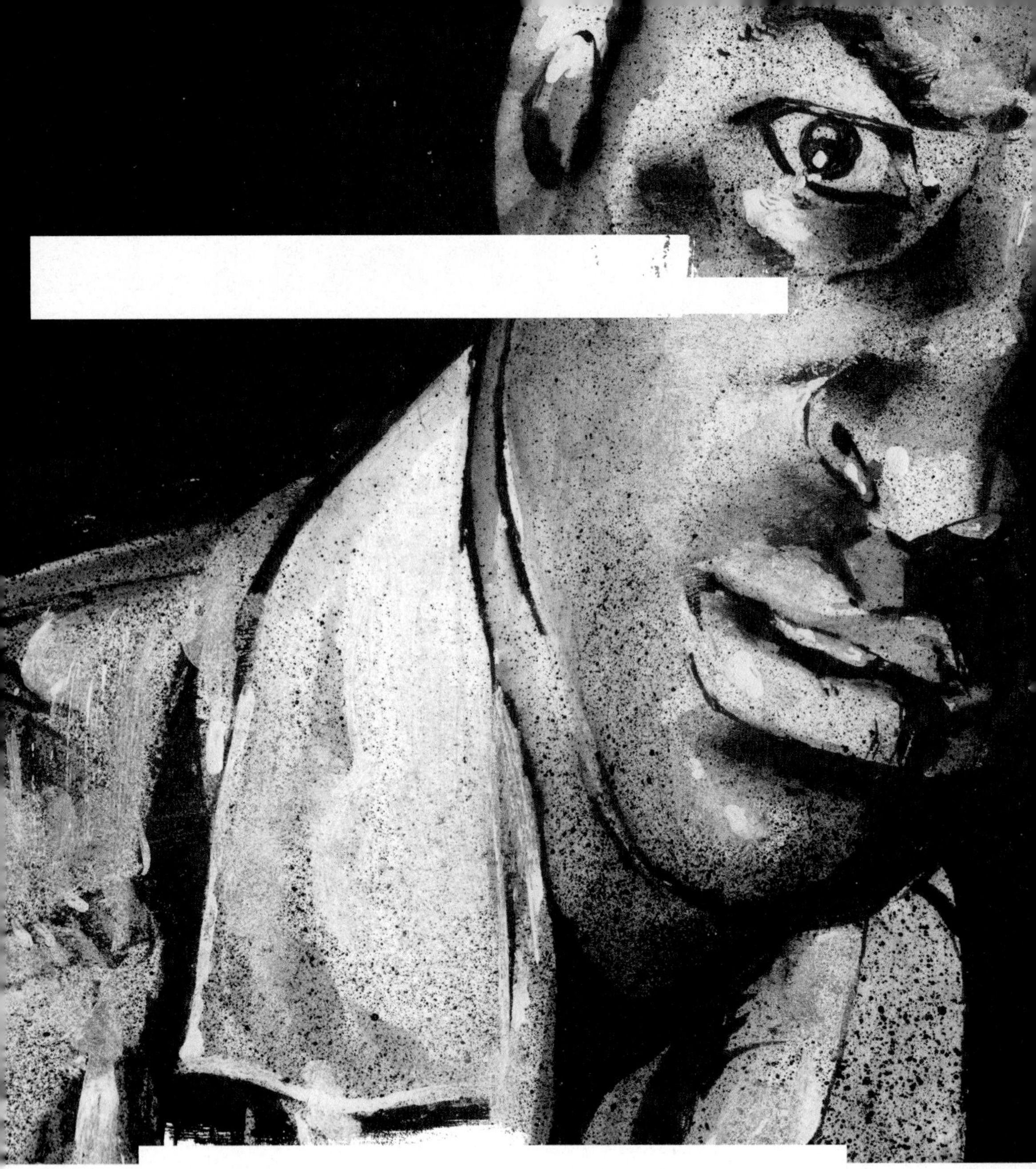

1_MAIN VERSIONS [01-06 +LCSD]
2_VARIANT EDITIONS [01-06]

COVER GALLERY

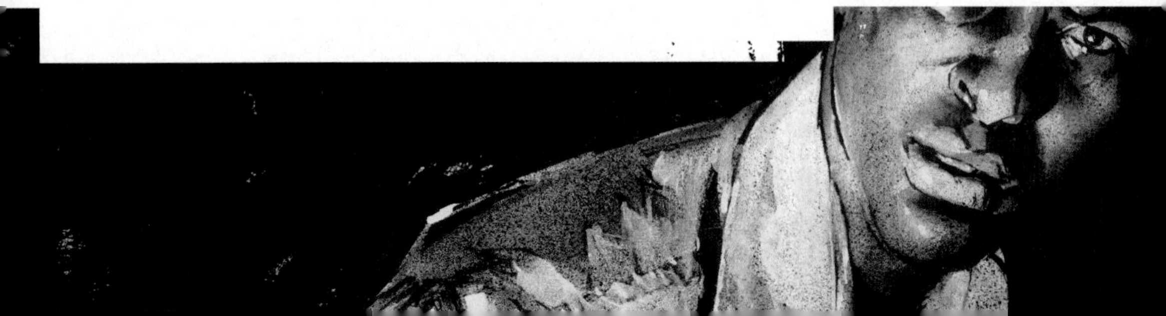

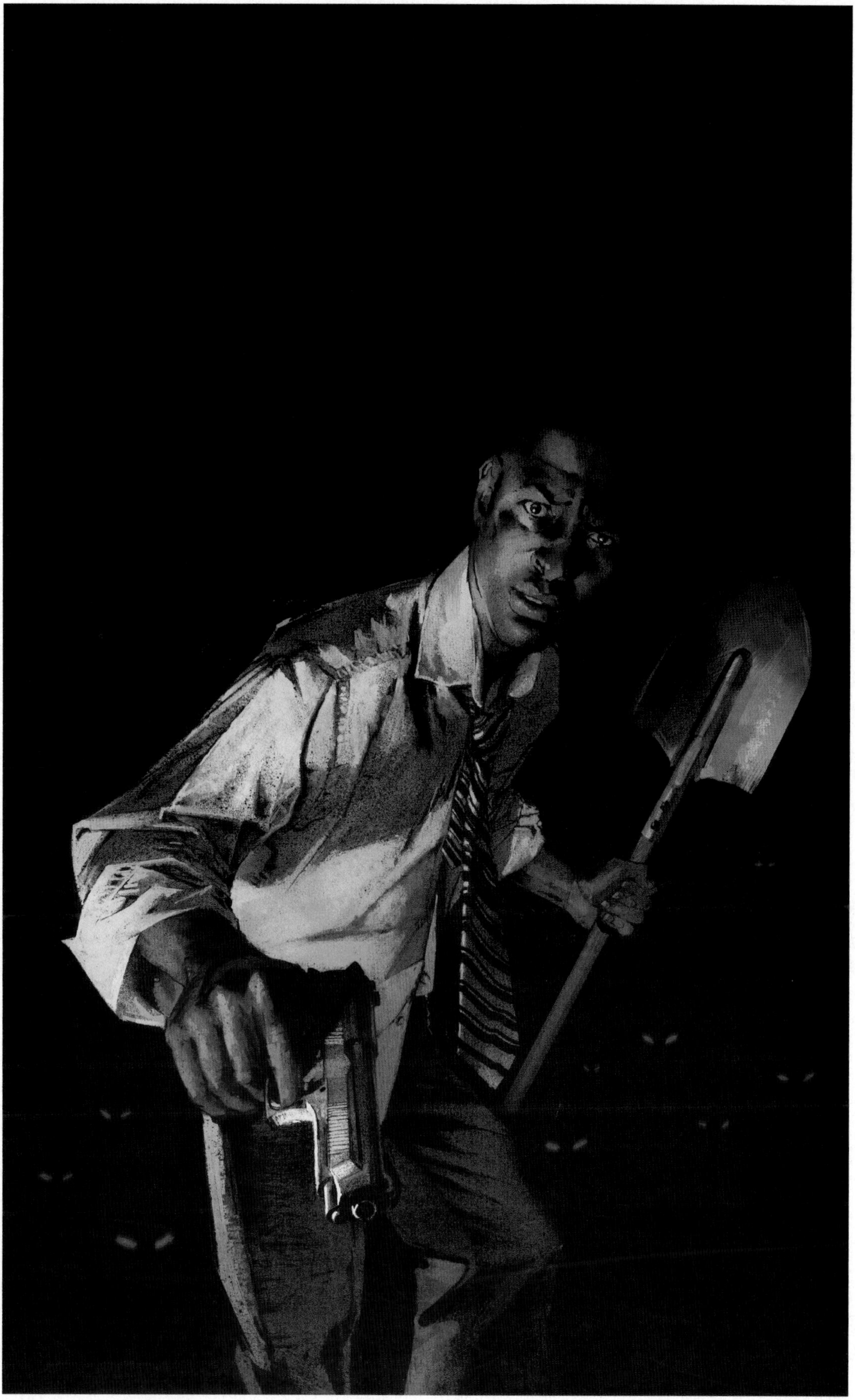

[01 MAIN] Jason Shawn Alexander
Luis NCT

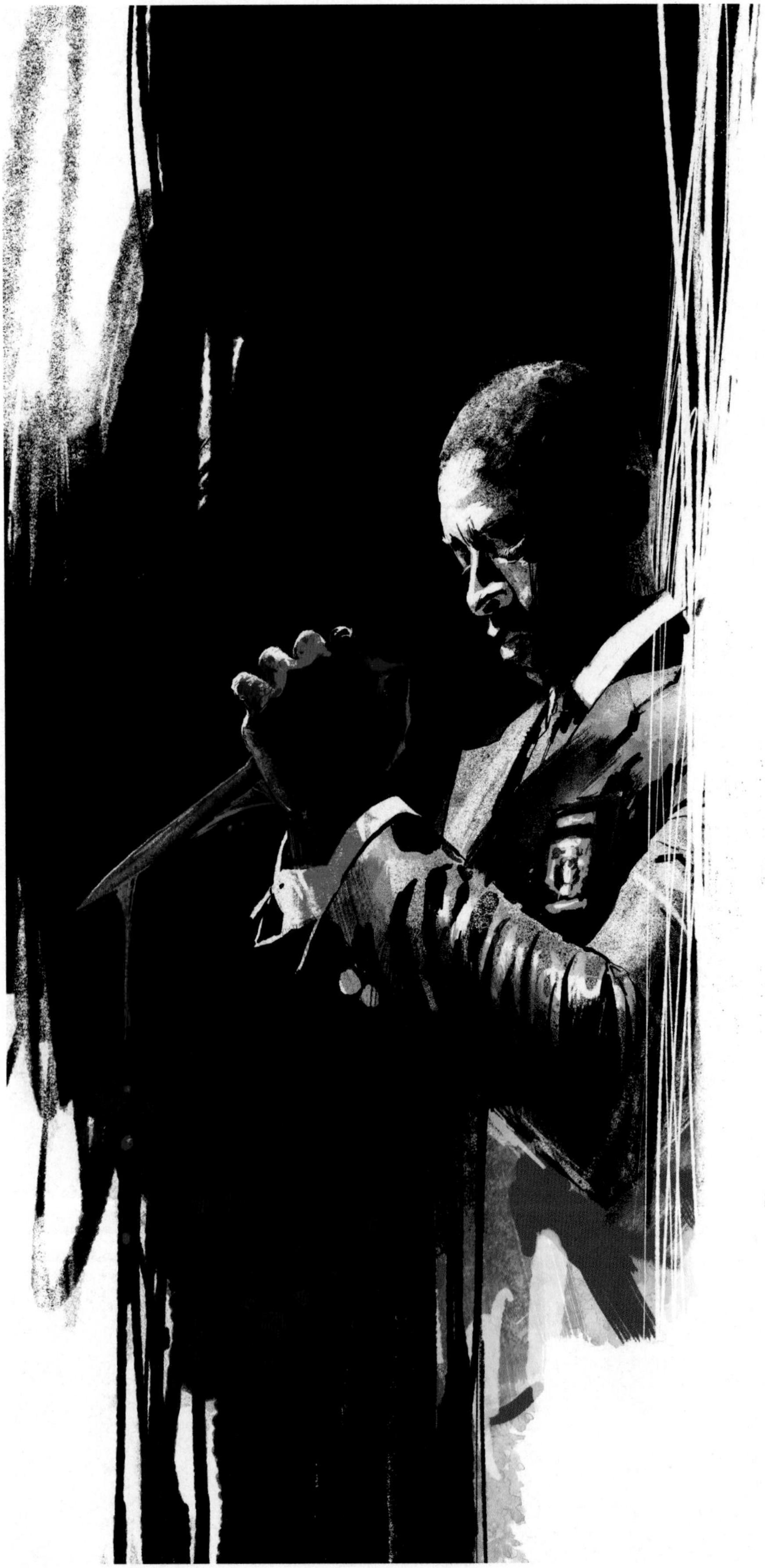

[01 LCSD] Jason Shawn Alexander

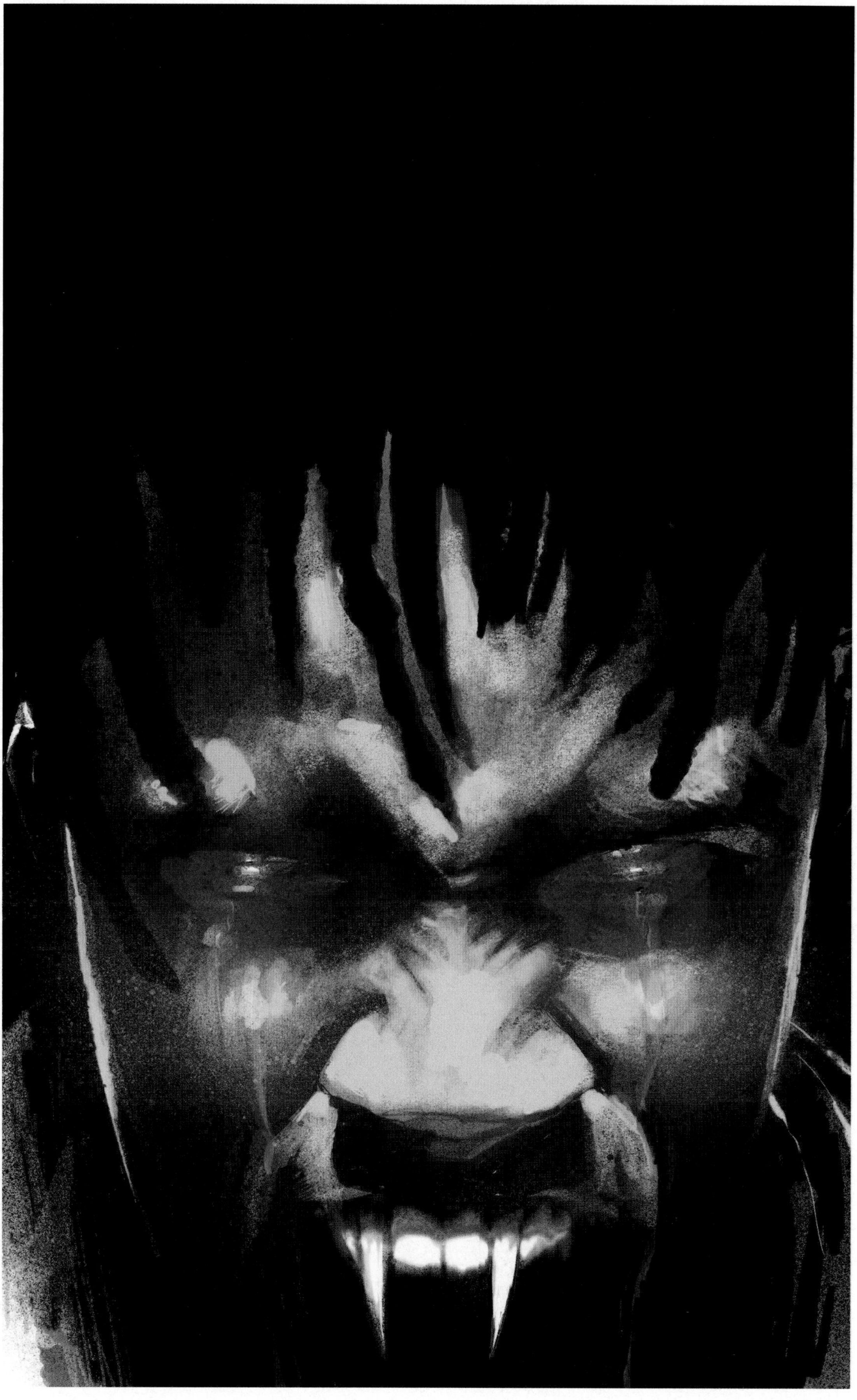

[02 MAIN] Jason Shawn Alexander

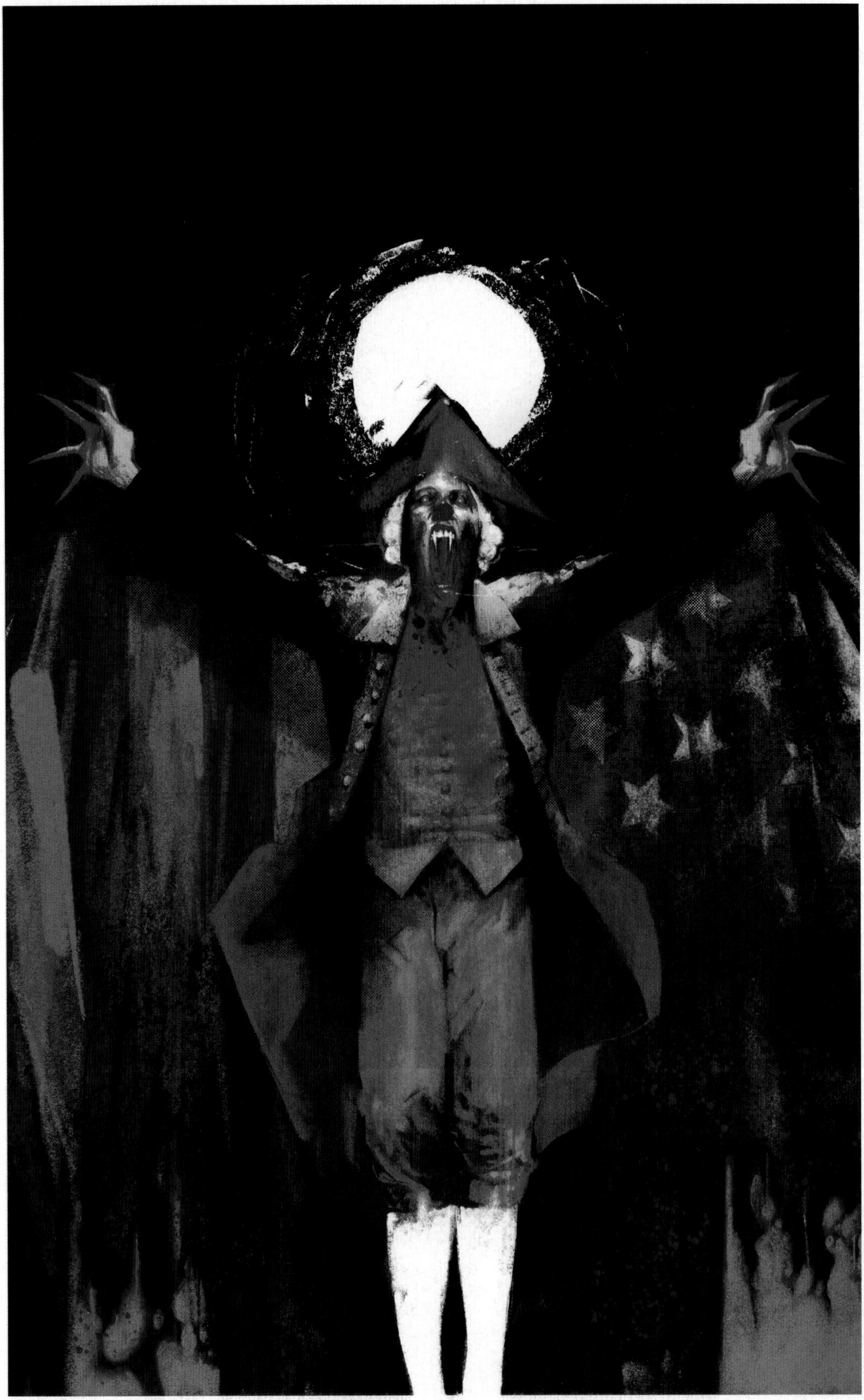

[03 MAIN] Jason Shawn Alexander

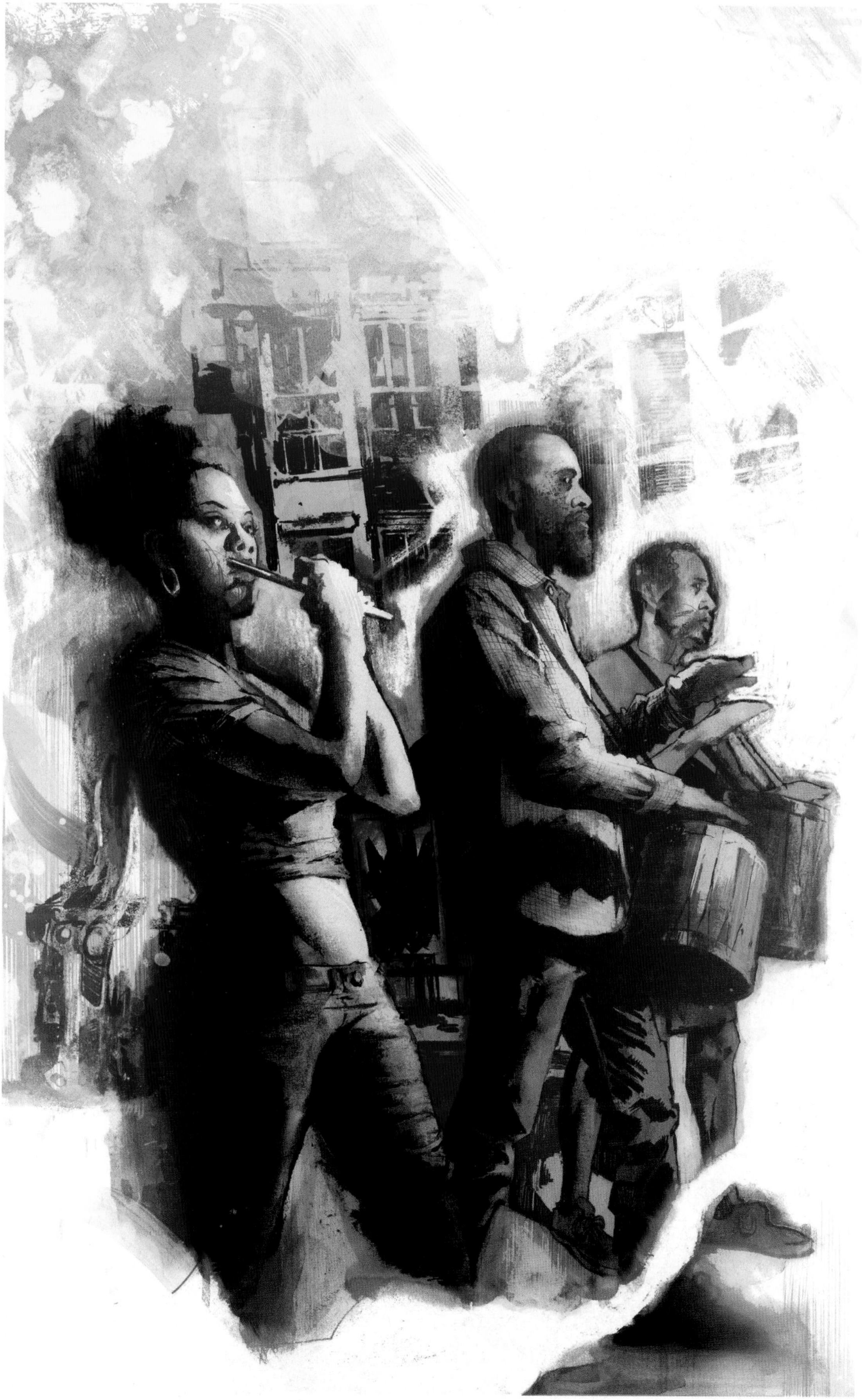

[04 MAIN] Jason Shawn Alexander
Luis NCT

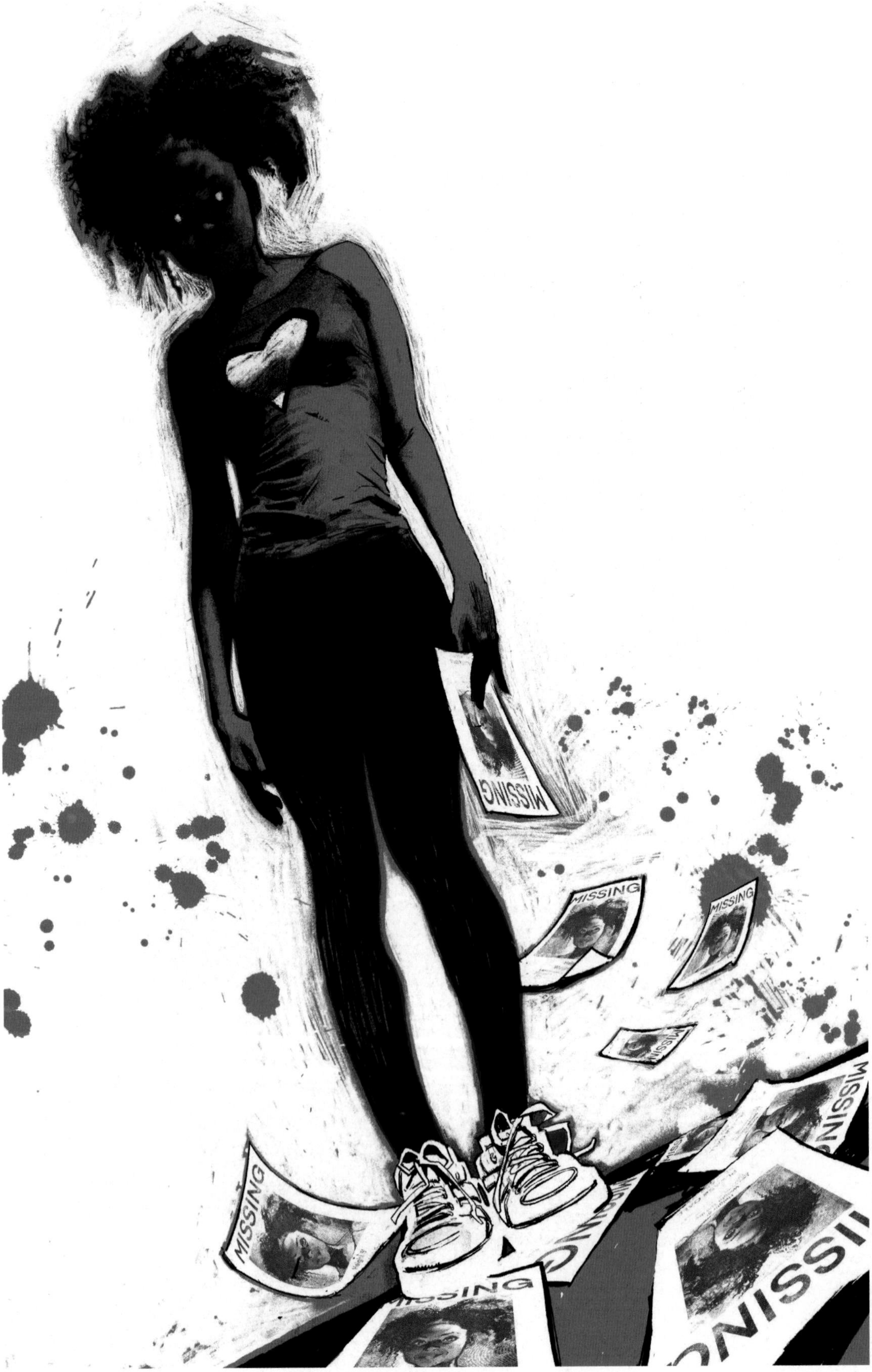
MISSING
MISSING
MISSING
MISSING
MISSING
MISSING

[05 MAIN] Jason Shawn Alexander

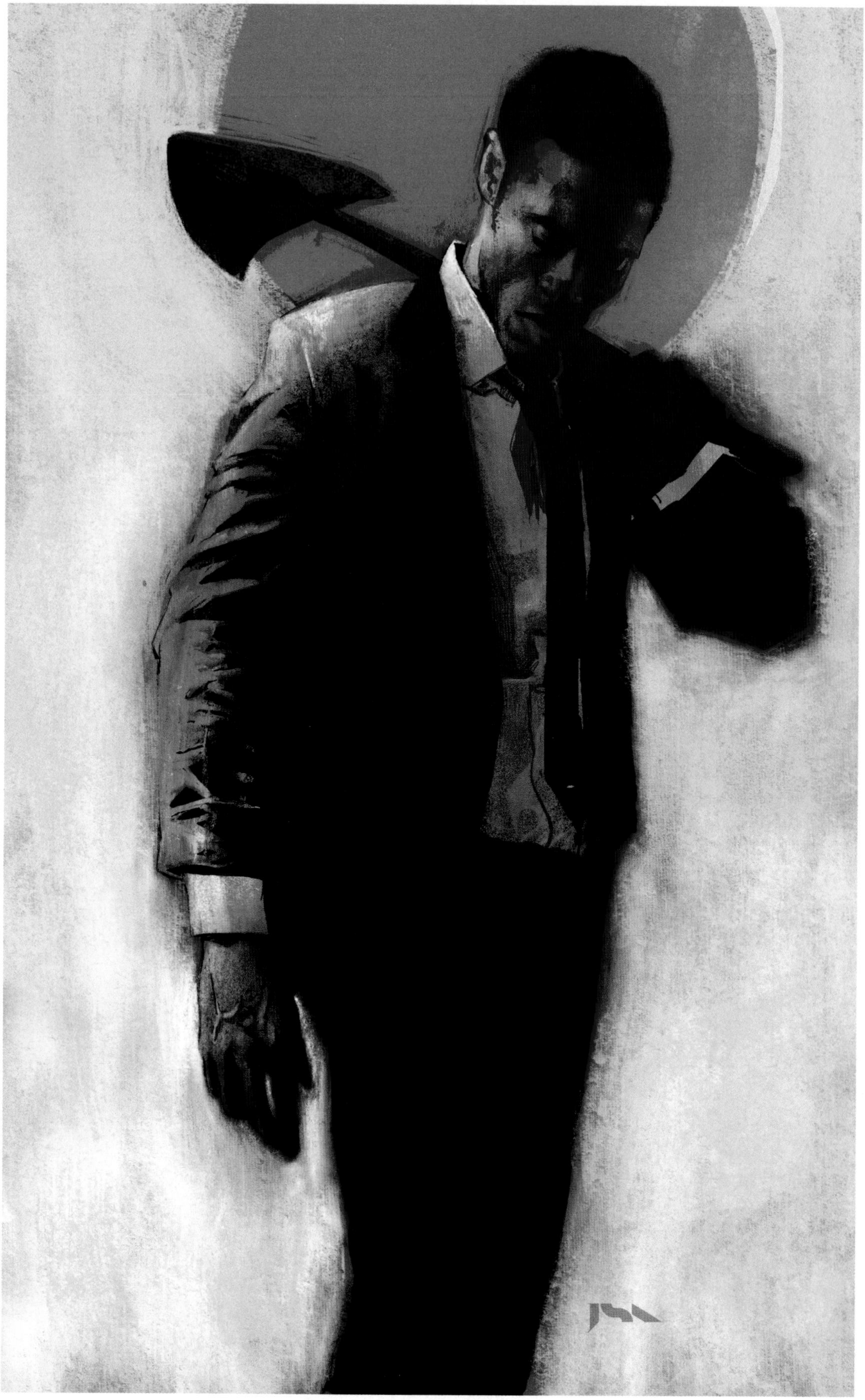

[06 MAIN] Jason Shawn Alexander

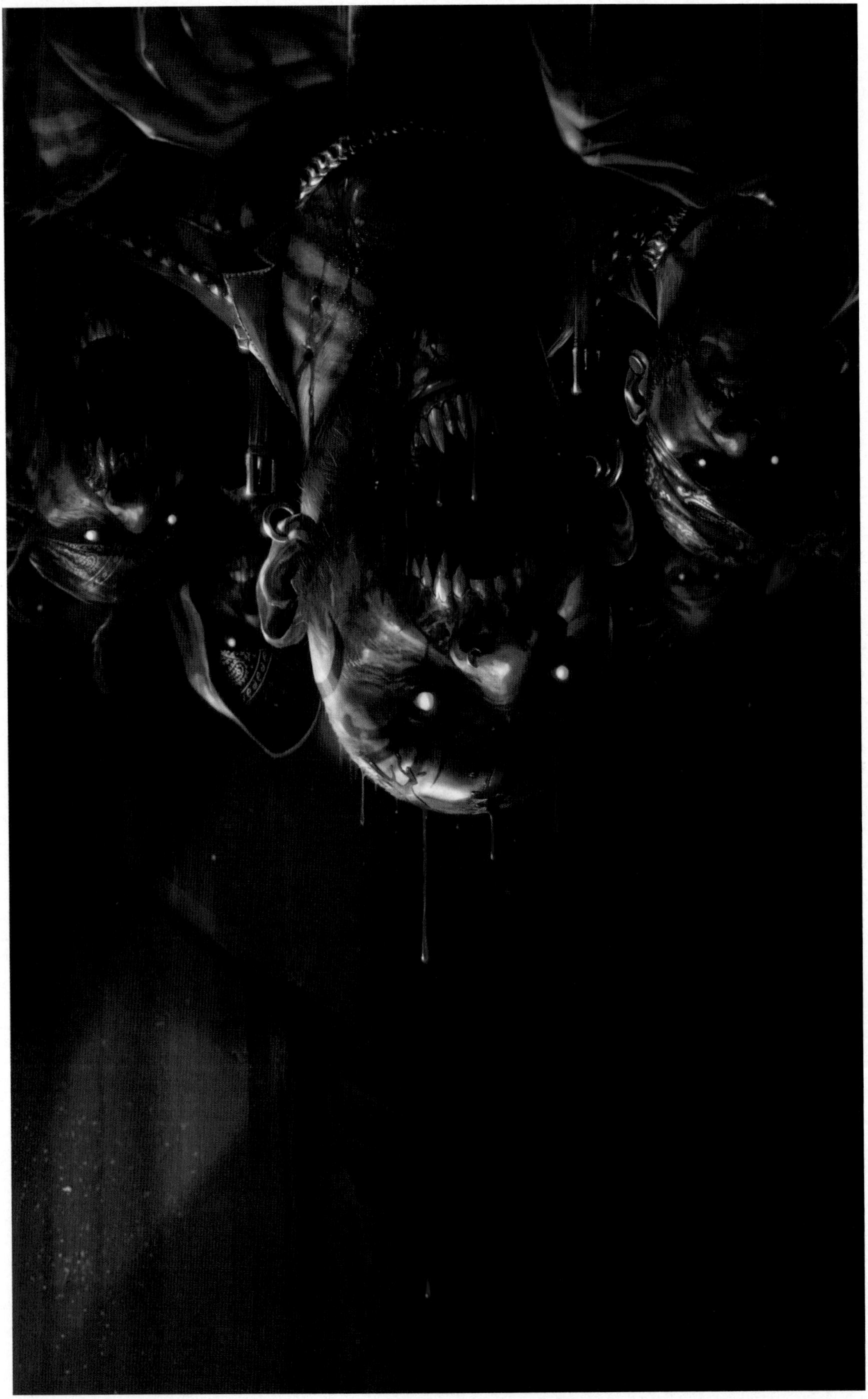

[01 VARIANT] Francesco Mattina

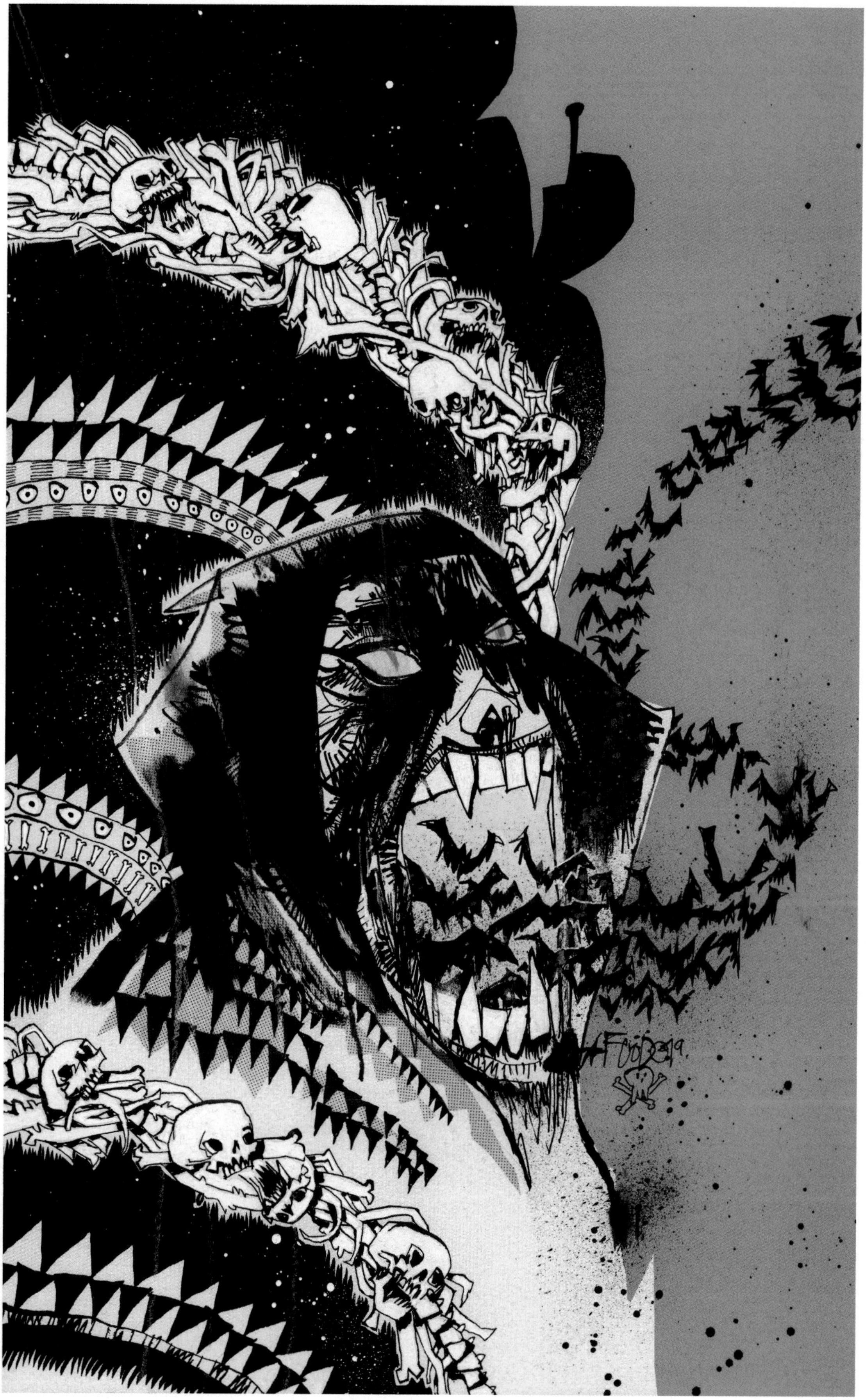

[02 VARIANT] Jim Mahfood

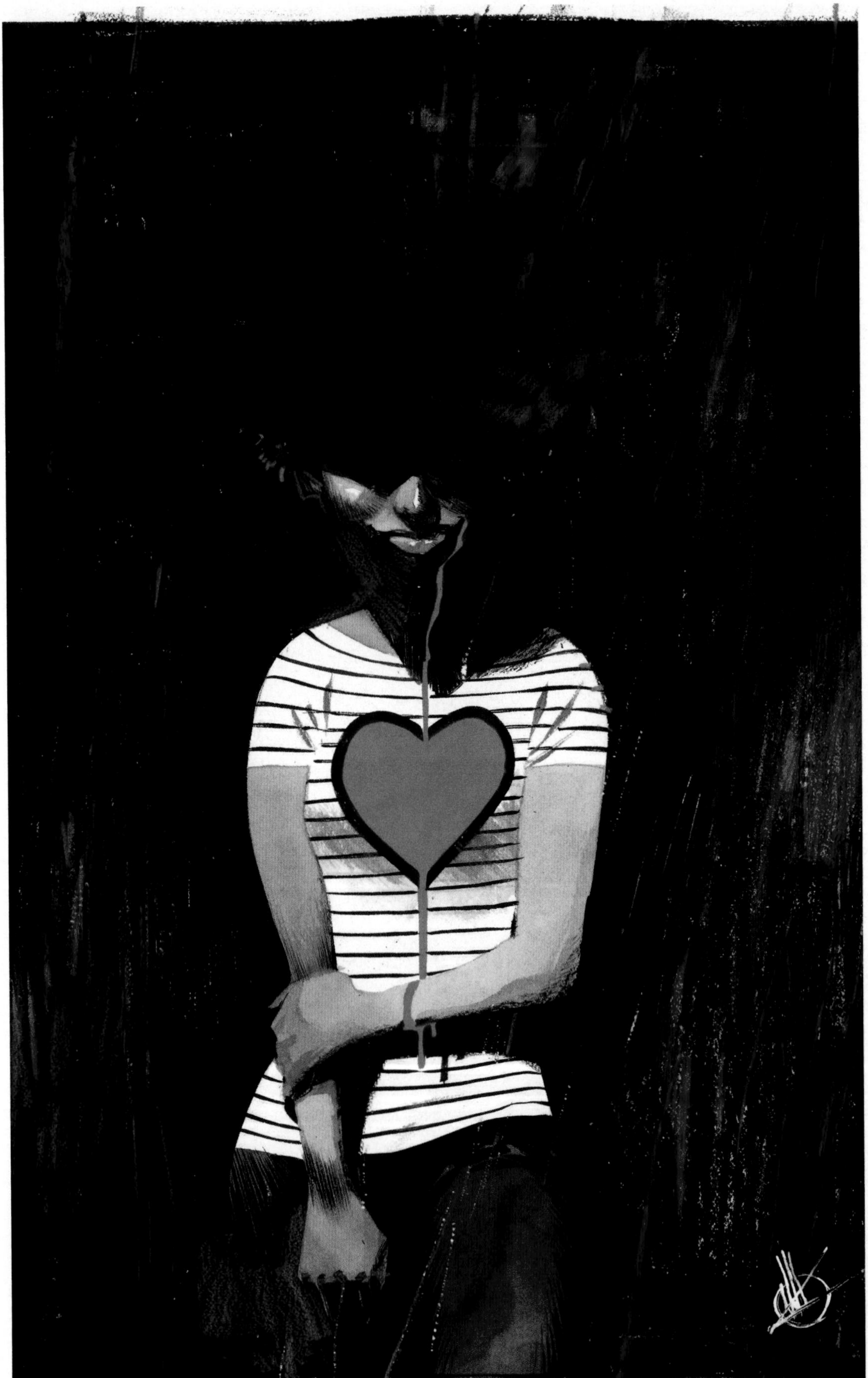

[03 VARIANT] Matteo Scalera

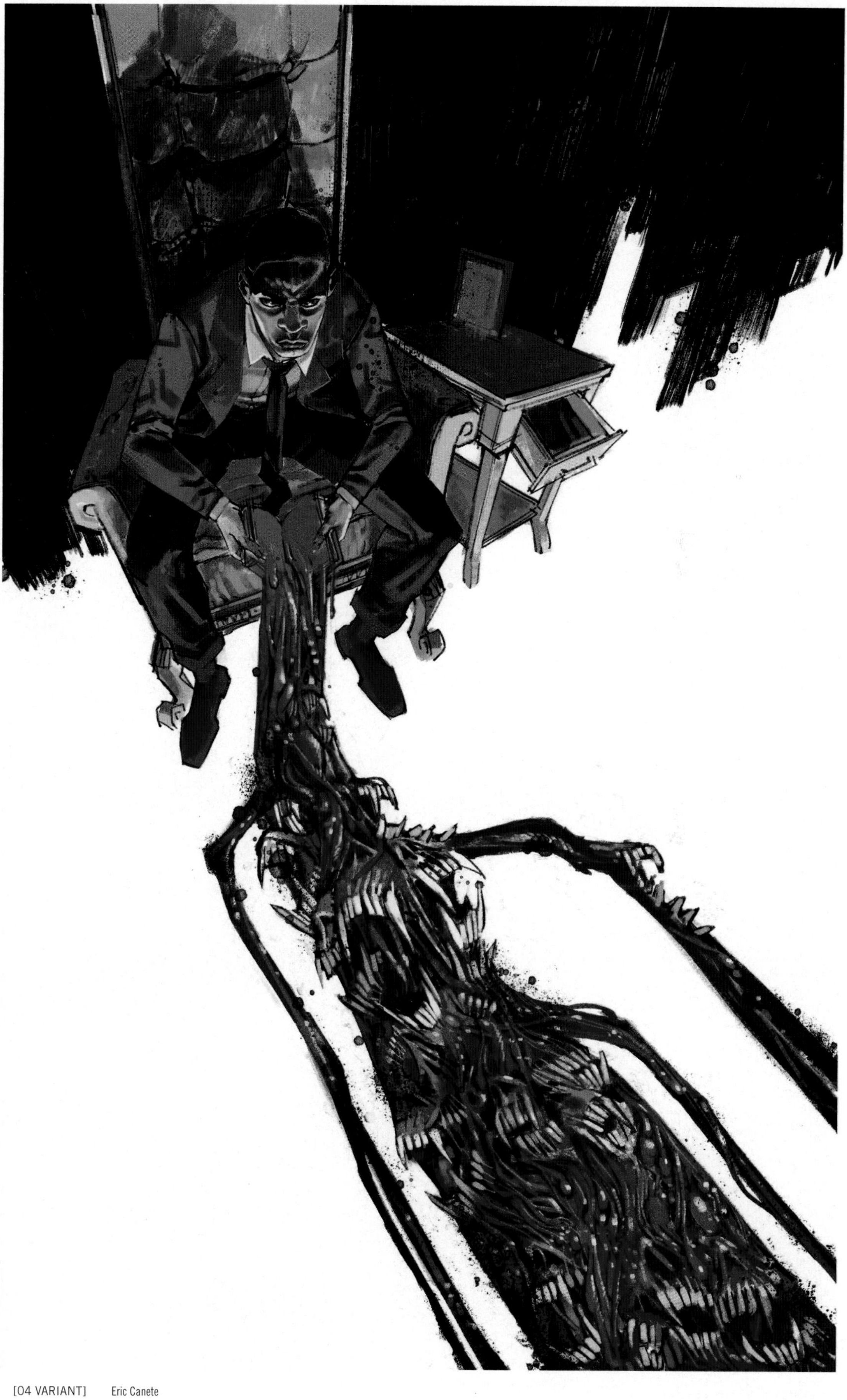

[04 VARIANT] Eric Canete

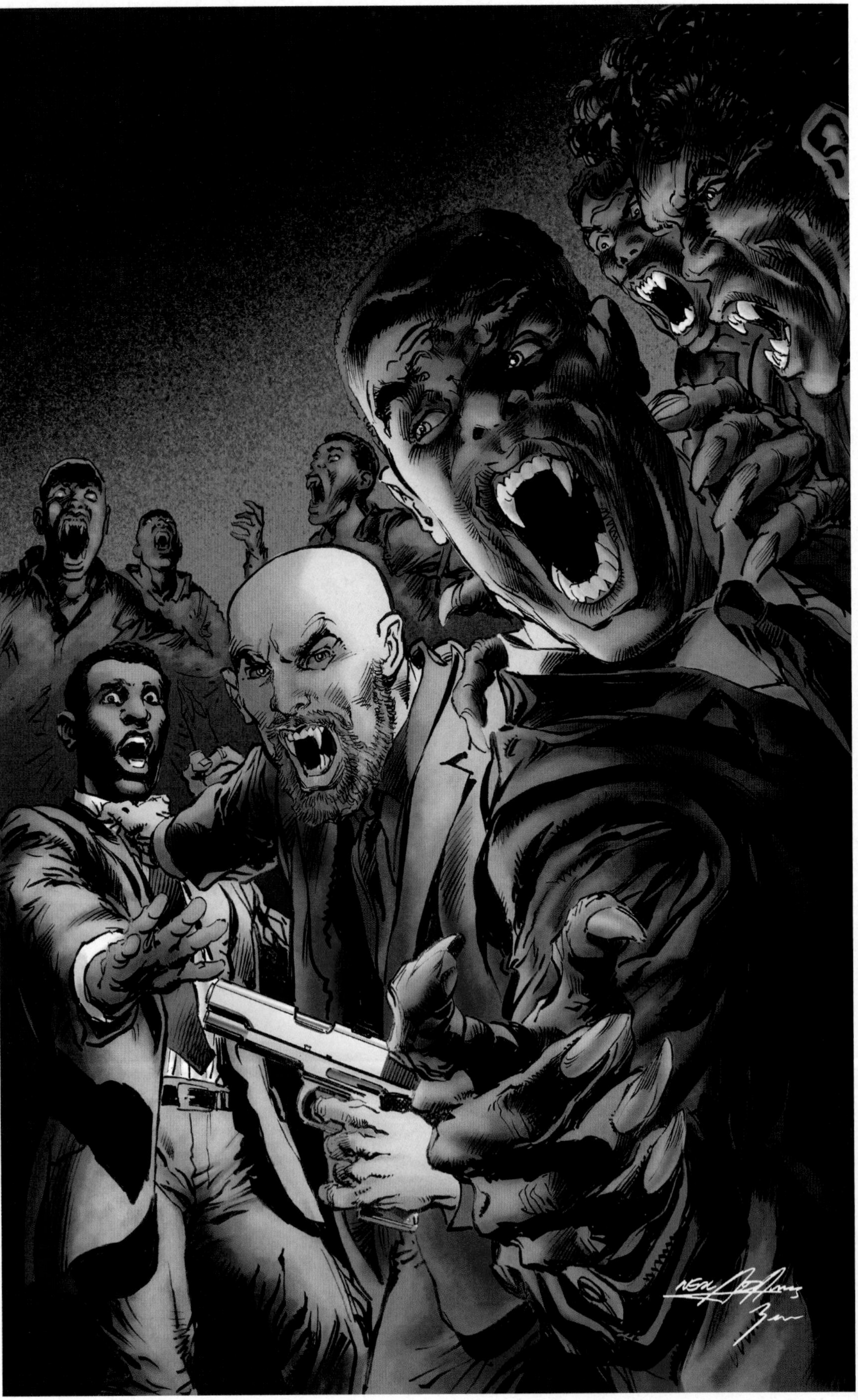

[05 VARIANT] Neal Adams
Zeea Adams

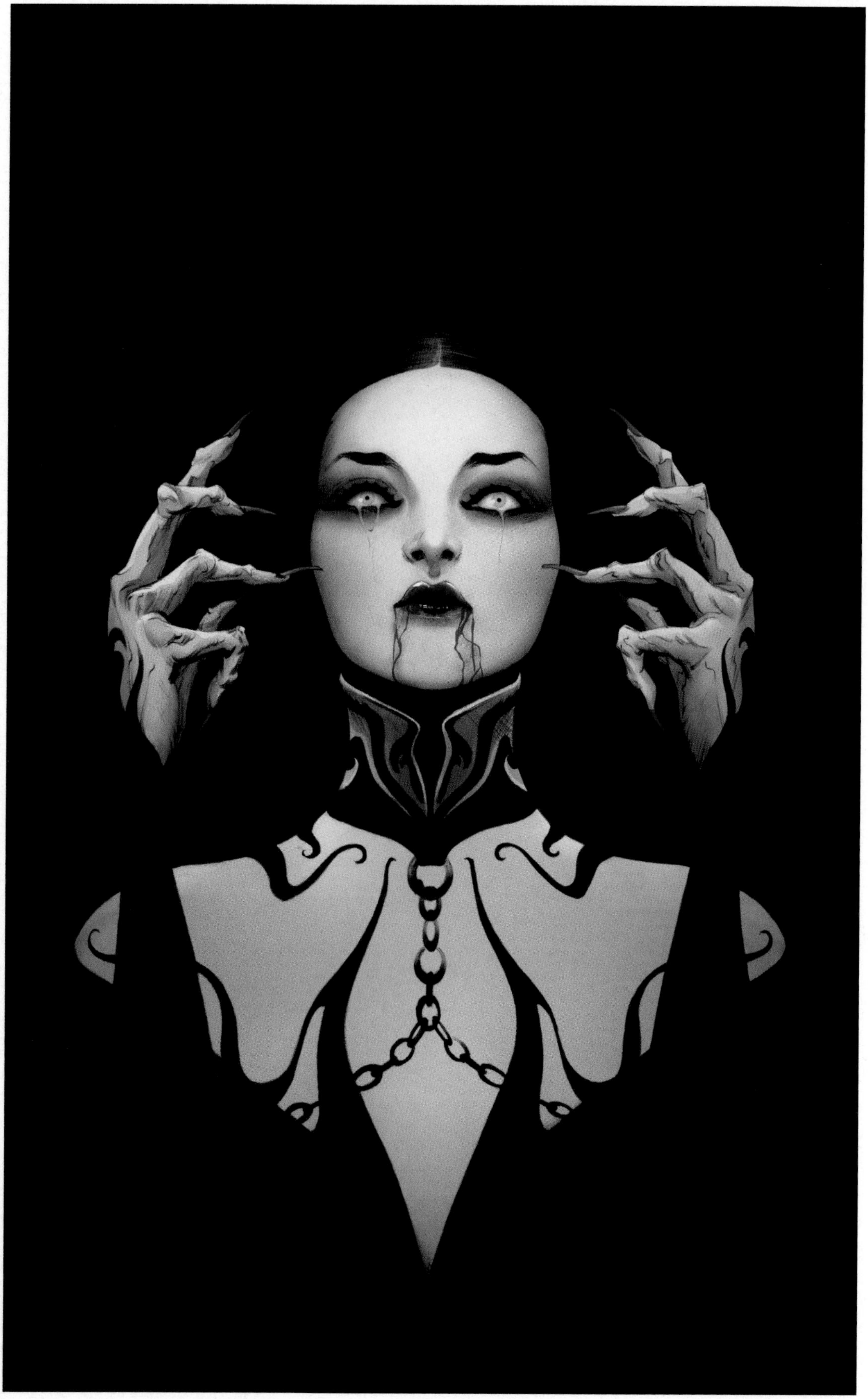

[06 VARIANT] Jae Lee
June Chung

Page Three

1/   Chaos abounds at the morgue as vampires attack our trio
Jimmy fires at them with his service revolver, but the bullets
pass through the bodies like a knife through hot butter.
The vampires, nude, display the ravenous ferocity of savage
animals deprived of food. Jose swings a surgical scalpel as
Sangster lifts a biting vampire high over his head.

2/   Sangster flings the vampire into an oncoming trio, creating
space between himself and the other attackers. He's looking
at Jimmy.

Sangster: Use the stakes for God's sake!

3/   Jimmy picks up a stake just in time to plunge it into the
chest of an oncoming vampire.

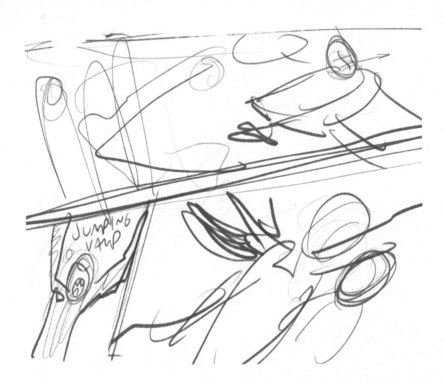

JASON SHAWN ALEXANDER

First, I read the entirety of Rodney's script for the issue, before I even start to sketch anything. This is the only time I get a chance to experience it as a fan. Every script brings the reader deeper into this horrifying world and this first read is where I get to really soak it in and experience the nuanced twists and turns before I start stressing over how to visually bring it together. Then, I go page by page, doing loose thumbnails and layouts.

Part I: Script, Thumbnails and Photo Reference

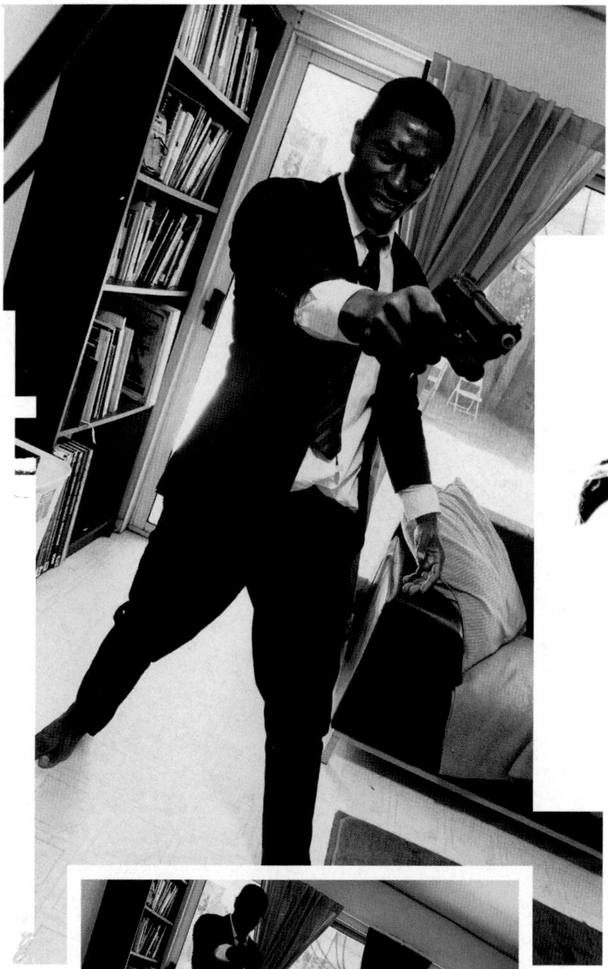

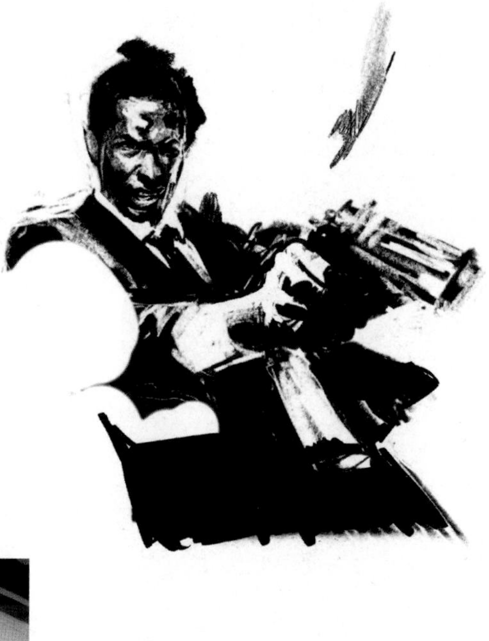

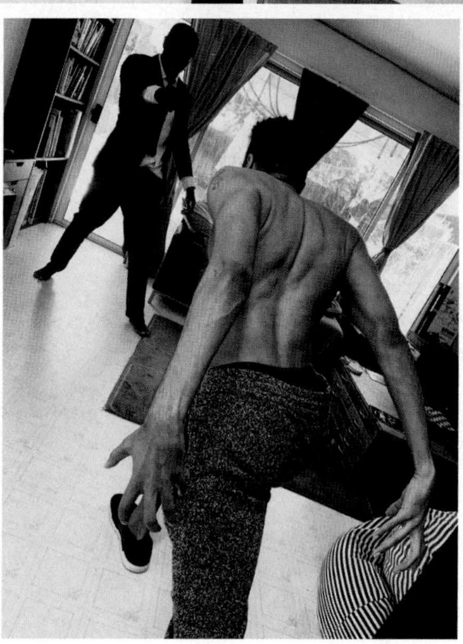

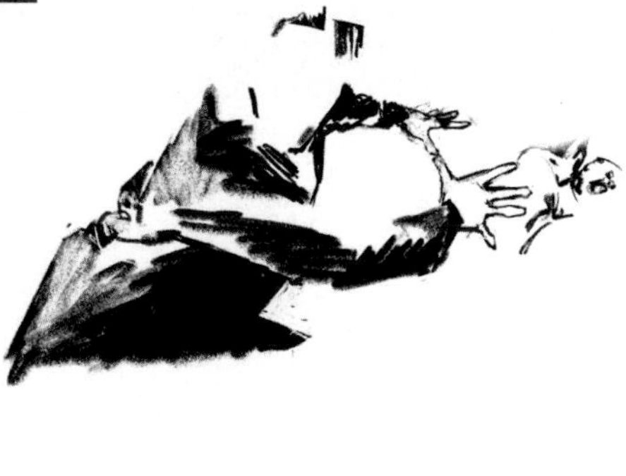

From there, I schedule a photo shoot with the main models I use for this series. The photo shoots are like stop motion movies. I read the scripts to the models and have them pose panel by panel. They're an amazing group of expressive, talented people.

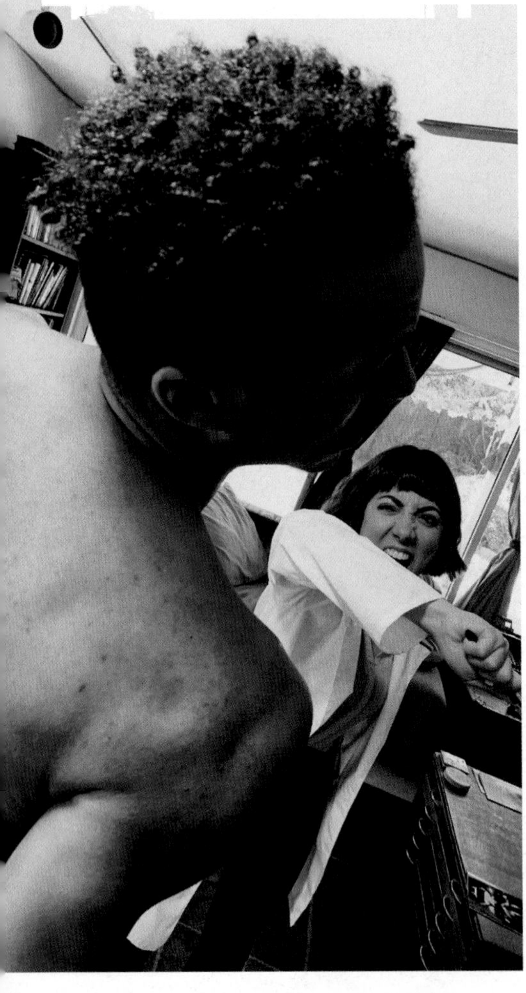

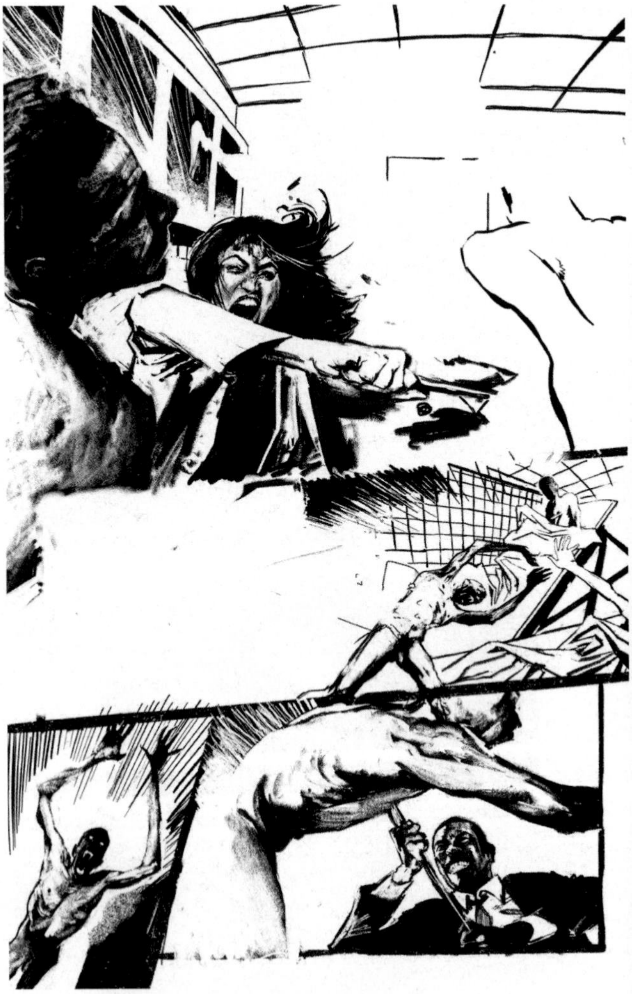

Keep in mind, the photo reference is more of a jumping-off point than anything else. I like to exaggerate and abstract from the reference as much as I can. The reference photos serve to ground the rendering in realism. My goal has always been to make the fantastic also believable.

Part II: Storytelling Composition, Inks and Refinement

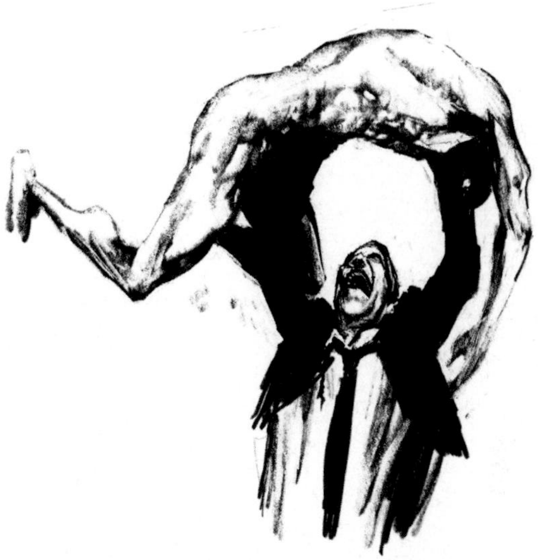

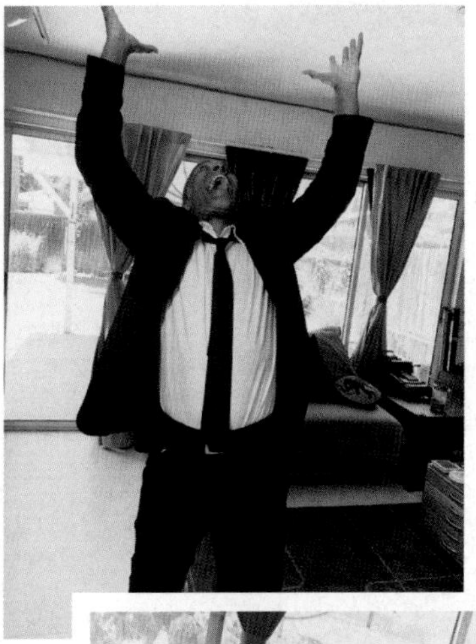

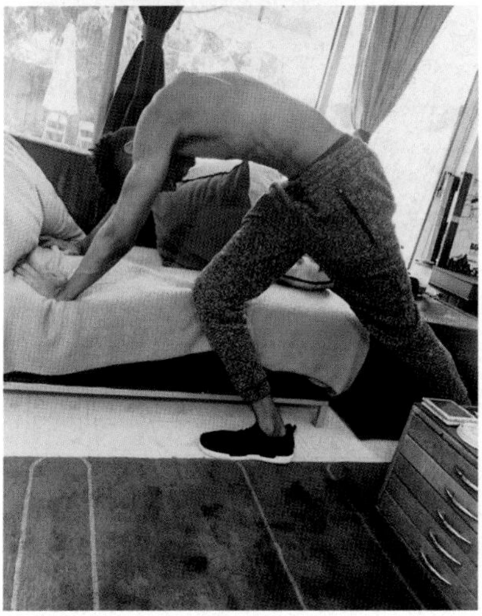

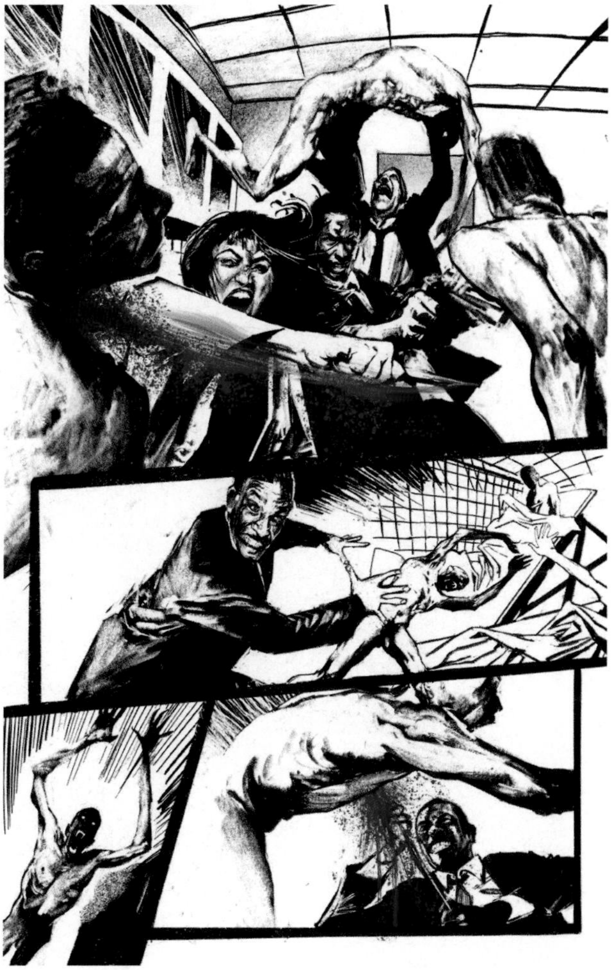

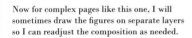

Now for complex pages like this one, I will sometimes draw the figures on separate layers so I can readjust the composition as needed.

After I've done my thing, Luis NCT comes in and brings this dark noir world of *Killadelphia* to light... or dark, with his incredible pallet and rendering of color. Luis and I have worked together for a good number of years now. He's an incredible artist on his own graphic novels as well.

Part III: Final Colors and Lettering

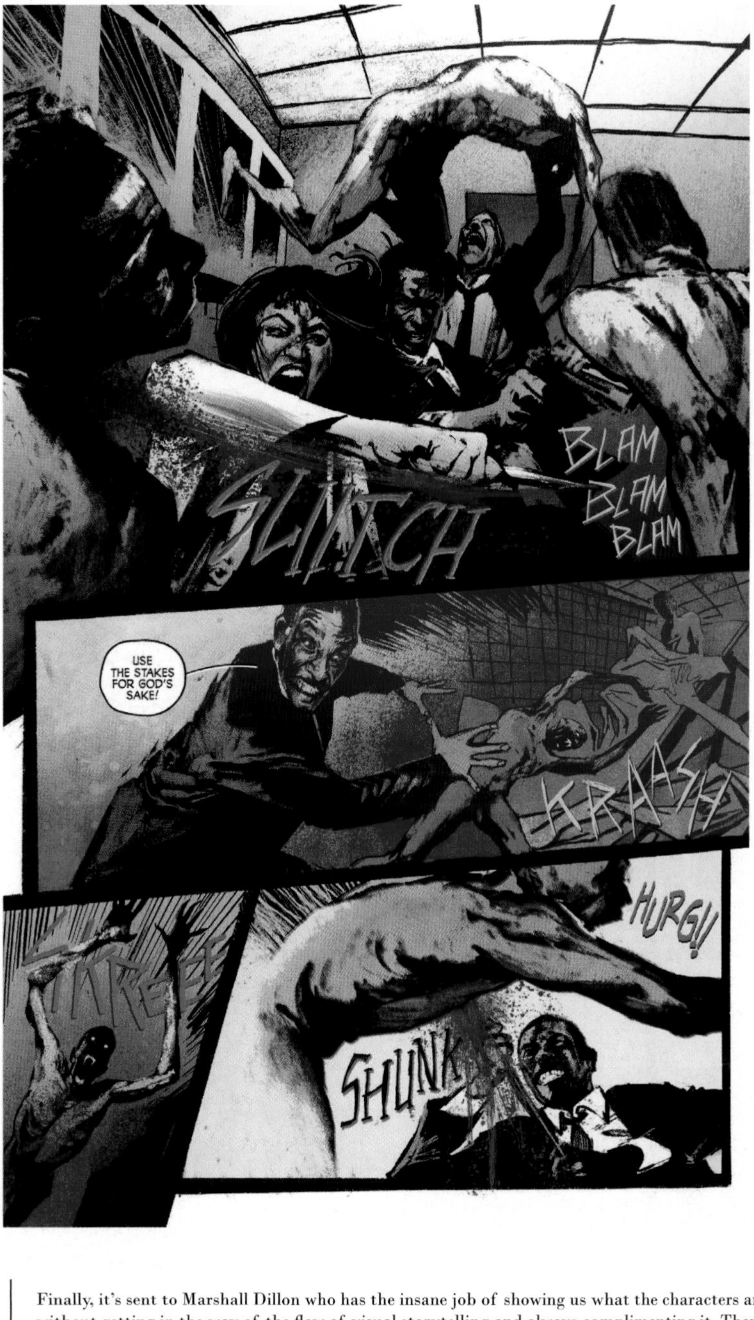
BLAM
BLAM
BLAM
SLIIITCH
USE THE STAKES FOR GOD'S SAKE!
KRAASH
HURG!!
SHUNK

Finally, it's sent to Marshall Dillon who has the insane job of showing us what the characters are saying without getting in the way of the flow of visual storytelling and always complimenting it. Then it's off to you, dear reader, who we hope gets as much fun and fright out of reading our tale as we get out of making it.

JSA
Los Angeles, 2020

BIOGRAPHIES

RODNEY BARNES

Rodney is an award-winning writer/producer of television, film, and comics. His credits include HBO's *Showtime*, Hulu's *Wu-Tang: An American Saga*, Marvel's *Runaways*, Starz's *American Gods*, *The Boondocks*, *My Wife and Kids*, *Everybody Hates Chris* and the Academy Awards.

He has received recognition from AFI, the NAACP Image Awards, and the Peabody Committee for his work as a writer and producer. Along with *Killadelphia*, Rodney has authored graphic novels for Lion Forge's *Quincredible* and *Star Wars -Lando: Double or Nothing*, as well as *Falcon* and *Secret Empire: Birth of a Patriot* for Marvel Comics.

JASON SHAWN ALEXANDER

Jason is an artist/writer who has worked in comics for over twenty years, receiving two Eisner Award nominations and the Silver Medal from the Society of Illustrators. Alongside his comics career, Jason exhibits his fine art work in galleries in Los Angeles, New York, London, Berlin and has shown in the National Portrait Gallery at the Smithsonian.

Along with *Killadelphia*, his series *Empty Zone* has garnered much critical acclaim. Among his list of credits, he is co-writer and artist of *Spawn*, and has contributed his art to *Hellboy*, *Abe Sapien*, *Batman*, *Superman*, *The Escapists*, *The Shadow*, *The Secret*, *Frostbite*, *30 Days of Night*, *Queen and Country*, *Marvel Zombies*, *Hellraiser* and more. He's also created art for motion comics for such films as *Pan's Labyrinth*, *Predators* and *Mad Max*.

LUIS NCT

Luis is a Mediterranean storyteller, illustrator, painter, writer and colorist who has been creating and self-publishing comic books since high school. He studied at Polytechnic University of Valencia and began his career as an illustrator creating artwork for roleplaying games and short films.

His recent works include coloring American comic books such as *Empty Zone* for Image and *Frostbite* for DC. He's published several creator-owned graphic novels, including *Sleepers* and *Wahcommo*, and many short stories, including a critically acclaimed manga *Mina No Uta* that appeared in Japanese magazine *Tezucomi*. He also worked as concept artist and character designer on the animated feature film *Another Day of Life*.

MARSHALL DILLON

Marshall has been in the comics and entertainment industries for 25 years, with notable clients including the U.S. Army, the Department of Health, the BBC, Intel, and AT&T.

Franchises and properties he's worked on include *G.I. Joe*, *Transformers*, *Street Fighter*, *Mega Man*, *Finding Nemo*, and *The Muppets*, as well as various movie tie-ins and video game properties. He's very excited to contribute to *Killadelphia* and to be a part of such a dynamic and energetic team.

GREG TUMBARELLO

Greg has over fifteen years professional experience in the comics and entertainment industry, having worked as an editor, writer and producer for MTV Networks, Disco Fries Music/Liftoff Recordings, The Comic Book Legal Defense Fund, Image Comics, Tokyopop, Marvel and DC Entertainment, among others.

He spent seven years as an editor at Legendary Entertainment after cofounding and structuring their successful comic book division. During his tenure, he worked on New York Times best-selling graphic novels such as *Godzilla: Awakening* and *Pacific Rim: Tales from Year Zero*. He was an integral part of the team that brought to life Grant Morrison and Frazer Irving's *Annihilator*, which garnered an Eisner Award nomination and Frank Miller's *Holy Terror*, which launched the division as a top ten comics publisher.

SHANNON BAILEY

Shannon has been Publishing Coordinator at Todd McFarlane Productions for the last five years, producing over 50 issues of *Spawn*, including the book's historic 300 & 301 issues, as well as other titles. Prior to that, she taught eighth grade English for several years, which prepared her for the crazy career of artist wrangling.

BRENT ASHE

Brent is a Canadian-born art director and designer specializing in branding, print and packaging design. His style is recognized around the world via his collaborations with clients such as Ubisoft, ArtStation, Mondo, Hasbro, Devolver Digital, Bungie, threeA, McFarlane Toys, Marvel, DC, Sony, Valve, Microsoft and Warner Bros.

He began his career by defining a signature presentation design for Todd McFarlane Productions, while winning Spectrum awards for his art direction work with artists such as Kent Williams and Jon J Muth. From there, he brought his talents to the video game industry, working on the *Assassin's Creed* franchise for Ubisoft before forming his own design and consulting agency in 2013.

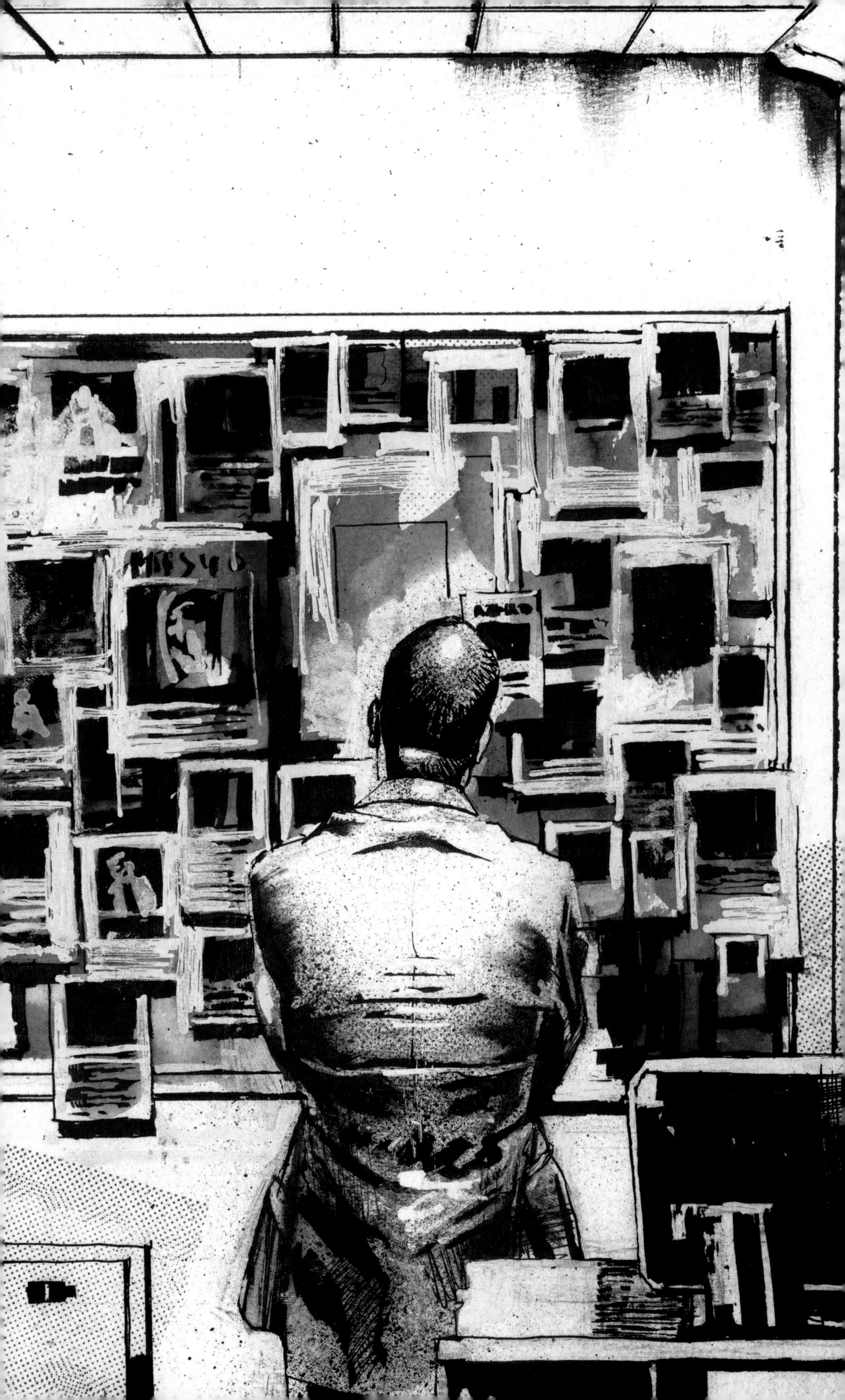

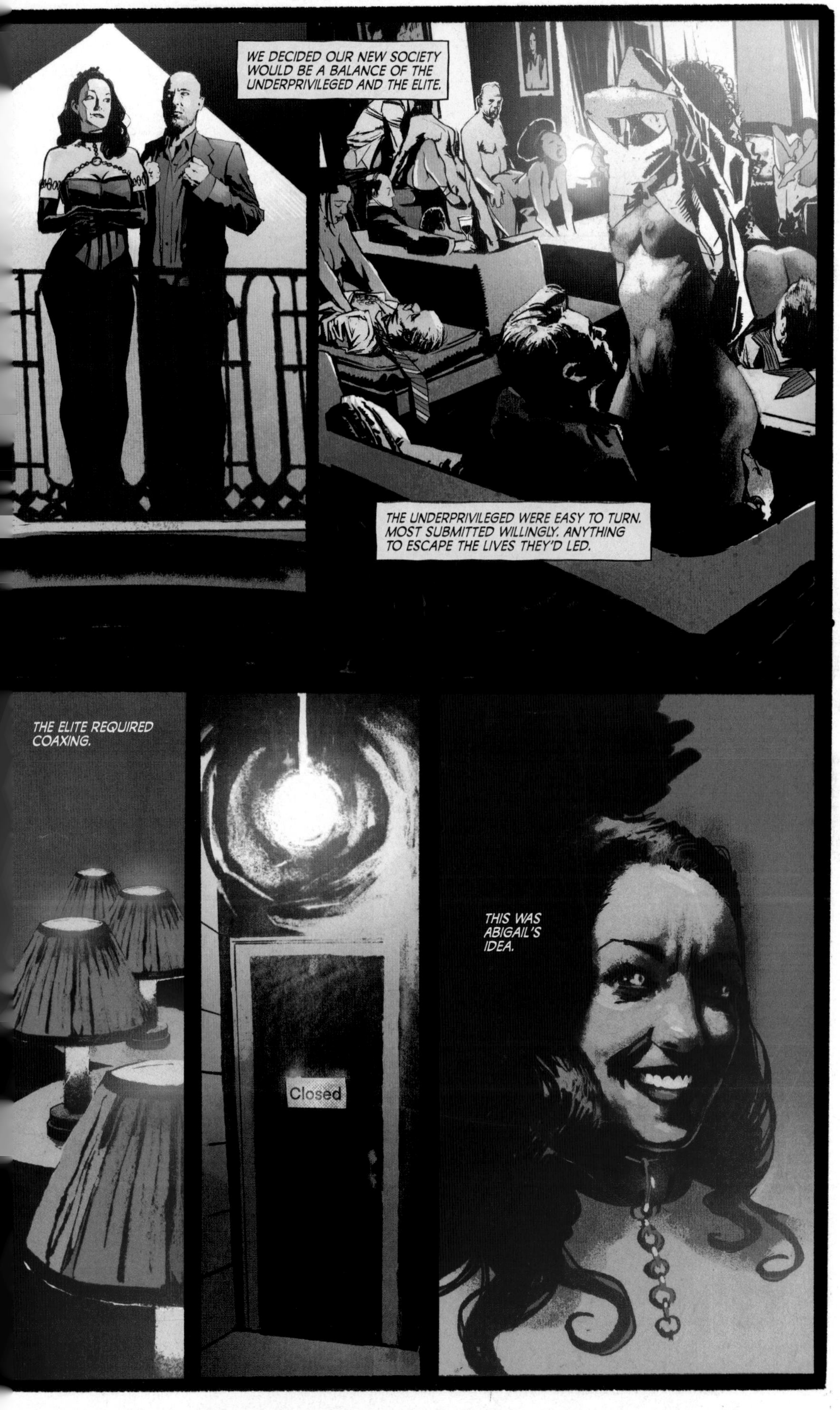
WE DECIDED OUR NEW SOCIETY WOULD BE A BALANCE OF THE UNDERPRIVILEGED AND THE ELITE.
THE UNDERPRIVILEGED WERE EASY TO TURN. MOST SUBMITTED WILLINGLY. ANYTHING TO ESCAPE THE LIVES THEY'D LED.
THE ELITE REQUIRED COAXING.
Closed
THIS WAS ABIGAIL'S IDEA.

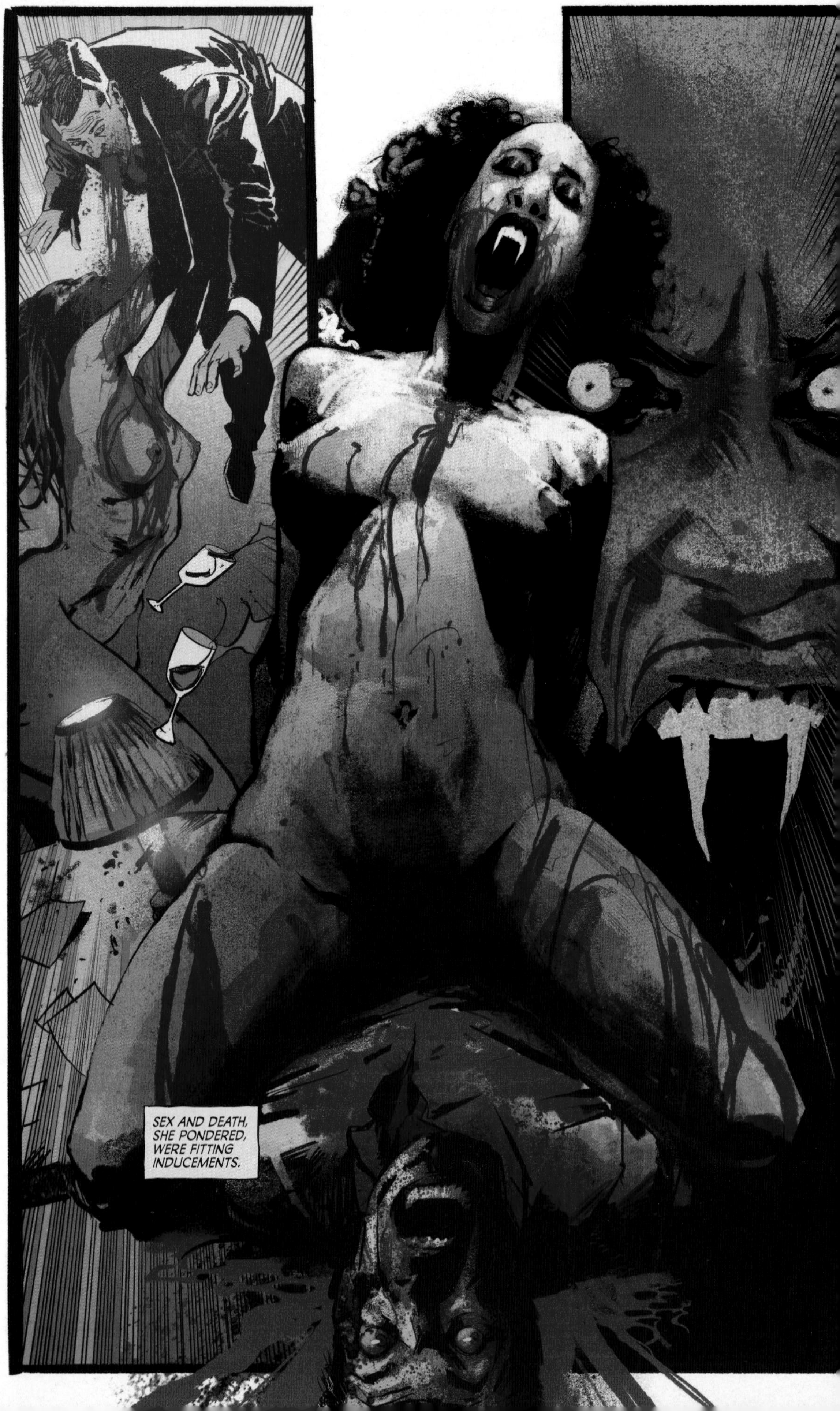
SEX AND DEATH, SHE PONDERED, WERE FITTING INDUCEMENTS.